# THE DELIVERY OF DÉCOR

*Shiloh Ridge Ranch in Three Rivers, Book 7*

## LIZ ISAACSON

# The Glover Family

Welcome to Shiloh Ridge Ranch! The Glover family is BIG, and sometimes it can be hard to keep track of everyone.

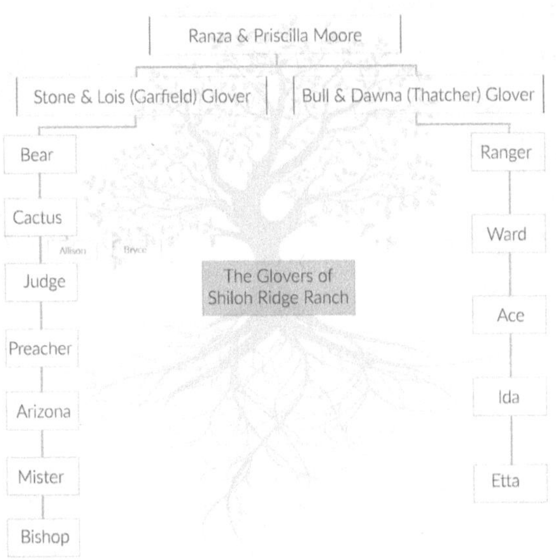

**There is a more detailed graphic here, on my website.** (But it has spoilers! I made it as the family started to get really big, which happens fairly quickly, actually. It has all the couples (some you won't see for many more books), as well as a lot of the children they have or will have, through about Book 6. It might be easier for you to visualize, though.)

HERE'S HOW THINGS ARE RIGHT NOW:

**Lois & Stone (deceased) Glover, 7 children, in age-order:** (Lois is engaged to Donald Parker)

1. Bear (Sammy, wife / Lincoln (9), step-son, Stetson (2), son, Russell (6 mo), son)

2. Cactus (Allison, ex-wife / Bryce, son (deceased) // Willa, wife / Mitch (10), step-son, Charlie (6 mo), son)

3. Judge

4. Preacher (Charlie, soon-to-be wife)

5. Arizona (Duke Rhinehart, husband, living at the Rhinehart Ranch, just south of Shiloh Ridge / Shiloh (2 mo), daughter)

6. Mister

7. Bishop (Montana, wife / Aurora (18), step-daughter, Robbie (3 mo), son)

**DAWNA & BULL (DECEASED) GLOVER, 5 CHILDREN, in age-order:**

1. Ranger (Oakley, wife / Wilder (18 mo), son)
2. Ward
3. Ace (Holly Ann, wife / Gunnison (4 mo), son)
4. Etta
5. Ida (Brady Burton, husband / Johnny and Judy, (twins, 6 mo), son and daughter)

BULL AND STONE GLOVER WERE BROTHERS, SO THEIR children are cousins. Ranger and Bear, for example, are cousins, and each the oldest sibling in their families.

THE GLOVERS KNOW AND INTERACT WITH THE WALKERS of Seven Sons Ranch. There's a lot of them too! Here's a little cheat sheet for you for the Walkers.

**MOMMA & DADDY: PENNY AND GIDEON WALKER**

    1. RHETT & EVELYN WALKER

Son: Conrad

Triplets: Austin, Elaine, and Easton

2. JEREMIAH & WHITNEY WALKER

Son: Jonah Jeremiah (JJ)

Daughter: Clara Jean

Son: Jason

3. LIAM & CALLIE WALKER

Daughter: Denise

Daughter: Ginger

4. TRIPP & IVORY WALKER

Son: Oliver

Son: Isaac

5. WYATT & MARCY WALKER

Son: Warren

Son: Cole

Son: Harrison


6. SKYLER & MALLERY WALKER
Daughter: Camila


7. MICAH & SIMONE WALKER
Son: Travis (Trap)

THE GLOVERS KNOW AND INTERACT WITH THE SEVERAL of the cowboys and their families at Three Rivers Ranch too... There's a lot going on in Three Rivers!

You'll see:

1. Squire and Kelly Ackerman

Mother / Father: Heidi (owns Ackermans bakery) / Frank

Son: Finn

Daughter: Libby

Son: Michael

Son: Samuel

2. PETE AND CHELSEA MARSHALL (CHELSEA IS SQUIRE'S sister)

4 sons: Paul, Henry, John, Rich

3. REESE AND CARLY SANDERS: THEY'RE THE ADMINS FOR Courage Reins, Pete and Chelsea's equine therapy unit at Three Rivers Ranch.

# Chapter One

Ward Glover paced in the hospital. How long did it take to have a baby? Honestly, he'd been here for three hours and his sister's babies should be tiny, seeing as how there were two of them being born at the same time.

He cast a look at his eldest brother, but Ranger didn't seem concerned about anything but the game on his phone. "You should sit down," he said when Ward went by again. "Pacing won't make Brady bring the twins out faster."

Ward simply grunted at him and kept walking. This time, he didn't turn around and go back by the chairs and couches the Glovers had claimed in the maternity waiting area.

He rounded a corner and pressed his back into it, breathing in deeply through his nose. He pushed it out the way the counselor at Courage Reins had taught him. He'd been going to the equine therapy facility for a few months now, and he'd doubled his sessions over the past three weeks.

Since Thanksgiving, when Dorothy Crockett told him she "liked him and all, but she didn't want to mix business and pleasure."

Ward didn't even know what that meant. She still didn't have the gravel he wanted, and they'd only been out a few times since he'd gotten brave enough to be straight with her. He'd held her hand and spent plenty of time talking and flirting with her, but he hadn't kissed her yet.

He'd been texting her in the twenty-four days since she'd told him that, and she responded. He suspected there was more at play than she'd said, but he hadn't been able to get anything more from her.

Thinking quickly, before he could change his mind, he took out his phone and tapped on her name right at the top of his app. He'd pinned her there, and he wasn't embarrassed about it.

*Ida's having the babies. I thought you might like to know.*

Dot lived only a couple of blocks from Ida and Brady, and one of their dates had been a double with Ward's sister and brother-in-law.

Since Dot was literally the nicest woman on town, she'd become fast friends with Ida, and Ward knew the two had spent some time together over the past few months.

*How exciting!* Dot said in response. *She must be thrilled. She was really hurting a couple of days ago.*

His sister had been experiencing some labor pains, as well as the reduced ability to breathe and swollen legs and ankles in the recent past. All pregnancy-related.

Ward stared at the conversation, wondering how he could get Dot to talk to him.

*You can't*, he told himself. She was a grown woman who was older than him, and she got to make her own choices.

And she hadn't chosen him.

The realization cut through him like an electric knife, made his breath catch somewhere between his throat and his lungs.

She *hadn't* chosen him.

*You'll never guess who I just spoke to*, Dot said, and Ward seized the opportunity to talk to her.

*Who?*

*Lionsgate Gravel. They have the thirty-five in bulk, and I got as much as I could.*

Ward's hopes lifted, and instead of texting her, he tapped the green phone icon to call her.

"I knew you'd call," she said, and she sure sounded downright flirty to him. "Nothing excites you as much as thirty-five gravel."

Ward cleared his throat. "Oh, I can think of a few things more exciting," he said.

She giggled, and Ward knew for certain she was flirting with him now. What he didn't know was *why*. Or why she'd turned cold a few weeks ago.

"You want the gravel, right?" she asked after she'd stopped laughing.

"How much do you have?"

"Enough to fill the order you put in a couple of years ago."

"Wow," he said. "Yeah, I want that. All of it." He

stared across the hall to the bland hospital wall looking back at him. "Maybe you'd let me take you to dinner to discuss delivery?" He almost coughed but managed to suck it back at the last second. "I mean, I'm already in town."

"At the hospital, Woods."

He grinned at her sarcastic tone and the use of his real name. "The cafeteria here has great food," he said.

"I'm not eating somewhere called a cafeteria. I'm not in grade school."

No, she wasn't. *Not even close*, Ward thought as he imagined the curvy blonde. And the first time he'd seen her rumble up in her dump truck and climb down like she owned the world....

Ward could barely breathe just remembering it. He didn't want to say, "Name the time and place, and I'll be there, darlin'."

He absolutely would not say that.

"I'm hungry almost all the time," he said. "If I can, I'll meet you somewhere."

Meeting her somewhere. That was low-key, right?

His brain misfired when he realized what else he'd said. *I'm hungry almost all the time.*

*My word, Ward,* he thought. *Get off the phone right now.*

"Hey, I have to go," he said, actually pulling his mouth away from the phone as if someone else needed his attention. "Let's talk later about the gravel delivery."

"Sure," she said. "Tell Ida hello."

"Yep." Ward hung up before he could tell Dot to come over and tell Ida hello herself. Then he'd get to see her, learn the color of her tank top, and what box of dye she'd chosen at the grocery store that week.

Dot never wore anything but jeans and a tank top, even in the winter. Not that Ward had much experience with her in the winter. "Or the spring, or the summer," he muttered to himself.

He thought about her flirty tone and teasing nature as he rounded the corner and went back toward the other Glovers. He sat next to Ranger, who didn't look up from his phone.

About twenty minutes later, right when Ward's patience was about to snap, Brady appeared at the mouth of the hall. The smile on his face couldn't be described in words, but the look of adoration and wonder could only be achieved by a new father.

"Here they are," he said, passing the baby boy wrapped in the blue blanket to Ward. "That's Jonathan Ryan Burton." He gazed down at the baby girl. "This is Judith Dawna Burton." The tiny baby gurgled, and Brady handed her to Ranger.

Ward couldn't look away from the sleeping child in his arms, and the little boy captured his whole heart in less time than it took for Ward to draw a breath. He knew Etta desperately wanted children of her own, and he'd have plenty of opportunities to see Ida in the next few weeks.

So he turned to Etta and handed her baby Jonathan. The boy's face scrunched up, but Etta cradled him right against her chest and cooed at him. "You're okay, baby," she said. "It's Auntie Etta, and you and I are going to be great friends."

Ward smiled at her, and she grinned back at him. "How's Ida?" Ward asked, stepping over to Brady as Ace and Holly Ann crowded in around Ranger and Oakley, who now held Judith.

"She did great," Brady said, looking a bit overwhelmed now. "They put her in a recovery room with a bunch of heated blankets when she started shivering. They think she may be having a bad reaction to the epidural."

"But she'll be okay, right?"

"Yeah, they didn't seem worried." Brady watched as Oakley gave his daughter to Montana, who rested the infant on her own pregnant belly. Bear and Sammy hadn't come to the hospital today, because they'd just left it yesterday. They'd had their second baby boy four days ago, and they'd named him Russell, which was Sammy's mother's maiden name.

Montana went to sit by Mother and Aunt Lois, and Etta wandered that way too. The four of them sat on a single sofa, the twins more loved than they even knew.

"Stay there," Ward said, dropping to one knee right there in the hospital. "Look at me, and let me take your picture for Ida. She'll like that."

The women looked up at him, and he tapped his phone to get several pictures. "Perfect," he said, looking at the picture as one of the infants started to cry.

A flurry of activity happened around him as Brady got loaded up with both babies so he could take them back to their mother. Ward stayed down as he used his favorite editing app to make everyone look better by taking down the shadows and pushing up the contrast.

"Why are you down on the floor like that?" a woman asked, and Ward's attention got jerked from his device. "Are you praying or proposing?"

He looked up at Dorothy Crockett, his pulse shooting through every vein in his body simultaneously. "Dot," he managed to say. The problem was, he tried to get up at the same time, and shove his phone in his pocket, and combined with his sudden nerves, he stumbled forward.

He managed to catch himself before he fell flat on his face, but he had to grab onto Dot to do it. She grunted and braced herself, and because she owned and operated a landscaping company and shoveled bark and gravel for a living, she was strong enough to hold him for a moment. Long enough for him to get his footing, release her, and clear his throat.

"Sorry," he said.

Dot looked around at his family, most of whom were watching the two of them. Preacher looked mildly horrified, and Ward suddenly knew why Preacher had kept his relationship out of the Shiloh Ridge limelight. Then he didn't have to deal with awkward situations like this.

Of course, he now held hands with his fiancée, and Charlie fit right in with all the Glovers.

Ward turned his back on the group and stepped over to partially shield Dot too. "Did I miss a text?"

"You said we could talk about the delivery of your gravel." She looked from him to his family and back, a hint of nerves in her eyes. "I thought I might get to see the babies."

"You just missed them," he said. "Look." He turned his phone toward her, and she took it from him.

"Oh, they're perfect." She looked at him again, and as he'd crowded in beside her, their faces were only a few inches apart. He took a breath of her and got something green with dirt and something cottony fresh. Her tank top was a dark eggplant color, and it clung to all of her curves and revealed the muscles in her arms.

"What did they name them?"

"Jonathan and Judith," he said.

"Judith sounds just like Ida," Dot said with a smile. She focused back on the picture, studied it for a moment, and then handed it back to Ward. "Are you staying here for a while? I know you and Ida are close."

"I'd like to see her," he said, glancing over his shoulder. "But her husband said they had her in a recovery room. She'll be here overnight for sure. I can come back." He took a step closer to her, though they were already practically touching. "Might be better, since there's so many of us. We can be a lot to handle."

"You're kidding," she said without the trace of a smile. "I had no idea you Glovers could be hard to deal with."

"Hey, I'm not hard to deal with," he said. "Am I?"

"Oh, Ward," she said, patting his chest and sending excited tremors through every muscle in his body. "You're the worst one."

# Chapter Two

Dorothy Crockett could admit that a day hadn't gone by since she'd smashed her raspberry cream whip into Ward's white church shirt that she hadn't thought about him. She'd seen a different version of the cowboy that day at the church potluck, and when he'd called and said she intrigued him, Dot had changed her opinion of him completely.

At the same time, he still used his good looks against her, along with that Texas twang she found so sexy. Of course, Dot had always been a sucker for a strong, tall cowboy, and Ward had all the strength and all the height in the world. He could wear a cowboy hat like no man she'd ever met, and she'd never seen him without jeans and cowboy boots too. He changed up his shirts, and as the weather had cooled, he'd started wearing a leather jacket that made her heart pirouette every time she thought about it.

Today, he wore a T-shirt with the outline of Texas on it, and he must've bathed in pine needles and sugar, because he smelled masculine and delicious all at the same time.

He looked at her with those blue eyes that had probably broken dozens of women's hearts, and Dot saw the confusion he harbored there.

"I'm the worst one?"

Dot blinked, trying to remember what she'd said to him and what he'd said before that.

"What have I done that's been hard for you to deal with?" he demanded, and he fell back a step. Two, then three. He looked like she'd insulted his dog and his daddy, and Dot regretted teasing him.

"Do you know how many times you've called my office about gravel?"

"Do you know what it would've taken to get me to stop calling?" He folded his arms, and Dot didn't want to have a stand-off with him in the hospital. Especially not the maternity wing, with his whole family watching.

"One returned phone call, Dot," Ward said, rolling his eyes. He turned from her as if he'd really walk away.

"I'm returning your latest call," she said, and that got him to face her again. Something sparked in those eyes now, and Dot really wanted to get burned by it.

*No*, she told herself. *You don't.*

She'd told herself that a lot when it came to Ward Glover, and every time, she hadn't been able to convince herself.

"You want to go to dinner?" he asked.

Dot shook her curly hair over her shoulders as she drew them back, making herself taller. "Yes."

He took one step toward her, and it almost felt menacing. "Okay," he said. "But if we go to dinner, you have to tell me why you quasi-broke up with me three weeks ago."

*Twenty-seven days*, Dot thought. *That's four weeks.* But she didn't argue with him. She searched his face, wondering how he'd take the news.

"I thought we were going to discuss the delivery of your gravel."

"Oh, we are," he said, giving her a smile that made her stomach quake. "Are you okay to hang out for a minute? I need to talk to my brothers for a sec."

"Yeah, okay," she said.

He nodded, his hand finding hers and squeezing before he walked away. That simple touch was what made Ward so extraordinary. It wasn't the things he said, but the small, minute details he did that told her what was really on his mind.

She didn't mean to stare after him, but she did. Her diverted attention meant she didn't notice immediately when two women sidled up to her and paused.

"I'm Etta," she said. "Ward's sister."

"Zona," the other woman said. "His cousin."

"Hello," Dot said, disappointed with herself that she'd let her guard down. She'd never gotten along all that well with other women, as she'd been a tomboy and an athlete her whole life. She was taller than the average woman, and she towered above Etta but not so much Zona. She'd dated a lot throughout high school and college, but she'd made bad decision after bad decision that had taken her a long time to come to terms with. Sometimes, she wasn't sure she'd made peace with her past, and she wasn't sure the Lord had forgiven her.

Then, every so often, she felt utterly loved and worthy of that love from On High. In those moments, she allowed herself to date again, but eventually, the things she'd once done sneaked back into her life and caused her grief.

"Do you have a name?" Zona asked, and Dot looked at her with a cocked eyebrow.

"Yes," she said. "Dorothy Crockett."

"Are you going out with Ward?" Etta asked.

"Just for dinner," Dot said. "We're not like...going out." She had no idea what that even meant, and as Etta cocked her head to the side and frowned, she obviously didn't either.

Zona snapped her fingers. "You own From the Ground Up."

Dot grinned at her. She could talk about her landscaping company forever. "Yes," she said. "Have you used us?"

"No," Zona said. "But my brother said you guys are great. I guess you put in a bunch of rose bushes and sod at one of our ranch houses."

"Oh, sure," Dot said. "I remember that. Something about relandscaping after termites?"

"That would be us," Etta said with a smile.

"You look so much like Ida," Dot said.

"Oh, you know Ida?" Etta asked. "We're twins."

"Oh, *duh*," Dot said, trilling out a laugh. "I can't believe I forgot Ida had a twin. Ward's mentioned it too."

"How do you know her?" Etta asked. "Did she introduce you and Ward?"

"No," Dot said, cementing her smile in place, though she liked these two women. They weren't firing questions at her about Ward, at least. "Ward and I went on a double-date with Ida and her husband. Turns out, I live only a couple blocks away from them."

"Oh." Etta looked like Dot had thrown icy water in her face. "I see."

"Etta," Zona said.

"I have to get back to the ranch," she said, already walking away. "I promised Bear and Sammy I'd watch Lincoln and Stetson tonight."

Dot watched her retreat to the couch and pick up her purse. "What did I say?" she asked quietly. "I didn't mean to make her feel bad."

"It's not you," Zona said with a sigh. "She's going through a rough time right now, and she sometimes feels left out. That's all."

"I'm sure if I'd have kept dating Ward, we'd have gone out with Etta and her boyfriend. Husband. Whoever."

Zona watched Etta gather her things and hug a few people. "She doesn't have a boyfriend or a husband."

"Oh." And she was Ida's twin. Ida, who was married and now with two babies.

Zona put her hand on her own pregnant belly, and Dot nodded to it. "When are you due?"

"Not until April," she said, smiling down at her stomach. "Three and a half more months."

"Boy or girl?" Dot smiled at her, but Zona's smile slipped away completely.

"It's a girl," she said, and she looked like she might cry.

"Do you live up at Shiloh Ridge?" Dot asked, because she was really good at making small talk with strangers. She'd literally built her business doing such things, and she could ask someone questions forever.

"No," Zona said. "But I grew up there. I married Duke Rhinehart, and we live on his ranch."

"I know the ranch," Dot said. "I did some tree removal up there a few years ago."

"Mm." Zona nodded, and she put another smile on her face. "Excuse me. I need to go talk to my mother. So nice meeting you."

"You too," Dot said, and thankfully, Ward returned a moment later. "Ready?" she asked.

"Yep." He hooked his thumb toward Zona. "You met my sister and my cousin?"

"Yes," Dot said. "You have a lot of family."

"Yes, I do." Ward indicated the sterile hall in front of them. "Do you have a restaurant in mind?"

"What about Small Plates?" she asked. "Or are you the type of man that doesn't share his food?"

"I can share food," he said. "Small Plates is getting great ratings on Two Cents."

"You use that app?"

"Ranger invented it," Ward said. "I work with him on the back end of it, pushing out notifications and polls. I update the infrastructure of it. That kind of thing." He gave her a devastating grin that made Dot's pulse skip and hop through her ribs. "I get to see the results before anyone else."

"Wow, Ward, that's great." Sexy and smart. It so wasn't fair to bring so much to the battle, and Ward Glover seemed to have it all.

He led her to his truck, opened her door, and waited while she climbed in. He didn't touch her again, a fact Dot was keenly aware of as the man rounded the front of his truck and got behind the wheel.

"Listen," she said. "I didn't mean to say you were difficult."

"What did you mean to say?" He buckled his seatbelt without looking at her, and Dot didn't like that. She also had no idea how to answer his question.

"I was just teasing," she finally said. "It wasn't very funny, obviously."

"You do think I'm difficult though," he said. "It's fine," he added quickly. "I know I can be a little intense about certain things. I guess I just didn't realize I'd done that with you." He shot her a look out of the corner of his eye as he left the hospital parking lot.

"I thought we'd been gettin' along real nice, Dot. Slow, but nice. And I'm fine with slow." He kneaded the steering wheel with those big hands, and Dot swallowed when she thought about holding one of them again.

*Tonight*, she thought. *Hold his hand tonight.*

"I am," he said. "I...like taking my time to get to know a woman, and I've been real busy at Shiloh Ridge." He finally relaxed as he finished talking, and Dot reached up to tuck her hair.

A smile formed on her face. "We do get along real nice," she said. "For a while there, before we really knew one another, yes, I thought you were demanding. I thought you were really arrogant. *So* good-looking, and you knew it. Boy, did you know it."

He turned and looked at her fully, blinking quickly. "What?"

"Come on," she said with a light laugh. "You know you're gorgeous."

"Am I?"

Dot coughed, because she suddenly felt like she'd say the wrong thing and Ward would pull over and demand she get out of his truck. Find her own way home. "Anyway," she said, clearing her throat. "It was nice getting to know you better. Intense is a better way of describing you, and I don't mind intense."

"You're not exactly the Queen of Relaxation," he said.

Dot burst out laughing, thrilled when Ward joined in. They quieted, and Ward drove steadily toward the restaurant. She'd been able to find something to eat every time they went out, and she'd already given herself a shot of insulin tonight.

"Ward, I...I thought maybe we...Okay." She took a deep breath. "I said we shouldn't mix business and pleasure, because I don't really know how to have a relationship with a man that lasts."

"Oh."

"And I'm diabetic, and I didn't want to tell you."

"Dot." He looked at her again, swiveling his head from the road to her and back. "Why is that a deal-breaker?"

"I don't like talking about it," she said to the passenger window. "I can manage it on my own, and I don't need someone fussing over me."

Ward didn't say anything for a few moments. He made a turn and came to a stop at a red light. "I think one of the nicest things about having a partner is that they can fuss over you. It's something I really miss."

Dot turned toward him, stunned at the vulnerability in his voice. "Who did you have fuss over you?"

"Mother," he said with a smile. "My sisters. It's why Ida and I are so close. I got the flu—like the demon flu. So bad I couldn't get out of bed for anything—once right after I'd graduated from high school and moved to town for a bit. Ida was still in school and living at the ranch."

He pressed on the gas when the light turned green. "I went to sleep on a Monday morning and woke up Wednesday night. Ida was right there, taking care of me. Fussing over me." He smiled to himself, and it only made him more attractive in Dot's eyes. "I've had a girlfriend or two along the way like that too." He cleared his throat. "Nothing's ever worked out though. Never been married or engaged."

"Me either," she said, and Ward nodded. This was definitely a deeper conversation than the ones they'd had on their previous dates, and it painted Ward in a whole new light.

"I don't mind fussing over the ones I care about," he

said. "And that would include you and anything you needed with your diabetes."

"Thank you," she murmured, because Dot had very few people she'd call on if she needed help. She had two really good friends she worked with, and a couple of people from church. Her brother and parents. And now...Ida and Ward.

Warmth moved through her, and she clasped her hands in her lap. "I'm sorry I said I didn't want to see you anymore. I think I was in complete denial when I sent that text."

"And now?"

"You ask a lot of hard questions," she said, grinning at him.

He returned the smile and ducked his head. "You don't have to answer that last one."

"I think I already did, Ward."

"I suppose you did, darlin'," he said. He slowed as Small Plates came up on his right. With his blinker on, he made the turn and found a place to park. "It's a miracle there's anywhere here." He peered through the windshield. "We might have a long wait. I forgot about the holidays, and it's smack dab in the middle of dinnertime."

"I don't mind waiting," she said. *With you*, she added mentally.

"All right," he said. "If you wait, I'll come open your door for you."

Dot nodded, and Ward killed the engine and slid from the truck. When he opened her door, he crowded right into the gap created between it and the truck. "Your fainting episode at the church makes so much more sense now. You had low blood sugar."

"Yes," she said. "I carry candy in my pocket everywhere I go. That's how serious it can be."

"Good to know," he said. "I've seen you eat dessert."

"I can eat whatever," she said. "I have to monitor the blood sugar and inject myself with insulin if I go crazy and have chocolate cake."

"But you love Black Forest cake," he said. "If I remember right." He gave her a smile that stole her breath again.

"You remember right." She smiled back at him. With her still seated in the truck, and Ward standing beside her, they were very nearly the same height. Dot reached out and ran her hand down the side of his face, the softness from his beard sending a thrill through her. "You really are extremely handsome," she said.

"Thank you," he said. "I think you're downright gorgeous yourself." He ducked his head, but he only kept it down for a moment before meeting her eyes again.

Without thinking or second-guessing too much, Dot curled her hand around the back of his neck, feeling the thick hair there too. She could only think about kissing him, and he clearly knew it.

Of course he did. Men like Ward Glover weren't strangers to women.

He reached up with one hand and swept his cowboy hat off his head. His other hand cradled her face, and he pressed his hat to her back at the same time he touched his lips to hers.

Explosions and waves of heat moved through Dot, and if she'd known kissing Ward Glover would be this magical and this blissfully intense, she'd have done it weeks and weeks ago.

She thoroughly enjoyed herself until an all-too-familiar *whoop! whoop!* of a police warning siren filled the air.

Ward broke the kiss at the same time the bright blue and red lights filled the parking lot.

"Sir," a man's voice said over the loudspeaker coming from the police vehicle. "Step away from the truck and keep your hands where I can see them."

"What in the world?" Ward asked, falling back a step.

Dot rolled her eyes and got out of the truck. "It's just my stupid brother," she said.

"Brother?" Ward asked, pausing near the hood of the truck and facing the cruiser.

"Yeah," Dot said, moving to stand next to him. She folded her arms and cocked her hip, glaring toward the windshield, behind which Tyson sat. "He's the third thing I didn't want to tell you about, because he gives every man I go out with a hard time."

"I didn't even know you had a brother," Ward said.

"You're about to find out why," Dot said dryly, hating that Tyson had interrupted the best kiss of her life and hoping that later that evening, she and Ward could pick up what they'd been doing before Tyson's rude intrusion.

# Chapter Three

Ward stuck his hands in the pockets of his denim jacket, wishing he'd worn a coat. He'd reasoned that he'd be spending most of his time indoors, and he hated wearing the big parka if he didn't have to. Since he ran hot most of the time, he usually didn't have to.

Right now, he looked from Dot's frowning face to the flashing lights on the cop car.

"I have a younger sister too," Dot said, her voice seeping right into Ward's eardrums and embedding itself there. He sure did like this woman, and he hoped he could keep her interest this time.

*It's not that you couldn't before*, he told himself as a tall man unfolded himself from the police vehicle. Ward glanced at Dot again. *She has walls up.*

Ward had worked his generational family ranch for decades. He knew how to re-landscape a field to be able to feed more cows. He knew how to build and fix fences. He knew how to make a piece of land that was wild into something cultivated, with roads, homes, and flowerbeds.

He could work on Dot until she realized how much she wanted to be with him.

He reached up and wiped his mouth, as if Dot wore lipstick and it would be on his lips now. He certainly didn't want Tyson to see that.

"Tyson," Dot said, stepping forward without taking Ward with her. He ended up moving a step or two later, because he wanted to meet this unknown brother. The sister too, if he could. He knew Dot's parents lived in town and that they'd been in Three Rivers for about six years, same as her.

She lived right around the corner from them, as they were getting up there in years, and the three recipes Dot had admitted to being able to make came from her elderly mother.

"You're such a loser," Dot said, swatting at her brother. He stood about six inches taller than her, close to Ward's height. Tyson flinched away from her hands, but his chuckle indicated he didn't view her as a threat.

When she linked her arm through his and faced Ward, he could see the similarities in them. Dot had a softer, more feminine face, with beautiful, high cheekbones and those wide, gorgeous hazel eyes. Everything about her seemed tinted a bit orange because of the street lamp in the parking lot, but Ward still found her stunning.

His mouth dry, he said, "I'm Ward Glover," and extended his hand for her brother to shake.

"Oh, I know who you are," he said. "My Sergeant married your sister."

"Brady," Ward said pleasantly as Tyson shook his hand. "He's great. They just had their twins tonight."

Tyson cocked his eyebrows. "And here you are, standing in the parking lot at Small Plates, kissing my sister."

Ward looked at Dot, who rolled her eyes. "I'm almost forty, Tyson. I can kiss who I want." She released his arm and switched sides, linking her arm through Ward's as she stepped to his side and turned to face her brother. "So if you'll excuse us. I'm starving, and Ward has to get back to the hospital soon."

She started to move away from him, her hand dropping to Ward's, who caught it and tightened his hold on her fingers so she couldn't go too far.

Pure heat flowed through his veins, as if someone had removed the blood and replaced it with lava instead. "Nice to meet you," he said. "I hope I'll get to know you better another time."

"You know enough for now," Dot said. "He's been tormenting me about the men I date my entire life."

"Someone has to watch out for you, Dot," Tyson said with a chuckle. His eyes danced with delight as he met Ward's again. "You two have fun."

Ward tipped his hat at the man and finally moved to follow Dot. She wove through a couple of parked cars before arriving free of them so they could walk side-by-side. She said nothing, and questions piled up behind Ward's tongue.

"How long has he lived in town?" he asked, thinking he'd seen him at Ida and Brady's wedding.

"Same as me," she said. "He got appointed to the Three Rivers Police force as their Deputy Chief six years ago." She glanced up at him, her silver blonde hair swinging as she then reached forward to open the door.

Ward's manners had failed him, but his mind still reeled from so much new information. "Does your sister live here too? How old is she?"

"She lives in Amarillo," Dot said. "Kassie's thirty-five and married. They have an eight-month-old baby." She smiled then, and Ward sure did like the way it filled her face with joy and light. He'd seen that gesture without those emotions too, and Dot had a wicked sarcastic smile that made his stomach quiver.

"Any other secret siblings I should know about?" he asked as he held the door for her to enter. "Secret diseases? Anything like that?"

Dot filled the doorway but didn't go inside. Her eyes widened, and Ward's heart kicked out an extra beat. "I lied earlier," she blurted out.

He settled his weight on his back leg, shifting away from her. "About what?"

"Can we get a table first?" She turned away from him and walked inside the restaurant. He let her hand slip away, frowning at the way she got to dictate everything.

"She lied to you," he grumbled to himself, thinking of the text that had semi-ended things between them weeks ago. That had been a lie too. Was he opening a chamber in his heart that she'd completely destroy?

Still, he followed her, because she'd left a wake of flowery perfume that made his male hormones fire like they never had before. He remembered the way she'd kissed him back, and the touch of her lips against his had initiated an entire fireworks show that was still exploding through his body.

Plenty of spark there, that was for dang sure.

She stood at the hostess station, and she glanced at him as he joined her. They didn't speak as they followed the woman to an intimate booth in the corner with windows on two sides and a circular table with a curved bench that went around it.

Dot slid in first and sat with her back to the corner. Ward entered the booth on the other side and moved all the way around to sit directly beside her. He took the menu and pretended to study it while the hostess said Marc would be their waiter.

"Thanks, Bentley," he said.

"Are you gonna need any seasonal help this winter?" she asked, leaning her hip against the tall side of the booth's seat.

"Always," Ward said, smiling at the woman. "You want me to call you?"

"For anything," she said, returning his grin. "I think I showed you I can handle the work."

"That you did," he said. "I'll be sure to put your name on my list."

She nodded and turned to leave. She nearly hit the man approaching the table, and he looked at her with a massive smile and stars in his eyes. Ward had great vision, and he could see something going on between Bentley and Marc.

"What was that about?" Dot asked, but Marc had arrived at the table.

He tossed down two cardboard drink coasters and said, "I'm Marc, and I'll be helping you out tonight. Anything to drink? Have you had a chance to look at our appetizers?"

Ward had eaten at Small Plates several times, as the women he'd gone out with sure seemed to like it. He could admit he did too, because it was fun to sample lots of different things with just a bite or two.

"I want the biggest Diet Coke you can bring me," Ward said. "Lots of ice." He looked at Dot, who wore a line between her eyebrows. "What?"

"Nothing." She buried her gaze into the menu. "I'll have the Lime Rickey with ginger ale, please."

"No problem," Marc said.

When Dot said nothing else, and the man looked like he'd leave, Ward said, "I want the loaded tray as an appetizer." He glanced at Dot again, noting her wide eyes. He swallowed and added, "Please."

"You got it." Marc grinned and walked away, finally leaving Ward and Dot to themselves. He didn't pick up his menu again, and he wished he had his drink right now. He needed something to do with his hands.

With one, he reached over and took Dot's. The other went in his pocket. "I just want to say something real quick."

"I'm sure you do."

He met her eyes, a storm brewing in his chest. "First, I

don't appreciate the sarcasm. I get that you're kind of like that, and it doesn't normally bother me, but it's annoying me tonight."

Her mouth dropped open a little bit, and Ward felt like he was setting their relationship on fire. At the same time, he had to be honest with her. If he couldn't be honest, what was the point?

"Second, if you're going to make it a habit to lie to me, I'm not real interested in perpetuating the relationship past this meal." He spoke quietly but with plenty of power. So she wouldn't accuse him of being intimidating again, he dropped his eyes to their joined hands, which he could partially see before the table concealed them.

The silence thickened between them, and Ward wondered if he should get up and walk out now. It would probably save him a lot of trouble in the future.

*Sometimes trouble can be good.* His daddy's words flowed through Ward's mind, and he stayed right where he was.

"Okay," Dot said, her voice equally as quiet as his had been. It also didn't contain a single ounce of sarcasm. "I apologize for the sarcasm. It is a default for me."

He nodded and kept his eyes down.

"I don't want to lie to you. It's just that you're so… perfect. I feel inadequate."

"That's ridiculous," he whispered, lifting her hand to his lips. "That kiss was pretty dang perfect for me."

She laughed almost under her breath, and Ward dared to lift his eyes back to hers. The dark depths of the brown sparkled, and he sure did like that.

"I've been engaged before," she said. "That was the lie.

I said I hadn't been, but I have." She swallowed and looked out into the restaurant. Ward followed her gaze, feeling removed from the entirety of it with the big, round table between him and everyone else.

"I see," he said. "You don't have to tell me about him right now, obviously."

"It was a long time ago," she said. "In Albuquerque where I used to live."

"You had another landscaping company there," Ward said. "Right?"

Dot nodded, her expression far away, almost like she could see that past life playing before her eyes. "We co-owned it...this other man and I. When we broke up, he sued me for the company. Tyson had just gotten his appointment here, and it was a huge promotion for him. My parents wanted to move here with him, and I figured that was a great time for me to make a clean break from everything in New Mexico."

So many pieces of Dot fit together in that moment, especially the part where she said she didn't want to mix business and pleasure. She'd done that, and it had ended terribly for her. Ward squeezed her hand, hoping that would convey his acceptance of her confession. Of her as a woman.

"So he's running that company in Albuquerque?" Ward asked.

"Yes," she said. "From the Ground Up does better though."

Ward put a smile on his face, glad to see Marc coming

with their drinks. His throat felt like baked sandpaper. "I see how you are. You spy on him."

"Maybe a little," Dot admitted as Marc put the sodas on the table.

"Your app is coming up in two minutes," he said. "Do you want to order?"

Ward looked at Dot, who didn't pretend to study the menu this time. "I know what I want. Do you want to go first, and I'll add on whatever you don't order?"

A smile entered her expression and touched that mouth he wanted to kiss again. "Sure." She switched her gaze to Marc. "I think we'll want the Tour of Texas, all twelve plates."

Marc nodded, didn't write anything down, and looked at Ward. Shock moved through him, because he'd been out with Dot before. They didn't agree about much, though they managed to get along.

"I'd have ordered that," he said. "I think we'd like the Dark Chocolate Express too."

"All six?" Marc asked, glancing to Dot.

Ward did too, catching Dot nodding. "All six plates," he said, grinning from ear to ear now.

"You got it." Marc left, and Ward released Dot's hand to sling that arm around her shoulders instead.

"I think we should eat at Small Plates all the time," he said, leaning down to whisper the words against her hair.

"Yeah? Why?"

"Because we agree on the food," he said, following the words with a chuckle as she snuggled further into his chest. That movement caused a sigh to slip from his lips, and he simply sat with Dot for a few moments in blissful silence, the shape and warmth of her next to him creating a memory he wouldn't soon forget.

Then she said, "You will go back and see Ida tonight, won't you?" and they started talking about his family, something they'd done in the past too.

---

A COUPLE OF HOURS LATER, WARD KNOCKED ON THE heavy hospital door and nudged it open a couple of inches. "It's just me, Ida." His eyes caught on his sister's, who held a baby in her left arm as she nursed him.

Brady held the other baby, this one wearing a pink hat and fussing for all she was worth. She wouldn't take the bottle her father tried to give her, and Brady looked beyond relieved to see Ward.

"Come in," Ida said, and Ward committed to entering the room.

He smiled at his sister and her new family, his heart warming with love for all four of them. "Looks like the waiting room cleared out." He moved over to Brady and took baby Judith from him.

"Yes, finally," Ida said with a sigh. She watched Ward settle the infant girl in the crook of his arm. He took the bottle from Brady and practically collapsed into the only chair in the room. A sigh came from his mouth and a wave of exhaustion pulled through him.

He had so much to finish for the Cowboys Provide Christmas program he participated in each year, but he reasoned that emails could go out in the morning. He could also do them from his phone, though using the computer in the office at Bull House would be faster.

He thought of Preacher driving when he was too tired, and as he bounced the baby and then tried giving her the bottle, he asked, "Can I sleep at your place tonight? I'm not sure I'm fit to make the drive up to the ranch."

"Of course," Brady said, staring at him as Judith took the bottle and quieted down to eat. "How did you do that? I've been trying to get her to eat for ten minutes."

"He has a way with babies," Ida said fondly. "They love him."

"It's the body heat," Ward murmured, gazing down at the perfect, tiny human in his arms. "I think she has your nose, Ida. She looks like those baby pictures of Mother."

Ward had been going through a lot of the family photo albums in the past month, digitizing them and uploading them to a folder his siblings could access. No one loved family history as much as Ward, and he'd been working on books for each of them, with childhood pictures and stories from Mother's journals specific to each of them. It was a slow process, and one that Ward couldn't spend as much time on as he'd like.

At the rate he was going, he figured he'd have a couple of the books ready for Christmas gifts next year. Maybe.

"Body heat," Brady said.

"She does look like Mother," Ida said.

Ward simply watched Judith suck on her bottle, finally asking, "Are you going to call her Judy?"

"Yes," Ida said. "And Johnny. Maybe JR. We haven't decided."

Ward closed his eyes and rocked baby Judy in his arms as she ate. He dozed slightly, his mind never straying too far from Dot and the near-perfect evening they'd shared. A kiss, though not another one when he'd delivered her to her truck right here in the hospital parking lot. He'd learned about her family, and she'd told him something deeply personal about her past.

"I heard you went out with Dot," Ida said, and that brought Ward's tired eyes open.

"Yeah," he said, smiling as he turned his head to meet his sister's eyes.

Ida smiled too. "She's done with that bottle, brother. Let's switch, and you can tell me about Dot while she nurses."

# Chapter Four

Dot bustled around the kitchen while her coffee brewed. She put together a plain peanut butter sandwich, tossed it in a brown lunch sack, and reached into her pantry for the sugar-free fruit snacks she loved.

Her diet may be closer to that of a twelve-year-old boy, but Dot knew how to maintain her blood sugar. She disliked eggs and yogurt, which made eating breakfast really hard. Dot also hated sitting down to eat. It felt like such a waste of time to her, and she liked things she could grab and eat on the go.

She thought of the dinner with Ward last night. That had been a nice, sit-down-and-eat affair that had taken almost two hours. She'd thoroughly enjoyed herself too, a fact that made her frown when she thought of some of the bumps in last night's date.

How could she enjoy herself so much when the man lectured her about her sarcasm?

"Probably because of that hot kiss," she muttered, returning to the coffee maker now that it had completed its job. She poured herself a tall thermos of the stuff, skipped the sugar and cream, and twisted the lid on tight. She would nurse it all morning, along with a few bites of a high-fiber breakfast bar here and there, and she wouldn't need insulin.

She packed it with her anyway, and she checked her jeans pocket for the hard candy that went everywhere with her. With her breakfast and lunch in her hands, she headed out to her truck.

She made the drive from the older, prettier East side of Three Rivers to the more industrial West side. From the Ground Up sat on a huge plot of land on the corner of Tenth West and the highway that ran toward Amarillo.

Piles of decorative rocks, bark, and pavers made a nice display for customers, and Dot had worked hard to make the lawn and trees and flower beds in front of the building look amazing. She decorated it for the holidays, and right now, since Christmas was only a couple of days away, she'd put a family of light-up reindeer in the front garden area that surrounded the pond.

She'd done all of the landscaping there, and she periodically changed out the bark and decorative rock so she could keep things fresh and show off new products.

Bella's sporty coupe sat around the back of the building, as did Wendy's sensible SUV. Wendy had been with Dot from the very first day she'd opened From the Ground Up, and she'd been a valuable asset in helping Dot acclimate to and understand the culture in Three Rivers, Texas.

Born and raised in New Mexico, Dot had had to become a Texan, something she felt sure she'd accomplished some days while on others she felt absolutely certain it would never happen.

As Dot got out of her truck, Calvin turned to park next to her on the passenger side. She waited at the back tailgate for him to get out, noting the Batman lunch box he used. She smiled at it. "You and Trevor use the same lunch box."

"He likes to be like his daddy," Calvin said, grinning. "What's on the schedule for today?"

"I have no idea," Dot said. "Wendy will have everything printed, I'm sure."

The older woman liked doing things old-school, and that included printing delivery receipts though From the Ground Up had the software and devices needed to do digital signatures for the receipt of orders. Dot could admit she didn't mind having something physical for her older customers to sign and for herself to look at when she was navigating around town in her huge dump truck, which she'd named Brutus.

"It's Bella's birthday," Dot said, though she wasn't sure how Calvin could've forgotten. Wendy had sent no less than seventeen texts about the lunchtime party she wanted everyone to attend. From the Ground Up employed six people besides Dot, and noon was when they were finally all there.

"I got her a gift card," Calvin said with a nod. "You?"

"I hope it's not to Small Plates," Dot said. "Because that's what I got."

"Nope, for Wilde & Organic. She loves to go to their cooking classes with Dover, and I thought they'd like to go to a couple on me."

"Good idea," Dot said, wishing her gift card was that personal. She'd only chosen Small Plates because she'd been there last night. She wasn't even sure Bella liked the restaurant.

As she entered the building, her phone rang. Dot tucked her lunch sack under her arm, thinking she needed a hard lunch box so she wouldn't smash her sandwich, and pulled her phone from her back pocket.

Ward's name sat on the screen, along with that pretty-boy cowboy face, and Dot's pulse rioted with the need to hear his voice.

"Ward Glover?" Calvin asked. "I thought you broke up with him."

"They're back together," Bella said, taking Dot's coffee and lunch so she wouldn't drop them both. Bella's dark green eyes shone like deep emeralds. "At least the gossip network says they are. They were spotted at Small Plates last night. Together."

"Together?" Calvin asked. "On purpose?"

"I think when you're caught kissing someone in the parking lot, it's on purpose," Bella said over her shoulder as she took Dot's things toward the office.

Her phone rang again, and Dot blinked her way out of what the gossip network of Three Rivers knew and tapped to answer Ward. Her arm felt encased in cement as she lifted it to her ear, and she was sure Ward had said hello twice before her brain caught up.

"Hey," she said.

"Can you hear me?" he asked.

"Yep." Dot turned away from Calvin, who was walking toward the staff room. He'd put his lunch in the fridge there, and Dot could see Wendy in there hanging decorations for the party later that day.

"I stayed in town last night," he said. "I'm using Ida's computer for a bunch of admin work this morning, and I wondered if you'd have time for lunch before I go back up to Shiloh Ridge."

Dot wanted to blurt out yes, of course she'd have time for lunch. She'd *make* time for lunch with him. Wendy left the staff room, a fist full of papers in her hand.

"I don't really know my deliveries yet," she said as Wendy made a beeline toward her.

She handed Dot four papers and said, "The cake will be here at eleven-thirty. You'll be good until one." She turned back to her desk, which sat just outside the staff room. Bella was Dot's personal assistant, and she helped with deliveries if necessary, but she really acted as the administrative assistant.

Wendy handled the phones and the filing, the ordering of new products, and the inventory. The bell on the door Dot had walked through a minute ago rang, and she turned to find Amber walking in. She was the morning sales person, and she'd manage the floor and the register for anyone who came into the store looking for fertilizer, potting soil, or a new garden hose. She'd send anyone who wanted rocks, pavers, trees, and more to the outside sales person, who was Holden Bickmore.

"Morning," Amber trilled, stopping right in front of Dot. "I heard you had the *hottest* date last night, with the hottest cowboy bachelor in *all* of Three Rivers."

Dot's mind blanked, though she was very aware of Ward's low chuckle on the other end of the line.

"She did," Wendy said, taking Amber further into the store. "Now come on, she's talking to him right now, and I need you to...." Her voice faded as they moved further from Dot.

Her face burned and her stomach swooped. She turned away from her store and her friends and stepped back outside.

"Lunch, sweetheart?" he asked. "I'm assuming Wendy just handed you your deliveries."

"Amber is twenty-three," Dot blurted out. "She's just a little...eager to know the details of my love life." She sucked in a breath, the last two words that left her mouth making embarrassment shoot through her. "I mean—"

"Love life?" Ward asked, his voice that rough, demanding one that annoyed Dot.

She pressed her eyes closed and took a deep breath. "Are you aware there's a gossip network in Three Rivers?"

"There is?"

"You cowboys are always a little dense about this kind of stuff," Dot said, hoping her voice sounded flirtatious enough. She honestly wasn't sure how to flirt with Ward Glover. "Everyone seems to know we went out last night, and that you...that I...that we kissed." Her voice lowered with every word until she whispered the last couple of words.

"Do they?"

"Yes," Dot said. "Bella knew, and Wendy, and you heard Amber. That's women from twenty-three to sixty." Dot wiped one hand through her hair before realizing she'd pulled it back into a ponytail like she normally did for work. She exhaled, trying to decide if she cared about this or not. At least everyone in town would know who Ward Glover belonged to.

She pushed against the thought, because a man like Ward didn't belong to anyone. He was his own man, and Dot could barely think of him as hers to begin with. She also wasn't one-hundred percent sure she wanted to keep dating him.

Her heartbeat shouted at her, and Dot warred with herself.

"I guess I'm kind of isolated up at the ranch," Ward mused. "I had no idea people would be talking about us."

"Tyson did cause a scene," Dot said. The breeze kicked up, reminding her of the winter temperatures. Calvin came outside, his deliveries secured in his folder, reminding her she had work to do.

"I can't have lunch with you today," she said. "It's Bella's birthday, and we're having a big party for her here at lunchtime." Her mind spun, and she thought of feeding some new gossip to the mill. "How about you come here for that?"

"Really?" Ward asked, plenty of surprise in his voice.

"We won't be alone," Dot said. "Obviously. But then you can talk to Wendy about scheduling your thirty-five."

"Mixing business and pleasure, I see," Ward commented, his tone full of meaning.

Dot smiled to herself and the weak winter sun filling the sky with gold and light. "Yes," she said. "I think you're seeing that right."

"All right, Dot," he drawled, her name in that delicious cowboy voice almost more than she could handle. "I'll be by around noon? Is that when the party is?"

"Noon, cowboy," she said, ending the call. She drew in a deep, cold breath and turned back to the building. She needed her coffee and breakfast bar to go with her on her morning deliveries, and she couldn't even pick up a shovel without her leather gloves.

---

"ALL RIGHT, ALL RIGHT," WENDY LEWIS YELLED. SHE'D raised five children, and she had a loud voice and a no-nonsense personality when it came to business. Dot had let her handle Ward's demands over the past couple of years, and she stayed out of the way now too.

She leaned against the wall near the back of the room, facing the only way in and out. Ward should've been here five minutes ago, and the man wasn't known for being late. At least Dot had never known him to be tardy.

The group, which included all the employees of From the Ground Up, a couple of their major contractors Dot used when she couldn't handle her business herself, and Bella's boyfriend, settled down.

Dot cast one more look toward the doorway and told

herself not to do it again. She felt like she'd been stood up, and she couldn't help the pinch behind her lungs.

"All right," Wendy said again, this time smiling around at everyone who'd obeyed her. "We have a very special musical number planned for Bella's birthday, and then we'll eat. It's simple. Sandwiches and cake."

Dot had already taken her insulin so she could enjoy the chocolate cake Wendy had ordered from Three Cakes —and Holly Ann Glover. Those Glovers seemed to be everywhere, that was for sure.

Silence covered the room, and then Amber said, "Oh my...." and let the words drip there.

Before Dot could find the woman to see what she was looking at, the strumming of a guitar filled the room. Her eyes flew to the doorway she wasn't going to look at again, and this time, Ward Glover's tall frame and broad shoulders filled it.

He'd already fitted the neck of his guitar through the doorway, and as a smile exploded onto her face and her heartbeat crashed against her ribs, his voice started the first strains of "Happy birthday to you...."

Everyone joined in by the third or fourth word, but not Dot. She couldn't tear her eyes from the best-looking cowboy in the state. Maybe the country. Fine, perhaps the entire world. He called to her in a way no one else had, not even her fiancé.

She could only stare as Ward played and sang, his fingers moving easily on the strings without him having to look. It was as if he knew one of her kryptonite weaknesses was a man with a guitar in his hand.

As the song ended and Bella leaned forward to blow out the candles on her cake, Dot finally took her eyes from the cowboy. She felt everyone watching her, not Bella, and that shifted in a single breath too. She still caught the way Wendy watched her, that matronly smile on her face that said she knew exactly what was going on in Dot's mind and body.

Dot felt like she needed to step outside and get some air, because her normal bodily functions had stopped working properly. Part of her wanted to run, though her tall frame had never enjoyed the activity much. Her knees were too knobby and her chest too big, and running was actually painful in a lot of ways.

But if she didn't have to greet Ward in front of all of her employees? Running away sounded like her best option while everyone cheered for Bella. They surged forward then, picking up paper plates and chattering with one another.

Dot stepped around them and over to Ward, who removed the strap from around his shoulder and head and set his guitar in the corner. He straightened to face her, hope and handsomeness streaming from his face. "Hey, there," he said, easily taking her into an embrace.

He didn't hold it for too long. Just long enough for her to say, "Hey, yourself, you country music star."

He chuckled as he stepped back. He wore a dark brown cowboy hat today, and Dot asked, "Do you keep a spare hat at your sister's?"

"All my spares are in my truck." He indicated the guitar.

"I just picked that up from the music store. They were restringing it."

"It sounds amazing," she said, glancing toward the instrument and back to the man. "You're a great player."

"I took lessons growing up," he said with a shrug. "They were from my grandfather, but he was a great guitarist, so I think it still counts."

Dot agreed and reached for his hand. "Are you ready to meet everyone here?"

"I think I've met them all before," he said, glancing past her to the fray surrounding the six-foot sub sandwich Wendy's husband had brought in. The two of them already sat on the love seat in front of the window close to where Dot had been standing.

She tugged him in that direction. "I don't think you've met Amber," she said. "She's pretty new."

The redhead appeared in front of them, her brown eyes as wide as a deer caught in the headlights. "My goodness, Ward Glover! You're *so* talented. I've never heard *anyone* play like that before."

Ward looked at Dot, who looked right on back at him. He faced Amber with a kind smile on his face, though Dot wanted to burst out laughing. "Thank you, ma'am," he drawled, really laying on his Texas accent. "You must be Amber."

The girl giggled and tucked her hair like she could get Ward to ask her out. Dot simply smiled and shook her head, though she was impressed by Ward's attitude and demeanor toward Amber. In fact, Dot was the one with gossipy thoughts in her head, and she watched as Ward dropped her hand and linked his through Amber's.

"I play so well because I was in this band once...." He led her toward the end of the table where the paper plates were, and Dot watched them go, once again in awe of the magnificent Ward Glover.

*So you like him*, she conceded. She started to argue with herself—after all, the man was demanding and arrogant *and* he'd once ruined her mother's raspberry cream whip before a church potluck—and stopped.

"Yeah," she whispered as Ward started introducing himself to Calvin and Holden. "You like him *a lot*."

# Chapter Five

Ward kept one eye on Dot as he took a section of the sub sandwich and a hefty piece of chocolate cake. She'd barely moved from just inside the doorway, and he smiled at Bella, wished her happy birthday, and turned toward the silver blonde who'd kept him awake far past his bedtime last night.

"Are you going to eat?" he asked, approaching her. He extended his plate toward her, and she took it. "Pick somewhere to eat and save me a spot, okay?" He turned before she could say anything. Back at the table, he got another plate, another piece of sandwich, and a larger piece of cake. He did love chocolate cake, and this wasn't the bakery kind with the greasy frosting. This was homemade chocolate cake, with thick, rich, chocolatey frosting that he'd been able to smell the moment he'd stepped inside the building.

Ranger, his older brother, had always teased him about having the nose of a bloodhound, and sometimes it served

Ward well. It could be a curse too, but right now, his stomach growled at him and his mouth started to water.

He once again kept track of Dot as she chose a spot down at the other end of the table from where the food sat. Calvin, the other truck driver here at the landscaping company, sat on one side of her, with Holden taking the seat next to him. No one took the one on Dot's right, and it sure seemed like everyone knew Ward fit there.

He slid into the chair and glanced at Dot. "How did your deliveries go this morning?" He poked his fork into his cake and took a bite.

"You're eating dessert first," she said.

"Mm hm." He'd been absolutely right about the nature of this cake, and he let his eyes drift closed. A moan came from his chest, and he wasn't even aware of it until Dot started to laugh.

"Now I know what to get you for your birthday," she said, the light radiating from Dot's face made Ward feel like a million bucks. She sobered the moment by meeting his eye. "When is your birthday?"

"February," he said, his throat a bit narrow due to the gorgeous woman gazing at him like she'd very much like to kiss him again.

---

WARD WHISTLED AS HE STRODE TOWARD THE NEW BARN Bishop and Montana had finished a week or two ago. They'd been working non-stop around the ranch for a while now, and Ward had a feeling it was all going to come to a screeching halt once Montana had their baby. She wasn't due until March, and that still gave everyone three months to see what they could do.

They'd moved on to building Arizona and Duke a new house on the Rhinehart Ranch, and all the initial designs for Preacher's new house down the hill at the Kinder Ranch had been finalized.

Ward had sat in the meeting where Bishop had detailed the permits he and Montana had filed with the town and he'd been on-site with Preacher and everyone else as the well had been removed and the first sewer lines brought in.

He'd spent the morning sending out reminder emails that he needed any receipts from the Cowboys Provide Christmas related to the gifts, food, and shipping they'd provided. He was acting as the treasurer this year, and while he didn't do a whole lot leading up to Christmas, he had to make an accounting of what the program had spent for farmers and ranchers across Texas by February fifteenth.

The previous treasurer had said that it took several emails and sometimes some phone calls to get everyone to turn in their accounting forms and receipts. Ward didn't understand that, as he always sent his receipts the moment he finished shopping and shipping. He saw no reason to hold onto them, and then he didn't get hounded to do it.

He kept everything in a folder in the filing cabinet in the office at Bull House, and Ward told himself as he pushed into the barn that it was time to go through his files and clean out things he didn't need anymore.

His phone chimed, and he tugged it free from his

pocket. His brother had texted to say the new update for Two Cents was ready to go out, and he'd just pushed it to Ward's app. *Check it, would you?*

*On it*, Ward texted back, though he had a full day's work to do on the ranch and only a few hours of daylight left. Spending an hour with Dot during her lunchtime—even with her friends and co-workers there—had been worth feeling harried now.

He opened Two Cents and gave it a few seconds to download the update. It restarted while he went down the aisle in the barn and checked the clipboards from his crew. They moved the animals for the rotational ranching, and he found that all five groups had been rotated today, as required.

Ward loved the rotational ranching concept. He liked utilizing the land the Good Lord had given his family in the best way possible. It felt responsible and honorable to him, and if Ward couldn't feel like that about his job, he'd have quit at the ranch a long time ago.

After all, it wasn't a job that got a lot of accolades. No one even really knew what he did up here, out in the barns, or why he'd needed meat birds and chickens. He knew though, and he'd wanted to continue to increase the value of their ranch, the value of their cattle, and the value of his role in all of it.

He looked down at his phone, which told him the new features inside the Two Cents app. Users could now submit businesses to lists instead of having to vote on existing ones. With the growth in Three Rivers, it had become impossible for Ranger, Ward, Ace, and Bishop to keep up with all the new companies, stores, services, and more that were housed on the Two Cents app.

With this new feature, owners, employees, or anyone could enter a new business. With a website and a physical address, along with three top categories for the new entity, the business would be added to the database. Users could then vote for it on any list, people could leave comments, and everyone got a fair chance to be noticed around town.

Ranger sent another text: *Try to add a business.*

Ward swiped away the message and closed the notification window. This new round of updates also included stronger security measures, and the ability to link a phone number to the app, so he could call Down Under straight from the app if he wanted to order barbecue baby back ribs.

He actually tried that first, and the line at Mack's Motor Sports rang easily from the app. "Mack's," a woman said, but it wasn't Ranger's wife. Oakley owned the car dealership and ATV rental, but she'd been working about half-time since having Wilder last March.

"Just checking something," he said. "Sorry to bother you."

"No problem, sir," and the call ended. Ward made a mental note to tell Oakley that her receptionist did a great job on the phone as he went back to the list and tapped on Restaurants. From there, he chose fine dining, and he found a new button sitting on the top right. It was a blue circle with a plus sign through it, and while he and Ranger had poured over what to make the "add a business" button look like, he still thought he'd know exactly what to do with it.

"Especially with the instructions in the notification pop-up," he muttered. He tapped on the plus sign and went through the user experience of adding a business. He'd tell Ranger the name of it, and his brother would delete it.

He'd implemented a review process for the submissions, as he anticipated having multiple submissions for some businesses, and he wanted the app to be as accurate as possible. He'd worked incredibly hard on the app, and he'd kept it a secret for a long time. Now that it was out in the open, the ranch actually invested in the app and the infrastructure pieces that ran it.

Ward could get lost in the app, as well as the backside of it. He loved computers and organization, and nothing kept things cleaner and clearer than writing code to make it be that way.

He was self-taught, mostly by studying what Ranger had written and listening to his brother talk. He'd been working on Two Cents with him for the past three years, and Ward did love seeing the advancements and ideas that came from their pow-wow sessions—all of which happened on horseback.

Ward longed to ride his horse right now, but he tapped on *submit* and texted Ranger the name of the fake business. Then he got to work in the barn, setting task lists for the following day and heading out to check on the pig pens that had been slowly eroding over the years.

Cactus loved pigs, and the man wouldn't let them get

rid of the oinkers yet. All that meant for Ward was a foul smell in the heat of summer and a new set of stalls as the old ones continued to deteriorate.

The wind gusted out on the ranch, and Ward flipped up his collar. Out at the pens, which sat beyond the barns and the chicken coops, the hay loft and all the stables, Ward found that the roof had collapsed on one of the pens.

"Good thing Cactus took those pigs to his barn," he muttered, trying to lift the roof right up off the pen. He managed to get it up a few inches—enough to see no pigs had been left behind and then smashed—before dropping it again.

He exhaled as he got out his phone to call Bishop. "Heya, Ward." A wild rushing across the speaker of his phone told Ward that Bishop was outside in the wind too. "What's up?"

"We need new pigpens," he said. "Cactus was right, and the ones we've got are useless." He glared at the splintered wood in the corner, where the roof had broken.

"Uh, okay," Bishop said, clearly distracted. "I don't know when we're going to do that. Where are the pigs? Didn't Cactus take them?"

"To his barn, yes," Ward said, turning his back to the wind. It pushed him forward, and he didn't resist it. "I could call Leon." He waited for a moment, and when Bishop didn't object, he continued. "He's great with this kind of stuff, and he could probably use the work."

"As long as I don't have to work with him," Bishop said. "He insulted Montana the last time she called him, and she vowed not to use him again."

"I know." Ward sighed. "Who are you guys using once Montana goes on maternity leave?" She'd been insistent that she wouldn't quit around the ranch entirely. Zona and Duke's house wouldn't be done before the baby came, and surely they had a plan for keeping the construction moving despite the arrival of their baby.

"She's meeting with the Lowensteins today," Bishop said. "We've been talking to Lira and Barney. They're nice, their portfolio is impressive, and they have great references."

"They're also out of Pampa," Ward said, because he knew the Lowensteins. He'd worked with them on projects around the ranch before Bishop and Montana had started doing the construction full-time. "That's a long drive."

"They'd come set up a trailer," Bishop said, and the wind rushing across his phone ceased. "They don't have kids, and they work the way Montana and I do. We told them we have RV hookups and they're welcome on the ranch. Duke said they can stay at his ranch too, and we've even got hookups at Kinder now."

"That should work then," Ward said, marveling at how much Bishop and Montana could achieve. He thought they got along together so well, and not just professionally. A lump of jealousy formed in his throat, and he was glad when Bishop simply kept talking about the negotiations they were in with the Lowensteins.

"I finally told Montana to give them what they want." Bishop chuckled. "It's not like we can't afford it."

"Right?" Ward laughed with him, finally reaching the safety of one of the oldest buildings on the property. He ducked inside the stable, and he wasn't surprised to see all the horses safely in their stalls.

Three Rivers had experienced quite the wind storms this winter, and Ward was already ready for spring to arrive. He kept a religious eye on the weather, and he knew it was going to snow overnight from Christmas Eve to Christmas.

"Talk to you later," Bishop said, and Ward ended the call.

The child inside him couldn't wait for a white Christmas, and the man inside him would work like a dog for the rest of today and tomorrow so he could have Christmas Eve and Chrsitmas Day off.

Not totally off, as animals had to be fed no matter what day of the year it was. But off enough that he could go next door to the homestead and enjoy the family party on Christmas Eve. This year, Holly Ann and Ace were hosting Christmas dinner at their house, which they'd moved into just last week.

The only thing that seemed to be constant around Shiloh Ridge these days was how often things changed.

Ward checked all the horses, his mind moving through what they needed without a checklist. When he'd first learned how to take care of a horse properly, his daddy hadn't allowed him to do anything without a checklist.

Straw, food, water, hooves, flesh, teeth, eyes. Ward made sure everyone in all the stables had what they needed, and he fed and watered any horses that required it.

Back home, he cleaned the kitchen, saw a note from Mister that said he'd be up at Duke's until late, and Ward started making dinner for just himself. For a while there, he'd thought he'd like to live alone, because he was never really alone. This ranch housed dozens of people, from married couples, to families, to single cowboys in over a dozen residences.

But cooking for himself? That was akin to torture, and he should've pulled out a bowl and a box of cereal instead of spending thirty minutes opening cans and browning beef to make taco soup. With it bubbling away on the stove, he left it to go into the office on the other side of the main floor.

The gift for Judge sat there, and Ward picked it up. The man adored gardening and photography, and Ward had bought him a book about taking pictures of landscapes. He'd also contacted Whitney Wilde and asked her if she'd be willing to consult with Judge and teach him a thing or two about his camera.

His cousin had bought the camera a couple of years ago, but every time Ward asked him about it, Judge said he hadn't shot a picture in months. "Always months," Ward said, running his fingers down the spine of the book.

Honestly, he hoped this gift would remind Judge of something he loved and spur him to action. He flipped open the front cover and found the envelope with the training sessions with Whitney there, and then he set it down and reached for the wrapping paper.

He wasn't sure who'd drawn his name this year, as it was a secret thing until the family party. They usually held it the Sunday before Christmas, but this year, it had been scheduled on Christmas Eve as Christmas itself fell on the Sabbath. They'd be going down to town for church that day, and then having lunch together at Ace's, and everyone had wanted to keep them as two separate events.

He thought of Dot, instantly wanting to invite her to the family party. Lots of his siblings and cousins had brought their significant others to family get-togethers. Maybe it was his turn to finally bring someone.

"Is she significant enough?" he asked himself as he folded and taped. They'd had a great lunch, and he'd asked her to dinner. She'd declined, saying she kept From the Ground Up open until eight o'clock on Thursdays, and she had to stay and close up.

*She's significant enough to you*, he thought, but he wasn't sure if he was significant enough to her. He couldn't help getting a tad bit ahead of himself when it came to Dorothy Crockett, and he finished wrapping Judge's gift and sat in the desk chair, his mind entirely consumed by her.

She'd been wearing jeans today—of course. The woman always wore jeans. Her tank top had been light green, with a peach-colored sweater over that. She stole his breath even now, and Ward wondered what that meant.

"Ward," Preacher called, appearing in the office a moment later.

"Yep." Ward stood up, glad his cousin could walk here by himself now. He'd been in a terrible car accident that had left him with a broken hip only a couple of months ago.

"Are you going to invite Dot to the family party?" He held his phone away from his mouth. "Ace and Holly Ann are grocery shopping and he said you must be in here, because he couldn't get ahold of you." Preacher's light eyes searched Ward's face, but he had no idea how to answer.

"Does one more mouth really make a difference?" he asked, thinking only of the gossip network Dot had mentioned and how his sisters-in-law were clearly part of it.

"Holly Ann says to invite her," Preacher said, turning. He limped slightly, and Ward saw it all. He'd gone on enough walks with Preach to catch the carefully controlled pain in his eyes too. "He's going to invite her," he said as he moved into the kitchen. A moment later, Preacher called over his shoulder, "Hey, Ward, can I have some of this taco soup?"

## Chapter Six

❧

"Come on, boy," Dot said, coaching her big, noisy dump truck to kick into a lower gear so she could get up this final hill to Shiloh Ridge Ranch. Beside her on the seat, her hound dog George panted and looked out the window lazily, not a care in the world.

Dot had a few cares on her mind, truth be told. First, she hadn't seen Ward in a couple of days. She'd had to work late on Thursday night, so she couldn't go to dinner with him. Friday, he'd texted several times but nothing had worked out, especially after he'd said he needed to check his turkeys and then he'd gone dark.

He'd called last night to say he'd found an entire pasture of them missing, and it had taken him and his brothers—or cousins, Dot wasn't really sure—a few hours to find them. By then, he'd been "exhausted and freezing," in his own words.

When she'd asked him what he was doing, he said he'd

collapsed on the couch in front of the fireplace to let his clothes get a little drier before he showered. She'd then asked him what he was wearing, and he'd laughed right out loud and asked her if that was a pick-up line.

Humiliation had muted her last night, and she shook her head again now, just as Brutus kicked into the lower gear and steadily climbed the hill. She'd been up to Shiloh Ridge before, and she'd admired the arch over the road as well as all the outbuildings and houses she'd seen.

The men and women up here took good care of their land, their animals, and each other. Dot could feel the love and attention to detail rising straight from the very dirt she drove over and she wasn't even there yet.

The road seemed to go on and on, until finally, her headlights caught on the metal poles holding up the wooden sign that signaled her arrival at the ranch. She hadn't told Ward she was coming, and nerves rolled across her shoulders as if she needed to stretch out the muscles there.

"Please don't let him be too busy," she prayed, glancing over at George again. The hound looked at her, his eyes doleful and his tongue lulling out of his mouth. She grinned at him and reached over to scrub his head. "He's going to be happy to see us. He is."

She gripped the steering wheel and silently prayed that what she'd just said would be true. To give herself an even greater edge, she'd brought double cheeseburgers from The Burger Barn. Ward had mentioned a couple of times that he loved the doubles there, because they came with toasted buns and no pickles. Apparently, in the world where Ward Glover lived, pickles could ruin any good sandwich.

Dot smiled to herself—or maybe to her hound dog. Either way, she was smiling as she trundled onto the ranch and dang near got blown off the road by a strong gust of wind. The weather this Christmas Eve was supposed to be nasty, and Dot had purposely come in the early afternoon so she wouldn't have to drive home in the dark.

She had the distinct thought that she better get the gravel she'd brought with her unloaded quickly and get back on the road if her desire to be home before the sun sank could become reality.

She made the wide right turn on the graveled road to go in front of the homestead, seeing plenty of trucks there. They'd been parked side-by-side, and she counted seven before she'd passed them all.

Perhaps all the Glovers had already gathered for lunch. Dot eased off the accelerator, though she knew Ward lived in the house a hundred yards past this one. He'd mentioned it would be easy to find, and Dot hadn't had a problem any of the times she'd come to Shiloh Ridge.

Now, though, she couldn't even see Ward's house, and it couldn't be more than a hundred and fifty feet from her. Her nerves sang out again, this time for an entirely different reason. Her mind flashed through the supplies she kept in Brutus—a sleeping bag, a blanket, an emergency first aid kit. She had a box of MRE's, but she had never eaten the ready-to-eat meals and she didn't want Christmas Day to be when she started.

Dot and Brutus took up the whole road, and she eased

the dump truck forward and off to the side in front of a garage. She put the beast in park and turned to the living, slobbering beast on the seat. "I'm just going to run in and see if he's here. Maybe Bear or Ranger can radio him if he's not."

Ward would be thrilled to see the gravel. Dot wasn't worried about that. She did harbor some trepidation about how Ward would react to seeing *her*, and she glanced down at her jacket. It covered a blue tank top that had a rainbow on it. She wore her usual jeans and steel-toed work boots, and she'd whipped her hair into a ponytail that morning before her first delivery to Payne's Pest-Free.

Marcy Walker had met her there, her baby strapped to her chest. The woman was a powerhouse if Dot had ever seen one, and she liked Marcy a whole lot. Number one, she owned a pest-control business as a woman, dusting all the fields at the dozen or so ranches surrounding Three Rivers. She dealt with a lot of men and she did so just fine.

Dot admired that, because she'd had to learn to do the same. The cowboys in New Mexico were a bit different than the headstrong ones here, as if the men in Texas believed themselves to be the only true cowboys on Earth.

Dot didn't think so, but whenever Ward came to mind, he was definitely the cowboy god among other men who wore cowboy hats.

She jumped from the dump truck and got flung right back into the metal door. Pain shot through her hand, but Dot didn't take the time to examine her fingers. She better get inside quickly.

She couldn't see much, so she cupped her hands around

her eyes and ran, keeping her gaze on the gravel. When there was a break in the fence, she darted through it, her feet meeting cement. Then a set of wide, wooden steps.

Wow, the wind up here was twice as deadly as the small gusts they'd had in town. It was like Dot now existed entirely on another planet. She panted as she reached the porch and faced the massive front door.

Something ran down her face, and when she wiped it, her fingers came away bloody. Alarm pulled through her, and Dot got woozy fast. She stumbled forward, pressing both hands against the wooden door. "Help," she said, her heartbeat sprinting through her chest.

She had the mental capacity to step to the side and ring the doorbell, something she did once, twice, and then three times before she told herself to stop. She'd barely taken her hand from the little button when the door opened.

Ward's younger brother stood there, and the surprise on Ace's face switched to concern in less time than Dot could blink. She didn't have time to say anything before he yelled, "I need help here," and rushed out onto the porch to support her with one arm sliding under one of hers. "Okay, Dot, can you walk with me?"

Ward appeared, and his shock doubled as he took in Dot's bloody face. Why did she have to show up with a bloody face? That wasn't in the plan. Nothing she was doing was according to her plan, as she'd left the bag of cheeseburgers in the dump truck.

"George is going to eat the cheeseburgers," she said as Ace passed Dot to Ward.

"I have no idea what that means," Ward said, and Dot remembered she hadn't told him she had a dog. She hadn't told him much of anything. "Oh, wait," he said. "George is your dog. Where is he? Did he come with you? Is he hurt too?"

"I left him in the dump truck," she said as he guided her to the right of the stairs, past a flocked-white Christmas tree with charming crocheted ornaments on it, to a spot where he opened a door seemingly out of the wall itself. A half-bath sat there, and Dot marveled that it was so white and so clean. "I brought lunch for us, with a load of your thirty-five. I thought it would be a good Christmas surprise."

"It's a surprise," he assured her. "Ace, will you go get George? He's a hound dog, but he's really nice."

"I parked in front of the garage just north of the house," Dot said.

"I'll take Bishop and Mister," Ace said, and Dot caught sight of the three men leaving in the mirror.

She looked at herself and drew in a sharp gasp.

"Tell me where it hurts," Ward said, wetting a washcloth before he wiped it down the side of her face.

"It's not my face," she said. "At least I don't think so." She looked down at her fingers, and they were definitely the culprit of the blood. "Oh, I can't look at my own blood." Her words slurred, and the world spun. She could give herself a shot and be fine. But this much blood?

She reached out and grabbed onto the nearest solid object, which thankfully, was the bathroom counter and not Ward Glover.

Dot yelped at the pain that tore through her right hand, and Ward said, "Let me see, Dot."

"I think...the wind blew the door on Brutus and my hand got cut." She could see it all in clarity now, and she pressed her eyes closed and focused on pulling in breath after breath as Ward's rough fingers handled hers gently.

He put a warm cloth on them. He cleaned them up. He wrapped them in bandages. "Good as new," he said. "You've got some blood on your face still. Do you want me to...?" He turned on the sink again and Dot simply kept breathing while he finished making her presentable.

"You can open your eyes now."

Dot drew in another breath and did what he said. His bright blue eyes had never been classified on the color scale, and they dove right into Dot's heart. She reached up and cradled his face. "You're so handsome."

"Thank you," he whispered, his hand mirroring hers on the side of her face. "You're beautiful."

"No one's ever called me beautiful," she said.

"I don't believe that. Your former fiancé? Never?"

She shook her head. "I'm not beautiful, Ward. I'm manly. I have these boxy shoulders and hair that's fifteen different colors. It's wispy if I let it grow too long, and my nose is way too big."

"So is mine," he said.

"Fits your face though."

"And yours fits yours."

"Ward," a man said, and Ward jumped away from Dot as if he'd been electrocuted by the voice. Dot looked past him too, catching sight of Bear Glover. "Sorry. Hey, Dot.

Uh, the tornado sirens are going off. Mother put on the radio, and they're calling a severe storm warning for the next several hours. Winds up to eighty miles per hour. Snow coming earlier than they thought."

"Okay," Ward said.

"I should go," Dot said.

"We're splitting up early," Bear said. "Everyone's headed home to shelter so they'll be in their own beds. Ace is taking your mother; Bishop is taking mine."

Ward strode out of the bathroom. "What do I need to do?"

"Go home," Bear said. "Make sure you have wood. Check the gas on your generator. Preach, Judge, and Mister left."

"What about my dog?" Dot asked, her panic rising up. "Mister left to get my dog." She joined the two men in the foyer as Ace helped his mother out the front door.

"See you, Bear," Ace said. "Bye, Ward."

"See ya," Ward said. "What about Etta? Have you heard from Ida?"

"Ida's good," a woman said as she headed for the open door. A chill had worked its way into the house, and Dot shivered. "She texted us girls to find out where we all were."

"She just went home today," Ward said.

"She'll be okay," another man said, and Dot recognized Ranger too. He came down the steps with a baby in his arms, and he smiled at Dot. "Hey, Dot."

"Hello." She wasn't quite sure what to do with her hands, and the urge to get back to Brutus and then home to her familiar surroundings drove her to take a step toward the front door. "I should go, Ward."

George barked at the same time Ward looked at her. "You can't go," he said.

"I agree," Bear said. "You'll never make it back in this weather."

"The sirens are going off right now," Ranger said.

Dot looked at the three of them, then crouched down to scrub George's face between her hands. "What should we do, bud? Huh?"

"Do you think Brutus can make it down the road to my house?" Ward asked, joining her in a crouch. He too stroked George, and the dog's eyes closed in bliss. Ward kept his head down, his cowboy hat concealing his face. "I've got loads of food and four empty bedrooms." He met her eye, and something like lightning struck her straight in the chest.

"Okay," she said.

Ward stood up and extended his hand toward her. Dot had the very real feeling that if she took it, she'd be sealing her fate, whether good or bad.

She slipped her hand in his and let him help her to her feet. "Come on, George," she said, barely glancing at the other Glovers still in the foyer. "We only have to go a little further."

# Chapter Seven

Ward felt like his brain was bouncing against his skull. "My word," he said. "This is like getting blended up." His teeth knocked together as Dot continued the pilgrimage down the lane Ward couldn't see. Not only was Brutus's front end massive, but the wind had blown loose dirt into the air from all over the ranch, mixing it with the snow that had started to fall in earnest.

Dot said nothing as the truck bounced along, but the tightness in her white knuckles spoke volumes.

"Right there," Ward said. "See my truck?"

"You don't park in the garage?"

Annoyance sang through Ward, but he couldn't pinpoint why. "Not today," he said. "I was in a rush, and I figured I'd pull it in later." The need to do so now rang like a gong in his ears, and he could barely hear Dot's next question.

Several seconds passed as he struggled to comprehend

what she'd asked. "Yes," he finally said. "We have firewood. We might have to bring it in, but we've got lots."

"I can build a mean fire," she said.

"Okay." Ward couldn't settle down and make his mind focus on any single thought. Instead, they raced through his mind, everything from what he could feed to Dot for dinner, to what the guest bathroom looked like, to whether or not the guest bedrooms were made up.

He couldn't recall anything at the moment.

Dot finally brought the truck to a stop, but they both stayed right where they were. Ward enjoyed the sensation of stillness, and he glanced over at George as the dog put his head on Ward's shoulder. "Hey, buddy." He smiled softly at the dog. "Dot, would you...would you mind if I said a prayer?"

Only a beat of silence passed before she said, "Of course not."

He reached up and swiped off his cowboy hat. Pressing it to his chest, he closed his eyes and managed to get a silent prayer out to help him align his thoughts. Another breath. Another moment of silence, with only the wind battering the truck and screaming past the shut windows.

Ward's mind quieted, and he opened his mouth. "Dear Lord, we love Thee and we put our trust in Thee during this storm." He'd never been very eloquent like Mother. His thoughts came out in short sentences, and he realized he'd made a mistake by asking her to pray with him.

"Bless any outside still to get home or to somewhere safe, where they can be cared for and kept from harm. Bless Ida and Brady and the babies. Bless Tyson and Dot's parents in town. Bless all of us here at Shiloh Ridge to have the power, fuel, and food we need to have the merriest Christmas possible."

He cleared his throat. "Amen."

"Amen," Dot said quietly, and Ward opened his eyes and busied himself with putting his hat back on.

A horrible alarm buzzed on Ward's phone, startling him and making him jump a mile if he moved a foot. Dot's phone joined the shouting, and he quickly looked at the alert on his.

"It's the winter storm warning," he said over the noise. He tapped *okay* so he wouldn't get the message again, and Dot did the same, basking them back in silence. "Let's get inside and take stock of what we've got." He looked at her. "How about you slide over and get out on this side? Then we can stay together." He looked out the passenger window and couldn't see the house.

Alarm pulled through him. "Does George have a leash?"

"He'll stay with me," Dot said.

"Okay." Ward took a deep breath and opened the door. The wind grabbed it and yanked, and Ward yelped as his arm went with the door. He jumped from the truck, and yelled, "Come on, George."

The dog leapt out of the truck and Ward waited for Dot to slide over and get down too. He grabbed onto her hand and started in the direction he thought the house sat. The gusty wind had blown snow across the sidewalk and driveway, and Ward nearly smashed into his truck before he saw it.

He put his hand on the vehicle and guided himself and

Dot around the front of it. "Let me open the garage door!" he yelled, unsure if Dot could even hear him. He held her hand as tightly as he could as he flipped up the keypad cover on the electronic pad. He pressed in the four-digit code and hit enter.

The door started to open. "In, in, in," Ward said, urging Dot to go low and get inside. "George!" he yelled. "Come on, George!"

The wind blew dirt and snow into the garage, and Ward didn't stop until Dot had gone up the four steps to the small cement pad that led into the house. "Go in, Dot. I'll get George." He joined her on the pad, ready to punch the button the moment the brown and white hound dog made his appearance.

He didn't, and Ward's pulse throbbed through his whole body. Could he leave her dog outside?

Dot whistled through her teeth, nearly deafening him, and he actually ducked his head to get his ears further from the sound.

"Dot," he said after several more dogless seconds.

"He's coming," she said, her voice desperate. "George! Come on, George." She whistled again, but Ward was ready this time.

The dog came running into the garage, skidding when his wet paws hit the slicker cement. Ward hit the button to close the garage, and he opened the door and herded everyone inside.

He closed and locked the door behind him and flipped on the lights. "All right," he said, his mind whirring through a list. "Let's get the heat turned up. Close all the doors to the rooms we won't be using. I'll get firewood and check the gas supply for the generator."

"I'll wipe down George and do the doors."

"Pick a room," he said. "Mine will be obvious. The other one that's lived in is Mister's, but it's downstairs. We'll just block off the basement."

She nodded, and Ward strode into the living room to get the leather sling he used to bring in firewood. He grabbed the gloves from the hearth too, wishing he'd tied a rope from the back door to the woodpile. It was only ten steps, but Ward had lived through a blizzard before, and he knew a man could get disoriented in a single step when a white-out came to play.

"Be right back." He didn't go out the sliding glass door and to the right. Instead, he went into the garage and collected a rope. Then he went out the back door in the corner of the garage and kept one hand planted against the house at all times as he stepped toward the wood pile.

He reached it and filled the sling while inhaling snow and gasping against the wind. That done, he put down the wood and tied the rope around the end pole of the rack. He collected the wood and took painful step after painful step, never moving without one hand solidly against the house. He took the few steps up to the deck and reached the sliding door. He tied the rope to the door handle, leaving some slack so he could open the door and get inside.

A sigh of relief slipped through his lips as he entered the house, and he quickly shut out Mother Nature behind him. He didn't see Dot as he crossed through the dining room to the fireplace. He didn't see her as he unloaded the wood. He didn't see her as he went back outside.

Following the rope, he brought in four loads of wood and stacked it on the hearth before he decided he had enough. That should get him and Dot through at least twenty-four hours of continuous fire should they need it.

He stood in front of the dark fireplace and removed his gloves, finally calling, "Dot?" He shook from head to toe though the furnace pumped hot air into the house. "George?"

"Right here," she said, and Ward turned toward the mouth of the hall. "He was muddy, so I put him in the tub." She looked like she'd gotten in with him, and Ward's mouth turned dry at the way her hair tumbled over her shoulders. She'd let it out of its ponytail, and all Ward could think about was running his fingers through it as he kissed her.

"I got all the doors closed. I just took the only other bedroom on this floor, on the other side of the bathroom there. I closed the vents in all the other rooms, and I made sure the bathroom had towels in it."

"Thank you," he said, rubbing his hands together.

"Ward, you're frozen." Dot darted forward. "Sit down. George, come sit with him."

Ward started to protest, but Dot put one palm against his chest, and he fell back despite the light touch. George jumped up on the couch next to him, and the warmth from the animal seeped into him instantly.

"Take off your wet clothes," Dot said. "I'll get a fire going."

Ward shrugged out of his jacket and tossed it on the linoleum in the kitchen since it was so wet. He kicked off his boots and discarded his hat behind the couch. He ran his chilled fingers through his hair, which was also wet, and watched Dot shave down a larger piece of wood into kindling.

She built a teepee out of it and stuffed newspaper from the basket in between the shards of wood. She struck a match and lit a tail of newspaper, the smoke lifting into the air. She tended to it, caring for it, giving it the oxygen it required to grow and breathe and crackle to life.

Ward watched the flame as it danced, and he said, "I love fire."

"Ah, a bit of a kleptomaniac, are you?" Dot looked at him over her shoulder, her smile beautiful in the firelight.

He shrugged, chuckling. His mind felt whole again, most of the shock of the situation wearing off. He closed his eyes, and he saw Dot standing on the front porch at the homestead, seemingly bleeding from everywhere on her head.

Then the storm warning. The bouncing ride. The absolute cold and fear of not making inside the house. The dog. The firewood.

"I loved going camping as a boy," he said. "Because we got to have a campfire. My daddy would bring marshmallows and graham crackers, and the only time we had s'mores was when we went camping."

"I'm surprised you had much time for camping as a rancher."

"We didn't," he said. "But my dad and uncle would take us a couple of times every summer. All of us."

"You've told me about your siblings," she said. "But you have a million cousins too."

Ward chuckled again. "Just seven."

"And four siblings. And you. So that's twelve."

"A lot of them are married now," he said. "So that makes us bigger."

"Were you all there at the homestead?"

"Yeah," he said, sighing as he opened his eyes. "We were doing our gift exchange."

Dot had the fire positively roaring now, and she sat back on her haunches to watch it for a moment. She stood and turned to face him. Ward wanted to invite her to sit with him on the couch, curl right into his chest the way she had in the booth at Small Plates a few nights ago.

He didn't have to speak to get his point across, and Dot took the two steps to the couch at the same time Ward lifted his arm. She exhaled heavily as she sank into the couch and then into his side. He did too, because holding her like this was really nice.

Really, really nice.

Ward thought about what his life would be like had he come back to Bull House alone. *Miserable*, he thought. But with Dot there, the house held new life he hadn't felt in it for years and years.

"You grew up in this house, didn't you?" Dot asked.

"Yes," Ward said. "It's obviously been updated over the years, but yes. I had a bedroom in the basement I shared with Ace for a couple of years." He smiled at the fond memories. The glass in the windows behind them rattled and shook, making a sound like they'd shatter at any moment.

Ward looked that direction and then faced the fire again. "The wind is really bad up here. Worse than in town."

"That was the first thing I thought when I got out of the truck." Dot tilted her head back and smiled at him. "You don't hear the sirens up here, do you?"

"No." He shook his head. "We have a ranch network that sends messages out, and my mother and Ida live in town. We have a twenty-four-seven family text that annoys me more than I like it." He gave a light chuckle. "But it's useful in emergencies."

He wished he had something hot to sip, but he couldn't drink coffee past dinnertime. With a start, he realized it wasn't anywhere near dinnertime. The sun had just been blocked by thick clouds, making everything darker than it should be at two o'clock in the afternoon.

"Do you want some coffee?" he asked. "Hot chocolate? We probably have some leftover tea from when one of the twins brought some."

"What kind of hot chocolate?"

"Let's see what we've got." Ward eased himself away from Dot and went into the kitchen. He first filled the electric kettle with water and set it on the element. He plugged it in and then dug into the cupboard.

"Hazelnut," he said. "Mexican hot chocolate. Mint truffle. Special dark." He set can after can on the countertop.

"And…white." He frowned at the last can. "Ace loves mini marshmallows, so we have tons of those."

He opened a different cupboard and pulled out half a bag of marshmallows. He got down two mugs and pulled out two spoons. When he turned to put everything on the island, he found Dot standing at the dining room table, examining the photo albums he'd left there.

Instant embarrassment filled him, but Dot looked up with wonder in her eyes. "Is this you as a boy?" She held up a four-by-four square inch picture that was mostly brown and white. Orange seemed prevalent in the older pictures too, and Ward hated how the pictures had aged without someone to properly care for them.

"Yep," he said, his voice somewhat clipped. "I'm five or six." He left the hot chocolate supplies on the counter and approached the table. "I'm trying to match up the pictures with Mother's journals. She kept a pretty detailed record of things for our branch of the Glover family."

Dot set the picture on the album it had come from. "These are so amazing." She ran her fingers down the side of one of Mother's journals.

Ward swallowed, trying to decide how much to share with her. Part of him wanted to sweep the journals and albums into the box he'd taken them from and rush them into the office. The other part yearned to share his project with someone. He'd told all of his siblings about it, as well as Bear, Preacher, and Mister, who obviously had to live with the mess constantly on the kitchen table.

They all thought it was a great thing he was doing, but they didn't share his excitement over things old and past.

"My dad died young," Ward said, clearing the emotion from his throat. "He's been gone for seven or eight years now, and a couple of years ago, my cousins all got a letter from their dad. He'd written them to his kids before he died, but my daddy didn't do that. At least not that we know of."

Ward's throat stuck to itself, but he thought it best to just get the story out. "I was kinda jealous of them, to be honest. I know Ace had a hard time with it too."

"Makes sense to me," Dot said, threading her fingers through Ward's. "You miss your daddy."

"I do," Ward admitted. "We've had all these albums in the basement for years and years. This past summer, I pulled them all out, and I started reading them. I started putting the stories in Mother's journals together with the pictures in the albums. I have good memories of growing up here, and I'm making a book for each of my siblings with the journal entries and photos. It won't be something from our dad, but it'll be something to remind us who we are."

He thought of the angel tree, because he claimed a pair of running, wild mustangs for his father every year. Sometimes he hung a star too. Sometimes an apple pie, because his daddy had loved apple pie with cheddar cheese.

Ward smiled just thinking about it. "It'll be a long process," he said. "I don't have much time to work on it."

"It's sweet," Dot said, glancing up at him again. Ward froze, as did time itself. He gazed at her, her face only a few inches from his. He could easily bend down and kiss her, and yet, he didn't.

He wasn't sure how long they stood there, but he finally broke out of the trance when the electric kettle behind him began to bubble and boil, sending a hissing, steamy sound into the air. He drew a breath and turned from the table. "What's your poison, Dot? And please don't say white hot chocolate."

## Chapter Eight

D ot had just finished brushing her teeth with a brand-new toothbrush Ward had produced from a linen closet in the hall when the lights flickered, flashed, and went out. "Great," she muttered. As if today hadn't already been disastrous enough.

Ward had commented earlier that he was surprised the power hadn't gone out yet with as strong as the winds were. He said they often lost power during the wind storms, and since the ranch sat thirty minutes south of Three Rivers, up in the hills, the power company didn't make Shiloh Ridge their first stop. But he and Dot had enjoyed heat and power all afternoon and into the evening. He'd put a frozen pizza in the oven and served it with a bag of her favorite salad—sunflower seed broccoli crunch.

She'd teased him about having salad in a cowboy bachelor pad, and he'd shaken his head and smiled while he mixed in the poppy seed dressing. He'd asked her what her favorite foods were, and she'd admitted to macaroni and cheese, pepperoni pizza with ranch dressing, and her peanut butter—extra-chunky only—sandwiches.

"So basically you're a teen boy," he'd teased.

"Basically," she'd said. He hadn't had a much more refined palette, but he did admit that he could put together a few meals that weren't entirely composed of carbs. She'd said she'd like to see that, and he'd promised her spinach and mushroom quiche for breakfast.

That so wasn't happening without power. Dot couldn't even see to rinse her mouth, so she opened the bathroom door, hoping for a glimmer of light from the fireplace to penetrate the darkness in the hall.

This house—Bull House, Ward called it—was far too big for low firelight to travel as far as this bathroom down the hall. Ward lived in the master bedroom, and when Dot had peeked inside it when she'd first arrived, she'd been somewhat surprised to see his bed made, his cowboy hats hung on a long row of hooks next to the door, and not a stitch of anything out of place. He lined his boots up by the back door too, and while he'd brought in wood, Dot had actually started to look for a room with any sort of chaos in it.

She'd found it in the office, though even the folders and papers there seemed to have some semblance of organization. Her opinion of Ward Glover changed by the minute, and she found it once again morphing as he came down the hall with a spotlight that could illuminate the whole house.

"You okay down here?" he asked.

"Yeah," she said, quickly filling the glass in the bathroom and rinsing her mouth. Ward kept the blinding light pointed at the ground, which cast the two of them in strange, upward-reaching shadows. "Thanks."

"It's only eight-thirty," he said. "It feels like midnight." He gave a low chuckle, and Dot smiled at the sound of it in his chest.

"I get up early," she said. "Shovel rocks all day. I could go to bed right now." That was what she'd been preparing to do.

"I found some sweats and put them on your bed," he said. "You can take this torch. I have another one in the pantry I can use. And the generator should kick on any minute now." He actually cocked his head as if it would simply because he'd commanded it to.

The house stayed stubbornly dark.

Dot stepped to leave the bathroom, but Ward didn't back up. She reached up and put one palm against his chest, the very real beating of his heart bumping through his T-shirt. "Thanks for everything, Ward."

"Of course," he said. "How are you feeling? Everything good with the insulin?"

"Yep." Dot didn't want to talk about her diabetes. She knew which foods were high in glucose, and she'd given herself a dose of insulin before eating the pizza and salad. Bagged and boxed things tended to have more additives and extra sugar, both of which threw her body out of whack.

But she had insulin, and she'd stored it in Ward's fridge the way she did at home. He didn't have a dog, but he'd scrambled some eggs and put them into a plastic container of leftover stew he said he was going to throw out anyway. George had been pleased as punch, and Dot had said Ward would spoil them both with homecooked meals, and then the hound dog would howl at her for the same thing once she took him home.

Which, hopefully, happened tomorrow.

Dot had not brought a change of clothes with her, and she didn't carry such things in her dump truck. She had a single pair of socks that had gotten wet coming into the house, and she'd laid them over a heat vent to dry out. They had, and she currently wore them, as well as her jeans and tank top. She had a sweater and a jacket to wear as well, but that was it. No shoes but the steel-toed boots she worked in.

"All right," Ward drawled. "I'm gonna grab that other flashlight and head to bed."

"Okay." Dot let her hand drop, but it slipped down his chest because of how close they stood.

His breath entered his lungs in a sharp gasp, and then he swept one hand around her waist and brought her even closer to him. "We'll have to see how the weather is tomorrow."

"It's Christmas," Dot murmured, too close to him to focus on his face. She relaxed into his half-embrace and laid her cheek against his shoulder.

"It sure is." Ward's breath wafted across her ear and Dot's skin prickled with desire. "See you in the morning, Dorothy." He swept his lips along her forehead and stepped gently away. How someone so tall and strong could move with so much grace astounded her, and she took the light from him and watched him walk back toward the kitchen.

"Don't stand here staring," she muttered to herself. She'd taken one step when the lights flickered and flared back to life.

"Generator's on," Ward called. "I'm going to turn off all the lights we can, okay? That way it'll focus on the furnace." He appeared at the end of the hall, his eyebrows up as if seeking her permission.

"Good plan," she said, as he knew how to keep his house functioning for as long as possible. She reached over and flipped off the lights in the bathroom, as well as the hallway, plunging herself back into the darkness that perpetually clawed at the spotlight's power.

She went into the bedroom she'd chosen, which was the one closest to the rest of the house—the first door on the right. It held a ready-to-sleep-in queen bed, a dresser she'd already dug through, and a nightstand with a single lamp on it.

She hadn't asked who'd slept in here before, but it didn't matter. Everything looked and smelled clean and fresh.

Dot closed the door behind her and set the spotlight so the light shone toward the ceiling. It illuminated the room decently, and Dot stripped out of her clothes and picked up the T-shirt and sweat pants Ward had found for her.

The T-shirt said TEXAS across the front of it, along with a pair of longhorns. It was bright orange, and Dot couldn't believe this was what he'd chosen. He couldn't be playing a joke on her, because Ward didn't strike her as the type of man to even know how to joke. He could tease, sure. But a joke?

No way.

The sweat pants were gray, with a similar T down on one ankle.

A knock sounded on the door, and Dot gasped as she spun toward it. "I'm not dressed," she said, her voice an octave higher than normal.

"Do the clothes fit?" he asked through the closed door. "They're from my college days, and the smallest stuff I've got."

"I'm trying them right now," she said, still holding the ugly T-shirt in front of her like a shield. She quickly put her arms through it and stepped into the pants. They were still too big, but not so large that she was drowning in cloth.

She opened the door and put one hand on her hip like a real supermodel. "They're not terrible," she said. "Except for this color. What *is* this?"

Ward's eyes dripped down to her toes and back to her eyes. A smile formed, and it wasn't so dark that Dot couldn't see the glint of attraction in his eyes. It surprised her a little bit, though Ward hadn't been shy about how he felt about her.

The memory of kissing him filled her mind, and Dot leaned into the doorway for support.

"I did this accounting certificate from the University of Texas," he said. "It was a two-year program, distance education, and I don't know. I wanted to feel a part of the university." He shrugged and reached out to touch one of the sleeves on her shirt. "I bought all this Texas stuff and I'd wear it when I did my classes."

Dot grinned at him. "You have many layers, Mister Glover."

"I think that's a compliment."

"It is." Dot didn't have anything else to say, so she straightened. "I'm still trying to figure out who you are."

"Me too," he said, dropping his eyes. He was softer without the cowboy boots and hat on. Right now, he wore a pair of shorts made out of the same material as her sweat pants and a T-shirt with the words *Home is Where the Herd Is* splashed across the front of it in a western font.

"Yet another layer to uncover," Dot said. "But we'll have to do that tomorrow, Woods. I'm exhausted even though all we did was watch movies and talk this afternoon."

Ward lifted his eyes to hers when she used his first name. She needed to use it more often so she'd start to think of him as a Woods. The name didn't quite fit though, and she knew why he'd looked up at the use of it.

"Why don't you use your first name?" she asked.

"It's a long story," he said. "I'll have to tell it another time." He nodded at her and turned toward the kitchen. "Good night, Dot."

"Night," she said, retreating into the bedroom. She didn't close the door though. If the generator went out, she'd need the heat from the fireplace to keep warm.

She gathered her torch and put it on the nightstand with her phone, which was nearly dead. She'd put it on power saving mode hours ago, and that was the only way she still had any battery life left. She had a charger in her truck, but Ward said he'd get it in the morning when the storm had calmed down.

Dot climbed beneath the thick quilt on the bed and reached over to switch off her light. She was physically exhausted, but the moment she closed her eyes, she was wide awake. Ward had said he'd be going to bed right away too, but he bumped around in the kitchen and living room for several more minutes before the house dropped into silence. Even then, Dot didn't hear him go past her bedroom to his.

She lay there thinking about what life would be like if she and Ward really shared this house as husband and wife. She wouldn't be so still and rigid, waiting for him to go to bed so she could relax. He'd be with her, and she'd fall asleep to the steady thumping of his heartbeat in her ear.

Dot sighed, because the fantasy was almost too good to be true. Ward himself was almost too good to be true, despite some pretty obvious flaws. She'd seized onto those in the few months they'd started seeing each other, but Dot now knew they were surface defense mechanisms. Or simply how Ward was, though he certainly *wasn't* demanding or arrogant. He seemed surprised when she told him he was good-looking, and he softened considerably in his "demands" with every interaction she had with him.

He was definitely an enigma to her still, and she tossed and turned for what felt like a long time. Finally, she got out of bed and pulled off the blanket, taking it with her as she left the bedroom in favor of the living room.

The front door hulked in front of her, the kitchen to her right. Ward's office sat to the left, and Dot caught the sliver of pale light shining from under the closed door. So he'd gone in there.

The rest of the house sat in darkness save for the firelight, and Dot settled onto the big couch they'd moved closer to the hearth. With the blanket all tucked in around her and the crackling flames whispering new fantasies about her and Ward, Dot finally fell asleep, the gentle strains of guitar music acting as a lullaby to pull her into deeper water with the gorgeous, hardworking, and smart cowboy who strummed from inside the office.

# Chapter Nine

Etta Glover stood at the bottom of the huge staircase that led up to the apartment-suites on the second level of the main homestead at Shiloh Ridge Ranch. She loved living at the homestead with Ranger and Oakley and their baby, Wilder. Bear and Sammy and their family took up the other suite, and Etta actually wondered how long they'd be able to stay.

With Lincoln, Stetson, and now Russell, their three-bedroom suite was full. She'd heard Stetson fussing when she'd gotten up to get a box of crackers from the kitchen. She kept some staples in her smaller suite behind the living room and actually mostly under these stairs, but she'd been out of her favorite chicken-flavored crackers, and she'd seen Oakley with a box earlier that week.

She'd texted Sammy and Bear that she'd take Stetson so he wouldn't be bothered by their newborn, who woke a couple of times in the night to be fed. They'd only been home for four nights now, and Etta wanted to help them if she could. What was the point of living here otherwise?

Not only that, but she adored Stetson, and the boy loved her too. Bear had said he'd bring the child down to her, and Etta heard his footsteps a moment later.

"Thank you, Etta," Bear whispered as he approached, a sniffling chunk of a boy in his arms. Etta reached for Stetson, glad when the twenty-month old cuddled right into her chest the way he normally did.

"Any time," she whispered back. "I can't seem to sleep anyway, and this way, we'll both be better off." She gave Bear a smile, but the man looked utterly exhausted. Etta wished she could wrap him in a hug and tell him he didn't need to shoulder everything that happened in the Glover family. Such a task was impossible, but Bear kept on trying.

"Everyone's good and safe," she said, hoping that would be enough to get him to relax and get some sleep.

"That they are." Bear returned her smile, though his was weak, and they went their separate ways. Etta took Stetson and her crackers through the cavernous kitchen and around the furniture in the living room. The entrance to her suite sat right beside the fireplace, and the door was seamless, making it almost impossible to see. If not for the knob, she wouldn't know it was there.

She had a small living room with big windows in it, and she'd put her recliner there, a basket of board books for Stetson beside it. She didn't go there right now, but headed through the sitting area to her bedroom. The master suite was also large, with plenty of windows and a big, attached bathroom.

With a television and a kitchenette in the sitting room, it was a suite the perfect size for someone single like Etta. She couldn't entertain, but she had the entire homestead to cook in if she wanted to. She had done lunches with the ladies in the past several months since moving here, and she thanked the Lord each day for the life He'd given her.

As usual, she thought of Noah Johnson, as the man still crept into her thoughts on a daily basis. She often wondered what her life would be like had she married him last April as she'd planned to do. She wondered where he was, and if he was happy.

She prayed for his happiness every single day, morning and night. She prayed that he'd be able to forgive her every single day, morning and night. She was still working on forgiving herself.

"All right, baby," she whispered to Stetson as she reached her bed. She pulled down the blanket on the left side where she didn't sleep and laid the boy down. "There won't be any little brothers crying down here and waking you up." She smiled softly at the child, his eyes closed and his chest lifting and falling slowly. She brushed her fingers through his hair and covered him with her blanket.

Etta took her crackers to her side of the bed but before she climbed in, she dropped to her knees. She didn't pray vocally, but the Lord heard mental prayers. She prayed that Mother would be safe and happy at Ace and Holly Ann's. They didn't have a generator in their house yet, as it had literally been finished only a week or two ago.

But they did have a large fireplace that should keep them all warm should it come to that. The homestead still had power, but they also had a built-in generator that came on after five minutes of continuous power loss. It was attached to the house, and Ranger nor Bear had to do anything if the power went out. The generator simply kicked on.

Bull House, where Etta had grown up, also had a whole-house generator. Ward and Dot had gone there, and Etta prayed with all the energy of her soul that Ward would find happiness with Dorothy Crockett. They did make a handsome couple, as Dot was tall and strong like Ward. Etta felt like a dwarf next to her older brother, and while she didn't have quite the same relationship with him that Ida did, she still loved him fiercely.

Ida had just taken the babies home that day, and Etta had missed her more than anyone at the Glover family gift exchange. She'd been planning to video call Ida so she could still participate, but the weather had turned too soon after lunch. None of the gifts were actually exchanged, and many of them remained in the house.

Etta herself had gathered them up and put them under the angel tree. Once Mother Nature blew herself out, everyone would return, and they'd do their traditional gift-giving then.

She prayed for Ida and Brady, for Johnny and Judy, and she hoped they would stay safe down in town. She prayed for Ranger and Oakley, as Etta knew they were already trying for another baby.

She prayed for Montana, Willa, and Zona, as the three of them were currently carrying babies. Zona especially disliked storms, and she and Duke had one of the longest drives to get to their safe house at the Top Cottage. It had been damaged in a tornado a few years ago, but the roof had been rebuilt. Zona had still admitted her concern on the ranch ladies' text instead of the family string that all the men saw.

So Etta prayed for comfort for Zona. She prayed Willa, Cactus, and Mitch and all their animals would be safe and protected out on the Edge. That was the longest distance from the epicenter of the ranch, without much for protection.

She prayed Bishop and Montana would be able to take care of Lois and Don, who'd gone to stay in their house for the duration of the storm. She thanked the Lord that He'd allowed so many new people to join the family, and that new homes had been constructed so they each had a place to shelter in times like these.

She prayed for Judge, Mister, and Preacher in the Ranch House, and not only because Judge and Mister sometimes didn't get along. That house had a built-in generator too, but no fireplace, as Bishop had taken it out during the remodel.

Charlie Perkins, Preacher's fiancée, had gone to the Ranch House too, as there was no way she could make the hour-long drive from Shiloh Ridge to her house in the northeast hills with the tornado sirens going off.

Exhausted now, Etta finally thought about herself. *I don't know what I need, Lord,* she thought. *But You do. Help me to recognize it when it comes into my life, whatever it is. Even if it's simply being the best aunt to all the babies coming to the family, that's fine. I can do it. I'll do what You want me to do.*

It had taken Etta thirty-five years to learn that lesson, and most days she still struggled. She had things she wanted out of her life. She wanted a good, strong man at her side. She wanted to be a mother more than anything.

She didn't understand why the *good* things she wanted weren't coming true. She prayed to be good enough. She served others. She worked hard around the ranch. She fought against the jealousy when it came, and she never gossiped. She simply wanted to be good enough for the Lord to bless her with the true desires of her heart.

*You are good enough.* The thought came to her, and Etta started to weep. She'd been working so hard to keep in touch with her spirit, to feed it the words of God every day, to attend church, to think of others before herself.

"Thank you," she whispered, and with that assurance that the Lord knew her and loved her, Etta got into bed with Stetson. She reached over and made sure the blanket covered him adequately, and she kept her hand lightly on his arm, the human connection something she needed powerfully in that moment.

She closed her eyes and let herself drift, finally infused with comfort and peace though the storms of life raged on around her.

THE NEXT MORNING, ETTA WOKE VERY EARLY. HER bladder tended to do that to her, and it didn't care that the clock only read five a.m. or that it had taken her a long time to fall asleep.

She sat up in bed while Stetson slumbered on and swiped on her phone. She'd joined the main dating app for Three Rivers, which was a localized app for the men and women living specifically in the Texas Panhandle.

She'd tried the bigger, national apps, but they felt full of dishonest people or profiles that hadn't been updated in a while. She'd chatted with a man for a couple of weeks before he'd said he'd moved to Dallas from Amarillo two years previous.

Etta didn't need to expend energy she didn't have, so she'd retreated to the local app. It didn't have as many options, but Etta didn't get on very often. Christmas morning felt like a great time, though she hoped it didn't make her desperate.

She read through some of the profiles she'd seen before, a couple which she'd actually tapped on to indicate she liked them. The men hadn't responded to her tap, and Etta deleted them, the silent rejection almost as harsh as someone coming right out and saying they weren't interested.

A new profile came up when she scrolled, and she paused on the name Marshall Redmond. He was a cowboy, as most of the men were—the app itself was called Cowboy Connection—and he had a nice smile. A little crooked, but Etta actually liked it.

Feeling brave, she tapped on the heart on the top right, next to the brim of his black cowboy hat, and kept scrolling.

Not two seconds later, a heart flashed across her screen

too, with the words *Marshall Redmond likes you! Chat with him now.*

She tapped the heart and the chat part of the app opened up.

Etta's heart tapped out a quick staccato rhythm. She hated meeting men this way. It felt so unrefined to her, but a message popped up that said, *Merry Christmas Etta*, with a Christmas tree emoji and then a bright yellow star.

A smile formed on her face, because at least he hadn't led with how pretty she was. She quickly tapped out a message too. *Merry Christmas, Marshall. What are you doing today? Family activities? Just trying to stay warm and dry?*

Next to her, Stetson snored in the cutest little boy way, and Etta glanced at him, pure love filling her. When she focused back on her screen, she found Marshall typing, and a new hope entered her heart that perhaps this year, she could fully heal and find the things she wanted in her life.

# Chapter Ten

❦

Judge Glover sat in front of the desktop computer in his office, the dual screens brightening the room enough to see. The sun hadn't quite come up yet, and the office faced northwest, which made the sunset more striking than the sunrise anyway.

The moment he'd gotten home last night, he'd powered down his light show. He couldn't even imagine what mess he'd find once it was safe to go outside. His stomach knotted just thinking about what could be damaged. At the same time, it would be a very good reason to get all kinds of new things for next year's show.

On the Three Rivers website, he was third for the Christmas light display, and familiar bitterness and disappointment cut through him. He should be glad for a top three placement, but the problem was, he could never get higher than that.

A lot of people didn't make the journey out to Shiloh

Ridge to see the show, and he'd considered doing something right down on the highway, closer to town. It wouldn't be his house, though, and he'd need to have a piece of land he owned, could set up copious amounts of lights on, and get the best WiFi in the known universe so the show would run.

He'd need a laptop to code it all, because he certainly couldn't be making changes on this computer, driving down the hill to watch the show, and then back to the Ranch House to tweak things.

And heavens above, Judge tweaked and tweaked and *tweaked* his Christmas light display show. Even once the voting had started, Judge made minuscule changes that probably only he'd notice. The perfectionist in him really wanted the show to be the best it could be. If someone left a comment in the voting bracket about his show, and he felt good about making the change, he did.

One year, he'd changed the color of lights that marched with the soldiers from red to blue, and he'd liked the show better.

Weariness ran through him now, because his creativity was starting to wane. He'd been designing, setting up, and programming the light show for sixteen years now. Sixteen. That was about fifteen too many not to have won yet.

The drive to win tasted like metal in the back of his throat, and every time he considered giving up, he'd be reminded of how far he'd come, how much he'd learned, and that next year could be the one.

He'd prayed to win for the past five years, and he was beginning to think the Lord simply didn't care if he won or not. *Of course He doesn't*, Judge thought. God had much bigger problems and the people of the world had much bigger cares than the piddly light show in Three Rivers, Texas.

At the same time, Judge had been taught from boyhood to pray to the Lord for what he wanted. Talk to God, and tell Him what he was grateful for. Ask for help. Listen for guidance. He'd been doing that for almost forty years, and the things he wanted still sat out of his reach.

He glanced at his phone, looking for a message from Etta. They'd become closer in the past six months, after Judge had followed a prompting he believed came from the Lord. He'd felt like he needed to get over to the homestead or call Etta and go to lunch with her for about a week before he'd done it.

They'd been texting, calling, and getting together at least once a week since, even if it was just sandwiches out in the office Etta used in one of the barns to run the school programs. They'd cried together. They'd laughed together. They'd told each other what they really wanted and asked one another why God seemed to be ignoring them.

Deep down, Judge knew the Lord wasn't ignoring him. Sometimes there was no right or wrong. His desperation told him he either needed to try again with Juniper Nichols —really try—or he needed to move on.

With all of his brothers, sisters, and cousins finding lifelong partners, Judge didn't want to be the only single Glover remaining. He already had to work so hard to get noticed, and he didn't want the spotlight on him for being single when everyone else wasn't.

He'd given up the practical jokes in the last year, and while he still made a big deal at family parties about being first in line, the joy of that had started to fade too. Really, Judge just wanted a normal life. Average was fine by him.

"June's not average," he grumbled to himself, clicking away from the window where he coded the light show and over to social media.

Judge was fairly social, especially online, and he scrolled through a few posts from friends who'd already posted pictures of their Christmas morning. It was barely seven a.m., but Judge didn't have little children excited to see what Santa Claus had brought them.

He smiled as he saw new skateboards and bicycles, video games and drones. Judge himself worked with a lot of drones around the ranch, and he loved flying model airplanes. His last one had crash-landed in some bushes out at the Cornish Plantation, and Judge hadn't found time to rebuild it yet.

The light show consumed him from June to December. January was usually dedicated to taking down the decorations and properly storing them, so he only had a few months where he could dedicate his time to other hobbies.

His eyes caught on June's name, and he stopped scrolling. "Best Christmas gift ever," he read, his eyes skipping to the picture of her and her daughter, their faces pressed cheek-to-cheek. He pulled in a breath, because Juniper Nichols really was the most beautiful woman in the world. At least to Judge.

She had soft, wavy dirty blonde hair and the biggest, brownest eyes. Joy poured from her when she smiled, and she'd recently cut her hair barely long enough to keep it in a ponytail. This morning, it had been parted right above her left eye and fell in dark golden waves luscious enough to make Judge's fingers curl into a fist.

She had black eyelash extensions that always made her look perfectly made up, and Judge sure liked how big her eyes were. She could devour a man with a single look. His heart pounded as he glanced at Lucy Mae, her sixteen-year-old daughter. She'd be seventeen in a couple of months, if Judge remembered right, and he did.

She had another year of school, and then Judge might have a chance with June. She'd told him she didn't want to get involved with a man or remarried until Lucy Mae was graduated and gone to live her own life. Judge wasn't sure what the difference was, because it wasn't like Lucy Mae was never going to come back to Three Rivers to visit her mother. Either way, she'd have to make a family with whoever her mother started seeing.

He looked back to the text above the picture. "My baby announced that she completed her online classes and will graduate from high school a whole year early. She's applying to colleges across the state, and she's already gotten in to UT."

There were multiple exclamation points, though June didn't normally use such punctuation marks. Judge sat back from the computer, realizing he'd been leaning forward to read the screen faster.

His heartbeat boomed at him, saying things like *a year early. Lucy Mae is going to be graduated and gone in only six months.*

*Six months.*

*Six. Months.*

Judge's hand flew out in the direction of his phone, and he hit it in his haste to pick it up. He had to talk to June right now.

He tapped, her texts always pinned to the top of his app, and the call connected. His brain fired at him, telling him the clock had barely ticked to seven, but he argued back that June had posted already this morning. She was obviously awake.

"And not answering," he muttered, hating that her phone would tell her it was him calling. He didn't want to think that he was one of the people she screened for.

He was just about to hang up when she said, "Good morning, Judge." She sounded really happy, and his voice lodged in his head.

"June," he managed to push through his narrow throat. He cleared things away and breathed. He'd been out with this woman before. He'd held her hand before. Heck, he'd kissed her before.

The fact that he wanted to do all of those things again made him very, very nervous. June had turned him down in the past, after she'd broken up with him, and Judge really didn't need this to be his third strike.

He'd been playing things cool for months. Over a year. Maybe two years. Time had a way of flowing by him without him noticing, but he tuned in keenly when she said, "Merry Christmas. What are you doing during the storm?"

"Just hunkering down," he said. "I'm with Preacher and

Mister, and Preacher's fiancée." He leaned back in the chair and looked up at the ceiling. "Mister said he'd make bacon, cheese, and egg kolaches this morning, so I was just playing around with something on the computer."

"Yeah, I know what you were playing around with," June teased. She'd been out to the ranch over the summer too, to help him upgrade his network. She was brilliant with routers and WLANs and all kinds of other things Judge could've figured out if he cared to. He didn't. He'd rather call June and have her come help him.

Judge chuckled, though neither of them said he'd been messing with his light show. "I saw your post about Lucy Mae," he said, wondering what would come out of his mouth next. He did a lot by feel, based on his mood, and liked being spontaneous. He also liked to have a plan, especially when it came to June. "That's so great for her."

June laughed again and said, "I'm so proud of her. She's worked so hard."

"I know she has."

"I didn't put this online," June said, gushing now. "But she got accepted into this summer internship for the engineering school at UT-Austin, and I'm just dying for her to accept."

"She hasn't yet?" Judge asked, hoping June would keep talking. She had the kind of voice that made him happy, and he simply liked listening to her.

"She's waiting on a couple of other things she applied to," June said.

"Well, tell her congratulations from me," he said.

"I will."

The conversation stalled, and Judge's pulse jumped up into his throat. "Did your parents come into town?"

"They tried," she said. "But Amarillo grounded all their flights yesterday morning, before the storm. So they didn't make it."

"That's too bad."

"It's just me and Lucy Mae," she said. "We're going to video call my parents and my sister at nine."

"Oh, that's a good idea," he said.

"What about you Glovers?" she asked.

"We're all spread out," Judge said. "We were about to do our gift exchange when Ida—you remember my cousin Ida? She lives in town?"

"Yes, Ida," June said. "I think everyone knows Ida Glover."

"Do they?" Judge asked, interested to know why that was. Ida and Etta did a lot of community outreach programs through the ranch, but usually through the schools.

"Seem to," June said. "Lucy Mae knows her and Etta because they come talk to the students. She said Ida is real funny."

"Funnier than Etta—I can see that," Judge said. Etta definitely liked rich things and she was more refined than her twin. She wasn't stuffy, but Judge could see how she might come across that way. "She's changed a lot in the past several months, actually," he said, suddenly feeling protective of Etta and her scarred heart.

"They're both very nice," June said diplomatically. "Anyway, Ida did something?"

"Oh, right." Judge centered his thoughts. "She lives in town, and the rest of us were up here. We can't hear the sirens up here. We usually get a text—you know like one of those Amber alert type of texts that buzzes at you?—about ten or fifteen minutes after the sirens go off. But Ida texted to say the sirens were going off and the town had issued a major wind warning. So we split up."

"So you're at the Ranch House."

"Yes, ma'am. Everyone went to their own houses. We figured that would be better than trying to find beds and food for everyone at the homestead."

"Smart," June said. "I just checked the weather, and they keep extending the warning. Originally, it was only supposed to go until nine a.m. this morning, but now it's nine p.m."

"It certainly hasn't let up here," Judge said, realizing with horrifying clarity that he and June were talking about the weather.

The *weather*.

He wanted to hang up and cut out his own tongue. The windows rattled at him, as if telling him not to say another word about the wind.

"Here either," she said.

"Maybe when it does let up, we could...." Judge slowed down, wishing he hadn't started the sentence. He didn't know how to finish it.

"Go to dinner?" June supplied.

"Or lunch," he said. "Or even breakfast. I know you sometimes go really late on your appointments, but you rarely go out early."

"You know what, Judge?"

He couldn't tell what tone she'd used. Was she being sarcastic? Inquisitive? Kind? Was she going to tell him never to call her again and to please stop asking her out when she'd made her wishes known?

"What?" he asked.

"I'd like to go to breakfast, lunch, or dinner with you."

"You would?" Judge's eyes rounded, and he got to his feet. He couldn't have this conversation sitting down, and he paced over to the window and looked out. He couldn't see farther than two feet, and only a whooshing grayness stared back at him.

He faced the room as she said, "Don't sound so surprised."

"I am a little surprised."

"I am too," she said with a light laugh. "I don't know, Judge. There's just...something about you."

"Something good, I hope," he said.

"Something good," she confirmed.

"So we'll keep in touch," he said, basically his way of asking her if he could text her between now and when they went out.

"Yeah," she said slowly. "We'll keep in touch."

"Who are you talking to?" someone on her end of the line asked, and it was definitely her daughter.

June obviously moved the phone away from her mouth, because when she said, "Judge, now hush," it came through quieter.

"Oooh, Judge Glover," Lucy Mae teased. "Did he ask you out? Did you say yes?" Her voice grew louder with every word she said. "Judge, ask her out! She told me she'd say yes if you'd ask her again!"

"Oh, my word," June said. "Judge, I have to go find a way to mute my daughter."

Judge started laughing, but he managed to say, "Talk to you later, June," before she ended the call. He let his hand fall to his side and he stared at the open doorway that led into the hall.

He quieted as warmth spread through him. June had been thinking about him. June had been *talking* about him.

"With Lucy Mae," he said under his breath. She'd been talking about him with her daughter.

A whoop came from his mouth, and he darted out the doorway and into the kitchen, where Mister whisked eggs in a bowl.

"What are you cheering about?" he asked.

Preacher entered the kitchen too, only one arm in his shirt. "What's going on? I heard someone yell."

Judge looked at his brothers, who both stared steadily back at him. He almost didn't want to tell them. He'd let Preacher have his privacy while he'd dated Charlie for months and months.

He didn't want to hold things too close to his heart. He might need their help. So he said, "I just called June and asked her out, and she said yes."

"She said yes?" Preacher asked, his eyebrows shooting toward the ceiling.

"You're kidding," Mister said, the whisk coming to a stop.

"I'm not kidding," Judge said, his face stretching with a

wide grin. "She said *yes*." He felt like he was floating on a cloud, and it didn't matter that they couldn't get together for lunch at Ace's house that day. It didn't matter that the perfect gift for Ward sat at the homestead, unopened. It didn't even matter that he'd come in third for the Christmas light display show again.

He'd asked, and Juniper Nichols had said yes.

# Chapter Eleven

Ward stared at the assortment of food in the fridge, trying to find something diabetic-friendly he could make for Christmas Day breakfast.

Pancakes, waffles, and French toast were out.

Dot didn't like eggs or yogurt.

He really liked oatmeal, but that was carbs with plenty of sugar, and both of those could send her into a diabetic coma.

He had avocadoes, and according to the research he'd done last night, they were a diabetic-friendly food. If she'd eat eggs, he could make a killer omelet with smoked salmon, broccoli, and an avocado crema.

He closed the fridge and glanced over to the couch, where Dot slept. He'd seen her there when he'd finally finished soothing himself with online research and a few newly written bars of the song he was working on with his guitar. He'd expected her to rise before him, but she'd been snoozing when he'd arrived back in the living room.

She continued to sleep even though he'd already made coffee and the scent of it was starting to fill the house.

George came padding into the kitchen, and Ward reached down to pat the dog. "What does she eat for breakfast, bud? Do you know?" The hound probably needed to eat too, and Ward reopened the fridge and took out the eggs. He bought them in crates of five dozen, because he and Mister could eat them for every meal.

It was Christmas, and while Ward didn't normally spend it alone in Bull House, the day still held some magic to it. He cut open the two avocadoes he had and started to mash them together with garlic, salt and pepper, and a touch of olive oil.

He started cracking eggs, glancing over to the couch when he heard Dot moan. The darkness had ebbed away, but the sun hadn't fully claimed the day. Ward didn't think it would either. He'd checked the weather on his phone from his bedroom, and the winter storm warning and high wind advisory had been extended another twelve hours.

He and Dot would most likely be stuck together for another night. He certainly wasn't complaining about that, though he had beat himself up a little bit last night for not kissing her. Somehow, he wanted the next time they kissed to be more magical than standing in the doorway of the bathroom. That didn't feel romantic to Ward, though he'd definitely wanted to kiss Dot right after she'd brushed her teeth last night.

"Coffee smells good," she said, her voice lower and filled with a definite frog.

"It's ready any time." He didn't go too far with the avocadoes, because he wasn't making guacamole. "I'm trying to decide what you'd like for breakfast."

Dot rose from the couch and lifted her arms above her head as she stretched. Ward watched her body lengthen, and he forgot himself for a moment. Her eyes met his, and she tugged on the oversized T-shirt though it hadn't revealed any skin. "What are my choices?"

"You said you didn't like eggs the other night while we were at dinner," he said. "But I could make a pretty great omelet with smoked salmon and broccoli. That's diabetes-friendly. Or I could make you an English muffin with avocadoes. Kind of like avocado toast, but obviously better."

"Obviously," she teased. "Because English muffins are far superior to bread."

Ward blinked, liking the female conversation first thing in the morning. "Obviously," he said in a dead pan.

Dot smiled and laughed, and Ward looked down at the avocadoes. "But that's a lot of bread," he said.

"I'm okay to eat an English muffin," she said, entering the kitchen to stand beside him. "Those avocadoes smell good too."

"I do love avocado."

"Me too." Dot leaned against his arm. "I told you that you didn't have to fuss over me."

"And I told you I like fussing over the people I care about." He leaned his head down, but she didn't tip hers back. He felt utterly exposed in the house with her, as he didn't wear his hat indoors very often and he didn't have any of his traditional cowboy garb on. When he went out with women, he made sure every piece of himself was situated in exactly the right spot. The hat, the belt, the jeans, the boots. His wallet, his cologne, his beard. All of it.

"I think you're a very fussy man, Mister Glover," she teased.

"Am I?" He stepped away from her, though he didn't really want to. He bent to open the bread drawer, where he took out the package of English muffins. "Do you like yours toasted or barely warmed up?"

"Toasted," she said. "Especially if you're putting that delicious avocado mixture on it."

"Toasted it is." He split a couple of muffins and put them in the toaster. "I'm fussy?" he asked as he got down mugs and poured coffee for the two of them.

"I maybe snooped while you were bringing in wood," she said.

Ward reset the coffee pot on the burner and looked at her, his right eyebrow cocked. "What did you find?"

"I've always wanted to do that," she said, gesturing to his eyebrows.

He lowered his and said, "By the way, your phone was beeping, so I plugged it in out here. We have tons of extra cords, Dot. All you had to do was ask for one." Ward had felt like an idiot for not suggesting it last night. He'd been...off yesterday after she'd shown up dripping blood from her fingers.

"Oh, great, thanks." She didn't move to go get it from

where he'd placed it on the counter. "It seems like every-thing in this house has a designated spot, and you've committed to making sure that item goes there."

Ward stirred in a couple spoonfuls of sugar to sweeten his coffee the way he liked it. "Mm."

"You didn't deny it."

"Nothing to deny," he said. "I do like things on the organizational side, I suppose."

"Do you make your bed every morning?"

"Yes," he said. "My mother made us. If we left for school without making our bed, she'd come get us out of class." He lifted his mug to his lips and took a sip. "We didn't forget but once, and Ace and the twins never did. They'd seen Ranger and I get the punishment."

"It meant that much to her?"

"Mother wanted us to learn to take care of things," Ward said, going for more sugar. "It was important to her that we knew how to do household chores and not just ranch chores."

"Why's that?"

"She wanted us to be good wives and husbands." He glanced at Dot, who nodded. "Daddy educated us about the ranch. Mother taught us about the house. They weren't strict, not really, but I know I didn't want to disappoint them." He grinned and tasted his coffee again. It was defi-nitely better with more sugar. "I especially didn't want Mother to march into my class and announce to everyone that I'd forgotten to make my bed, and she was so sorry, but she needed to take me home so I could."

Dot giggled as she stirred her coffee. She didn't add

anything to it before taking a drink. She didn't flinch or grimace, but Ward had no idea how she drank it so bitter. "How old were you when she did that?"

"Fifth grade," he said. "I had a crush on this girl named MaryLou." He shook his head. "She was *so* pretty, and I was *so* embarrassed."

"MaryLou, huh?" Dot's dark hazel eyes glinted. "Did you and MaryLou ever have a thing?"

"I was ten," he said. "So no."

"Lots of kids would 'go together,'" she said. "You never did that?"

"No, ma'am."

"Your mother scarred you, is that it?"

"That's totally it," Ward said. "No wonder I haven't been able to find a girlfriend all these years." He grinned at her and sipped his coffee again. The English muffins popped up, and Ward got busy spooning on the avocadoes he'd chopped and seasoned.

He took the plates over to the table and set them in the only two clear spots. He and Mister used them, and Mister never said anything about the photo albums on the table.

"No girlfriends?" Dot asked. "A tall, strapping cowboy like you?"

Ward dang near choked on his avocado muffin. He managed to swallow and wipe his mouth. "I mean, I've gone out with a lot of women." Especially recently, but he wasn't going to tell her that.

"How many?"

Ward shifted uncomfortably. "Uh, let's see." He started

to count on his fingers, Dot's eyes growing wider and wider. "About eight in the past couple of years."

"You're kidding."

"I am not." Ward took an overly large bite of food so he wouldn't be able to talk for a minute.

Dot stared at him. "You didn't like any of them?"

"No," he said. "I liked them, but not all that much. There was no...spark."

Dot nodded as if she understood. He wanted to ask her if she could feel the sizzle between them, but he managed to keep the embarrassing question quiet. "What about you?" he asked instead. "Who have you been out with?"

"Just me and Brutus for a while now," she said, ducking her head and taking a large bite of muffin too. He recog-nized the tactic, and let her have a minute to chew and think.

"You know," he said. "I'd gone to the potluck lunch after church specifically after praying I'd meet the right woman for me there. Then I ran into you."

"Yeah, and you ruined my raspberry cream whip."

"You ruined my shirt," he threw back at her, along with a smile. "Can you make that raspberry cream whip? Seems like the perfect thing to have on Christmas Day."

Alarm crossed Dot's face. "Do you think we'll be stuck here all day?"

"Yes," Ward said matter-of-factly. "I do. Holly Ann just texted to say she can keep the food until we can get together, but that they aren't hosting a meal today, because the wind is still howling out there."

Dot got up from the table and walked to the window as

if she didn't believe him. Ward didn't even have to move to see outside. The snow still swirled through the air, and the glass in front of her rattled right on cue.

She went over to the built-in desk and picked up her phone. After returning to the table and taking another bite of her breakfast, she said, "Three Rivers is reporting eight inches overnight in town." She looked up. "Has to be more than that here."

"Probably," Ward said. "I haven't been outside yet today."

"Then we'll just stay in," she said. "We have power."

"I need to go check on the gasoline for the generator," he said. "I don't know how long it had to be used last night."

"I think...were you playing the guitar?"

"Yes," he said. "I didn't mean to bother you."

"You didn't," she said. "For some reason, I couldn't fall asleep in that bedroom. I came out to the couch, and I was out like a light."

Ward smiled at her. "I'm glad." He finished his toast and reached over to cover her hand with his. "You were warm enough?"

"Plenty warm," she confirmed.

Ward watched her as she ate with her free hand, the warmth and silky quality of her skin touching his magical and heartwarming. He wanted to run his hand down the side of her face and draw her close for a kiss.

She looked up and met his eye, and Ward's face grew instantly hot. He told himself she couldn't see the fantasies inside his head, but that didn't stop his embarrassment.

He stood and picked up his plate. "I'm going to go check on the gasoline right now. You can shower or whatever. There are clean towels in the drawers in the bathroom. You've got a toothbrush. There's shampoo and conditioner and body wash in the shower. All of it."

"Okay," she said.

Ward went down the hall to his bedroom without another word, wondering why he'd turned so awkward around Dot. He'd *already* kissed her, for crying out loud. He changed into his jeans and a long-sleeved T-shirt. He covered that with a sweatshirt and pulled on wool socks.

He'd wear work boots, but they were out by the garage exit, as was his coat, hat, and gloves. Dot stood eating the leftover avocadoes with a spoon when he re-entered the kitchen. "You have to go outside?" she asked.

"Just to the shed," he said. "It's maybe fifty feet. I'll take a rope like I did with the wood." He pulled on his boots and continued getting dressed to face the elements. Ready and sweating, he turned toward her. "I'll be back in a few minutes. Like I said, go shower."

She nodded, and Ward wondered what she'd put on if she did shower. The clothes she'd worn yesterday? He'd hate that, but he didn't say anything. He just nodded and left through the garage door, went quickly down the steps, and moved over to the gas cans in the corner of the garage.

They were all empty. Every last one of them. "Great," he said with a sigh, though he hadn't truly thought any of them would have gas in them. They didn't store cans full of gasoline in the garage. If there was a fire, the whole thing could go up in flames in a matter of seconds.

He had gas in a tank out by the shed, and the ranch had a massive gas tank behind their main barn. They used it to fill tractors and trucks, and they got it wholesale for a much cheaper price than he could get at any station in town.

He picked up two cans and faced the back door in the corner of the garage. He first had to check the generator, but it sat just around the corner from the door.

The wind dang near clawed off his face the moment he tried to step outside. It cut straight through his hat and gloves and seeped through the fibers of his coat. His jeans felt frozen now, and he hadn't even left the garage yet.

In fact, he closed the door and took a deep breath, steeling himself to try again. After a few seconds, he opened the door again, ready for the sharp teeth of the wind and the blustery quality of the air. It didn't seem to go into his lungs right, no matter how hard he sucked at it.

He kept one hand on the house as he went right this time. Around the corner he inched, until he finally arrived at the generator. A steady red light on the panel indicated it was out of gas. If the power went out, the generator would be of no use to them.

Ward turned and put his left hand on the house, switching the empty gas cans to his right hand. In clear weather, he'd be able to see past the old, rickety swing set his daddy and Uncle Stone had built for the boys to the big red shed in the corner of the back yard. Daddy had never wanted a big yard, because it was just more work, and Ward had made the trek from garage to shed dozens of times. Probably hundreds. It was only a few strides with his long legs, and he reasoned that he didn't have to hit the door to find the barn.

He stepped away from the corner of the house, his eyes searching the misty, snowy soup in front of him. Another step. Nothing. Then another.

He made sure to keep his feet moving in precisely the same direction as when he'd stepped away from the house. Finally, the shape of the swing set—which now had no swings—came into his view. He reached out and grabbed onto one of the poles and took another step. Then another.

He reached the back of the swing set. The shed was only a few more paces.

It was then that Ward realized he hadn't brought a rope with him, and he'd have to make this blind trek on the way back too. *It's okay*, he thought, stepping away from the swing set. *Keep going. You're almost there.*

*Almost there, almost there, almost there...*

# Chapter Twelve

❧

Dot did shower, and the water rolled down her back nice and hot. She stayed in for a long time, and then she curled up in bed and called her mother. "There you are, honey," her mom said. "I was hoping you'd call before too long."

"You got my texts, right?" Dot asked. "I'm safe. I'm up at Shiloh Ridge."

"Yes, yes," Mom said. "I got them."

"How are you and Dad?" Dot asked. "Did you lose power?"

"Only for about fifteen minutes," Mom said, and she proceeded to say that Dad had roasted off four pounds of chicken breast before she could convince him that they weren't going to lose everything in the freezer. "So we have shredded chicken for about an army." She trilled out a laugh, and Dot smiled.

"You love shredded chicken tacos," she said.

"I'm making chimichangas today," she said. "It's not very traditional, but I suppose it could be."

"Why not?" Dot asked. "You're from Mexico. I'm sure someone down there had chimichangas for Christmas dinner." They laughed together, and Dot got an update on her father's health. He'd been diagnosed with mild dementia earlier this year, but Dot hadn't noticed any symptoms when she spent time with him. Mom had some good stories though, and the baking off of dozens of chicken breasts probably had something to do with his mental health.

"Have you talked to Tyson?" Mom asked. "Or Kassie?"

"Nope," Dot said. "I called you first, Mom." Her mom would like that, and Dot smiled as her mom told her that she was sure Dot's siblings would love to hear from her. "We saw Ty last night. He brought over some hand warmers to appease your father."

"During the storm?" Dot asked, shocked that Tyson would risk himself or his car for hand warmers.

"Yes," she said. "It hadn't gotten too bad yet."

"Mom, it was bad at one o'clock when they rang the siren."

Her mom said something else that didn't really make sense to Dot, and then said, "The timer on the oven is going off. I have to go."

"What are you cooking now?" Dot asked, but her Mom hung up a moment later. "Bye," Dot said grumpily. "I love you too."

She glared at her phone like it had cut them off and her scatterbrained mother hadn't been behind the abrupt end to the call. Dot slid out of bed and got dressed in yesterday's clothes. Thankfully, she'd only done one delivery before coming up to Shiloh Ridge, so her clothes weren't visibly dirty. Didn't mean they were clean, especially to Dot.

She rubbed her hair as dry as she could get it without an appliance and hung the towel on the back of the doorknob before going out into the living room again.

Ward wasn't there, and Dot's eyes immediately flew to the office. The door sat open today, and while the light pouring in the huge back windows wasn't made of golden rays, it was definitely bright enough to see everything.

"Ward?" Dot called, glancing into the kitchen. His boots didn't sit by the garage exit, and the house felt deathly still and far too quiet. She walked through the living room toward the office. The front door rattled in its battle against the storm outside, but Dot ignored it. Surely Ward would be sitting behind his computer, his earbuds in while he worked on his song.

He'd told her a month or two ago, when they'd still been dating, that he was writing his own tune, and that he sometimes recorded himself playing right into the computer. Then he'd cut the music and let a program write the specific music in bars and notes for him. Later, after he'd finished the tune, he'd write lyrics for the song.

Dot had marveled at such talent, because she was barely a step above tone deaf, without a single music note in her blood.

"Ward," she said as she stepped through the double-wide office doors.

He wasn't there.

She spun around, her heart hammering in the back of her throat now. He'd been gone for far too long for anything good to have happened. "How long does it take to get gasoline from a shed?" she asked herself, her mind taking her ten different directions.

She wasn't an expert, but she didn't think it would take as long as she'd taken in the shower, then laid in bed to talk to her mother, and then got dried and dressed. He'd been gone for at least thirty minutes. Maybe longer.

Dot ran through the house to the bedroom and picked up her phone. Her fingers shook as she called Ward. His phone rang while she hurried back into the living room and to the sliding glass door that assumedly went into the back yard.

He didn't pick up.

"Dang it, Ward," she said, her voice pitching up. Dot retraced her steps once more to get her socks. She yanked them on and then hurried to get her boots on. She shouldered into her jacket, but she didn't have a hat or gloves. The small area just inside the garage held a bank of lockers, and Dot nearly ripped off the door of one so she could look inside.

Ideas raced through her mind. She could call Tyson and get the number for one of Ward's brothers. She could request an ambulance. She could pray the Lord would make the wind lighter for just five minutes so Ward could find his way back—or she could find him.

"Please, please," she pleaded, reaching to grab the first hat she saw. It was bright yellow and hideous, but she jammed it over her hair. A pair of gloves fell on the floor, and Dot picked them up and put them on. She had big, manly hands, but they were still too large. She didn't care.

She faced the back door, only one goal in mind. Find Ward and get him back inside.

She wished she had time to build up the fire. Heat some water for coffee or hot chocolate. Hot apple cider would be amazing too. She wanted to throw a bunch of towels and blankets in the dryer so they'd be warm when Ward made it back inside.

Dot pulled open the back door, the screech of the sliding mechanism grating against her already raw nerves. The door didn't open all the way either, because Ward had tied a rope to it.

She ducked underneath it and slid the door closed. Then, grasping the rope with both hands, Dot turned into the storm and yelled, "Ward! Ward! Where are you?"

After following the rope down a couple of steps to the woodpile, where it ended, Dot lifted one hand to shield against the swirling blizzard in front of her. He'd said the shed was in the back yard.

"Fifty feet," she told herself, but she didn't dare take the first step. She should've brought out her torch. Maybe he'd be able to see it. She fumbled in her pocket for her phone, and she dialed him again, desperation coating every cell in her body. "Come on, Ward," she said. "Dear Lord, let him pick up. Help me find him. Help me find him."

She repeated the words while his line rang and rang. It ran through her mind as she hung up.

"I'm going to take the first step," she said, tipping her

head back and catching the icy cold gust against her bare neck. "Guide my feet."

*Guide my feet. Guide my feet. Guide my feet.*

Dot actually closed her eyes and took the first step away from the wood pile. She felt the crunch of snow under her boot, and she took another step.

"Guide my feet. Tell me what to do."

She paused, because her mom and dad had taught her to ask for something and then give God time to answer. So she stood very still, the wind and snow and sleet and rain whipping around her, and she closed her eyes again, listening with everything she had.

*Call him again.*

Dot's eyes snapped open and she stabbed at her phone four times before it registered her fingerprint and dialed. She took a step, holding the phone very close to her face. Another step. "Ward," she yelled. "Talk to me, Ward."

He didn't answer. Dot ended the call and immediately dialed again.

Another step.

"Ward!" she screamed into the storm.

In that moment, she saw something glowing up ahead. She had no idea how far, as she couldn't judge distance among so much chaos. "Ward," she called again, hurrying now and not bothering to count her steps.

She found him grasping the pole of an ancient swing set, his eyes closed. "Ward." She reached him and shook his arm. "Ward, wake up. Ward!"

His eyes opened oh-so-slowly, and Dot saw anguish and

confusion there. She grabbed onto his arm and said, "Come on."

She marched back the way she'd come, keeping her eyes on the ground so she could see her footprints. After three steps, they disappeared, but she kept going. She'd have to hit the house soon enough.

Ward felt like dead weight behind her, and he stumbled forward. Dot couldn't catch him, and they both fell to their knees.

"Ward," she said desperately. "I need your help to get back inside." She got to her feet and took both of his hands in hers. "Come on, sweetheart. You can do it."

He lumbered to his feet, a bit more comprehension in his gaze. "Dot?"

"Yes," she said. "Come on. I can't carry you." She turned and took three more steps before she reached the wood pile. "Right here. Put your hand on this rope. It goes right to the back door."

"I left the gas by the swing set," he said.

Dot faced the storm, wondering how necessary the gasoline was. She made a quick decision. "That's just fine, Woods," she said. "We don't need it."

"We do if the power goes out."

"Nope," she said. "We have a huge fireplace and each other. Hand over hand, cowboy. Hurry up. I'm freezing." She followed him, and he moved so slowly. She couldn't even imagine how he'd survived so long, and when he finally got inside, he just stood there as if he didn't know what to do.

Dot did, though.

"Come on," she said, ripping off her gloves and hat. She dropped them without a second thought and started removing his wet, frozen clothes. "Hat off. Gloves. Coat." She actually took it all off of him while he stood there, his teeth chattering.

"I'm c-c-cold," he said.

"Yes, I know." Dot tugged on his sweatshirt. "It's all coming off, Ward. We're past modesty." She got him out of his shirts and boots, and he managed to use his white fingers to undo his jeans.

He stepped out of those, and Dot really tried hard not to admire his body. Boy, ranching did a body good, and Dot supported him as she moved him in front of the fire. She'd taken her blanket back into the bedroom, and she said, "Stay here. I'll be right back."

She ran to get the blanket, returning ten seconds later to see Ward had closed his eyes again. "Stay awake," she commanded, and his eyes opened slowly again. "Tell me about the shed out back. What color is it? Did you build it?"

"My dad," he said. "He b-b-built everything we used for a long time."

Dot nodded and got to work on the fire, stoking up the coals and adding a couple of handfuls of wadded up newspaper. "Did you help him paint it?"

"He made us all help," Ward said. "His name was Bull, and that should tell you a little bit about what kind of man he was."

Dot shrugged out of her coat and added some smaller pieces of wood to the fire. She worked so quickly that she didn't build the fire as carefully as she would have otherwise. It didn't matter. She needed it to flame up quickly and start putting out some major heat.

"You sound like you didn't like the work."

"I loved it," Ward said. "My dad worked so hard, and I wanted to please him."

"I think he'd be pleased, Ward," she said, turning to look at him. He wasn't quite as blue anymore, but she was worried about his extremities. "I'm going to move the couch closer." She got up and rounded the furniture, leaning her whole body into it to move the sofa with the muscled cowboy on it.

The flames danced and crackled, and Dot was happy with them. She put another huge log on and asked, "Where's the dryer?"

"Basement," he said.

She'd seen all the towels in the linen closet, and she bent down and got in his face. "You are *not* to move. You are *not* to fall asleep. I will be gone for five minutes, maybe less. Promise me you will not even *blink* for longer than it takes to breathe in."

He studied her, and Dot wasn't moving until he promised. She needed to get a hot shower going and get him in it. She needed to then meet him at the bathroom door with super-heated towels. While he got warm in the shower spray, she'd make hot apple cider and force it down his throat.

"Ward," she said. "Promise me."

"I won't move," he said. "I won't fall asleep."

Dot stared at him for another few seconds, and then

she spun and ran down the hall. She gathered as many towels as sat in a stack on the shelf, and she practically slid down the steps to the basement she went so fast.

She found the dryer and tossed the towels inside, twisted the knob, and started the appliance. She took the steps two at a time back to the kitchen, where she said, "Talk to me, Ward. If you're asleep, I'm going to lose my mind."

His sexy chuckle filled the room. "I'm not asleep."

"Tell me your greatest fear." She filled the electric kettle with water and switched it on.

"I'm terrified of being inadequate," Ward said, and Dot looked over to the couch. He was lying on it, and she couldn't see him.

"Cider or tea?" she asked, puzzling over how in the world Ward Glover could ever be inadequate.

"Tea," he said. "I hate hot apple cider."

"Good to know," Dot murmured. She opened the same cupboard that he'd pulled hot chocolate from last night and found a box of herbal tea. She put a bag in a mug and hurried to the couch. She leaned over the end of it and looked into Ward's eyes. "Warm or cold?"

"Getting warmer," he said.

"Do you want me to put you in the shower?" she asked. "It'll warm you right up."

"No," he said, his eyes drifting closed. He pulled them back open again. "Just come lay with me."

"Give me another minute," Dot said. She returned to the sliding glass door and made sure it was locked. She took off her boots and wet jeans too. She picked up everything she could and then dropped it on the counter when she saw the steam rising from the kettle.

She poured the hot water over the tea bag and then reclaimed the wet clothes. Back in the basement, she swapped out the now hot towels for the clothes, restarted the appliance, and hurried back upstairs.

Her heartbeat sprinted around her chest as she lifted the blanket from Ward's body and started tucking the hot towels around his torso and legs, reserving one for his head and neck.

"We have rice bags in the cupboard beside the microwave," he said. "They heat up and get real nice and toasty."

"I'll get you one for your hands and one for your feet," she said. "I'm going to change so I'm dry, and then I'll come lay by you."

Her hair dripped, because it had been wet when she'd gone outside, and it had frozen. She fetched his tea and handed it to him. "Sit up and drink, Ward."

"Those towels feel great," he said, taking the tea. His eyes caught on her bare legs. "You're not wearing pants."

Dot grinned at the shock on his face. "Neither are you, cowboy." She hurried into the kitchen and started two rice bags in the microwave before going into her bedroom and put on his college clothes she'd worn to bed, kicking her wet shirt out into the kitchen so it wasn't resting on carpet.

She finally joined him on the couch, lifting the blanket to tuck a rice bag against his bare feet. She handed him the other one, added another log to the fire, and slid beneath the blanket to share her body heat with him.

"Better?" she asked, noting that he'd wrapped all ten fingers around the hot mug and that he inhaled the steam rising from it too.

"Getting better," he said, his eyes darting around the room without looking at her. "I feel so stupid."

"You should," Dot said. "But not as stupid as me. I showered and chit-chatted with my mom while you were —" She cut off, because she could not imagine how she'd feel if he'd died while she was lying in bed, safe in his house, talking to her mother about cooking too much chicken.

Tears filled her eyes, and Ward moved. He switched position on the couch so he could wrap her in his arms and hold her against his chest. Dot allowed herself to shed a few tears while Ward stroked her hair and whispered, "I'm sorry, sweetheart. I'm so sorry, Dot," over and over again.

Eventually, she quieted and so did he. Dot didn't close her eyes. She watched the fire to make sure it blazed heartily, and she listened to the cadence of Ward's breathing to make sure he didn't fall asleep.

He didn't seem to be lethargic and about to lose consciousness anymore, but he didn't say anything either. Dot wondered what he was thinking, but she enjoyed this cocoon they'd made for themselves, and she didn't want anything to break into it or disturb it.

# Chapter Thirteen

❧❦❧

"Are you awake?" Ward asked.

"Yes," Dot said. She shifted and sat up. Ward was very aware that he only wore his boxer shorts and Dot was fully clothed. "I'll get you some clothes, okay? Should I reheat the towels?"

"I think I'm good," he said, watching her rise. He felt five thousand percent better than he had thirty minutes ago, and he was well-aware that Dorothy Crockett had saved his life. "I'd love some clothes, and then I'd love to know how you found me."

Dot nodded and went down the hall without saying anything.

Ward sighed and leaned his head back against the couch. "Idiot," he chastised himself. "You shouldn't have gone out there without a rope or without telling Dot to call Ranger if you weren't back in ten minutes."

He didn't know how long he'd been outside, but it had

felt like years. He'd lost feeling in his toes and fingers, though he could definitely feel them blazing now. They pricked with life, and he closed his eyes and said, "Thank you, Lord, for preserving my life. For sending Dot, who seems to know exactly what to do."

"Amen," Dot said, and Ward's eyes shot open. She stood at the end of the couch, holding the shorts and T-shirt he'd worn last night. "I found these on the chair in the corner. Seemed safe."

Ward reached for the garments. "Thanks." He stood and stepped into the shorts, covering the most private parts of himself. He fumbled with the shirt, though his fingers were working just fine. They trembled a little bit, and he looked up to find Dot watching with those eagle eyes of hers.

Her gaze switched to his chest, and she licked her lips and swallowed. Ward's face burned, and he should be glad for the extra body heat. He was, and he was glad to know Dot seemed to like what she saw.

"More tea?" she asked.

"No, thank you," he said. "I could use some more to eat though."

"Cold cereal?" she asked. "I can do that like a pro." She gave him a grin and walked into the kitchen. He liked her wearing his clothes, and he liked her presence in his house. He managed to get himself dressed before she returned with the honey nut Cheerios doused in milk.

He sat back down on the couch and she sat on the other end of it. "You're real good at building a fire," he said.

"I worked as a boy scout camp counselor for a few

years," she said. "We had to teach the boys how to do stuff like that."

"A boy scout camp?"

"I can assure you that I don't like campfires or s'mores as much as you do." She gave him a brilliant smile and Ward dang near threw his bowl and lunged at her. He had to kiss her again soon, but he wasn't going to do it with milky breath, only a few minutes after an embarrassing encounter that could've ended his life.

"I think you're the one with all the layers," he said. "Boy scout camp?" He smiled and shook his head before taking another bite of cereal. "Did they teach you about hypothermia there too?"

"Yes," she said simply.

He nodded and kept eating, suddenly ravenous.

"Ward," she said, her voice clear and serious.

He looked over to her, the honey and nut and milk one of the best things he'd eaten in a while. Maybe he just loved honey nut Cheerios. "Yeah?"

"I have another confession."

His heart tried to squeeze itself into a box two sizes too small. He took another bite and ate it before speaking. "Go on then."

"Don't you have any confessions?"

"Probably," he said, thinking of one he liked to get out of the way when it came to women. At least women he was serious about, and he'd never been as serious about anyone as he was about Dot. He cleared his throat. "Yes, I have one I can think of."

"Maybe we can swap confessions this morning."

"Then will you let me take a nap?" He grinned at her, and Dot giggled and shook her head.

"I think you're in the clear for hypothermia," she said. "So we can probably take a nap, yes."

"We? Together?" he asked. "Right here?" He gestured to the couch with his spoon.

"If you'd like," she said.

"I'd like." He took another bite of cereal.

"I haven't even made my confession yet."

Ward glanced up and into the fire while he chewed. He swallowed and faced her. "You think I won't want to be in the same room with you after I hear what you have to say?"

"I have no idea."

Ward lifted his bowl to his lips and drank the extra milk. "I'm ready." He set the bowl on the hearth and started bundling himself back in the blanket and towels. The rice bag was still hot, and he'd have to tell Mother her crafts had saved his toes.

"Remember how I was kind of...standoffish with you in the beginning?"

"Yes," he said. "And you know, like, three weeks ago."

"Yes." She reached up and tucked her hair, the gesture of the nervous kind that Ward had seen her do before. "There's a reason for that."

"Okay."

"You see...my ex-fiancé and business partner's name was Ward."

Ward opened his mouth to say something, but his brain honestly misfired.

"Ward Rogers," she said with an exhale. "Sometimes

your name still triggers me a little." She looked at him with doe-eyes, and Ward didn't know what to think.

"I see," he said, but he didn't. Not really. There were probably a thousand men named Ward.

"That's why I asked about your name so early," she said. "And why I wish you'd go by Woods."

Ward wanted to tell her he'd go by Woods from that moment on. At the same time, the name had never fit him, and everyone in the family had known it. "Woods is my great-grandmother's maiden name," he said. "That's why my mother chose it for me. But my name is Ward."

Dot nodded. "I know. I'm dealing with it."

"Dealing with it?" Ward didn't mean to sound so harsh. "It's just a name, Dot." He got to his feet and took his cereal bowl to the sink. He didn't want to make his confession now, because he suddenly felt inferior due to something he absolutely couldn't control.

Something pinched in his chest, and he placed both palms against the strip of counter in front of the sink and leaned into them. He strained to see beyond the window, but the wind felt never-ending.

It annoyed him, because they had animals to tend to. He'd probably find some of them dead due to the cold snap and lack of food, as no human could get out to the barns and stables to feed the animals. All he could do for them was pray, and he took a moment to do that.

"Praying again?" she asked.

"Yes," he said without opening his eyes. "For the animals out on the ranch. I've got a horse named Nickers I'm quite fond of."

"Knickers? Like underwear?" She giggled, but Ward wasn't done with his prayer yet. He added a bit about him so he wouldn't push Dot too far away while he dealt with his feelings about her confession.

Ward didn't get to have feelings sometimes, and he hated that. He'd learned to be steady, and he'd adopted his daddy's attitude of worrying about things when they happened and not a moment before. But the truth was, he did worry about things from time to time, and he felt like he had no safe place to do so.

"No," he said, exhaling and opening his eyes. "Like the sound a horse makes. He nickers at me. He can nod too."

"He can?"

Ward grinned at the faint reflection of himself in the glass. "Yep." He turned toward her and said, "Thank you, Dot, for saving my life. Really." He didn't move toward her, and she hadn't gotten off the couch. "I'm going to go work on some stuff in my office, if that's okay."

That got her to her feet. "Wait. I thought you had a confession."

He shook his head. "I don't want to say it quite yet."

She looked like she'd protest, then she snapped her mouth shut. She nodded, and Ward did too. Then he walked toward the office in what he hoped was a normal gait, not something that looked like him running away from her.

WARD LET HIS FINGERS WANDER OVER THE STRINGS, plucking if they wanted to and strumming chords in no order whatsoever. He loved sitting on the back deck with his guitar in his hands, and he wished he could escape these walls and find a breath of fresh air.

"There's a road no one knows about," he sang under his breath, though he hadn't started writing the lyrics for this particular song yet. He'd written dozens of songs over the years, but he'd taken a break in the past couple of years since becoming foreman here on the ranch.

Now that Preacher had taken some of that load, Ward thought he'd get back to putting harmonies and melodies together. He still had the contact information of the music producers in Nashville, and he'd sold plenty of songs to them.

Only Etta and Ida knew that some of the biggest country rock, country pop, and pure country hits were written by him. No one ever scrolled to the "written by" credits in music, and a lot of the big-name artists were just singers and guitar players. They weren't song-writers.

Ward was all of the above, but he'd learned his lesson early in his life. The Lord simply didn't want him to be a country music star. He had the talent, but he didn't want the lifestyle. He'd thought he had, once, but time and experience had taught Ward that some things were far more important that money and fame.

"It's a road I walk alone," he added, thinking he should write these words down. "I don't know if I'll stay on it. Maybe the Lord will take me in a different direction."

He strummed for a few bars, thinking about Dot and

why her confession had bothered him so much. He had zero control over it, that was why. He couldn't rename himself because she'd had a bad experience with a Ward at some point in her past.

He hated the injustices in the world, and he felt like he'd been blamed for this other Ward's actions. That so wasn't fair, and he honestly didn't see how Dot couldn't see the difference between him and her ex-fiancé.

"Maybe there's no difference," Ward said, breaking off the music. The office echoed in the resulting silence, and Ward looked toward the window as the light coming through it brightened. His heart took hope that the sun would peek through the clouds, and he set his guitar aside to go look.

Before he arrived at the glass, the room darkened again. The flat gray light made him frown and only worsened his mood. He sat behind the computer, but he wasn't interested in checking his email or filing any receipts for the Cowboys Provide Christmas program.

It was Christmas Day. He should've been out in the stables handing out carrots and sugar cubes. After that, he'd shower and head to Ace's house, where he'd get to spend the day with his family, the people who reminded him who he was and kept him grounded.

Ward couldn't remember the last time he'd gone all day without seeing his brothers. He pulled out his phone to check the family thread. Several people had been on this morning already, sending out happy holiday wishes. Bear had sent several photos of Lincoln and Stetson opening their gifts, and the joy on Stetson's face reminded Ward of all the good things in the world.

The sight of those wide, wonder-filled eyes and pure joy in the child's smile, reminded Ward of how very much he wanted a son of his own. By the time his father was Ward's age, he'd had five children. He and Mother had gotten married very young, and both of them had told their children not to rush into marriage.

All of them had taken such advice seriously, as none of them had even started looking for a companion until they were well into their thirties. Well, maybe Etta had, but she'd had the worst time of it so far.

Ward's fingers flew across the screen. *I'd love to see everyone today*, he said. *Let's video in and sing our carols together. Before lunch? After? Maybe Preacher or Charlie can set up a private video chat for us.*

Before he could second-guess himself, Ward sent the message. He kept his head bent as the replies came in.

*We're in*, Ace said. *Great idea, Ward. Holly Ann said she'll keep the feast for when we can get together. Can't be too much longer.*

*Charlie has a ton of video stuff*, Preacher said. *She's on it and will text out a link to everyone.*

*We're in*, Bear said.

*I guess I can stand to see your faces*, Cactus said with a winking emoji.

*Will you play your guitar, Ward?* Judge asked. *I can jump on the piano here at the Ranch House.*

*Sure*, Ward said. *I'll text you a set list, Judge.*

*A set list?* Bishop asked. *How formal is this? Do I need to get dressed, because I really don't want to....*

*At least put on a shirt, Bishop,* Arizona said.

*I'm crying over this,* Ida said. *I hate that I'm the only one not up there.*

*We're all in separate houses, Ida,* Mister said. *Don't feel bad.*

Ranger and Etta didn't answer, and Ward navigated over to a note-taking app and started making a list of songs he could play on the guitar. Judge was quite an accomplished pianist—as was Willa, though Cactus didn't have a piano out at the Edge Cabin—and he could play anything.

"Nothing too long," Ward said, knowing that video could be tricky sometimes. People forgot to mute themselves, and the Internet connection could be bad. Sometimes a link wouldn't work, or it would only allow a few people into the chat.

He made a list of six songs and sent them to Judge. The Glovers always sang Silent Night last when they did their family caroling, and Ward saw no reason to change that.

*Amazing list,* Judge said. *I'm going to suggest eleven-thirty if that's okay. I think a lot of people got up and made breakfast, and that way, we'll be free for lunch or naps or whatever.*

*Sounds good to me,* Ward said, and then he went back to the family text string. Ranger had commended Ward for a great idea, and he said any time was fine with him.

Etta had said she'd join Bear or Ranger, and others had started suggesting songs. Bishop had sent pictures of his mother and Aurora with matching necklaces, as well as a huge spread of French toast, bacon, and fresh strawberries and cream.

Judge had been right about breakfast, that was for sure.

Ward thought about his trek through the snow that morning. He'd been so scared to go past the shed. The back yard ended with the shed, and the land beyond that went down at a steep decline to the road that went around to the Ranch House. If he'd fallen down that....

Ward knew he was lucky to be alive, and he should probably tell his family about the incident. At the same time, he didn't want anyone to know his girlfriend had come to save him, and she'd been smart enough to get the job done.

Ward looked up from his phone, his eyes landing on the closed office door. He couldn't be upset with Dot because she had a past. He supposed everything he'd experience had shaped who he was in this moment, and she hadn't said she blamed him for being named Ward.

"Stupid name," he muttered to himself as he stood. His name had always been a sore spot for him, because Grandmother had given everyone else a special name that meant something. Ward had felt overlooked and insignificant, and he hated that. He'd been inadequate, and he absolutely didn't want to feel like that.

He didn't have a letter from his daddy explaining his name. He didn't know why Grandmother had never chosen something for him. As he picked up his guitar and went to rejoin Dot, he told himself that none of the girls had gotten nicknames either, and not having one didn't make him better or worse.

He'd been telling himself that for decades, and he still

didn't quite believe it. He wasn't going to stay silent with Dot. He wasn't.

He found her on the couch, and he lifted his guitar. "Would you like to hear one of my songs?"

"Absolutely," she said, getting to her feet. "But first, Ward, I'm sorry if my confession upset you. I'm working past—I'm—it's my problem, not yours." She put her hands on his chest, and it would be so easy to slide his hand along her waist and pull her closer.

So he did. "Mm, this is nice," he whispered. "I'll tell you my confession after I play, okay?"

"You've got yourself a deal, cowboy."

# Chapter Fourteen

Dot helped Ward push the couch back so it wasn't quite so close to the fire. He then sat on the hearth, and she retook her place on the sofa. His fingers played over the strings, but he clearly wasn't fully committed to making beautiful music with the guitar yet.

He shifted and cleared his throat. "I guess I have two confessions, and this is the first one."

"Bonus," Dot said, grinning at him.

"This is a song I wrote about five years ago, and I sold it to Columbia Records. They gave it to Carrie Underwood."

Dot's eyes widened at the same time her heart started booming in her chest. "You're kidding."

"Do you listen to country music in all its forms?" he asked. "The rock, the pop, the more twangy, traditional stuff?"

"Sure," she said.

"Then you'll probably recognize this." He stopped playing and looked down at the neck of the guitar. A moment later, he started to play, and Dot could tell the difference. Every note sat in exactly the right place, and his fingers moved effortlessly along the strings.

She recognized the first strains of the song, and awe streamed through her that the man in front of her had written this tune. She knew the words, and Ward came in right on time. She'd imagined his voice to be a deep bass, but it wasn't. He sang tenor, and Dot sighed and closed her eyes to experience the music in its purest form.

When he finished, and the last reverberations of his guitar still hung in the air, Dot started clapping. She opened her eyes and grinned at him, finding him even more attractive than she had previously.

Her attraction to him went deeper than just how beautiful the man was. He had a good heart, and plenty of talent, and some skills in the kitchen she sure did like. "That was amazing," she said. "Seriously, Ward, I have no idea how your mind works like that."

He seemed to have a glow about him as he set his guitar next to the hearth. He smiled back at her and extended his hand toward her. She leaned forward and put her hand in his. "I'm going crazy in this room," he said. "Do you want to see the office?"

"I snooped in there, remember?"

"It has huge windows," he said. "We can pretend we'll be able to leave this dang house."

"Ah, someone doesn't like being inside all the time."

"Do you?" he challenged.

"Not at all," she admitted. He secured her hand in his and gently tugged her to go with him. "How many songs have you sold to big country stars?"

"Uh, let's see." He didn't count on his fingers this time, and Dot found him absolutely adorable. "I haven't done it for a while, since becoming foreman. But for a while there, I was selling every song I wrote."

"Dozens?"

"Yeah," he said. "Probably thirty or forty."

"I just can't...I don't know what to say."

Ward smiled at her as they entered the office through the double-wide French doors. A couch sat in front of the massive desk, and she saw a guitar stand there as well. "By the way, we're doing a family caroling event at eleven-thirty. I'm playing the guitar. You can...you don't have to participate if you don't want to."

"I want to," Dot said. She wanted to participate in all areas of Ward Glover's life. "Do you guys normally go caroling?"

"No," he said. "We just sing either before or after our big family meal on Christmas Day. We usually take down the angel tree, but Etta texted to say she thinks we should leave it up a few extra days because of the storm. So we'll go take it down then."

"Is that a family event too?"

"Usually," he said.

"Do you guys do everything as a family?"

"No," he said. "We have some big things—traditions, like most families. Other stuff is way more loose, especially as the family grows."

"Like...?"

"Like Sunday dinner," he said. "Sometimes Bear will say he doesn't want a crowd at the homestead. If someone wants to cook, we'll meet at True Blue. If someone doesn't, we make our own Sabbath meal."

"Who cooks for the whole family?" Dot couldn't comprehend that either. Of course, she couldn't even make her own meals, let alone enough food to feed dozens of people.

"Bishop loves it," he said. "He's my youngest cousin. He actually won the Christmas cake bake-off this year." He released her hand and rounded the desk to sit down. "I'm the treasurer for this program I've been doing for a while. Cowboys Provide Christmas?" He raised both eyebrows and met her gaze.

"I haven't heard of it."

"It's a great organization," Ward said, his voice slipping into a somewhat more professional tone. "Cowboys from ranches around Texas provide Christmas for other cowboys and ranches and their families also in Texas."

"I'm assuming you provide and not receive." She perched on the edge of the couch, refusing to remove her eyes from his.

He dropped his head, but he wasn't wearing his cowboy hat, and he couldn't hide anything from her. "Yeah, yep." He nodded quite aggressively and shifted some papers around. "That's my second confession. I, uh, we all have, um, I'm a billionaire."

He leaned away from the desk and steepled his fingers. "All of us are. We invest a lot of money to make more money, and we have healthy calf sales every year. We sell our extra hay. We reinvest any profits. My daddy and my uncle started that decades ago, and we're quite well-off at Shiloh Ridge."

Dot thought she'd been hit with a load of bricks with the songwriting. That alone was something she needed time to wrap her mind around.

But this?

She exhaled all of the air out of her lungs and slid all the way back on the couch. "Okay." She wasn't sure why she'd said okay. It's not like she could make it not okay. He wasn't going to give away all of his money if she didn't approve of him being rich.

*Really rich*, she thought.

"That's all?" he asked.

"I don't know what to say. You hit me with really big things."

"You told me my name is a trigger for you," he shot back, his gaze turning dark.

Dot opened her mouth to argue but found she couldn't. Anxiety streamed through her, and fear had frozen her vocal cords.

"I'm a little sensitive about my name," he said, looking toward the windows and softening. "My grandmother gave all of the other boys these perfect nicknames. I just got my middle name."

Dot rubbed her hands down her thighs. "Maybe you did get a perfect name for you. You take care of everything and everyone. I can feel how heavy it is for you sometimes. You're like the ward of the family."

He frowned. "That doesn't make sense."

Surprise coursed through her. "With your experience with lyrics, I'd think you'd know all the meanings of the word ward," she said gently. "It's a noun and a verb. One of the meanings of the verb is to like, you know, protect. Guard over something or someone. Like, you're the ward of the ranch. You guard it. You protect it."

His gaze came slowly back to hers. "You really think so?"

"Absolutely," she said.

"Seems like Bear's forte, not mine."

"And yet, you're the foreman, and you literally know every inch of this ranch, every human who comes here, all of it." Dot gestured behind her, toward the wall but really at what lay behind it. "You're making those books for your siblings, because they need the memories. You're protecting them. You're guarding them."

Ward seemed puzzled, and then the emotion melted right off his face. He swiped and tapped on his phone, and then he said, "It's an archaic meaning of the word."

"Old fashioned," she said.

Ward met her eyes again. "To guard or protect. This says, 'it was his duty to ward the king.'"

Dot gave him a small smile. "That's what you do, Ward. And you do it really well."

"You don't know that."

"But I do," she said. "You've told me other things on other dates. You help your brothers and cousins. You protect Ida and Etta. You provide a great place to live for animals and people alike up here. Who does more on this ranch than you?"

"Preacher used to," Ward said. "Before his car accident. We all work hard here, Dot."

"I'm not saying they don't. I'm just saying maybe your grandmother *did* give you the perfect name for you."

"Maybe," he said. "I'm going to ask Mother and Aunt Lois about it."

"Good idea." Dot continued to smile at him, and he finally got up and joined her on the couch.

He lifted his arm around her and said, "I'm going to put in a turkey breast for lunch. I can make baked veggies to go with it. Does that sound diabetic-friendly?"

"I can eat whatever," she said, because she didn't want to think about her diabetes so much. She had insulin, and she'd be fine. The wind storm couldn't last much longer, and after Ward had disappeared to the office for a few minutes, she'd checked the weather. The advisory had not been extended again.

"Okay," he said. "Maybe I'll pull out a cherry pie too."

"From where?" she asked. "Do not tell me you bake."

He grinned and leaned down to brush his lips along the side of her face. He said something, but she had no idea what. White noise buzzed in her ears with his touch, the scent of his skin, the warmth from his body.

He got up and left her on the couch, and only then did she hear what he'd said. *I can bake a few things, but cherry pie isn't one of them. Etta put one in my freezer a couple of months ago. It's a heat and eat.*

"Heat and eat," she said, reaching up to touch her

face where he'd kissed her. Before she knew it, he'd returned, and he started clicking around on the computer. He turned the monitor so it faced the couch, and he settled on the other end of it with his guitar on his knees.

Another man blipped to life on the screen, and Ward said, "Ranger. Wow, it's good to see you."

"This is nuts, right?" His older brother looked at Dot. "How are you holding up, Dot?"

"Good," she said.

"I hate being trapped inside," Ranger said. He leaned closer to the screen, his eyes darting left and right. "Bear and everyone are coming into the conference room, but my word. You should see him. He's like a wild bear in a too-small enclosure."

Ward chuckled, and Dot watched him with his family, even if they were on a screen. "He's got a newborn, Range. Remember when you brought Wilder home? You were a snapping zombie for at least a couple of weeks."

"I didn't want to kill the child," Ranger said.

"You never slept," Ward said. "Cut Bear some slack."

"Some slack would be nice," someone said from off the screen, and Ranger leaned away. The monitor got turned, and Bear grinned at Ward.

He held a tiny infant in his arms, and his wife sat next to him, their other child on her lap. "Lincoln got a tambourine for Christmas," Bear said. "I'm not sure who's great idea that was, because I've had a headache since six a.m." He still grinned like it was great. "He wants to play with you and Judge."

"Sure thing," Ward said. "I'll text you the set list for him."

"Of course," Bear said as another screen popped up and another Glover joined the video chat. "The set list."

"How many songs on this set list?" the third man asked.

"Glad to see you have a shirt on, Bish," Bear said.

"Oh, be quiet," Bishop said. "You know what I meant."

"How's Montana?" Sammy asked. "Her back hurt yesterday when y'all left."

"She's okay." Bishop looked to his right. "She doesn't want to be on screen. Mother and Donald are getting coffee. Aurora is sending Ollie the link. Hope that's okay." While he'd been talking, three more people had joined the chat.

Some of them kept themselves muted, but some greeted everyone and someone asked if Oliver Walker was going to marry Aurora.

"You dang near killed Montana," Bishop said, his eyebrows drawn down. "We don't know. They have several months of school left."

More people joined, and finally, Bear asked, "Is everyone here? Who are we missing?" He leaned closer to the screen too, obviously counting. "We're all here. Ward?"

"You should introduce Dot," Ida said, smiling as she held one baby in her left arm and Brady held one in his. Dot smiled at the pair of them, because they were great people, and she'd had fun going out with them.

Ward looked at Dot, and Dot looked at Ward. He shifted like he'd done out on the hearth before playing his Carrie Underwood smash hit. "All right," he drawled, and that caused Dot to grin. She managed to tame the giggle, thankfully, as most of the other women on the screen in front of her seemed made of refinement.

"This is Dorothy Crockett," Ward said. "Or Dot. She owns From the Ground Up, and we've been seein' each other for a few months now. Give or take a few weeks. On and off." He cleared his throat. "I'm hopin' it'll stay on, but I've done some pretty dumb things in less than twenty-four hours, and I'm pretty sure she can't wait to make a break for the exit."

Several people laughed, Dot herself included. She reached over and took Ward's hand in hers, knowing it was in plain sight of everyone on the screen. "Thanks, Ward." She faced all the Glovers, and even virtually, it was a sight to behold. "It's nice to meet y'all. I hope we can do it in person when I'm not bleeding."

That prompted a few questions about why she'd been bleeding and how her fingers were doing. She and Ward answered them, and then he released her hand and lifted his guitar into place.

"Let's sing," he said. "Judge is going to put the set list up on his screen, and everyone can sing as much or as little as they'd like."

He gave Judge a moment to put in the list, and his cousin said, "We're starting with something the kids will love. Frosty the Snowman."

A little boy of probably eleven or twelve raised both hands and made a sound like an elephant. His parents laughed, and Ward leaned toward her and whispered, "Mitch is deaf, so he'll sign the song."

"Oh, that's great," she said, grinning back at the screen. Judge started to play the introduction, and a very loud tambourine came on the scene too. Ward fiddled around with his strings, and right when it was time to start singing, he added a beat with his palm against the box of the guitar.

Dot sang every word to every song, because singing Christmas carols with the Glovers was one of the most enriching experiences of her life. She felt herself slipping down the slope toward being in love with Ward Glover, and she had no idea how to stop herself.

She wasn't even sure she *wanted* to stop herself.

# Chapter Fifteen

B ishop Glover honestly didn't mind that his step-
daughter, Aurora, had included her boyfriend on the
family caroling. He couldn't fathom getting married at
eighteen, but the truth was, Aurora would be an adult
soon. She didn't need his permission, and she didn't need
her mother's.

He sang the last few words of Silent Night, his soul
filled with wonder and gratitude. He'd gotten up from the
desk where he kept his laptop, and he'd sat next to his
beautiful wife during the caroling. He squeezed her hand
and leaned over to kiss her temple.

"I love you," he whispered, his joy complete this
Christmas Day.

"Love you too, Bishop." Montana rested her free hand
on her belly and smiled at him with exhaustion in her blue,
blue eyes. He swept a lock of her bright blonde hair off her
face.

"You should take a nap, baby, while I make dinner."

"Already on my agenda," she said, leaning her head against his shoulder. She wasn't due until March, but she looked like she'd swallowed an extra-large beach ball already. With only ten weeks left in her pregnancy, she'd claimed she was on the home stretch, and she'd make it just fine.

Bishop had still taken her off the heavy construction schedule they'd been keeping around the ranch for the past three years—since she showed up on the doorstep of the homestead and asked him if there was any work for her to do.

He wondered if she regretted her decision to come to Shiloh Ridge that day. He sure hoped not, and he'd worked hard to give her and her daughter the best life possible.

"We could call Uncle Bob and Aunt Jackie like this," he said, gesturing to the computer screen. "Wish them Merry Christmas."

Hope entered her expression, and she nodded as Ward started thanking everyone for being there.

"I wanted to ask Mother and Aunt Lois something," he said, and because he was speaking, he took up the whole screen on Bishop's laptop. He put down his guitar and edged closer. "If you need to go, that's fine. I don't care if everyone hears though."

No one left, and Bishop certainly had nowhere to be. He'd actually really enjoyed the past day trapped in his home with his family. Mother and Donald had come to his house, and he was pleased as punch to host them. Of him and Montana, he definitely liked entertaining more than she did.

She allowed him to pamper everyone who walked through the door, and that was good enough for him.

"Mother," Ward said, clearing his throat. He glanced at Dot, who nodded at him encouragingly. Bishop had known his cousin was seeing someone, but he hadn't realized it was Dot Crockett. The woman was tall like Arizona, and Bishop could see why Ward had been attracted to her in the first place.

She had thick, silvery blonde hair that would've drawn his attention too.

"First," Ward said. "I wanted to let you guys know about something that happened this morning. I'm fine, obviously, but I got stuck outside in the blizzard. Dot had to come rescue me and get me warmed up again."

"My goodness," Aunt Dawna said, and the screen switched to her. It jumped around as others expressed concern too and questions got asked.

"The generator is out of gas here," he said. "We keep it in the shed, so I'd gone out there to get it. I forgot a rope, and I couldn't get back." He glanced at Dot again. "Dot has some sort of blizzard vision, because she found me clinging to the swing set in the back yard and since she worked a boy scout camp in the past, she knew how to get me warmed up."

"I bet she did," someone said, and a couple of people chuckled. Ward was not one of them, and neither was Bishop.

The mood turned awkward, and then Ward said, "I

want to know about my name. Specifically, I'm wondering why Grandmother didn't give me a special name." He dropped his chin toward his chest, and Bishop could taste the sadness coming from him.

He'd never realized how much the names in the Glover family meant to their owners. He'd literally never thought about why Ward didn't have a different name that wasn't one of his given names.

"His real name is Ward?" Montana whispered.

"No, it's Woods," Bishop murmured. "But Ward is his middle name."

"That is odd, then."

Bishop nodded as Aunt Dawna came up again. "Grand-mother thought you'd already been named appropriately, son. It's not that you didn't deserve one."

"I don't have one either," Zona said.

"Sure you do," Bear said. "I used to call you spitfire growing up."

"I called you all kinds of things," Preacher said, and that got significantly more laughter.

"The twins don't have nicknames either," Mother said, and Bishop looked over to her and Don. He jumped up and turned the screen so it showed her and not him. "It wasn't that your grandmother didn't love you the way she loved the others. You'll notice that Dawna has three children who didn't get totally new names. She was simply better at naming her children than I was."

She smiled, though Bishop didn't think that was true at all. "Grandmother adored old names, and she actually suggested Etta and Ida to Dawna. I was there when we were talking about what to name the twins if they were boys, girls, or one of each."

"Right," Ward said. "But Bartholomew is a great name, and he still got Bear. And Richard is respectable—and old. Why Ranger?"

"I wrote about this in my journal once," Aunt Dawna said, clear worry on her face. "I'll have to see if I can find it. My memory has too many holes in it."

Bishop exchanged a glance with Mother. She was older than Aunt Dawna, but the other woman suffered from more health problems—and this new mental issue as well. She'd always been sharp as a whip, with plenty of wit and a no-nonsense attitude. Bishop had hung around with Ace a lot growing up, as they were close to the same age, and he'd never thought for a moment he could get away with something at Bull House that he couldn't at his own.

Concern rode in Mother's eyes, and she gave an almost imperceptible shake of her head.

"I have your journals, Mother," Ward said quietly. "I can look for the story."

"Grandmother told me once that I was unique," Arizona said. "My name was already unique for a woman, and she thought if I could grow into it properly, I could do it justice someday." She glanced at her husband, who sat beside her in the Top Cottage. "I have no idea what that means. How do you do Arizona justice? Like, the state?" She shook her head. "I think by the time the twins and I came along, Grandmother was too old and too tired to think of new names."

She grinned, and Bishop did let a laugh come from his

mouth. What she said didn't ring entirely true though. He was younger than Arizona, and he'd gotten a name. The twins were another year behind him, and Grandmother had died when they were only eight years old.

"Okay, that's it," Ward said. "Merry Christmas, everyone. I do miss seeing you today, so this was nice."

Bishop felt the love of his cousin, and he wanted to radiate it right back to him, to everyone. The goodbyes started, and Bishop didn't need to say anything, not right now. He left the group video chat and faced his wife, stepdaughter, Mother, and his new step-father.

"We're having bison stew for lunch," he said. "It'll be ready in about an hour, and I'm going to go shape the rolls. You guys are okay here?"

Montana usually picked a place in the house on her days off and didn't move much. They'd come into the office off the front door for the caroling, and she nodded. "I'm going to take my nap right here."

"I'll come help in the kitchen," Mother said, using her hands to push herself to her feet. "Don's going to call his kids."

"I'm going to stay here with my momma." Aurora got up and got a blanket out of the ottoman and covered her mother with it, pure love in her eyes. "I'm going to try to whisper the name I want for the baby while she sleeps."

Bishop laughed with Montana. "Like, subliminal messages?" Montana asked. "Good luck with that." She exchanged a look with Bishop, who kept his mouth shut. He and Montana had already chosen a name for their son; they simply hadn't told anyone yet. They'd decided not to, because in a family as big as the Glovers, everyone had an opinion and Bishop didn't want to hear any of them.

He got to work on the dough, letting his fears and worries about becoming a biological father for the first time knead their way out of him. On the outside of his life, everything looked amazing and great. Bishop didn't want to say it wasn't. But even when things were going well, Bishop wondered if he was doing enough.

He rolled out the dough and cut it into neat, even rectangles. Those got sliced diagonally, and he rolled them up from the small tip to the wide base. Each roll then got put on the baking sheet.

Bishop had finished about half of them when his phone rang, and Ranger's name sat there. He wiped his floury hands on his apron and reached over to tap on the call with his knuckle.

"Hey, Range." The app business never slept, and it seemed like Ranger didn't either. He worked a ton on Two Cents, though he still completed a few chores around the ranch, and Bishop had been helping him with some back-end things as he had time.

"I'm worried about Ward."

All of the seething inside of Bishop suddenly made sense. "Me too."

"I didn't know he cared so much about the names."

"I didn't think anyone did."

"Bear was surprised." Ranger exhaled. "I wish I could go over there."

Bishop looked up and out the windows to his right. "The weather will break tonight," he said.

"Yeah, and then we'll be swamped with clean-up and animal care."

Bishop was used to both, as he loved to cook, and that usually left the kitchen looking like a bomb had gone off. "Yes," Bishop said. "But we'll make sure we talk to Ward. Find out where his head is."

"I know he likes Dot a lot. Maybe he's just too far inside his head."

Bishop picked up another piece of dough. "I don't think Ward does that."

"Yeah, maybe not." A baby cried on his end of the line, and the speaker scratched. "Hush now," Ranger said in a smooth, soft voice. "Let me tell you, it's a good thing Etta's here," he then said under his breath. "Bear actually suggested we have grilled cheese sandwiches for Christmas dinner."

Bishop burst out laughing, because he'd lived with Bear and Ranger before. It wasn't an easy job, and they did love to eat. None of them over there, besides Etta, liked to cook or even knew how.

"What are you making for dinner?" Ranger asked.

"I don't want to say," Bishop said, still chuckling. "But it's not grilled cheese sandwiches."

"I'm going to suggest everyone send photos of their meals, and it might be like we're eating together."

"I had no idea I'd miss getting together as much as I do," Bishop said, finally reading between what Ranger was saying.

"Me either," Ranger said. "Usually, I can't wait to get

everyone out of the homestead, but today, I just want everyone I care about here."

Bishop knew exactly how he felt. "I'll save you some bison stew," he said. "And these lion house rolls I'm making right now are going to be perfect."

"Rub it in," Ranger said, though his voice carried a smile. "If you talk to Ward before I do, maybe see how he's doing."

"I will," Bishop said.

"Let's keep each other informed," Ranger said. "He tells us different things."

"He sure does." Ward worked a lot with Ranger too, and they were brothers, so sometimes Ranger got more information than Bishop. On the flip side, sometimes Ward didn't want all the fussing Ranger would bring, so he'd tell Bishop more sensitive things.

Both of them just wanted Ward to find happiness, because it was clear to anyone who could see even slightly that he wasn't very happy right now.

Bishop thought of the light he'd seen in his cousin's eye as he glanced at Dot. The small nod she'd given him. They had something, and as the call with Ranger ended, Bishop took a moment and closed his eyes to pray for Ward.

*Help him find the peace and information he needs*, he thought. *Bless Montana and I to know what to do with Aurora. Bless Montana through this last leg of her pregnancy.*

Bishop kept rolling dough until it was all done, and then he turned toward Don as he came into the kitchen. "How are your children?" Bishop asked, putting a smile on his face despite his own worries and fears.

Don smiled at him and set his phone on the countertop. "They're doing well," he said. "Of course, they can all leave their homes. We're the only ones shut in up here in the Panhandle." He came right over to Bishop and put his hand on his shoulder. "I'm worried about you. How are you holding up?"

Bishop wasn't sure what the older gentleman saw when he looked at Bishop, but it was obviously something.

"I'm tired," Bishop whispered, glancing toward the door way that led out of the big kitchen and living room at the back of the house. "But I'm trying."

Don gave him a kind smile. "I think that's the motto of life, son. Tired but trying. I like that. I'm doing that too."

"I think we all are," Bishop said. "I just keep telling myself that nothing lasts forever. Montana won't be pregnant forever. The wind won't blow forever. The construction won't go on forever."

"You're certainly right about that," Don said. "Once, when I first started my business...." He continued to tell a story about something that had happened many years ago. Bishop liked listening to him talk, because the man had a powerful, quiet voice, and plenty of life experience. As Bishop often felt like he had no idea what his next step should be, he appreciated the steadiness and wisdom that Don shared with him.

He caught sight of Montana lumbering into the kitchen, and Bishop dropped the washrag he'd been wiping the counter with and went to help her. "Baby," he said. "Why aren't you asleep?"

"This baby is kicking me," she complained, and Bishop

helped her to the couch, where she lay down. She sighed and closed her eyes, placing one hand over them. Bishop looked down at her, his heart bleeding for his wife.

*Ten more weeks*, he thought. *Can we make it ten more weeks?*

# Chapter Sixteen

Ace Glover woke when his wife groaned. Her footsteps on the marble tile in their bathroom told him she'd gotten up, and he rolled toward her side of the bed. The scent of clean, crisp linens, fresh paint, and an overall new car smell filled the house.

He and Holly Ann had only been living in their new house for nine days, and he still wasn't quite familiar with everything.

"Did I wake you up?" Holly Ann asked as she returned to bed. She was tall, dark, and beautiful, and the way her belly rounded with his child made Ace smile every time he saw her.

"A little," he said.

Holly Ann smiled as she bent to get her pajama pants. She got too hot in the middle of the night now that she had a body growing inside her. "Go back to sleep. It's barely six. I'll go make coffee."

"Mm, okay." Ace closed his eyes like he'd really go to sleep but he had no plans to do that. Ace couldn't drift back to sleep the way Holly Ann could—at least before she'd gotten pregnant.

She left the master suite and closed the door behind her. Ace listened to the furnace come on and the whooshing of hot air as it came through the vents. He heard Holly Ann bumping and thumping around in the kitchen, though the master bathroom sat between him and the gourmet area where she put together fabulous meals.

Ace had gained ten pounds since marrying her last spring, and he wasn't sure he cared. She had dinner waiting for him every evening, even if she had a party or event off the ranch. Ace loved her for more than her cooking though, and he counted her as one of his biggest blessings.

He groaned as he rolled over too. He put his feet on the thick carpet and reached both arms up over his head. He stretched left and right, rolled his neck, and finally left the warm comfort of his blankets and pillows.

He slept in gym shorts and a T-shirt, and he only detoured into the bathroom because his mouth felt like someone had stuffed it full of dirty cotton. He brushed his teeth and drank a big glass of water before returning to the nightstand for his phone.

*Our house needs a humidifier on the furnace*, he sent to Bishop. *Hard to do? Could I do it myself?*

Cowboys rose with the sun, but Ace hadn't seen that in a couple of days now. He opened the door to the scent of coffee and cream, his stomach already growling. Holly Ann stood in the kitchen in her blue and silver pajamas, a billowing, silk robe on her shoulders that moved like water when she moved.

"Hello, my love." Ace ran his hand along her waist and kissed her neck. "Do you think we'll be able to leave the house today?" He needed to get out, though Holly Ann had been showing him where the guest towels were, and he'd enjoyed seeing his wife interact more with his mother.

"Go check," Holly Ann said, waving a whisk in the general direction of the front door.

He started that way, leaving behind the massive kitchen with yards and yards of counter space, double ovens, and a cavernous fridge that had more cubic feet than any other refrigerator on the market.

She'd gotten her hardwood lookalike flooring, her solid oak dining room table that seated twelve, and a new sectional couch that faced the fireplace. She hadn't wanted a television in the main room or their bedroom, and Ace was fine with that. Holly Ann was the one who spent most of her time at home, and he'd wanted her to have the house of her dreams.

They'd put a den on the main level, on one side of the foyer that housed a wide, eight-foot-tall door with two window panels, one on either side. On the other side sat an office, where Holly Ann put her corner desk and her computer. She ran Three Cakes from there, and one of the sexiest things Ace had ever seen was the beautiful brunette bent over a paper calendar. When she looked up and peered at him through her reading glasses, Ace's pulse accelerated.

He didn't use an office or a computer that often, but

she'd put a desk in the office for him too. His laptop sat there, dormant the way it usually was.

Ace put his hand on the front door and allowed the chill to move through him. It would probably be cold for another six weeks or so, and then February would arrive. Sometimes Mother Nature could pull a mean trick on the Texas Panhandle and send snow in the shortest month of the year, but she usually didn't.

This Christmas was one for the books, that was for sure.

He didn't feel any vibrations in the fiberglass door, and he unlocked the deadbolt and then the doorknob before opening the house to the outside world.

Cold air hit him in the face and chest, but the one thing he did not feel was wind.

"The wind has stopped," he called over his shoulder. The ceilings in the foyer and living room were vaulted, and his voice got stuck up in the rafters. "The wind has stopped," he repeated just for his ears.

Despite the cold, he stepped out onto the porch. Holly Ann had made him put a couple of empty planters there, though she wouldn't get anything planted until spring. She loved porches, and theirs faced west. Ace could admit to wanting to sit there in the evenings with his wife and watch the day end.

They'd ordered patio furniture for that exact purpose, but it hadn't come in yet.

Ace went past the empty spaces where all of their big plans would go and paused at the edge of the steps. The cold cement burned his bare feet, but he didn't care.

The wind had stopped blowing.

The clear sky sat before him, a dark gray that surely would grow more golden as the minutes passed and the sun rose.

"Maybe we can have our family party today," Holly Ann said behind him.

He turned, but she stayed inside the house. "Probably not, sweetheart. We'll have to be out on the ranch all day, checking the animals and buildings and fences. Ward and Preacher will work us to death today."

Holly Ann smiled, but Ace wasn't kidding. He wanted to get out on the ranch and see what the wind had done to his fields. To the barns. To the fences and stables. He hoped the cold hadn't cost them too many of their chickens, and he had no idea where all of their free range animals would be.

Ward had sheep, chickens, turkeys, meat birds, and goats that grazed with their cattle, and no one had had any time to round up everyone. Of course, most of their animals were in pens or stables during the winter, but Ace knew they'd be down some animals.

His phone rang, and Ace wasn't surprised to see Ward's name on the screen. "I'm on my porch," Ace said as Holly Ann said, "It's cold, baby. I'm closing the door."

He lifted his hand to acknowledge her as Ward said, "Meet me in the main stable? I'm rounding up my crews so we can see what the past couple of days did to the ranch."

"I'll get dressed," Ace said.

"Great." Ward was all business, and the call ended as abruptly as it had started.

"He could've just sent a text, the way he did for his crew cowboys," Ace grumbled as he turned back to the house. The cold finally got to him, and he shivered as he hurried back inside.

He went straight into the bedroom and got dressed in his long underwear and his regular ranch attire. He took the toast Holly Ann gave him on the way through the kitchen, kissed her cheek, and promised he'd keep in touch with her.

"I'm going to text about Christmas dinner," she said.

"All right." Ace went into the garage and started up his truck. He backed out and went around the circular driveway he and Holly Ann had chosen, and by the looks of things he was one of the last to arrive in the main barn.

About fifteen men loitered about, and Ace shoved the last bite of peanut butter toast in his mouth. Holly Ann scrambled eggs and made a sandwich out of the toast sometimes, but today, she'd just layered on apple slices and called it good.

"All right, all right," Ward called, holding a clipboard in one hand and raising the other one. "Settle down."

The cowboys and cowgirls did what he said, Bishop one of the last ones to stop talking to Cactus.

"I've split you up into teams of two," he said. A dose of anxiety immediately shot through Ace, though he knew everyone standing in the barn. He could get along with anyone, and he already knew what he'd be doing.

"Check everything," Ward said, and Ace could've said it. "Every inch of every animal. Bring the dead ones out so we can number them. If you need first aid, Cactus and Phil are going to be making the rounds." He surveyed the group, a sense of real seriousness on his face.

Ace wanted to tell him to lighten up. It was just a ranch. They were just cows. He said nothing as Ward told the group to note buildings that needed repairs, take pictures with their phones, and he wanted everyone back by noon. "Even if you're not finished, okay?"

*Noon?* Ace thought, glancing around. There were easily nine or ten partnerships here, and it wasn't even seven a.m.

Ward started reading off names, and relief hit Ace when his was matched up with Bishop's. He could handle Bishop today, because the man had a lot of the same concerns Ace did. They'd spoken several times about their nerves to be fathers, though they both wanted the babies their wives were carrying.

Ace just didn't know how a child would factor into his already packed schedule. Holly Ann had played Santa Claus again this year, and she hadn't needed the extra padding in the bodysuit.

"Phones on, ladies and gents. If Preach or I need to get a hold of you, we don't want it to be hard."

"Yes, sir," a few men chorused, and Ace grinned at Bishop, who stood across the space.

Bishop reached up and tipped his hat, his way of acknowledging Ward's authority too. The meeting broke up then, and Ace waited for Bishop to make his way over to him.

"Let's go see how many turkeys we can round up." Bishop lifted the paper. "Ward said we should have twenty-seven."

"Can we take horses?" Ace asked.

"Ward said only if we check them from head to hoof first." Bishop held up the sheet. "Let's get this done. It's not warm just because the wind settled down."

"No, it is not." Ace followed Bishop out of the barn, and they made the short walk over to the family stables where they kept their personal horses. Ace checked his from head to hoof, saddled him, and started out into the pastures. They had some enclosures and outbuildings out on the ranch, and he figured he might find the turkeys there.

The sun rose, and Ace tipped his head back to bask in the light and heat, weak as it was. He and Bishop chatted easily about trivial things, or they rode in companionable silence. They found twenty-one turkeys, and Ace tied the dead birds to his saddle before they headed back.

Later, after the accounting on the ranch and after Ward had said he'd need an hour to put together crews to fix the physical facilities that needed work, Ace headed home. He felt dirty, though he hadn't done much more than ride a horse and herd birds.

"Hey, baby," he said as he walked in. "What's for lunch?" He grinned at his wife, who sat on the couch, flipping through the cookbook he'd bought her for Christmas.

"I didn't make lunch." She gestured toward the kitchen. "There's leftovers from yesterday."

"Perfect." Ace got out the pasta salad and a couple of the bratwurst they'd had. "Where's Mother?"

"She went over to see Lois," Holly Ann said. "I think

they were going to have a little pow-wow about the names."

"Uh oh," Ace said, turning toward her. "That doesn't sound good."

"I talked to my dad," Holly Ann said, setting aside her book. "He wants to—" She cut off as the house started to shake.

Ace's eyes widened, because he'd never known Texas to have earthquakes—not here. There weren't even really mountains here. A few rolling hills was all.

"What in the world?" he said, turning toward the back of the house. A long, custom sliding glass door opened onto a deck that stretched out and over the edge of the cliff a little bit.

He strode toward it, seeing the far corners of the deck trembling like someone was shaking them with every muscle in their body.

"Ace," Holly Ann said as he opened the door. "Don't go outside."

He went anyway and started to cross the deck as the shaking started to lessen. He felt like he was walking across a suspension bridge, something he'd done several times before. The ground moving beneath his feet unsettled him every time, and he paused when he heard a horrible, fearsome sound of...rocks crashing against one another.

He stopped about halfway across the deck, his heartbeat pounding in his ears as the very real sound of a landslide continued to fill the sky with noise.

"Ace," Holly Ann said again, plenty of fear in her voice.

"I'm okay," he said. The rushing sound, combined with

the cracking, tumbling echoes in the sky faded until only silence remained. Once the Earth stood still again, he hurried to the railing, despite his wife's warnings.

The scene before his eyes looked like land and hill carnage. Great gashes had been clawed from the cliff that their house overlooked, and as his eyes moved north toward the road and the town of Three Rivers, he sucked in a breath.

"I can't believe this," he said. Things that should've been green were the color of rich soil. The gray rocks were white and jagged in brand new places. Down below, where the land leveled out, the debris from the landslide still moved, trying to find a place to settle.

"What's going on?" Holly Ann called.

Ace couldn't take in the chaos fast enough, but he knew one thing for certain: No one was leaving Shiloh Ridge Ranch any time soon.

"The hill sheared off," he said, turning back and hurrying toward his wife. "We lost the road off the ranch." He gathered her into his arms and held her close. They breathed together for a few seconds, and then he said, "I have to call Ward."

# Chapter Seventeen

W ard lifted his head from the clipboard he studied in the barn. The ground beneath his feet shook, as did the stalls and frame around him. "Dear Lord," he said. "What else can go wrong?"

He took the clipboard with him and left the barn, his footsteps somewhat stilted as he tried to figure out how to walk on ground that moved. Several others came out of the nearby stables and barns, and Ward held up his hand.

The sound of a full river rushing over rocks filled the air, and Ward actually looked up into the sky. He had the very real feeling that Dot would be staying with him a bit longer. She'd insisted on staying that morning to help with the ranch, and he'd left her in Bull House to shower and get ready for the drive back to town in Brutus.

Ward had admitted silently to himself that he was going to miss her and her hound dog too. Ward didn't mind making breakfast for the two of them, and he suspected the hole they'd leave in his life would be ten miles wide.

"Stay here," he called, breaking into a jog. Around the next building, Bull House came into view. Dot's big, burly dump truck sat there, so she hadn't left yet. Ward's feet slipped on the snow-covered ground that had already started to melt. The rocks beneath his work boots moved with the earth, and then, all at once, it stopped.

The front door of Bull House opened, and Dot appeared.

"Dot," Ward called.

"What was that?"

He passed the dump truck and arrived on the cleared sidewalk in front of the house. "You okay?"

"I've never been in an earthquake."

"I'm not sure that was an earthquake." Ward went up the steps and took Dot into his arms. "I'm...I think...." He honestly had no idea what to think. He'd never been in an earthquake either, but for some reason, he thought he still hadn't.

His phone started to buzz and chime, but Ward ignored it.

"I'm okay," Dot said, stepping back. "I think maybe I better get out of here before I curse the ranch with more of my bad luck." She grinned up at him, and Ward sure would like to kiss her as the last thing she experienced about Shiloh Ridge. Maybe then she'd come back.

He leaned down, and the smile slipped a little. Her hand curved up around the back of his neck right when his phone rang. He lifted it as he still held it in his hand. Ace's name sat there. "It's my brother."

"Better get it then." Dot fell back, moving out of his arms like smoke dissipating into the sky.

Ward saw his romantic kiss with the glorious Dot Crocket disappear the same way. He swiped on the call. "What?" he growled.

"It was a landslide," Ace said. "We lost the road leading off the ranch. The road from the Ranch House is gone too."

"Gone?" Ward asked, his mind screaming at him to get into the back yard and see what Ace was talking about. "What do you mean gone?" He met Dot's eyes, and she spun back to the house.

They both started inside, and her long legs kept up with his. She went out the sliding glass door as Ace said, "I mean gone, Ward. Covered in earth and rock. I'm standing on my back deck, and I almost lost it. The cliff is sheared off here, and you know how there's that last, final, steep rise before getting to the arch and coming onto the ranch?"

*Yes*, Ward thought, but he couldn't get his voice to work. He crossed the deck and jogged toward the barn. He couldn't believe how close it was, nor could he believe he'd very nearly died standing right there next to the swing set.

"It cleaved off," Ace said. "Slid down the hill toward the Kinder Ranch land. There's no way we're getting off the ranch. They can't get down from the Ranch House either."

"I'm in the back yard," he said, sucking at the air from all the running. He paused at the corner of the barn, aware that Dot had arrived only a few moments after him. "I don't believe this...."

Ward couldn't speak as he stared at the carnage in front of him. The road that branched off from the main road and led to the Ranch House was, indeed, "gone." The soil, bushes, rocks, and weeds that had once populated the steep decline from the back yard to the road—and beyond—had broken off and slid down.

A particularly big boulder—at least twice the size of Brutus the dump truck—sat right in the middle of the road, a small tree with its roots pointing toward the sky right beside it.

"Holy cow," Dot said, her voice just as awed as his.

Ward looked right, and while the homestead was now a hulking two story building he could barely see past, he believed Ace when he said that road was gone too. The part he could see a little lower had plenty of debris covering it.

It looked like someone had dug down to the bottom of the salad bowl to pull up all the veggies so everything got coated in salad dressing. Only this was soil and sand, sage-brush and stones.

It was all the innards of the Earth, and they were in all the wrong places.

"Guess I'm staying for at least another day," Dot said.

"Guess so," Ward said, realizing the call with Ace was still ticking along. "This is surreal."

His phone continued to chime, but Ward couldn't tear his eyes from the landslide that stretched from north to south, as far as he could see.

"Bear's called an emergency family meeting," Ace said, his voice on the haunted side. "Guess I'll see you there in ten."

"Yeah," Ward said, and he didn't bother to hang up. He shoved his phone in his back pocket and reached for Dot's hand. "I have lots of food. You can stay for as long as you want."

"Good," she said. "It took you six months to build a road out to Cactus's house, if I recall correctly."

She did, but that was hardly his fault. He smiled slowly at her. "Yeah, because I couldn't get a certain someone to call me back about some *very* important gravel."

Dot grinned up at him, and Ward did like the sparkles and sunshine that ran between them. She released his hand and reached up with both hands to grip the collar of his denim jacket in her fists.

She pulled him down to kiss her, and Ward was more than happy to oblige. So many things had irritated him that morning, but they all washed away the moment he touched his lips to Dot's.

A growl with the same ferocity of the landslide he'd just heard came from his throat, and he threaded his fingers through the hair he'd been dreaming of touching since the moment he'd asked Dot to dinner, months ago.

***

URGENCY EXISTED ON THE RANCH. IT HOVERED IN THE air, driving Ward to get as much done as possible. His leg bounced as he listened to Bear and Ranger talk. It didn't matter what they said. Everyone could see the landslide. No one could see the road. At least a twenty-foot drop now separated Shiloh Ridge from the rest of the world. They truly did exist on their own up in the foothills south of Three Rivers.

Ward wanted to shout when Ace stood up. They needed to stop talking. He had fourteen cowboys out there waiting for him to tell them what to do. In Ward's opinion, they needed to rustle up as many shovels as they could find and start digging.

Dot was here; she could help them know how to grade down the drop-off. Or they could go down the road from the Ranch House and start to clear that road.

In the back of his mind, a voice told Ward that it didn't matter if they cleared that road. It connected to the main road leading from the ranch to the highway, and a new intersection would need to be made. The current one was under tons of dirt and rocks.

"I've got Huey Howard on the line," Ace said, placing his phone on the edge of the conference room table. Ward had attended dozens of meetings in this room, but he'd never been here with this many people. Men, women, babies, kids. Every Glover on the ranch had packed themselves in the room, and it seemed like ninety percent of them had an opinion as to what the family should do.

"He's the road engineer for Three Rivers," Ace said. "Tell everyone what you told me, Huey."

"Hi everyone," Huey said, and he had no idea what he was getting into.

"You're on with the whole family," Ace said. He smiled as if this were a friendly chat. "Thanks for doing this for us."

Ward wanted to roll his eyes. He needed to retreat to Bull House and find something to eat. Take a shower. Then a deep breath. Then he could get back to work in a better mood so he didn't turn into Bear and start roaring and snapping his teeth at everyone he came in contact with.

Dot sat next to him, her knee practically touching Ward's. He wanted pull the woman onto his lap and kiss her again, but he knew that would only alleviate his anxiety for a few minutes. The moment she pulled away, his stomach would knot again.

He wasn't sure if that meant he'd started to fall in love with her or he simply had way too much work to do around the ranch.

*You've definitely started to fall in love with her*, he thought, glancing at her. She reached over and squeezed his knee, something surely half the people in the room saw. Ward didn't care. He put his hand over hers and curled his fingers around to her palm. Having a partner felt so good, and Ward didn't want to go back to being single ever again.

*Yep*, he thought. *Definitely falling hard for her already. Better slow down, Ward.*

The problem was, Ward didn't know how to slow down. He didn't know how to fall shallowly. He fell fast, and he fell deep, and having Dot in his house, at his side every minute of every hour for the past two days, had definitely accelerated their relationship.

"I'm glad y'all have cellphone service," Huey said. "All right." A big sigh came with that. "We've got some damage and things we're dealing with down here in town, but I saw the pictures Ace sent. I'm getting a crew together, and we're going to come up there and see what we're really dealing with. We'll get you guys situated and the road all worked out. I mean, you've got to be able to get on and off your property."

"Yes, we do," Bear said, along with a couple of other people.

Ward folded his arms, because Huey had only stated the obvious.

"I'm dealing with some things right now," Huey said, clearly distracted. "My crew can't come in today, as I've already assigned them out, and several people have personal issues to deal with too. We're looking at Wednesday or Thursday."

"You're kidding."

"That's two or three days from now."

"We can't wait that long."

"How much food do we have?"

"Stop it," Bear bellowed, and the chaos that had broken out quieted. He glared around the room, and a growly, glaring Bear was best avoided. "They'll come when they can come. There's nothing we can do about it."

"We should start to clear the ranch road," Cactus said, his voice half the volume of Bear's.

"You can certainly try to do some of your own clearing," Huey said over the phone. "I honestly wouldn't recommend it. You have no idea what the ground is like underneath the debris. What we think happened, just based on the pictures and what Ace described, is that everything froze in the storm, right? Then today, the sun came out and things started to thaw. You've got that hill at just the right angle, and something thawed underneath in a way that the ground below couldn't support the stuff above it. So the top layers sheared off. They slid down. Basically, your slope there from where all your homes and buildings and the ranch are is unstable. It could slide again. You could clear the road and get buried."

Huey stopped then, and this time, no one said a word. Down the table a bit, Wilder babbled and chewed on a pen Ward would've taken from the child. He was probably going to bite right through the plastic and burst the ink sleeve inside. Then Oakley would be dealing with that on top of a landslide that had trapped dozens of people on the ranch.

Ranger stood up. "We won't clear the roads. We won't do anything but *look* at that landslide." He leaned both hands into the table and gazed around the room, his eyes sharp and perfectly clear. "We need full agreement on this."

"Yes, sir," Ward said in a loud voice, drawing several pairs of eyes. He didn't mind the spotlight when he knew what he was doing. He felt wildly out of control, but he happened to agree with Ranger. The last thing he needed was to order his cowboy crews to start digging and then send them all to their deaths.

No, thank you.

He released Dot's hand and stood up too. He swallowed, cleared his throat, and said, "We have plenty of food and water here. Our sinks and toilets work. We have power and fuel. We can keep taking care of our animals and land. We won't go near the drop-off zone—and I hate to say it, but that includes the cemetery." He paused, because he could not fathom losing the family plots where his ancestors were buried.

Reality could be a bitter pill to swallow.

"All we can do is pray that Huey and his crew will be able to come help us quickly," Ward continued. "That they'll be able to preserve the cemetery and help us dig out the landslide safely. Preacher and I are in charge of fourteen cowboys, plus you lot. That's a lot of people to be responsible for, and I for one am not going to ask them to put their lives in jeopardy when it's absolutely unnecessary."

"I agree with Ward," Cactus said.

Preacher stood up too, pure nerves in his expression. For him to call attention to himself meant a lot, and everyone in the room knew it. Maybe not Huey or Dot, but the somber quality of the atmosphere spoke volumes. "We won't touch the slide," he said, leaning toward Ace's phone. "Okay, Huey? You guys keep in touch with Ace or Bear or whoever and tell us where to be. We'll be there when you can come."

"Sounds good," Huey said. "I'll be in touch, Ace."

"Thanks again." Ace picked up the phone and ended the call.

"I've got a basement storage room with food in it,"

Ward said. "I know my cowboys don't always have a lot on hand, so I'm going to let them come take what they need first. Who else needs food?"

Arizona raised her hand. "We just moved in a couple of weeks ago, and we've been living off whatever Etta or Bishop cooks and boxed granola bars."

"We've got food here too," Ranger said, standing shoulder-to-shoulder with Ward. "The pantry is stuffed with it. Take what you need."

"I've got a ton of food at my house," Ace said. "Holly Ann was making lunch for everyone, and you know how she is." He smiled softly at his wife. "We have enough for the whole ranch times two."

"Great," Bear said. "Let's do our big family meal tomorrow, at Ace's like we were going to yesterday. Okay? Cowboys too?"

"Everyone is welcome," Holly Ann said. "We can pull chairs over from True Blue."

"We could just have it at True Blue," Ace said. "Might be easier."

"Might be," Holly Ann said, but Ward could tell she didn't like that idea.

"What else?" Cactus asked. "We've got water, power, food. Does anyone need medical attention?"

Ward's eyes went to Dot, who'd been sitting quietly throughout the meeting. She said nothing now, and Ward certainly wasn't going to call attention to her. She did look a little...off, but that could be exhaustion or being completely overwhelmed with the situation. Heck, meeting twenty-five people all with the last name Glover could make a person turn gray.

"We've got first aid supplies in every barn and every stable on the ranch," Preacher said. "We have six homes we can access for anything. Sinks in barns and stables. Twelve cowboy cabins with power and water. This is fine. We can live up here for a lot longer than two days until the road crew comes."

"He's right," Ward said. "We've still got a ton of work to do on the ranch, and I was almost done putting together our tier one needs. I haven't eaten, and I might rip off one of your arms and start gnawing on it if that doesn't happen soon." He grinned around at everyone, and the sober mood broke as several people laughed.

Ward appreciated Dot's smile and giggle the most. "So I'm going to go eat. I'm going to shower off this morning's bad karma. Then, I'm going to get my men and women to work."

"What time should we show up for assignments?" Preacher asked, looking at his phone. "Your house? Say, two o'clock?"

Ward glanced at the clock on the wall beside him. It was five to one. "Two o'clock," he said. "My house. Preach, will you text the crews?"

"On it," he said, his fingers already moving.

"Get the food and supplies you need before you go," Bear said as people started standing and talking. "From either here or Bull House."

Ward backed up and stood next to Ranger and Bear, the three of them pressed into the wall so others could walk by them. Preacher joined them, and soon enough, only the four of them remained.

"Mister said he's going to stay at the Ranch House," Preacher said. "Just to give you and Dot some privacy."

"We don't need privacy," Ward said instantly. "No more than you and Charlie do."

"Mm," was Preacher's only response.

Ward's phone chimed, and he checked it. "Cactus would like a crew," he told the group. "For animal care." He looked at Preacher. "Who should we put on that? You work with him more than me."

"I'll take Judge, myself, Russ, and Angie. They're all real good with animals, and they've worked with Cactus before."

"He'll have Mitch and Link with him," Bear said. "And all those blasted dogs."

The growling disdain in his voice struck Ward as hilarious, and while he tried to hold back his laughter, he couldn't. It burst from him in a loud stream, and before he knew it, all four of them were chortling.

"Come on, Bear," Ranger said. "This isn't going to be the end of Shiloh Ridge." He turned toward Bear and hugged him, clapping him hard on the back. "And guess what, Grizzly? You don't have to deal with this on your own anymore."

He released Bear and faced Preacher and Ward. "In fact, we're not dealing with it at all. We'll write a few checks while we enjoy our wives and families. These two are taking care of it."

"He's got a point," Ward said, grinning at Bear.

A sea of emotions stormed across Bear's face. "Thank you both," he said. "I will be at Bull House at two, though. I can still work just like anyone else." He turned to leave the conference room.

"I don't know," Preacher said with plenty of teasing in his voice. "You're gettin' real gray, Bear. You're like a silver-back gorilla."

"Gorilla," Ranger said, laughing afterward. "Can we start calling him Ape?" He followed Bear out of the room, Bear snapping back at him to keep all primate comments to himself.

Ward shook his head, though he was glad the mood around the ranch wasn't buzzing at him to do something, get more done, anymore. Alone in the room, he took a moment to say, "Dear Lord, bless us all here at Shiloh Ridge. Keep us safe. Keep us healthy. Keep us from killing each other." He chuckled, because he could see some real rifts happening if certain people got cooped up together for too long.

The sound quieted, and Ward leaned his head back against the wall. He had so many more things to say to the Lord. He wanted to know how to deal with Dot. He'd like to know how he really felt about her, and how she really felt about him. He'd like to be at peace with who he was. He'd like to know if his father was proud of him.

Familiar, trembling desperation rose in his throat, and he swallowed against it. He said, "Amen," and left the conference room too.

Dot waited on the couch in Ranger's suite, and she

jumped to her feet when she saw Ward. "Can I have lunch with you?" she asked.

Ward practically ran at her and took her into his arms. "Of course," he whispered, thinking that perhaps Preacher was right. He did need privacy with Dot, because he leaned down and kissed her right there in his brother's suite, and he sure didn't want anyone to be a witness to that.

# Chapter Eighteen

Dot could honestly kiss Ward Glover forever. The man's lips were made of candy—the soft, sweet kind. He eventually pulled away, and Dot ducked her head to try to infuse some reason into her brain before she looked at him.

"I really do want to eat and shower," he said. "But not in that order. Shower first. Eat second." He took her hand and led her toward the exit. "Sound good? I can put a pizza in before I jump in the shower."

"Sounds great," she said, though Dot's hands had started to shake about twenty minutes ago. She wasn't eating or drinking enough, and she knew it. She told herself that Ward had convenience foods in his house, and she could eat something while he showered and then share lunch with him too.

She needed insulin, but she said nothing. Once again, she could take care of that injection while he cleaned up.

"We lost several turkeys," he told her as they went down the staircase to the first level of the homestead. "A few cows, though we didn't find them. They might be out there somewhere, and we'll get them back. A dozen chickens. Two goats. Four sheep—again lost, but not sure if they're alive or not. And one pig didn't make it."

"I'm sorry," Dot said, thinking that was a lot of deceased animals to have to deal with. "How's Nickers?"

"Good as ever." He smiled at her. "We didn't lose any horses or dogs."

"Don't your dogs live with you?"

"Not the ranch dogs," he said.

"I saw a couple here," she said, looking around like Benny or Frost would come trotting over to her.

"Bear's got a dog named Benny. He's really his son's. Link gave him to his mom for her birthday."

They went outside and down the front steps, bypassing the noise in the kitchen to Dot's right. The walk from the homestead to Bull House wasn't long, but Dot already felt so shaky. She said nothing, but her grip on Ward's hand tightened.

He slowed and looked at her. "Dot, you don't look good."

Things could change so fast for her, and she quickly dug into her pocket. "I need to eat," she finally admitted. She pulled out a hard candy and tried to unwrap it. Instead, it fell from her fingers, which felt prickly and numb at the same time.

Ward bent to get it, because everything in Dot's world was suddenly moving at half speed. She drew in a long breath, trying to make her diabetes behave with oxygen alone. The cold air shocked her lungs, but it didn't affect her blood sugar.

He unwrapped the candy and handed it to her. She stuck it in her mouth and took his hand again. "I'm okay."

"I don't think you are." He didn't move, but she didn't see anywhere to sit. Not that such a thing mattered. If Dot couldn't stand, her body would simply force her to the ground. She moved over to the fence, which separated the lawn from the graveled area in front of the homestead and leaned against it.

"What do you need to eat?" he asked, right there at her side. "I'll go grab it from the homestead right now."

Dot shook her head, her thoughts so foggy. "I...don't know."

"Okay," he said, as if she'd just told him she'd like a chocolate chip ice cream cone.

The candy tasted like lemons, and Dot normally loved it. Today, though, she could barely keep it in her mouth. She yelped as someone grabbed her, and the next thing she knew, she lay in Ward's arms.

"I'm taking you inside the homestead," he said as she wrapped her arms around his neck and shoulder. "Someone's going to feed you, and I'm going to call your brother. Where's your phone?"

"In my back pocket," she said, though she told her brain to tell Ward to put her down. *Don't you dare call Tyson. I'm fine.*

Dot wasn't fine, and she and Ward both knew it.

"I have insulin at your house," she said, but that didn't

make sense. She didn't need to lower her blood sugar...did she? Confusion riddled her mind, and she looked at Ward with a frown.

"I'll send someone for it," he said. "Talk to me, Dot. I don't really know how to take care of a diabetic."

Her lips tingled, and irritation flashed through her. "I have candy in my pocket."

"You already ate one of those," Ward said, his steps going up jostling her. How he opened the door with her in his arms, she'd never know. "I need help, please," he called, but he didn't slow down.

"What's going on?" Bear asked. "What's wrong with her?"

"She's diabetic. She needs to eat, I think."

"Orange juice," Dot said. "That helps a lot, usually." Her words slurred over the last couple.

"Do I need to call an ambulance?" a woman asked.

"And they'll do what?" Ward barked. "We can't get on or off the ranch." He sat down, but he did not let go of Dot. "She has insulin at Bull House. In the fridge. Link? Could you go get it?"

A dog whined, and Dot felt the cold touch of his nose to her arm. She jerked it away, but it just came back.

"She doesn't need insulin," someone said. "She needs to raise her blood sugar, not lower it."

"Orange juice," someone else said. Dot had met them all, and she recognized their faces—at least until they started to blur along the edges. A woman—Ward's sister, Etta—held out a glass of orange juice.

Ward finally slid her onto the couch instead of his lap

and took the glass of orange juice. He knelt in front of her and held it out. "Come on, now," he said. "You've got to drink this."

"This says a couple of sugary snacks," someone read. Cactus. His name was Cactus. Dot remembered, because it was such a funny name for such a tall, good-looking cowboy.

Ward held the glass even after Dot curled her fingers around it. She drank, and nothing had ever tasted as wonderful or as cold as that glass of orange juice. It went down easily, and Dot greedily drank the whole thing.

"Now we wait ten or fifteen minutes, and she needs to check her blood sugar," Cactus said. "She should have a glucose monitor?"

"I have one," Dot said, finally finishing the orange juice. "It's in the bedroom at Bull House."

"I'll go with the boys," Cactus said. "Link gets distracted by butterflies, for crying out loud." He walked away, barking, "Come on, Galaxy. Leave 'er alone."

The dog whined again, her big, black head in Dot's lap now. She smiled down at the dog and scratched her head. "I'm okay now," she said. "You can go."

"Gal," Cactus called, and the dog's ears perked up. She lifted her head and looked toward him, then trotted away.

Dot met Ward's gaze. "I'm feeling better already."

"Mm hm," he said, clearly not believing her.

"I just need to eat. I haven't eaten yet today, and that's not great for me." She took a breath, and the waxed paper that had enveloped her mind lifted.

"Do you need more juice?" Etta asked.

Dot tilted her head back and looked at her. "No, but thank you so much, Etta. It's helping a ton." She wasn't going to jump to her feet and do a jig or anything, but the confusion and the numb lips had already started to fade.

"Tell me what you want to eat," Ward said, oh-so-serious.

She hated that she'd blown up his plans—again. "You wanted to shower." Foolishness filled her. "Put in a pizza. That's fine. I need some carbohydrates, and that's perfect."

"I'm not leaving you alone," he said.

"You can shower here," Etta said, coming around the couch. "I'll sit with her if she doesn't mind watching me fill out forms." She wore a bright smile, and Dot didn't mind at all. "Plus, Sammy's bringing down the baby in a few minutes, and he is the cutest little thing you've ever seen."

Etta sat on the end of the neighboring couch, her blue eyes brilliant and beautiful.

"Et, Et," a little boy said, and Bear lifted him over the couch to Etta.

"He wants you too, Etta," Bear said. "You won't be able to handle Russell too."

"I will too," Etta said, settling the toddler on her lap. "The forms can wait. Besides." She looked at Dot. "Dot can help me with Stetson."

"Sure," Dot said, completely enamored by the little boy in her lap. He had dark hair that a lot of the other Glovers did, but his eyes were exactly like sapphires. He had round cheeks and chubby fingers, and he made a grunting noise as he lifted a toy lizard into the air.

He looked at Etta and said, "Et, Et," again, and Dot realized he was saying her name.

"Yes, you love Auntie Etta," she said, cuddling him close. "But I don't know what the lizard says, buddy. What about a dog? What does the dog say?"

Stetson barked, and that made Dot giggle.

"You're okay?" Ward rose to his feet and bent down to press a kiss to her forehead. "Really?"

"I'll put in a pizza," Etta said. She got to her feet and nudged Ward out from in front of Dot. "Go shower, Ward. You smell like goats and your girlfriend is okay now." She smiled at her older brother as she handed Stetson to Dot. "You sit with Auntie Dot and tell her what a cat says."

"Meow," Stetson said. "Meee-oowww."

Dot laughed again, and she watched Etta scurry into the kitchen. "I'm okay, Ward," she said.

"You tell her the moment you're not," he said. "I'm going to shower, and I'm fast."

"Don't hurry," she pleaded. "Please. I'm okay."

"I'm putting you on my crew for this afternoon," he said, making it sound like a punishment. Didn't he know spending the afternoon with him was a prize? "I want to keep my eye on you."

"Fine," she said, grinning at him.

He finally broke, said, "Fine," too, and went through the door which stood next to the fireplace.

Dot sighed and cradled Stetson close. "What does a frog say?" she asked.

The boy turned toward her, his eyes aglow. "Ribbb.

Ribb." He blew the letter B through his lips, and Dot burst out laughing again.

She watched the door as she continued to quiz Stetson about animals, because while she adored the little boy and liked Etta, who she really wanted to be with was Ward.

A flutter moved through her stomach and into her hands. It could've been a tremble from her blood sugar, or it could've been from excitement. Dot knew, though, that she'd had a little shake of fear.

What was she thinking? Falling for another man named Ward....

*Please don't let him break my heart*, she prayed, and she looked up as Sammy Glover arrived with a newborn in her arms. Etta clapped her hands and reached for the baby, her whole countenance lighting up.

"Thank you, Etta," Sammy said with plenty of exhaustion in her voice. "I just need an hour."

"Take all the time you need," Etta said. "We'll be right here, and we'll be fine." She tucked the infant into her arm and gazed down at him with such love, Dot could feel it filling the air in the house.

She'd thought about being a mother, but she hadn't truly seen what that looked like on the outside. Watching Etta, she saw it. She felt it. She did want a child of her own, and she started fantasizing about what a baby boy that came from her and Ward would look like.

# Chapter Nineteen

Ward watched Dot as she picked up a bag of chicken feed. She could lift more than a normal woman, and he wasn't complaining about that. He liked her strong arms and can-do attitude, but he sure didn't need her fainting on him again.

She hadn't passed out at the homestead, and when he'd come out of the shower, his hair smelling like strawberries and cream—a scent that literally made him gag—Dot had been laughing with Etta and feeding Stetson crackers in the shape of goldfish.

His sister had fed him, and Ward had put every able-bodied person to work around the ranch. He and Dot were a team, and right now, they were making sure the turkeys and chickens had food on the ground.

The birds could scratch through the snow, and they would. Bishop had built coops about four years ago, and the turkeys normally roosted on the roof while the chickens went inside. There were no fences for the birds, and Ward moved them from pasture to pasture following the cows.

The cows grazed with the sheep and goats, because all three animals ate different parts of the foliage in the field. The birds didn't mind rooting through the manure for grubs, and the fields turned over faster that way.

But while they weren't using a ton of pasture in the winter—it didn't grow nearly fast enough—the chickens and turkeys had to be fed in addition to them wandering free-range to find food.

"Right over there, sweetheart," Ward said, indicating the empty spot in the truck for her bag of feed. Dot hefted it into place and wiped the loose hair off her forehead. She stunned him with her beauty in the waning afternoon light, and Ward couldn't contain the smile moving through him.

It felt like a movie-moment, where he could declare his love for her, and she'd say it right on back. Then he'd kiss her, and the sun would set and the credits would roll.

He actually opened his mouth, and the word, "I—" fell out. He cleared his terrifying and ridiculous thoughts as he cleared his throat. "This is the last of it," he said. "Then we'll be done. We can check in with everyone and see who needs to finish up what."

He looked up into the sky. "We don't want to be out here too much past dark."

"No, we don't." She stepped over to him and wrapped her arms around his waist. "Will you build me a fire tonight, cowboy?"

"You bet," he said, grinning down at her. "Are you gonna make dinner?"

She trilled out a laugh, and Ward chuckled too. "I'm useless in the kitchen, Ward. But I can probably put together a hamburger. That's one of the things I can make."

"Hamburgers sounds great," he said. "Mother makes them with barbecue sauce in the meat. Then a healthy pinch of garlic powder and one of onion salt."

"Oh, so you have a recipe you like already."

"I mean, anything you make will be fine. I can cut up some potatoes and make fries too."

"So you'll show me up in the kitchen."

Ward grinned and shook his head. "It's French fries. Not French food."

"Who makes French fries at home?"

"People who can't get off their property."

She burst out laughing, and she clung to him like she needed his arms around her to stay standing. He sure did like that, and Ward held her tightly around the waist. She quieted, and Ward bent his head closer to hers.

He bypassed her mouth though, and skated his lips along her jaw to her ear. "Dot," he whispered. "Is it too soon to talk about serious things?"

She pulled in a breath, her hands moving up to his shoulders. A shiver ran down his spine, but Ward didn't put new distance between them. "What kind of serious things?"

"You know, like family things. Kids." He dang near

coughed, and he definitely made a choking sound. "Do you want kids?"

"Did you see me with that baby?" she asked, pulling away. Her face had lit up. "He was the most adorable thing on the planet."

"Stetson or Russell?"

"Stetson," she said. "I would've given him crackers for the rest of his life."

"He knew it too," Ward said dryly. Stetson was a rare breed of child, as he loved everyone and everyone loved him. Even Ward was already wound tightly around Stetson's tiny pinky.

"I've always wanted kids," Dot said easily. "Seeing those two boys today and helping Stetson, I could see myself being a mom." She smiled at him. "I can see you being a dad too. You'd be all stern with them, and then sneak twenty-dollar bills into their lunch sacks." She laughed, and Ward actually took a moment to think about what she'd said.

"Maybe," he admitted.

"One of us has to be the bad guy," she said. "In my family, it was my mom. She actually told my dad he didn't get to be mad at the kids. They needed one person they knew loved them all the time." She took his hand and tugged, like she wanted to walk around to the front of the truck so they could go deliver this feed and be done with their chores. Ward wanted that too, but she'd said something to freeze his feet to the ground.

"One of us?" he asked. His heart throbbed in his chest in time to the words. *One. Of. Us. One-one. Of-of. Us-us.*

Dot looked up at him, her eyes rounding. "I just meant...one of the parents."

"What if it is me and you?" he asked, his voice gruff. "You'd come live up here? You know I'm going to live in that house where I live now. One of my kids will probably live there after I die."

Dot made a show of gazing around the ranch. They did stand in a pretty part of it, with plenty of trees surrounding this supply shed. Directly on the other side, though, the ranch buildings spread out, with plenty of noise, people, vehicles, and animals. For the most part, ranch life was a good life, but it could be busy and it could be intense from time to time.

"Yeah," she finally said. "I think I could live in that house with you."

He had no idea what that really meant. Did that mean she loved him? Or that she thought she could live in Bull House and put up with him? Those weren't the same thing, and Ward knew it. Mister lived with and put up with Ward. They weren't sharing their lives with each other. They weren't building anything together.

Ward wanted to share his life with Dot. He wanted to build a relationship and a life with her. A family.

His phone rang, and Ward blinked his way out of his thoughts. "It's Ace." He answered the phone and went with Dot around to the front of the truck. She got behind the wheel as he said, "What's up, bro?"

"Where are you with that feed? It's all we need to be done."

"Comin' now."

"You got sidetracked by that pretty woman, didn't you?"

"No."

"Did I interrupt you kissin' her?" Ace teased.

"No," Ward said again. He got in the passenger seat and nodded to Dot. "It's too cold to kiss outside anyway. We do all of that indoors." He grinned at Dot as Ace threw laughter into the sky.

"Wow, Ward," Ace said, still chuckling. "You aren't shy."

"Nope," he said.

"So it's serious with Dot."

Ward looked out the window at the trees as they gave way to the rest of the ranch. "I mean, yeah. Why wouldn't it be?"

"Didn't she break-up with you a while back?"

"We did just get back together, yes," Ward said coolly. "But I think I'm growing on her." He turned toward her, and Dot rolled her eyes, her grin a mile wide.

"You're not a fungus, Ward. Don't say stuff like that," Ace teased.

"Okay, *Mother*. I see you. I'm hanging up." He did just that.

Dot parked in front of the group of cowboys, Ace included, and they started unpacking the feed from the bed. "Why do you always call your mom Mother?"

Ward looked at her in surprise. "Uh, I don't know. We just do. Daddy called her Mother. I grew up calling her Mother."

"It's very formal."

"Yeah, I suppose."

"I don't want to be called Mother."

Ward gaped at her.

"Doesn't feel like it fits. Does it?"

"No," he said, hoping that was the right answer.

"Maybe Mom or Ma. I like Ma. Very old west."

"Ma?" Ward repeated, sure she was joking. They laughed in the same instant, and Ward knew she was kidding then. They got out of the truck to help with the feed, and the whole time, all Ward could think about was how well he and Dot got along.

They'd had some rough patches here and there. She wouldn't call him back about the gravel. She'd found him arrogant and demanding in the beginning. She'd driven him absolutely mad.

But now...now he knew more about what made her tick, and while she wasn't perfect—no one was—Ward could see her fitting neatly inside his life for a good long while.

"Doughnuts at the homestead," someone yelled, and a cheer went up.

"Check off with Ward," Preacher yelled, and Ward got out his clipboard. Pair by pair, he checked off the things that had gotten done on the ranch that day.

Cattle secure.

Horses fed.

Chicken coop mended.

Chickens and turkeys fed.

Fences fixed on the north side.

Cowboy cabin roof repaired.

Windmill taken down for rebuilding later.

The list went on and on, with most of their physical facilities issues having to do with fences that had been compromised by the wind. The taller structures had some damage too, but the barns and stables had weathered the storm quite well.

"Come on," Ward finally said as he made the last checkmark. "Let's go see if Holly Ann saved us a doughnut or two." She usually did, because Ward had been the one to call her and tell her to come to Bull House so she could make up with Ace after they'd broken up.

"How do you know Holly Ann made the doughnuts?" Dot asked.

"I assumed," he said. "Sounds like something she'd do."

"Does it bother you that I can't cook?"

"No," he said.

"Are you sure?"

"Does it bother you that I'm bossy?" he asked. "What difference does it make? I'm going to keep ordering the cowboys around the way I do, just like you're not going to suddenly know how to make doughnuts."

Dot blinked at him, and Ward had obviously made the wrong move. Given the wrong answer. "I mean—"

"But does it *bother* you?" she interrupted. "Maybe I would take a cooking class." She indicated that he should drive over to the homestead, and he took her around to the passenger door. "I don't know what you'd do to sweeten up." She grinned at him and reached up to force his collar to lie flat. "But maybe you don't need to. Your men and women seem to love you."

"I pay them well," he said. "So they put up with me."

"Mm." Dot studied him, but Ward didn't like the scrutiny. He opened her door and let her climb in while he went around to the driver's side.

She said nothing on the way to the homestead, and it was a two-minute drive that Ward had done countless times. He pulled up to a regular barn raising crowd, and Dot got out before he could move a muscle. The truck door slammed behind her, and Ward wondered if he'd said something wrong by not saying anything at all.

"Lord," he said, leaning his head back and closing his eyes. "Do I need to sweeten up?"

His door opened, and Dot stood there. "Come on, cowboy. The doughnuts are almost gone."

WARD WOKE UP WHEN DOT LEFT THE BATHROOM FOR the fifth time that night. He wasn't sure why, as her presence in the house the other two nights hadn't bothered him. He'd slept like the dead.

Tonight, though, she seemed to be using the bathroom a lot, and his worry ate at him. He'd read a little bit about type-2 diabetes and what it meant to have high blood sugar and low blood sugar.

Dot had taken her readings every hour after her episode at lunchtime, and she'd assured him that her sugar levels supported the doughnut she'd eaten. She had made hamburgers for dinner, and she'd excused herself to inject her insulin before they'd taken a single bite.

*She knows what she's doing*, he thought, and he rolled over so his back faced his open doorway. He thought of Bear and how the man liked to don a red cape and fly in to save the day.

*Don't be Bear.* Ward closed his eyes and commanded himself to go back to sleep. Unfortunately, sleep didn't work that way, and while he was exhausted, he didn't seem to be getting any closer to unconsciousness.

He glanced at his alarm clock—the old school kind with the bright blue neon numbers—and sighed. Two a.m. He'd slept for a couple of hours on the couch while Dot had texted her brother and sister, then her mother. She'd finally put him to bed and gone to bed herself. Ward felt like he'd been dozing since then. Awake for a few minutes, asleep for a few.

The bathroom door down the hall closed again, and Ward sat up this time. He crept to the doorway and on down the hall. It would be okay to ask her if she was okay, right?

He leaned toward the door only to hear her retching. He frowned and knocked lightly. "Dot, honey? Are you okay?"

She moaned, and then the word sounded very much like, "No."

"Can I come in?"

"Please," she said, and Ward dang near ripped the door down to get it open.

Dot knelt in front of the toilet, pure misery on her face. A bit of white residue ringed her upper lip and the corner of her mouth. Alarms shouted in Ward's head.

"I don't feel good," Dot said, a single tear rolling down

her face. Her breaths came in shallow gasps. "I'm nauseous and vomiting. I'm dying of thirst, so then I have to go to the bathroom all the time."

He knelt on the floor with her. "I can get you something to drink."

She shook her head. "I can't drink any more. I've been drinking for hours." She leaned her head against his chest. "I can't cry, because I'm so dehydrated."

Ward put his hand against her heart and found it beating like hummingbird wings. "More insulin," he said. "That's what you need?" He could go grab it from the fridge.

"Yes," she said, gasping the word out. "But Ward." Gasp. Exhale. Shudder. "I don't have any more."

# Chapter Twenty

"Tell them you're not coming in," Ida said, plenty of annoyance in her voice though she hadn't spoken louder than a whisper. Brady's phone continued to ring, and she reached over and smacked his chest. Honestly, how the cop could sleep through the noise eluded her. "Your phone."

Her husband groaned and rolled over, moving right into a sitting position. The light from the nursery, which sat only fifteen feet to Ida's left and through a massive, arched doorway, spilled into their bedroom and illuminated Brady as he lifted his phone. "It's Tyson."

"Great. Tell him no." Ida closed her eyes, not even wanting to see what time it was. It was the middle of the night, that was what, and she'd barely strung together three hours of sleep since the babies had been born seven days ago. Brady wasn't even supposed to be on-call.

Brady got out of bed, and Ida knew he'd slip away from

her. She was okay with it; they'd talked a lot about his job before he'd asked her to marry him. He'd also asked his boss if he could have a few weeks off of the rotation for on-call emergencies, and he'd been granted his request.

No one should be calling him in the middle of the night.

Ida sighed in an exaggerated way and rolled over. She fumbled for her phone to check the time, though it blinded her, and she had to squint against the light. Two-ten. She'd need to be up in a half-hour to feed the babies anyway. Perhaps she could sneak in their feeding now and then sleep until morning.

Armed with that amazingly good idea, Ida set her phone down and swung her legs out of bed. She still needed an extra second to steady herself, as she wasn't pregnant anymore, and she didn't have thirteen extra pounds attached to the front of her body.

"Ida, it's Ward," Brady said, rushing back into the room. He flipped the light on, and Ida frowned and threw her hand up to shield her eyes.

"Ward?"

"Well, it's really Dot," Brady said, tossing his phone on the bed. He reached for his boots, the urgency with which he moved frightening Ida. "She's out of insulin, and she's got super high blood sugar." He pulled in a breath. "Ward called Tyson—that's her brother—and he called me. I'm going with him to get more insulin and take it up to the ranch."

"I'll come," Ida said, her heartbeat pounding in the back of her throat. It hammered against her tongue. Ward was her very best friend besides Etta, and she could help him.

"You can't come, sweets," Brady said, standing up and rounding the corner of the bed. He took her by the shoulders and smiled at her. "We'd have gone to the ranch today if we could get there, remember?"

"I have to go," she said. "Ward will need my help."

"Everyone else is there," Brady said gently, but that was exactly the wrong thing to say. She flinched from the extra salt in the wound. "Have you forgotten how many babies we have now?" He grinned down at her and leaned in for a kiss.

He pulled away almost the moment his lips touched hers. "You have to stay here with the babies. They need you."

She glanced toward the nursery they'd added on to the back of the house at Ida's insistence. She didn't want the twins down the hall and in a bedroom near the front door —the only other option for bedrooms on this level of the home. She could barely stand them several yards away.

"Of course," she said. "The babies." She went that way while Brady reached for his jacket. "I'll call Ward. How are you going to get the insulin to him if the road's out?" She hadn't heard differently about the road, and she'd stared at the pictures Etta had taken for a long time. She couldn't believe the hill had just cleaved and slid down the way it had.

"Ward says there's a service road that connects the Rhinehart Ranch to the south to the road up by the Top Cottage. He told Ty he'd call Duke."

"Okay," Ida said, thinking she better get on the phone too. She could reassure Ward that she was praying for him, and she could make sure Etta knew the situation—if she didn't already.

Ida loved her life in town, with her husband and her new babies. She'd never needed to be entrenched in the work at Shiloh Ridge, though she did enjoy going there to spend time with her family. But right now, being separated from them felt like the worst loss of her life, and she pulled back on the tears as Brady kissed her again, promised to call, and then jogged out of the bedroom, his phone back at his ear.

Ida retraced her steps and picked up her phone. She didn't have any missed messages or calls, and she quickly tapped to connect a line to her brother.

"Ida," Ward said, and she felt the anxiety all the way from the ranch. "You talked to Brady, I assume."

"He just left."

"She's almost unconscious," Ward said, and Ida imagined him to be pacing up there at Bull House. "I'm so mad at her. She shouldn't have eaten those dang doughnuts."

"Ward," Ida said as Johnny started to fuss. Ida had worried needlessly that she wouldn't know what her children needed or wanted. When she'd first learned she was having twins, she'd cried for three days. What if they were identical? How would she ever tell them apart?

She knew now that she'd have been able to easily.

"Ward," she said again when her brother didn't respond.

"What?" he barked at her.

"Take a deep breath and talk to me," she said. "Tell me what's going on."

"Dot's diabetic," he said. "She already had one bout where she almost fainted today, but that was because her blood sugar was too low. She didn't eat enough. Etta fixed her up with orange juice."

"Okay," Ida said, because she'd heard all of this from Etta already.

"Tonight, she took her level, and she was getting low again. She said that can happen when she works a lot. Something about exercise...I don't know. I feel like I need a crash course on diabetes and blood sugar and all of it."

"Another deep breath," Ida said, and she listened while Ward took it.

"So she ate the doughnuts. Two of 'em, which whatever. I don't care except that now she's in the bathroom, vomiting and crying and telling me that she might pass out."

"Really?"

"Apparently she can go into a diabetic coma," Ward said. "Her level is two-seventy-five, Ida. She says she's had higher, but you should see her. She looks like she's about to die. Dear Lord, I don't know what to do."

He sounded like he might break, and Ida's heart squeezed. "Ward," she said gently as she entered the nursery. She bent over and picked up Johnny. He'd get fed first today, though he tended to hog all of her milk and not leave enough for his sister. "It's going to be okay," Ida said as she sat down in the rocking chair between the two bassinets.

"Brady and Tyson are on the way. Duke's going to get the insulin at the Top Cottage, and you'll have it within the hour." Her voice shook, but she took a deep breath too. Ward had been strong for her. She'd nursed him back to health in the past. She could help him through this too.

"I'll stay with you on the line until you get it," she said. "I assume you're not going ot leave her alone for a single moment."

"No," Ward said quietly. "I'm not."

"Where is she?" Ida asked, positioning Johnny so he could eat. She toed herself back and let the two of them gently rock forward.

"In the bathroom," he said. "I'm sitting in the hall just outside of it, watching to make sure she's still alive."

"I'm still alive," Ida heard through the line, and she managed a small smile at the sound of Dot's voice.

"Dot is one of the strongest women I know," Ida said firmly. "And you're the best person to be there with her, Ward. You can help her with this."

"I need to tell everyone," he whispered. "Then they can pray. But I don't want to wake up Bear and Sammy. They never sleep as it is. Etta took Stetson last night, in the middle of the night, and she was so tired tonight. We've all been working our hands to the bone today."

"You sound tired."

"I am beyond tired," Ward admitted.

"Are you feeling better after your attempt to freeze yourself?" Ida couldn't believe Ward had tried to go to the shed in a blizzard. It didn't make sense, because Ward didn't take risks like that.

"Yes," he said. "I slept a lot on Christmas Day, and Dot kept me warm and hydrated."

"It's two-sixty," Dot said, and Ida realized Ward had her on speaker.

"That's going down," Ida said. "Is that right?"

"I've been moving a little bit," Dot said. "But you're not supposed to exercise if you think you might be in ketoacidosis."

Ida had no idea what that meant, but she didn't have to. She could look it up online later.

"Why would it go down then?" Ward asked.

"Maybe just pure movement," Dot said, her voice closer. "Can I sit here?"

"Sure thing, sweetheart." Shuffling came through the line, and Ida could only imagine her strong, somewhat stoic brother sitting in the hallway of their childhood home, right outside the bathroom, his girlfriend snuggling into his side.

"Tell me how the babies are," Ward said, his voice soft. At least he wasn't about to stab something or snap at Dot.

"I will if you tell me what's really going on with you and Dot," she said, smiling down at her son as he ate.

"She's on the line, Ida," Ward warned.

"Maybe she can tell me then." Ida knew Dot reasonably well. She didn't live far from Ida and Brady, and they'd gone a double date with her and Ward several weeks ago.

"I'll tell you," Dot said. "But you have to promise to keep it a secret."

"I can do that," Ida said.

"I'm falling in love with him," Dot said. "Don't tell him that though, because he's already got such a big head."

Ida blinked in the darkness, shock coursing through her. Then happiness. Pure joy, in fact. She started to giggle, and Dot joined in a moment later. Ward didn't protest, and while Ida didn't think her brother had an arrogant bone in his body, she also knew him. She'd known him his whole life, and she knew how pure and good his heart was.

"I'm also going to have to report this little incident to the DLD," Dot said. "They might make me go get one of those medical certifications that says I can keep my commercial trucking license."

"Oh?" Ida asked.

"No, no," Dot said. "You promised Ward you'd talk about the babies."

Ida smiled to herself, actually hoping Dot wouldn't remember this conversation once she felt better.

"So I'm feeding Johnny right now," Ida began. "He's definitely going to eat me out of house and home when he's a teenager, because he already takes more than his share of the milk...."

# Chapter Twenty-One

Jeremiah Walker didn't keep his phone on silent through the night. He was responsible for too many animals, buildings, and men for such a thing. So when his phone rang in the middle of the night, he heard it.

Whitney, his wife, heard it too, and she sucked in a breath and sat up.

"It's fine," Jeremiah whispered. "Go back to sleep." He swiped for his phone, knocking his hand against the plate he'd left on his nightstand. He couldn't go to bed on an empty stomach, and he'd been up late last night helping his brother with a toy ATV he'd bought for his daughter.

Since Christmas had been a couple of days of wind and weather, Liam hadn't been able to get the ATV out for his daughter. They'd gotten it going—finally—after two trips to town and after the girl had gone to bed.

So Jeremiah had required a bagel with cream cheese for his midnight snack. The plate fell to the floor, and he pressed his eyes closed as a form of swearing, and then looked at his phone. Bear Glover's name sat there, and the man wouldn't be calling just to chat. Jeremiah wasn't even sure Bear knew the meaning of the word *chat*.

"Bear," he said, getting out of bed and hurrying toward the door. "What's goin' on?"

He pulled it closed behind him as Bear said, "Do you still have that crane? I saw it drivin' by your place last week. Micah said y'all had rented it to haul in some pavers."

"Yeah," Jeremiah padded into the kitchen and looked at the clock. Almost three in the morning. He probably should've pulled on some pants before leaving the bedroom, because this didn't sound like an easy problem to solve.

"We had a landslide here today," Bear said, and Jeremiah froze.

"You did?"

Bear sighed, and it sounded almost like a growl. "Yeah. We can't get on or off the ranch. Well, we've got someone here who needs some medicine in a real bad way. She should probably go to the hospital too, but we're not sure how to get her there."

"Okay," Jeremiah said, nodding along.

"Her brother is here with the insulin she needs, but we can't get it from him."

Jeremiah leaned against the island. "What about that service road up at Rhinehart?"

"Wade's truck is stuck in the mud. We tried that. It's impassable until the road dries out."

"To get there from the west, you'd have to go all the way to Amarillo," he mused. "And drive back on dirt roads no one knows about."

"Too long," Bear said. "So I thought...we need something to extend over the landslide. The back yard of the homestead and Bull House overlooks the road leading around to Preacher's place. If we could get that crane there, and put the insulin in a bag or envelope or something...maybe it would extend far enough to get it to Ward."

"It moves real slow," Jeremiah said, pushing away from the counter. "But I'll be on my way in five minutes."

"We're getting out all the spotlights we've got. Brady's here with Tyson Crockett, and they both brought their cruisers. They have bright lights too."

"I won't miss them then," Jeremiah said. "Who's diabetic up there?"

"Ward's new girlfriend," Bear said. "Dot Crockett?"

"Got it. Give me a few minutes." Jeremiah ended the call before he went back into the bedroom. He detoured through the bathroom and into the master closet to get dressed, and he took a moment on Whitney's side of the bed to tell her what he was doing in three sentences.

"Be careful," she said, sitting up. "Do I need to call anyone?"

"Nope," Jeremiah said. "I'll call you when I can."

She fisted the blankets and nodded, and Jeremiah hurried to grab the keys and get to the crane.

Outside, he found Micah walking at a brisk pace down the lane toward the homestead. His brother lived across the dirt street from the main homestead, in a custom-built house he'd constructed with his bare hands.

"I'm going with you," he said. "There's room for two of us in that crane cab, right?"

"Two of us, yes," Jeremiah said, noting the huge duffel bag Micah carried. "What's in that?"

"Ropes and carabiners," he said. "Pulleys. Stakes. Anything else I could think of that could be used to build something to get that insulin across a gulf." He hefted it onto his shoulder. "I'll carry it if I have to."

"Okay," Jeremiah said. "Let's go." He'd parked the crane out in the field next to Micah's property, and they walked with purpose to reach it. The vehicle had big, round tires, and as Jeremiah got behind the controls of it, he looked down at the speedometer. "Oh, this thing can go fifty miles per hour."

"Doesn't mean you should go that fast," Micah said, stuffing his bag of supplies into the space at his feet. "But let's go. Apparently, Dot is in bad shape."

"Did you talk to someone?"

"Bear," Micah said. "He saw the crane and thought it was mine. I told him that we'd rented it, but you had the keys and he said he'd call you. I tried to tell him I could get them and come, but he was already gone."

Jeremiah nodded and fought against a yawn. "No problem. They all came to help with the fire. We can give up some sleep for this."

"I can't believe they had a landslide. They're barely up any sort of hill at all."

Jeremiah pulled the lever toward himself and the crane

backed up. It felt like it was swaying forward and back as the motion had to travel up such a long arm, but Jeremiah didn't slow down. He got moving in the right direction, and the moment he faced southwest, he could see the lights in the distance.

"They've got their lights out all right," he said. "Let's go see what we can do."

Only twenty minutes later, Jeremiah maneuvered the crane where two police officers indicated he should. They didn't wear their uniforms, but he knew Tyson Crockett and Brady Burton. Brady had married Ida Glover last year, and Jeremiah and Whitney had come to the wedding.

He got out of the cab and approached Brady. "Morning," Jeremiah said, shaking his hand.

"We're thinking we can put the insulin in a plastic bag." Brady indicated the other cop. "And attach that to the hook on the end of the boom. This is a big one." He looked up into the night, but Jeremiah couldn't see the top of the crane.

"I don't think we'll need counterweights. We just need to get from down here." Brady turned and pointed up to a flat section of land where two men stood. They had set up lights up there too, and one of the cop cars had positioned the lights up there too.

"To up there."

"How far is it?" Micah asked, joining them.

"It's hard to tell," Brady said, sighing. "A couple hundred feet probably."

"This crane reaches about two hundred feet," Jeremiah said. "Let's try it. I'll lower the boom."

"Tyson," Brady called, and the other cop turned toward them. He was on his phone now, and he approached Jeremiah while saying, "Yes, I know, but this is all we can do right now. We'll deal with that if we have to." He shook Jeremiah's hand but didn't stop for long.

Jeremiah reached into the crane and pushed the button to lower the boom. That seemed to take longer than it had to drive here from Seven Sons Ranch. He stayed out of the way as Brady and Tyson talked about how to make sure the plastic bag didn't fall off. Micah offered some ideas, and they ended up tying the bag to the hook and then using one of Micah's carabiners too. They pierced the end of it through the bag and then attached it to the hook on the crane. That way, if the bag ripped or came loose from where they'd tied it, the carabiner would still be in place.

"Let's go," Brady yelled. "Bear, we're sending it up."

Jeremiah had no idea if he'd parked the crane in the right place to get the boom in front of Bear. He told himself Bear could walk left or right, and he raised the boom, and then started extending the boom toward the spotlighted pair up on the ridge.

"Right a little," Brady called, and Jeremiah adjusted the direction of the boom. He told himself to breathe, as he'd started to hold everything so tight. He didn't want to be wound up so much, and when his third baby had been born in less than five years, Jeremiah had taken a giant step back from all the stress in his life.

He still ran Seven Sons—that wasn't going to change. But he'd given a lot more tasks to his brother, Skyler, who only had one child. His wife was due with their second baby in May, but Jeremiah had hired two foremen—two amazing cowboys who'd been working the ranch before the Walkers had even bought it. That way, Jeremiah, Skyler, Micah, and the rest of their family still owned the ranch and ran the ranch. But it didn't have to *consume* him the way it had in the past.

"It's actually too long," Tyson said, and Jeremiah thought so too.

Bear reached up to get the bag, but it wasn't low enough yet.

"Down," Brady called needlessly, but Jeremiah bit back on his irritation. The man was just trying to help.

Jeremiah made the required adjustments, and Bear backed away from the ledge and out of the spotlight. He eased up and let the crane barely move. A few seconds later, a loud yell of triumph filled the sky.

"Got it!" Ranger yelled down. "Thanks, you guys. Thank you *so* much!" He lifted both hands and waved, and then he hurried into the darkness too.

Jeremiah started to lift the boom, because he'd need to drive the crane back to Seven Sons. His adrenaline raced through his bloodstream, and he didn't think he'd be able to go back to sleep tonight.

"Well, I guess that's it," Brady said, coming to stand next to Jeremiah. "Thank you so much for bringing this. It literally saved us." He looked up to the ridge as Tyson turned off his police spotlights and the land up there went dark.

"Anytime," Jeremiah said. "Glad to help."

"Wish it wasn't three a.m.," Micah said, but he wore a

smile on his face. "Even though it is, it's fine. We take care of each other out here."

"I know Bear and Ranger and Ward appreciate it," Brady said, clapping Jeremiah on the shoulder.

With the crane ready to go, Jeremiah got behind the controls again. Micah sat beside him in silence. Tyson Crockett hadn't moved, and he stood in front of his car, his eyes trained on his phone.

"It's nice to have family around," Micah said quietly, and Jeremiah didn't think there had ever been truer words spoken.

"Say a prayer for them on the way back," Jeremiah said. "I'm sure they're not out of the weeds yet."

# Chapter Twenty-Two

Preacher looked up from the gaming forum when he heard Ward's soft snores. His cousin had sat with him for hours while Preacher had slept, and he could certainly do the same in return.

His heart squeezed tight at the sight of Ward's closed eyes and placid face. His chest steadily rose, and then fell, and he looked so at peace. So calm.

He hadn't been calm last night, though Preacher hadn't talked directly to him. He'd gotten a call about four-thirty in the morning, and Bear had explained the situation with Dot.

Preacher had thought life on the ranch would be boring for Charlie, but when she'd awakened and he'd told her he was going to spend the morning at Bull House with Dot and Ward to make sure they were taken care of, she'd said, "Wow, there's never a dull moment around here, is there?"

He'd grinned at her, taken her into his arms, and kissed

her. She'd promised to do her morning broadcast and then come sit with him, and a trickle of guilt moved through his stomach that he wasn't watching her on Nexus. He didn't usually have time, and she didn't want him there anyway.

He knew about her online video game life, and he participated in it regularly. But she was a different person online that she really was in person, and Preacher preferred having the blonde woman in person than sharing her with others on the Internet.

His phone vibrated, and he looked down again. *I'm here*, Charlie had said. *Do I just come in?*

*Yep.* Preacher sent the text and got to his feet to go greet her. He hadn't knocked on the door at Bull House that morning, though the sky was barely light and the clock had ticked to six on his walk over from the Ranch House.

Ward hard been in the kitchen, of course, because Ward couldn't start the day without coffee and over-hard eggs. He'd tried to feed Preacher, who'd turned him down repeatedly before Ward finally stopped.

Dot had been asleep in the bedroom just down the hall, and Ward checked on her every fifteen minutes. Her brother had brought a glucose monitor that could take readings of her breath, and she'd allowed Ward to tape it near her mouth.

They'd been steadily decreasing since the three a.m. delivery of insulin, and by the time Preacher had checked on Dot, they were normal. Ward had taped a piece of paper with the numbers on the nightstand next to Dot, along with Tyson Crockett's phone number, and he'd given

Preacher explicit instructions to wake him if Dot's levels got one stitch above normal.

Preacher had been there for four hours, and Ward had been asleep for three of them. Dot hadn't woken at all. He worried about that, but he wasn't sure what to do. He'd read a little bit about diabetes and glucose and blood sugar, but he didn't truly understand it.

The front door opened when he was a couple of paces away, and Charlie entered. Her presence made Preacher light up, and he took her into his arms. "They're both asleep." He buried his face in her neck and took a deep breath of the soft scent of her skin.

"I need to check Dot's numbers, and then maybe we can sit outside to talk."

"Have you been outside?" she whispered. "It's not warm, Preach."

"The office then." He indicated it on his left, and Charlie nodded. She went into the office while Preacher retraced his steps to the living room. Ward hadn't moved, and Preacher hoped he'd sleep for a long, long time. He hadn't silenced his phone before lying on the couch, but Preacher had done it the moment Ward's breathing had evened out.

Dot seemed to be in the same position as well, and the number on the breathalyzer fell in the range of normal. She'd told Ward, who'd told Preacher, that she'd need to eat at some point. She'd said to watch the numbers. The moment they started slipping low, she needed to be awakened and fed.

He jotted down the number on the pad of paper next to the cheat sheet and hurried to rejoin Charlie.

"How'd your broadcast go?" He opened the blinds on the big windows facing the ranch and settled next to her on the black leather couch. She snuggled into his side, and Preacher took a moment to thank the Lord above that he'd found her.

"Good," she said, but something carried in her voice that alerted Preacher.

"What did you talk about this morning?"

"Stuff."

"Uh oh," he said. "I don't like 'stuff.'"

"You already know about it," she said.

"The marriage thing."

"Yes." She sat up and looked at him. He gazed steadily back at her. "You have the setup here, Preacher. We're here. Your mother is here. Your whole family is here."

"Ida's not here."

"Ida will survive."

"Davie's not here."

She lifted her chin, her strength admirable. "I called her right after I finished my broadcast. I asked her if she'd be devastated if she watched me get married on a private, family-only video feed."

"And?" Preacher couldn't believe he was even entertaining the idea. Mother would be devastated, as she loved planning weddings more than the actual event itself.

At the same time, Preacher would love to have Charlie in his bed at night.

"She couldn't believe we haven't already tied the knot."

Preacher scoffed and shook his head. "Okay, first off, I don't believe that."

"She did," Charlie insisted. "Maybe not in those words, but she said she wouldn't be upset."

"Your parents aren't here."

"Preacher," she said, her voice pitching down. "My family is not like yours. Trust me when I say this is going to be okay. I've always marched to the beat of my own drum. They won't even be surprised."

"I find that very hard to believe," he said.

"You'll understand when you meet them."

"They'll hate me," he said. "Who marries someone without even meeting her parents first?" He shook his head. "That's not a great start for my relationship with them."

Charlie put one hand on his chest. "You want to marry me, right?"

"Of course I do." In May or June, like they planned. When they'd found out yesterday that they were stuck at Shiloh Ridge for several more days, Charlie had come up with this insane idea of getting married. Like, right then.

"I don't want to wait, Preacher," she said softly. "We're both here. Your family is here. I can livestream it if you want. My fans would love that." She grinned as Preacher shook his head. "I applied for the marriage license online, and we could literally get married here tomorrow."

She leaned forward and pressed her lips to his. She so wasn't playing fair, because Preacher couldn't think properly when she kissed him with so much precision. So slow, and so careful, like she was afraid he'd break if she moved too fast or pressed too hard.

"Tomorrow," she whispered. "Then, I wouldn't have to go down into that chilly, scary basement all by myself, and we could avoid the huge show you hate."

"My family is a huge show by themselves," he reminded her, tasting her lips again. He was going to say yes to this, and he knew it. He'd be surprised if Charlie didn't know it too.

"You can meet my parents on video right now," she said, tilting her head back so he could kiss her neck. "I'll call them right this second."

"They're not together," he said.

"Two phone calls," Charlie said, leveling her eyes with his. "Please, Preacher? I have all the ranch wives to help me get ready. You've got all your clothes, and heaven knows they're nice because you've been to like a billion family weddings in the past year."

She grinned with him as he started chuckling. He kept shaking his head no, though this crazy idea of hers had been planted in his mind and had started to sprout.

"Judge can marry us," she said. "It'll be legal and binding, and I know you want it over and done with. Just think how miserable you'll be talking about cakes and colors, guests and gifts, for the next *six months*."

"I'm miserable already," he joked.

"So let me text Judge." She got out her phone and looked at him, her eyebrows high and the hope in her expression bright.

Preacher gazed back at her. "Are you sure?" he asked. "Like, really, really sure? You have friends at HealNow."

"They'll think this is the most romantic thing in the world."

Anything and everything Preacher had been able to think of, Charlie had an answer for it. He still attempted to find one last thing that would convince her this was a bad idea. He wasn't sure why he wanted to talk her out of it, only that he didn't want her to have any regrets.

"And what? We'll live in my bedroom at the Ranch House? With Mister and Judge, mind you."

"They won't stay forever," she said. "Maybe Mister and Judge could move here with Ward—Mister lives here technically already—and we'll have the house to ourselves until Judge figures things out with June."

Preacher couldn't argue with that. The Glovers moved all over the ranch, and it wasn't like there weren't places to live. He thought of the Kinder Ranch and how beautiful that would be once it was completely redone.

But he didn't know what the landslide had done down lower, and it was still eighteen months away from being complete as it was.

"I'm texting Judge," Charlie said, her voice decisive and final. "I love you, Preacher, and I want to be your wife right now."

"I love you too," he said quietly, and that was as good as a yes for Charlie. She sent the text, and when their eyes met again, she searched his face.

"I'll make a private link for the people we want to be able to view the wedding. We can have a big party later."

"I don't care if it's just me and you," he whispered. In fact, for Preacher, that would be ideal.

"Your mother can plan the party."

"I'll tell her that."

Charlie threw her arms around Preacher's neck and laughed. He joined her, because he had some anxiety he needed to chortle away.

"Should we call my parents first or tell your family?" Charlie looked down at her phone. In the next moment, it rang, and she said, "It's Judge."

"He's going to think we're crazy."

She swiped on the call and tapped the speaker button. "Heya, Judge. You're on speaker with both of us."

Preacher expected his sensible, down-to-earth brother to launch into a speech detailing all of the reasons they couldn't get married tomorrow. Literally, *tomorrow*.

Instead, Judge said, "I'm in. What time were you thinking?"

# Chapter Twenty-Three

Cactus Glover entered True Blue, the family gathering barn he'd helped restore for his brother's wedding, through the back door. Ten minutes ago, he'd been elbow-deep in sawdust. Now, he was going to witness another of his brothers get married.

"Come on, boys," he said, turning back to make sure Lincoln and Mitch were with him. He signed the words and straightened Mitch's cowboy hat as the child went by. He loved the boy with his whole heart, because his heart was whole now.

*Where's my mom?* Mitch asked, and Cactus signed back to him.

"She should be here. She was helping get everything ready." He went past the bathrooms and toward the noise, something that would've taken a lot of courage only a couple of years ago. In the main hall of True Blue, eight or ten tables had been set up. There weren't any fancy bows or decorations on the chairs.

Each table had an ivory cloth covering it, and someone —most likely Mother—had set a vase in the center. There were no flowers or vines. No pictures of the happy couple. No table for gifts. No music playing.

Relief hit Cactus when he saw his oldest brother, Bear, chatting with Duke. They were both wearing the same thing he was—jeans, a long-sleeved shirt, and some sort of jacket. They'd obviously come in off the ranch too.

When Preacher had texted—*texted*—yesterday morning that he and Charlie would be getting married—*married*— on the ranch the next day—*the next day*—Cactus had read the message five or six times before he'd believed it.

They'd been engaged for maybe ten days. As far as he knew—as far as any of the Glovers had known until that moment—Preacher and Charlie were planning a late spring or early summer wedding.

"Can't complain about this," Mister said, walking toward Cactus. "This is the most comfortable I've been at any of these weddings." He smoothed his palms down the front of his red-and-white plaid shirt.

"Yeah," Cactus said, because he didn't know what else to say.

He stood next to a tripod that held a camera of some kind, maybe the kind that went on a computer, and noticed the cable connecting that to a speaker. "They're going to broadcast it."

"To her family and friends," Mister said. "She's a pro at getting things online."

"I've heard." Cactus marveled at the technology in the world. They could literally be cut off from the rest of civilization and still participate in important events. He had to admit he liked that, but he probably never would out loud to anyone except Willa.

"Have you seen my wife?" he asked Mister, turning back toward the doorway he'd entered through. To the right down the hall sat the prep rooms, and she was likely in one of those with the other women.

He scanned the crowd as Mister said, "There are no women here, Cactus."

He was right. Not a single female could be found in the hall, and Cactus wasn't that surprised. Willa had gotten the same text he had, and she'd come bustling out of the house a moment later.

"I'm going to Holly Ann's," she'd declared. Cactus had still been trying to figure out if Preacher was pranking the lot of them or not. When he'd looked up, all he'd caught was the dust behind Willa's tires as she drove away from the Edge Cabin.

She'd been gone all day, and when she'd returned home that night, she'd gushed and gushed about how "wonderful" and "romantic" this wedding was going to be.

To Cactus, a general sense of awkwardness hung in the air. Loud voices to his left drew his attention, and he and Mister turned toward the front entrance of the barn. They had a receiving foyer, but someone was bringing in something big.

"Careful," Preacher said, and he too wasn't wearing anything fancy yet. "It's caught on the rug."

Ace bent to free the rug, and then he, Preacher, Judge, and Ward continued to push in the baby grand piano that usually sat in the formal living room at the Ranch House.

Judge positioned it just-so at the front of the hall, and he nodded to Preacher before he sat down. Lilting, romantic music filled the air, chasing away all of the tension and awkwardness that had been there.

Ward placed a stool next to the piano, and after perching on it, Preacher handed him his guitar. The man could've been country star famous, but he'd chosen a different path for himself. Cactus smiled as Ward tuned his instrument and then came right in with Judge.

He couldn't play the piano or the guitar all that well, though Mother had tried to get him to learn both. He could read music, but his true talent lay in his voice.

Preacher approached, and Cactus took a couple of steps sideways to intercept him. "Hey, brother," he said, drawing Preacher into a hug. "Are you doin' okay?"

"Okay sounds about right," Preacher said, gripping Cactus tightly too. He stepped back, his smile nervous. "I just have to get dressed. We're on time to start, don't worry."

"I'm not worried," Cactus said. "It's the Grizzly you've got to please." They laughed together, and Preacher hurried off to get dressed.

Five minutes later, Bear looked up from his phone. "Glovers to the groom's room," he said in his roaring voice.

If all the blood relatives of Preacher went to the groom's room, the only people left here would be Donald, Duke, Mitch and Lincoln. Bear put his arm around his oldest son and Cactus assumed he could bring in Mitch too.

"We'll hold down the fort," Don said with a big smile, and Cactus fell into line with the others moving toward the back hall.

"Nope, everyone is included," Ward said, clapping Duke on the back. "Y'all are comin'. Let's go."

At the corner, Cactus looked back toward the front of the room, where the piano sat silent now, with Ward's guitar resting against it.

There was no altar. Nowhere for Charlie to march toward and arrive. Cactus frowned. Was this really happening?

He continued on, arriving almost last because of his pause.

"Thank you," Preacher said as Judge closed the door behind him. "Thanks for coming, everyone, really." He now wore the same suit he'd worn to Cactus's wedding, and surprise filled him. The navy blue did look nice, and though Preacher didn't have the fancy silk trim, or Daddy's string tie, or the fancy cowboy hat, he definitely looked good enough to get married.

Cactus edged his way toward Preacher, who said, "I know this is kind of crazy, but we're stuck up here, and it turns out that it's kind of torture to be stuck in a house with someone you love and not be as...close as you'd like."

He cleared his throat, his face turning red. "Charlie came up with this idea, and honestly, I hope I can keep up with her in my life."

"You'll be fine," Bear murmured, and Cactus agreed with that.

"I asked Mister to pray before we start," Preacher said, nodding at the man.

Cactus had left his hat on the back hook, so he just reached up and ran his hands through his hair to make it look less smashed. He closed his eyes and bowed his head as Mister began.

"Lord," he said. "We come before Thee as brothers and family."

Cactus drew in a long breath, feeling the bonds of brotherhood he craved. They formed and strengthened, and though they hadn't always all gotten along, right now, they did. For Preacher, they would. He was their glue, their bridge between older and younger, the path between the Stone Glover family and the Bull Glover family. Every single man here would do anything for Preacher, Cactus included.

Mister cleared his throat. "We love Thee. We love the land Thou has entrusted us with. We love the animals we're tasked with caring for, and we love the new men, women, and children who have joined our family in the past few years. Bless us with Thy spirit this day. Bless Preacher and Charlie as they start their new life together. Bless any in our company that need help at this time."

His voice broke, and Cactus cracked one eye to look at Mister. His whole face trembled, and Cactus wondered what in the world was going on with him. He needed to spend more time with the younger brothers, but the truth was, the family was huge. He had so much on his plate already, and he had family members he had stronger bonds with than Mister.

At the same time, something pricked at his heart, telling him to get to Mister's side and make sure he knew he was there. That Mister could count on Cactus. Anyone and everyone could count on Cactus to be there for him, the way they'd always all been there for him.

*I will*, he vowed to himself and to God. *I'll make sure he knows.*

Preacher moved over a couple of feet and slung his arm around Mister, who looked at him. "I can't," he said, the words choked in his throat.

Cactus expected Bear to fly in and save the day. He'd finish the prayer. He'd take care of everything the way he always did.

Instead, Bear stood silently too, and when he met Cactus's eye, he simply smiled.

Mister reached up with both hands and scrubbed his face. When he lowered his hands, he looked determined and resolute. "Bless us that our roads and land will be restored, and that we'll be able to come and go from Shiloh Ridge normally very soon. Amen."

"Amen," the rest of the group chorused, and then a new drape of silence covered them.

"All right," Preacher said a few seconds later. "Y'all go on now. Find a place to sit. I'll be out in a minute."

Cactus had already hugged him. He'd already asked Preacher how he was. His face shone with joy as he hugged Bear and then Ward, and Cactus didn't need any more of

Preacher's energy. He left with Don and Duke, and when they entered the hall, Cactus froze.

In the few minutes all of the men had been in the groom's room, someone had brought in an altar. The rough-hewn log sat on supports one could find all over Shiloh Ridge, as they were used to build their fences.

Two additional logs making an X, one on each end of the log, held it up, and a big, bold G had been carved into the front of it.

"Wow," Ace said as he flowed past Cactus. "That's great."

"Where did that come from?" Bear asked, pausing next to Cactus.

"No idea," he said.

"Let's go sit," Bear said. "I'm pretty sure those women have a video camera on this room, and they're not making a move until we do what they want." He grinned at Cactus and went to find a seat.

Cactus followed him, making sure there was room enough for Mitch and Willa before committing to sit with Bear and Don.

Bear was one-hundred percent right. The moment the last man sat down, the sound of female voices filled the hall behind them. They didn't appear though, and Cactus turned to watch.

Mister got up and fiddled with the camera at the back of the room. He signaled to it and then Judge and Ward, who started to play the wedding march. They definitely had more details than Cactus did, and he found himself relaxed and fine that he could just enjoy this ceremony.

Mother appeared, and he got to his feet. Everyone else did too, and she beamed with joy as she walked between the tables to the altar. She touched her finger to the top of it, and then the front, and when she moved, Cactus could see a blue smudge where she'd put her fingerprint.

Sammy appeared next, and she did the same thing. Willa appeared next, and Cactus sucked in a breath. She wore a light blue dress that wafted around her knees like fairies had enchanted it to never stop moving.

After she managed to lumber all the way to the altar, she turned and sought him out. The most beautiful smile filled her face, and he stepped out to cock his elbow to receive her. "You okay?" he asked, seeing the smile for what it was—a mask for the pain she experienced.

"I'm ready to have this baby," she whispered.

Cactus pressed his lips to her forehead, because he could only imagine. With her injuries from a car accident a few years ago, her pregnancy hadn't been the easiest. She walked with a limp and sometimes a cane as it was. Adding all the extra weight and bulkiness hadn't been a picnic for her.

One after the other, all of the women walked to the altar and put their painted fingerprint on it. They all wore dresses, and Cactus found such a thing unfair. He looked like a fool next to Willa, but he supposed every man was in the same boat as he was.

Finally, Charlie appeared, and Cactus found it so strange that Preacher wasn't standing at the altar waiting for her.

Then he stepped to her side, and they linked hands, the

two of them gazing at each other like other people didn't exist. The love Cactus felt between them warmed his heart, and he smiled as they passed him.

They too added their prints to the altar, and Cactus found he wanted to do the same.

The music stopped, and Judge rose from the piano bench. He took his spot behind the altar, and everyone sat down.

"Everyone should add their fingerprint to the altar today," he said. "Charlie and Preacher are going to put it on the Kinder Ranch, and they want everyone's touch in their lives." He smiled out at the family gathered there, and then focused on Charlie and Preacher.

"Time to get married," he said, and Cactus squeezed Willa's hand. They'd done this only a year ago, and that wedding day was the best day of his life. Watching Charlie and Preacher recite their vows and pledge themselves to each other, Cactus knew this would be the best day of theirs too.

# Chapter Twenty-Four

"Don't you think we should get back to the wedding?" Dot whispered, though she had no desire to do so.

Ward touched his lips to hers again, and Dot didn't want to do anything but kiss him. He'd stolen her away after the ceremony, after the luncheon, and after the recorded music had started to play for the family dancing.

He claimed not to be a great dancer, but Dot thought the man had some pretty good moves.

"How's your blood sugar?" he murmured. "We ate."

Irritation flashed through Dot. She knew she'd eaten. Because of her embarrassing—*super* embarrassing— encounters with low and then high blood sugar, she'd slept most of yesterday. Ward had too. His family members had come to check on them several times, and when she'd finally gotten up to eat, she found a chart of her blood sugar levels taken every fifteen minutes on the nightstand.

She was happy she'd been so well taken care of. She was.

She simply didn't want to make an accounting of her health to Ward every other second. She already had to go to the doctor and get a medical examiner's certification that she was safe to drive Brutus. She was glad the law had been changed a few years ago to make such an accommodation, or her diabetes would prevent her from doing her deliveries.

"I'm fine," she said, pressing one hand against his chest. She'd spoken with Tyson, and she knew the great lengths several people had gone to in order to help her. She'd already called Brady to thank him, and she'd spoken to Ida last night too.

She needed to write a card for Jeremiah Walker and Wade Rhinehart, both of whom had been awakened in the middle of the night to help.

Ward searched her face, but Dot couldn't meet his eye. "I really think we should get back to the wedding."

He said nothing, which only made Dot more uncomfortable. She'd borrowed the dress she currently wore from Arizona, who was close to her height. Ward's cousin had also brought down a few pairs of fresh jeans and shirts for Dot, apologizing all the while that she hadn't thought of it before.

Holly Ann had once again postponed the family dinner because of Dot, but it had worked out to serve it for the wedding. Dot had never eaten such good food, and she wished she hadn't been so out of it yesterday, so she could've participated in the planning of today's impromptu wedding.

Apparently, all of the other ranch wives had congregated at Holly Ann's the moment they'd found out the event was happening. They'd planned everything, and Ward, Judge, and Mister had put together the altar as a nod to Preacher, who liked to carve things.

All of these Glovers were really good at something, and Dot's own inadequacy spiraled through her. She'd been thinking a lot the past couple of days—since Ward's serenade and confession that he wrote and sold country music songs for some of the biggest artists.

What was she good at?

Did she have any special skills at all?

Shoveling gravel and picking out a paint color could hardly be considered a skill someone else would envy.

Dot didn't need to be envied. She simply wondered if she'd fit in here at Shiloh Ridge.

She stepped back into the dance hall where the rest of Ward's family was still congregated. One of Preacher and Charlie's first dates had been him teaching her how to dance so she'd attend his mother's wedding with him, and they'd wanted a big dance party at their wedding.

Charlie wore Montana's wedding dress, and Aurora— Montana's daughter—had taken it in for her. The girl was good with a sewing machine, and even the in-laws had special skills to set them apart from everyone else in the world.

Ward's hand landed on her hip, and it took all of Dot's

willpower not to lean into the sexy touch. "Are you upset with me?" he murmured, those sugar-coated lips so close to her ear.

"Yes," she said. Might as well get it out and over with. Perhaps then the man would know that he couldn't mother her to death.

"Why? What did I do?"

She turned toward him, letting his hand slide along her side. "Remember how you said you don't mind fussing over the people you care about?"

"Of course." His blue eyes blazed with an energy Dot had only felt a couple of times in her life. Once, when she'd employed her courage and walked away from the business she'd poured her heart and soul into in New Mexico. Again when she'd managed to pay off the small business loan she'd gotten to start From the Ground Up here in Three Rivers.

Again the first time Ward kissed her in the parking lot at Small Plates. Had that really only been six days ago? That couldn't be right. It felt like she'd known him forever. They'd been together for months and months.

"Has it occurred to you that I don't want to be fussed over? I've been diabetic for thirty years. I know how to handle it."

"Do you?" he challenged. "Because we swung from low to high to into a serious diabetic coma all in a single day."

"*We* didn't do anything," she said fiercely, edging her face closer to his. "I'm sorry I upset your life and caused you worry. Things happen. I didn't know I was going to be stranded up at this blasted ranch for days and days. I don't pack weeks' worth of insulin with me."

Ward glanced past her, and Dot didn't want to make a scene at this wedding any more than he did. "I know that." His voice barely left his mouth, but it vibrated through his chest.

Dot took a deep breath. "I just...you irritate me sometimes. I don't need you to ask me how I'm feeling. I *know* how I'm feeling, and I know what to do about it."

"I understand that. I—"

"You don't," she said. "You're mothering me. No, *smothering* me. You're not my nurse. I don't want you to be my nurse."

Ward fell back a step, his hand falling from her hip. "What do you want, Dot?"

She'd already told him that. Maybe not everything had been said in words. But plenty had been said. She'd told his sister that she was falling in love with him, for crying out loud. When Ida had told her that, Dot hadn't believed it.

But Ida had called and insisted, and Dot's blurred, sugar-high memories had rushed forward. She couldn't be responsible for what she'd said while nearly in a diabetic coma. Could she?

It didn't matter if she could or not. She hadn't lied, because she *was* falling in love with Ward Glover.

*He sure does know it too*, she thought.

She suddenly couldn't breathe. "I'm gonna go for a walk." She turned away from him and headed for the brides' room where she'd changed earlier.

"Dot," he said after her, but she kept going. She arrived

in the room, the only one there, and stepped out the stupid dress. She hated dresses, and tears formed in her eyes. All of the other ranch wives seemed to adore dresses. Dot would never fit in with them.

She sniffled as she stepped back into Arizona's jeans. The fact that she didn't have her own made her first tears fall. She didn't have anything here she needed, and she just wanted to go home.

"Can't I just go home right now, please?" she whimpered. She pulled the ponytail holders out of her hair and shook her head to get the curls to fall. She tugged on her work boots, the steel in the toes so heavy. She definitely wouldn't be able to walk very far.

*Just get back to Brutus*, she told herself. She shrugged into her jacket and left the room. Ward hadn't moved, and their eyes met across the distance.

"I'm fine, Ward," she said. "Really." She swiped at her eyes, a smudge of darkness coming off on her fingers.

"You're not fine," he said. "And you're a bad liar."

"Thanks so much," she said sarcastically, brushing by him. Honestly, the man must enjoy rubbing salt in wounds.

She left the barn only to be greeted by crisp, winter air. She turned north, because she couldn't really walk that far. Physical activity caused blood sugar to drop, and Dot already felt a little weak. She reached into her jacket pocket and pulled out three hard candies.

With them all in her mouth, she made the quick trek from the barn to Bull House. She gathered George, her faithful hound dog that hadn't left her side for longer than five minutes during her blood sugar episodes, and together, they climbed up into Brutus.

Dot maneuvered over the seat to the back bench seat barely wide enough for a human to sit on. She normally just threw her trash back here, and she'd clean it out every once in a while. She hadn't done that for a few weeks at least, so she had wadded up orders, soda bottles, empty granola bar wrappers, and even a sweatshirt she'd forgotten about.

She shook that out and rolled it up, making a little pillow for herself. She stretched out on her side and pulled her truck blanket over her body. She didn't need to start Brutus up to keep warm. The sun shone on Texas today, and the little cab held plenty of heat for right now.

Dot stared at the back of the seat in front of her. "Why does he make me so crazy?" she whispered.

Up front, George huffed and shifted, finally circling to sit down.

"Can a relationship between us really work when we irritate the other so badly?"

The hound dog had no answers for her, and it sure seemed like the Lord was going to let Dot figure this one out on her own. Her head swam, and Dot tasted the butterscotch in her mouth.

She'd already eaten lunch. She'd dosed with insulin before that. Ward had skipped the dancing and gone straight to the kissing. Maybe that had burned through some blood sugar. She'd walked over here, and it had probably taken her fifteen minutes.

She sighed as she sat up and leaned over the seat—and

George—to the glove box. She pulled out her glucose strips and tested her blood.

It was on the low end of normal, and Dot performed another bout of acrobatics to get a granola bar from the glove box. She ripped into that, forced herself to eat the whole thing though it tasted like cardboard, and then lay back down again.

She closed her eyes and let her mind drift, her desire to go home increasing with every breath she took. Her skin felt like a prison, and internally, she screamed. No one heard her, not even George.

Time passed, but Dot didn't know how much. The cab of the truck stayed plenty warm, and she heard other trucks grumbling by hers on the road. The Glovers could get around their ranch easily, as it was just the new cliffs to the east that prevented them from accessing the dirt lane that led to the highway—and her freedom.

Eventually, Dot sat up. Foolishness filled her, and she met George's eye. He panted in the front seat, his deep, brown eyes begging her to let him out. He loved to run and romp on the ranch, and she climbed over the seat and opened the door for him.

"There you go," she said, glancing around. He trotted over to the patch of grass in front of Bull House and took care of his business. Dot hated how petulant and childish she'd acted, and she pulled her phone from her pocket to send a message to Ward.

*I'm sure you need help somewhere on the ranch. Where would you like me?* Dot faced the sun and closed her eyes, letting the light warm her skin as the breeze tried to cool it. She suspected Ward would call, as the man tended to get right to the heart of the matter instead of dancing around and sending texts.

Sure enough, her phone rang within the minute, and the jazzy pop tune she'd set for Ward's ringtone met her ears.

"Hey," she said after swiping on the call. "Where are you?"

"The stables," he said. "We're settin' all the horses out for the afternoon. They'll like it, and we'll be able to get everything cleaned out."

"I can do that," she said, already stepping in the direction of the stables. They weren't hard to find, even if Ward hadn't given her a tour of the ranch the day after Christmas.

"We're letting out the last of them now," he said.

"I can shovel out stalls."

"I'm not going to say no," he said, the smile carrying in his in tone. He cleared his throat. "I promise I won't fuss over you."

Dot sighed into the sky. "It's fine. I just...."

"Got irritated," he said. "Which is fine too. Heaven knows there are things that irritate me."

"Yeah." She couldn't help wondering if they should be together if they bothered each other so much.

"I apologize," he said. "I may or may not be a little freaked out at the idea of watching you slip into a coma again."

Dot had never apologized for her health, because it really wasn't her fault. She'd brought the supplies she needed for a couple of days, but she couldn't plan for everything. She thought about what Ward had seen—thought about herself throwing up and crying in the bathroom through his eyes. What did he see when he looked at her?

"I'm sorry I got upset with you for being concerned," she said, swallowing her pride. It didn't taste as bad as she'd thought it might. "I'm sorry you had to watch me go into a coma—which I didn't really go into, by the way. I maintained consciousness the whole time."

"I know," he said quietly.

"Still, that can't have been easy for you, and I'm sorry. I'm going to write thank you cards to everyone who helped, and I'll make sure you get one."

He chuckled softly, and Dot watched him exit the stable up ahead. He really was stunning, especially when he stepped into the sunlight and raised his hand as if she needed help locating him. Ward stood over six feet tall, and his clothes seemed tailor-made for his broad shoulders and big biceps.

"I don't need you to write me a card," he said.

"No?" Dot grinned at him as they walked toward each other. She lowered the phone. "What do you need me to do?"

Ward hung up and shoved his phone in his back pocket, all while steadily striding toward her. He took her into his arms and held her against his chest. She listened to his pulse beat powerfully through his chest, and she tilted her head back.

"Kiss me," he said, grinning wickedly at her. "That's all I need."

"Hmm." Dot cocked her head as if truly considering it. "All right, I guess."

He laughed, his hands moving to cradle her face in both palms. He kissed her, and Dot did exactly what he'd asked her to do—she kissed him back.

# Chapter Twenty-Five

W ard stood on the edge of the cliff, the morning sunlight shining right into his face no matter how low he moved his cowboy hat. He normally liked this morning winter sun, but that was when he sat on the back porch and plucked chords while sipping his coffee.

Today, he felt like he could dive off this cliff just to get off the ranch. Thirty feet down, two Three Rivers city trucks came to a stop, and men started piling out of them.

"Ho there!" one of them yelled, donning his bright yellow hardhat. "I'm Huey Howard."

"Welcome to Shiloh Ridge Ranch," Bear called, and a glance to his left showed Ward that Bear actually wore a smile on his face. Shocking for this time of morning, and in the state they still found themselves in.

Stuck.

Stranded.

Isolated.

"Looks like y'all have a problem," someone else yelled, and Ward wanted to start throwing rocks. Of course they had a problem. The ranch leadership had met again last night, and Ranger had talked of driving out past the Edge, out past the Cornish Plantation, and up into Amarillo to get groceries. They had plenty of food for now, but if the roads would take a while to fix...all solutions had been outlined on the white board in the conference room in Ranger's suite.

One of those solutions had three little letters that had made Bear's eyebrows fold down.

ATVs.

Ranger owned two of them, and he'd fired them up this morning to see if they were still running. When they sat for a while, the batteries could go dead and the tires could get misshapen. But he'd revved the engines and zipped from Bull House to the Ranch House and back just fine.

They didn't need a very wide road to get off the ranch on an ATV. Ward had suggested the all-terrain vehicles, and he'd said if they could put a couple of trucks where the city ones now sat, anyone could get off the ranch, leave the ATV and take the truck to town, do what they needed to do, and come on back.

It might take three or four trips to get the groceries from the trucks back up to the ranch using the ATV, but they wouldn't be stranded. They could get Aunt Lois and Uncle Donald back to their own house. They could return Mother to the assisted living facility where she normally lived.

Dot could go home and get back to her regular life.

Ward's frown deepened at the very thought of that. He didn't want the gorgeous woman to leave him alone up at Shiloh Ridge, and he'd laid awake last night for at least an hour, despite his exhaustion.

She'd told Ida she was falling in love with him. He'd been present as she said it. Dot didn't remember saying it, and Ward wondered if the truth had come out when her guard was down.

He knew he was falling in love with her, and his blood sugar wasn't currently off the charts. Ward had always known how he felt about the woman he was seeing, and Dot ticked all his boxes. She lit him on fire, and he almost hoped it would be weeks before the road could be fixed.

*It will be*, he thought. But they needed a solution to get on and off the ranch sooner than that. He didn't want to cold call her brother in the middle of the night again, that was for dang sure.

Bear and Huey had been talking, and Ward noted that the conversation was about getting a couple of trucks down now, and then using the ATVs, as Ward had outlined the previous evening. Ranger's chest had puffed to twice its size during last night's meeting, and Ward glanced at him to find him nodding.

He'd wanted to use the ATVs around the ranch, but Bear had steadfastly refused. Ward had vetoed the idea a couple of times himself, but he could admit having a smaller method of transportation was going to be dead useful in this case.

"Okay," Bear yelled down. "So you guys will assess the

debris and start to move it? We'll hang tight and see how it goes."

"Yep," Huey called. His men had been poking around the gravel, dirt, and rocks during the conversation. "We've got an excavator coming up too. Louis just called for it."

"Could be a while," another man said. "But we should be able to clear a lane for y'all today."

"Have you guys spoken to a landscape architect?" Huey asked. "They'll help you design a plan to get the roads back in permanently."

"Not yet," Bear said. "I don't even know who to call for that."

"Best in town is Dorothy Crockett at From the Ground Up," Huey said. "I can get you her number. She's real busy all the time, but if you explained—"

"We know Dot," Ranger said, his eyes landing on Ward. "We'll talk to her."

"She's a landscape architect?" Bear asked, not bothering to try to throw his voice down to the men below. "I didn't know that."

"Makes two of us," Ward mumbled, his face heating with embarrassment. He always fell in love too fast. Heck, he didn't even know the big things about Dot. "I'll go get her. Maybe she can start right now."

He walked away from his brother and cousins, leaving Preacher, Ranger, and Bear behind to continue to deal with the city. Inside the house, George trotted over to him for a pat, but Ward barely looked at the dog.

"Dot," he said, though he didn't see her. "You still here?"

"Brushing my teeth," she said, though around the toothbrush it barely sounded like that. Ward waited at the end of the hall while Dot finished, and she smiled at him as she left the bathroom. "What's up?"

"You're a landscape architect?"

Dot's step slowed. "No," she said. "Who told you that?" She wore confusion in her expression, and she'd left her hair down. Ward folded his arms so he wouldn't rake his fingers through that hair as he kissed her. There was no time for kissing this morning.

"Huey Howard," he said. "Said you're the best in town, and we need someone to analyze our problem and help us get permanent roads in again."

"I can help with the permanent roads," she said, dodging into her bedroom and coming back out a moment later with her phone in her hand. "I've got an app that measures some things, and back at the office, I have software that helps me make the determinations for the grade, the material needed for that specific incline, and if we'll need to build up around the road to do it."

"So you do know how to design roads."

"I mean, yes?" She made it sound like she was guessing. "I've done it before, just not on this magnitude." She gestured in the general direction of the front of the house. "We did your roads out to the Edge, right? It's just like that, except it's on a slope."

Ward wasn't sure why his annoyance sang so loudly. "I wish you'd told me that. We could've been working on it the past few days."

"Not without the software," she said. "And taking

measurements is easy. I just need to be down on the road...."

"Not so easy," he said.

"With the ATVs, it will be," she said. "You could take one down and over the debris on the main road."

"You could?"

"Yep," Dot said. "I'll do it if you want." She stepped past him, putting one palm flat against his chest as she did. "I didn't keep anything from you, Ward."

"Okay," he said, turning to follow her. She collected her boots from the mudroom and put them on.

"Let's go." She grabbed her jacket and headed out the front door. Ranger and Bear stood near the pair of ATVs, which Ranger had not put away in the garage that now sat between the homestead and Bull House. "Morning, boys," Dot called.

Ranger and Bear turned toward them, both of them calling good morning back to her.

"I hear you need some help redesigning your roads." She stopped in front of them, and Bear started talking. Preacher came out of the garage, brushing his hands off. He still limped a little bit, but if Ward didn't watch for the hitch in his left side, he might not have seen it.

"It measures with a laser," Dot said, and Ward liked listening to her talk. He'd always liked working with Dot, because she was the best at what she did. "I just need to be down there where they are."

"I can get you down there," Ranger said. "We'll take an ATV and show Bear they're not useless." He grinned at

Bear like he'd said the funniest thing in the world, but Bear only rolled his eyes.

"I never said they were useless. I said I didn't want them on the ranch."

"I bet you're glad we have them now, aren't you?" Ranger clapped his hand on Bear's back as he moved over to one of the ATVs. "Let's go, Dot. You're with me." He climbed on, and Dot met Ward's eyes for a moment.

He leaned toward her and kissed her quick, right there in front of everyone. "Go be awesome," he said, and she grinned at him with all the power of gravity before practically hopping onto the back of the ATV with his older brother.

Ranger eased them out onto the road and down past Brutus. Ward watched them until they went around the curve that led to the Ranch House.

"Guess we'll see them down below," Preacher said, his eyes glued to Ward.

"Yep," Ward said. "Let's go see if that ATV can get past the debris."

"They've already moved a ton of it," Bear said, starting toward the back yard again. "Come see."

Everyone had come out to see, and Ward found Mister, Judge, Oakley, Sammy, Bishop, Ace, and Duke standing in the back yard of Bull House. He, Bear, and Preacher stepped into the group, and Ward asked, "Where are the kids?"

"Etta's feeding them," Sammy said.

Ward noted that all of the pregnant women were absent, and as he looked down toward the debris, he hoped they were all okay. The road crew Huey had brought had made great progress already, and the excavator had already arrived. It moved earth by the clawful, and Ward watched in amazement as a big chunk of dirt and gravel got moved from one side of the road to the other.

It crashed down the hill, but that didn't matter. They just needed the earth on the ranch-side of the road to be stable.

"We should put a retaining wall in," Ward said.

"Did Dot say that?" Bear asked, leaning out to see past the people who stood between him and Ward.

"No," Ward said. "Just seems like common sense to me."

"Yeah, probably," Preacher said.

"How are things?" Cactus asked as he strode to Ward's side. "I had a hard time getting out of the house this morning. Mitch isn't feeling well."

"Uh oh," Ward said. "How's Willa?"

"She's not feelin' too well either." Cactus wore a growl on his face as he looked below. "Looks good here though."

"Better," Bear admitted.

The buzzing whine of the ATV filled the air, and Ward looked north to find Ranger and Dot approaching.

"You know, Jeremiah has that crane," Preacher said. "He could lift the trucks down if we can't get them past the debris."

"They're gonna get that rock out of the way," Bear said. "Then it won't be a problem."

"Just something to consider if they don't," Preacher said.

Ranger brought the ATV to a stop, because there wasn't quite enough room to get by. The excavator took several more bites from the earth, and then the operator started to move it.

"Is there anything down below that we should worry about?" Huey called up.

"What do you mean?" Bear asked.

"We're gonna push this boulder over the side." He gestured to the main object blocking their escape from the ranch, as if they couldn't see it. "Is it going to hit anything?"

Bear looked at Ward, and Ward looked at Bear. "The Kinder Ranch is on the other side of the road," Ward said. "I can't imagine there's anything there."

"How far will it roll?" Preacher asked.

"I guess we're gonna find out," Bear said, almost under his breath, almost as a growl. "If I'd have known that's all they were gonna do, we could've been down there digging and pushing a rock over a hill."

Ward didn't think the men on this ranch could do the work of an excavator and road engineers, but he wasn't in the mood to deal with Bear's grizzly persona. He kept his mouth shut as Bear said there was nothing in the way of that rock.

The excavator operator brought in the arm of the machine, the claw buckled under as if he was putting it away for the day. Instead of shutting it down and jumping from the cab, he extended the arm straight out until it met the rock.

"All clear!" he called.

"Clear," several men shouted back. The machine started to hum and growl and groan. It clanked as it adjusted against the rock. A hiss sounded as the weights on the excavator dug in.

Ward started to pray. *Please, Lord, move that rock. Thou can move mountains and send down rain. Please move that rock.*

"Faith can move mountains," Preacher whispered, and Ward closed his eyes, putting every ounce of faith he had in God, and in that excavator.

He opened his eyes when Bear said, "Dear Lord, it's moving."

As if by magic and sheer will, the boulder moved. It moved and moved and moved, and the excavator followed it until gravity took over and it rolled down the hill.

Great, terrible noise rose from the earth as it did, and Ward was reminded of the feeling he'd had during the landslide. Fear, accompanied by something that felt otherworldly, coursed through him.

Cheers rose up from the ground below, and Ward joined his voice to everyone else's despite the fact that without that boulder in the way, Dot didn't have to stay.

# Chapter Twenty-Six

Ranger Glover loved his ATVs, he wasn't going to lie about that. He and Oakley had taken them out into the hills all summer, and it had been the perfect hour-long escape he needed from real life. They could get away from the crowd of family on the ranch. They could leave their baby behind and just be a couple again.

He loved the ATVs, and he loved his wife, and he loved his ranch. He really did. Sometimes, he just needed an escape from some of it, and the ATVs had provided that. Right now, they were also going to provide the way off the ranch for everyone in the family, and he couldn't help wondering if the Lord had foreseen this landslide and prompted Ranger to buy the ATVs years ago so Shiloh Ridge would have them.

"Your turn," he said to Preacher, and his cousin climbed on the back of the ATV to go with him down to the debris site. Ward drove the other ATV, and Dot had loaded up every available shovel on the ranch in the back of her big dump truck.

Bear and Bishop had each taken a truck full of men and water and granola bars down, and once Ranger got everyone else down there, he'd get to work alongside everyone else.

They were really just clearing away the debris off the lower road for right now. Huey and his crew had deemed it safe and useable, and they'd taken their excavator and themselves and left thirty minutes ago. Since Shiloh Ridge had plenty of manpower, their help was needed somewhere else for now.

When Ranger and Preacher arrived at the debris site, Ranger wasn't surprised to find several more trucks had arrived. Squire Ackerman stood at the tailgate of his truck, handing a shovel to his sixteen-year-old son, Finn.

He gave one to Pete Marshall and then Brit Bellamore, who took the tool and then stepped back over to his truck. "I've got sandwiches," he bellowed to the men, and Bear went to talk to him.

Ranger's heart filled with love for the other ranchers in Three Rivers. It was a solid ninety-minute drive to Three Rivers from Shiloh Ridge, and Squire certainly had plenty of work to do around his own ranch after a storm like they'd had over Christmas.

With a smile on his face and a song in his heart, Ranger went to greet everyone. "You didn't have to come," he said to Squire as he took a shovel. "But we sure appreciate it."

"If it were me, you'd be there," Squire said with a smile.

"Brit's the one with food. I just raided our toolshed and brought shovels."

*And men*, Ranger thought. And friendship. That was needed most of all sometimes.

"Put me to work, Ranger," Jeremiah Walker said. "I brought Liam, Tripp, Rhett, Skyler, and Micah."

Ranger gazed at the row of tall, strong Walker brothers.

"Wyatt got out of working because of his back." Rhett grinned at Ranger and shook his hand. "He's stopping at the bakery and Wilde and Organic, though. We gave him a shopping list."

"I bet he loved that," Ranger said with a chuckle.

All of the Walkers laughed too, and Skyler said, "I think Wyatt does like to shop, actually," which only set them off again.

"My dad's here," Duke said as yet another truck arrived. Wade Rhinehart got out, along with his two younger sons. They all had shovels too, and Duke went to greet them and put them to work.

With that many hands and that many shovels, Ranger seemed to barely move much earth before the job was close to done.

"Let's make a lot over here," Bear said from the other side of the lane. "And anyone who can move those rocks, let's get those lined up along the edge there, just in case more dirt starts to slide down."

Ranger was happy to be second-in-command during times like this, and he tossed his shovel back into the bed of Squire's pick-up before going with Mister to help move rocks. He bent, his back telling him to be careful.

"Got it?" Mister asked, and their eyes met.

"Got it," Ranger confirmed, his fingers getting as far under the rock as he could. They lifted together, both of them groaning to get the big rock up. With stilted, small steps, the two of them moved the rock from its undesignated spot in the middle of the road to the side.

Ranger kind of threw it and dropped it at the same time, and it very nearly landed where he thought it should. Mister, a much younger man than Ranger, bent and managed to move it right along the edge of the road, where wild grasses and wildflowers had once grown.

"Perfect," Ranger said, smiling at Mister. His cousin dusted his gloved hands together and grinned back.

"Yeah," he said. "This is just perfect."

"We'll be able to get off the ranch," Ranger said, locating Dot and watching her as she shone her laser up the hill and then down the road. Ward and Preacher moved a rock, and Ranger started looking for another one. The sooner they got this job done, the sooner he could eat lunch and then return to the homestead and his family.

He walked over to another rock, but when he turned back to see where Mister had gone, he found the man hadn't followed him. He stood stock still back beside the first mini-boulder they'd moved, glaring over at something near all the parked trucks on the lane.

Ranger turned to follow his gaze, surprised to see Liberty Bellamore standing there with her sister, Mildred. They'd brought hot coffee and hot chocolate, and Mister looked plenty perturbed about it.

Wyatt Walker rolled up just then too, and with his

larger-than-life personality, the work stalled for several minutes while he started handing out doughnuts and cream cheese Danishes. Along with the hot drinks and sandwiches the Bellamores had brought, Ranger thought they were having a regular party.

He stood next to Ward and Preacher, half a doughnut in one hand and a cup of perfectly brewed coffee in the other. "What's with them?" He nodded toward Mister and Liberty, who'd separated themselves from the group. Really, it looked like Mister had taken Liberty's elbow and dragged her away. She was clearly trying to get her arm out of his grip, and while Ranger watched, she wrenched her arm away from Mister.

"He's doing it all wrong," Preacher muttered.

"He's not going to convince her he likes her by doing that," Ward said.

"He likes her?" Ranger asked, surprised by that too. He sure wasn't acting like it, as Mister's fingers curled into fists and he said something with a dark, swirling storm cloud on his face.

Liberty shook her head and turned away from him. She marched back to the truck she and Mildred were serving drinks from, and she wore her own brand of darkness on her face. She said something to her sister, and Ranger lifted his coffee to his lips as Mister looked at the three of them standing there watching him.

"Incoming," Preacher said under his breath as Mister took the first step toward them. "This is you, Ward."

"Me?" Ward asked right out loud. "What do I know about this?"

"Everything Judge and I have said falls on deaf ears," Preacher said. "Ranger? Someone besides me." He barely got the last word out before Mister arrived. "Hey, Mister. Did you get some coffee?" Preacher sounded so upbeat that Ranger could barely contain his laughter. He wouldn't want someone laughing at his dating mishaps, that was for sure.

"No," Mister growled. "That woman is impossible." He turned more toward Preacher and less toward Ranger, but he didn't bother lowering his voice as he asked, "You're sure she asked about me last year?"

Preacher nodded, clearly not going to say another word. Ranger hadn't even known Mister liked Liberty Bellamore. They'd been friends for years, and Mister had never been interested before. In fact, Bear made it sound like Mister had asked Liberty to set him up with some of her friends in the past.

Ward drew in a deep breath and blew it all out, as if preparing to say something deep and wise. "I need to go talk to Dot," he said, and with that, he walked away.

"Coward," Preacher called after him as Mister took the spot Ward had occupied in the middle of the threesome.

"What am I going to do about her?" Mister asked.

"Any ideas, Range?" Preacher asked.

"Fill me in," Ranger said. "I'll see what I can come up with." Hey, it was better than breaking his back trying to move heavy rocks, and he listened as Mister started the story of his and Liberty's rocky love story.

# Chapter Twenty-Seven

✦

"Come on, Georgie," Dot said to the hound dog. "Up and in." That was the phrase she used to get George into a vehicle, and he jumped up into the dump truck. She closed the passenger door and turned back to Ward. "I guess this is the end of our little staycation together."

He smiled at her and opened his arms. Dot stepped straight into them, inhaling the strong, clean, crisp pine scent of his skin.

"I can't wait to use my own shower," she said. "Wear my own clothes."

"I bet," he said, holding her tight.

Dot already missed him, but she didn't know how to say so. She did want to go home. She'd been here since Christmas Eve, and tomorrow was New Year's Eve. She and Ward hadn't talked about what would happen now. He hadn't asked her on another date. He hadn't even said he'd call her later.

"Your crew needs you too," he said.

"Yeah." She sighed as she stepped out of his embrace. "I'm headed home to shower, change, and eat, and then I have to get straight over to From the Ground Up. Apparently, we've rescheduled a ton of deliveries because Brutus has been calling in sick." She put a smile on her face, because she didn't want to act like a needy female in front of Ward Glover.

"You better go then," he said, reaching for her again. "I'll talk to you later, okay?" He slid one arm around her as she agreed, and she tipped up to kiss him goodbye.

He kissed her, and Dot felt something different in the stroke of his mouth against hers. She wasn't sure what it was, because she'd kissed Ward a lot in the past several days. This felt more...intense, in a way Dot wasn't sure she'd ever felt from a man before, and all she could do was hold on and enjoy the ride.

He finally broke the kiss, his breathing coming quickly. He said nothing, and Dot almost wanted him to say he'd miss her. Or he wished she didn't have to go.

She missed him already, and she wished she didn't have to go. In the truck, George barked, and that got Dot to move. "I'll call you tonight," she said.

"Okay."

Dot walked around the front of the truck and got behind the wheel. Brutus started right up, his engine loud and filled with grumbles in the beginning. The main road off the ranch wasn't fixed yet, and Dot continued in the direction she was facing and went around the corner before she relaxed.

Ward certainly couldn't see her anymore, and she wasn't sure how she was feeling. She'd never felt like this before, and she frowned at herself.

Her truck was quite a bit bigger than the regular pickups that had been using the makeshift road in the yard of the Ranch House, but she fit just fine. Brutus stumbled over the spot where the yard met the road, but she evened him out easily once they were on the real dirt lane.

"Almost there," she told the truck and George. And herself. Back around the bend, and then another straightaway that usually led to the road that went up to the ranch and down the highway.

They'd gotten a row of rocks lined up along both sides of the road where the landslide had washed it out, and Bear had started a parking lot in anticipation of needing to use an ATV to get off the ranch to a regular vehicle. But when he'd seen the progress, and that full-sized vehicles could make it down past the Ranch House and then this road, they'd abandoned the idea of a lot.

To be safe, the Glovers had left two pickup trucks in the partial lot anyway, and Dot glanced at them as she made the left-hand turn and headed down the lane to the highway. A sigh of relief filled her lungs, and the drive to her house seemed to pass in the blink of an eye.

She fed George real dog food and got him fresh water. She checked her blood sugar, and it was starting to fall. She put a pot of coffee on for herself and she put a toaster waffle in to warm and crisp. She could have the carbs with her sugar where it was, and she even put butter on it and dipped it into some sugar-free syrup.

Once she'd eaten and made sure George was happy, she stepped out of the clothes she'd been wearing for so long, immediately wanting to burn them. Instead, she put them straight into the washing machine before she padded into her master bathroom and got in the rainfall shower.

"Ah, yes," she said, another sigh passing through her as she stood under the hot water in her own house. Everything was better in her own space, though she hadn't minded being at Ward's.

Bull House was spacious and wonderful, and it sat on a beautiful piece of land, with a great view of the town of Three Rivers to the northeast. She could only imagine what spring and summer would be like on that back porch, and as Dot showered, she found herself daydreaming about being there with Ward year-round.

Before she knew it, the water started to cool, and she hadn't even washed her hair yet. She quickly got the job done and stepped out of the shower. Wrapped in her own towels, she brushed her teeth, moisturized her skin, and headed into the bedroom to get dressed.

Her coffee waited for her in the kitchen, and Dot poured a familiar tumbler with her favorite drink.

She wasn't sure what she'd find at From the Ground Up, but everything looked so...normal. The wind clearly hadn't blown down here, because none of the trees even bent over. The piles of rock and bark had been raked back into order. Cars and trucks sat in perpendicular lines in front of the storefront.

Dot went around to the back, but Calvin and his truck

weren't there. Of course, she didn't really expect them to be. Since she'd taken a delivery up to Shiloh Ridge, they hadn't had her truck to do that for the past four days.

She could only imagine the state Wendy would be in, though she'd kept in touch with her staff via text and email. Wendy had told her they'd "make do," and she hadn't bothered Dot much.

Dot parked Brutus in his usual place and went toward the building. Inside, she expected streamers and people to jump out from behind racks of fertilizer. No one even looked in her direction, as Amber had a line three deep at the register, and Wendy wasn't at her desk at all.

She wasn't sure why her chest pinched, but it did. She waved to Amber as she went past, and the woman's face did light up. She'd come talk to Dot once the customers had been helped, and Dot passed into her office.

Once again, she expected something quite different than what stared back at her. As she stood just inside and recognized the desk had barely changed, she realized what had.

*She* had.

She'd changed since the last time she'd left From the Ground Up with the gravel Shiloh Ridge had ordered.

Ward had ordered it.

Dot drew in a breath and quickly stepped further into the office so she could close her door behind her. She just needed a minute to figure out what was happening. Who she was if she was no longer the Dorothy Crockett she'd always been.

*Not always*, she thought as she sat behind her desk. She'd changed when she'd left Albuquerque too. One of the great joys of life was that people could change. Even in the past week since she'd gotten back together with Ward, he'd changed. He didn't ask her about her blood sugar, and he didn't act quite so arrogant.

Dot looked at the invoices in front of her, something beating through her mind. *You love him. You're in love with him.*

She shook her head. "No," she whispered. She'd vowed once never to open that door inside her heart again. She knew what kind of bleeding could happen if she did. Just because she liked Ward and let him kiss her didn't mean she was in love with him.

To distract herself, Dot got to work. She examined the papers Wendy had left for her, and by the time someone knocked on her door, Dot was ready to leave the office and go do some deliveries.

"There you are," Wendy said with a warm smile when Dot opened the door. "How are you, dear?" She hugged Dot, who clung to her as if the older woman was Dot's mother.

"Good," she said, clearing the emotion from her voice. "What needs to go where?"

"Only one delivery this afternoon," Wendy said, handing her a paper. "I didn't know what time you'd be back or how you'd be feeling. We've rescheduled everyone else to next week."

"What about tomorrow?" Dot asked. "I can deliver on Saturday."

"It's New Year's Eve."

"I can do a half-day," Dot said. "That's three small deliveries."

"Everyone understood," Wendy said with a smile and a frown at the same time. "Are you okay, Dot?"

"Yes, I just...don't want anyone to be disappointed."

"They're fine." Wendy turned and went to her desk. "Just the one today, and remember, we're closing at two tomorrow."

"Mm." Dot looked out into the store. It had cleared out except for one customer, who stood with Amber back by the garden hoses. She didn't feel needed here, and yet, she was. She owned this company, and she wasn't going to let it go without a massive fight.

*Even for a life of wedded bliss with Ward Glover?*

She shoved against the thought, somewhat annoyed it had even entered her mind. She'd never needed a man to feel fulfilled and complete. At the same time, she now knew what waking up in the same house as Ward Glover felt like, and she couldn't stand the thought of going back to her empty, quiet house all alone.

So she made her delivery, parked Brutus back behind the building, and drove her sedan over to her parents' house. "Mom, Dad," she said as she entered their quiet house. "It's me."

"Dot's here," Dad said as if her mother wouldn't recognize the voice. They both appeared in the pass-through window that had a view into the kitchen.

"Oh, Dorothy, you're all right." Her mother hurried as

quickly as she could around the corner and hugged Dot tight.

"Yes, Mom," Dot said with a smile. "I'm fine."

"I guess you'll take a week's worth of insulin with you everywhere you go now." Her mother smiled at her and pushed her hair back off her face in such a matronly, loving gesture. Her happiness faded to concern the longer she looked at Dot. "What's wrong?"

"Nothing's wrong." Dot avoided her mother's eye as she stepped over to hug her father. "What have you guys been doing? Did you have some damage in the yard?"

"A little," Dad said. "Tyson came to help out. He's been working eighteen hours a day, helping everyone around town who needs it."

"I'm sure he has," Dot said, thinking of how he'd helped her by bringing insulin up to the ranch in the middle of the night. "He's a good guy like that." If she could keep the conversation topic off her, she might have a chance of escaping without telling them about Ward.

Unfortunately, her mom said, "Come, sit. Tell us about the ranch and Ward." She bustled off for the kitchen, adding, "I have lemon poppyseed bread. Phyllis dropped it off an hour ago."

Dot did love the lemon poppyseed bread from Mom's neighbor down the street. Phyllis Grandy made the bread to help her daughter pay for her competition dance classes, and every time the opportunity came up to order, both Dot and her mom usually did.

The bread carried a lovely vanilla icing, and Dot's mouth watered as she entered the kitchen too. "I need to check my blood sugar," she said, and another moment of clarity hit her. She'd never checked her sugar levels as much as she had in the past few days, but she found she wanted to. She needed to make sure she took care of herself...so Ward wouldn't ever have to see her in such a bad state again. She didn't want to scare him like that again.

She checked her levels, and she gave herself a shot of insulin before accepting the bread. Mom finished making dinner, and Dot stayed, telling them about the operation up at Shiloh Ridge. She could talk about the landslide and horses for hours, and she very nearly did that.

"I should go," she finally said with a yawn. "I'm exhausted." She hugged her mom and dad, holding them for several long seconds each. "I love you guys."

"We love you too, Dot," they chorused together, and Dot left their house. Upon returning to her own home, she found Tyson's police cruiser parked in her driveway. She pulled all the way into the garage and entered the house.

"I see you let yourself in," she said to her brother, who stood in the kitchen with a hunk of turkey in his hand and George sitting obediently at his feet.

"George was whining."

"Mm hm." Dot smiled at Tyson and hugged him hello. "Dad said you've been real busy. To what do I owe this great honor?" Dot continued into the living room and collapsed onto her couch. Her head ached, and she should probably check her blood sugar again, make sure it was right, and get to bed.

She'd promised Ward she'd call, but she honestly didn't know what she'd say to him. *Hey, everything is great down here.* No one had missed her. No one had really even needed her. From the Ground Up ran without her, and she honestly wasn't sure if that bothered her or made her proud.

Ward would only answer with silence.

*How's the ranch?*

He'd say, *Fine.*

More silence.

Dot shook her head at herself, paying more attention as Tyson too sighed heavily as he sat on the other end of the couch. "What's going on with you?"

"I have to tell you something, and you have to promise not to laugh."

Dot stared at him. They'd been close growing up, and he'd started conversations with those exact words before. Not for a long time, as they'd become adults decades ago.

"I can't promise anything," she said. "I did that one time you told me about this insane plan you had to breed snakes, remember? But I laughed, and then you got so mad and you wouldn't talk to me for a week." She grinned at him, glad when he returned the smile.

"This isn't about snakes."

"What's it about?" Dot watched her older brother squirm, and she had her answer. The only thing that made Tyson even bat an eyelash in fear was a woman. He faced criminals with grit. He could complete a high-speed chase without missing a single beat.

But put a pretty brunette in the room, and Tyson would duck and cover before he'd speak to her.

"What's her name?" Dot asked as gently as she could.

She even looked down at her phone, thinking perhaps Ward would call her. He had a phone, and he could use it too.

"Melanie," Tyson said with a sigh, and Dot knew she wasn't headed to bed any time soon.

# Chapter Twenty-Eight

J udge let the last note hang in the air, the music still moving through his soul. The echo of it lilted through the air, because the ceiling in True Blue, the family gathering barn at Shiloh Ridge Ranch, stretched for at least three stories.

He finally lifted his fingers off the keys the way his teacher from years past had taught him. "Thank you," he whispered into the silence. He had plenty of thanks to give for his ability to play the piano. Mother and Dad had driven him down through the hills to Three Rivers each and every week, sometimes at great sacrifice to them. Mother had seen and recognized his talent at an early age, and she wouldn't allow it to be squandered.

Judge had practiced hard to please her, as he still labored to do to this day. "Miss you, Dad," he said, finally standing. He worked his fingers to get the aches out of them, because he spent plenty of time using his hands around the ranch while he wasn't playing the piano.

Dad had always encouraged Judge to play for their family nights, after church on Sundays, and before every one of his concerts at school. He had to give the whole troop of Glovers a private concert, because not everyone could make it down to the auditorium to hear him play.

Judge had felt very loved and valued by his father, and he hated that he'd lost that too soon in his life. A wave of missing spiraled through him, making his breath catch somewhere behind his lungs. Dad had been gone for a long time now, and Judge wondered when the hole in his life would stop growing.

"I have a date with June in an hour," he said, looking up toward the ceiling his father and his uncle had built with their own hands. Bishop had led the restoration of the barn, but he'd kept the roof intact and employed the family motto of reuse, recycle, and repair on the shingles. He'd patched them and tarred them, and Judge could feel his father when he looked at the roof.

"It would be great if it would go well," he said. "It's been a long time since I've been on a date, and it especially has to go well because it's June." He'd been out with her before, but that was over two years ago now. Maybe three. Judge wasn't sure. Time didn't seem to register well without June, and he'd been holding onto the hope of this date with tight fingers for so very long.

His heart lifted as he walked toward the wide doorway that led to the door on the front of the barn. Mother and

Don should about be ready to go, and Judge wasn't surprised when he heard Mother calling him from outside.

"Coming," he said, hurrying to get to the door now. He found her and Don standing next to Judge's truck, a fond smile on her face.

"You've been working on that song." She beamed at him. "It sounds completely different than last week."

"I should hope so," Judge said. "I'd just started it last week." He hugged her and gave her a kiss on the cheek. "You guys ready to get back to your own place?"

"Yes," Don said with a smile. Judge shook his step-father's hand and gestured to the other side of the truck.

"Want me to help you, Mother? Should I get Cactus's sedan?"

"This is fine," Don said. "I'll help her."

They'd driven her SUV up to the ranch, but it currently sat in Bishop's driveway with a tree-sized dent in the roof. "Dent" wasn't the right word as the whole top had caved in. There was no reusing or repairing that. Oakley had said she'd sell them a very reasonable replacement, and Don had called the scrap yard to come get the SUV. He'd gotten a couple of thousand dollars for it, but now they needed a ride to town.

Judge was going that way, as were several others, now that the roads were fixed. June had been the first person Judge had called once the big boulder had been removed from the west ranch road. She'd readily agreed to dinner tonight, and Judge's nerves once again chittered at him not to mess up this second chance.

In reality, it was probably his third chance, and he was sure if he made one false move, he'd strike out. Game over.

He got behind the wheel of the car, and Mother must've been able to sense his anxiety, because she kept the conversation moving over trivial things all the way to Don's house on the southeast side of Three Rivers.

Once Judge had dropped them off, he hurried to Wilde & Organic, very near where they lived. The whole foods store had amazing organic produce, much of which they grew right here in Three Rivers and the surrounding areas on a family farm, but what Judge wanted waited in their floral department.

Several bouquets of red roses remained, but Judge didn't want something so formal. He wanted easy. Fun. Light. He didn't need to come across to June as too eager, though his whole body seemed made of eagerness.

He selected a pretty vase of purple, yellow, and white wildflowers that had a big violet bow tied around the glass. He paid for his purchase and headed back to the truck. He looked at himself in the rearview mirror, noting that his beard was neat and trimmed. He'd oiled it and taken time to get every errant hair off his neck.

Likewise, the hair on his head all stood in exactly the right place, and he told himself that he wasn't going gray; he simply had lighter brown hair than the rest of his brothers, even Bishop. Judge was probably the fairest of all the Glovers on both sides of the family. Just another way he stuck out—at least to him.

He'd been working for four decades to get someone in

the family to look his way, but he'd really calmed down in the past year. He had Preacher and Cactus, Ward and now Mister again too. Bear and Sammy made a point to come to the Ranch House for dinner, and Judge really appreciated them and loved their kids. No one had abandoned him just because they'd found women to love, though that was something he had to tell himself on a near-daily basis.

And now here he was, out on a date where he hoped he could convince Juniper Nichols to give the two of them a real chance to be a couple.

He licked his lips and reached for a mint. He sucked on that as he made the drive from the grocery store to June's house. She lived in one of the newer homes on the north side of town, having relocated just before he'd met her for the first time.

He could still feel how the world had narrowed to just her standing on his front porch. He'd stared for a good ten seconds before Mister had elbowed him out of the way and let the network technician into the Ranch House. Judge had sort of followed June around like a puppy after that, but somehow he'd managed to ask her out.

Sammy had helped with that, and he wouldn't be surprised if the woman was waiting up for him in the Ranch House when he returned tonight. At the very least, she'd show up before dawn with her newborn and Judge's favorite box of cereal.

He loved cold cereal more than life itself, and every time something happened to bruise his ego or worsen his mood, Sammy brought him a new box of breakfast food.

The last one had been miniature chocolate chip cookies, so he wasn't exactly sure if they counted as a healthy option for breakfast. He wasn't complaining, he knew that.

The only thing he wouldn't eat was raisin bran, and Sammy had been steadily moving through the entire cereal aisle to see if there was anything else he simply couldn't stomach.

The thoughts of Sammy's kindness caused a smile to come to his face, and Judge found himself in front of June's house only a few minutes later. "Here goes nothin,'" he said to himself, checking the mirror once more.

Still good.

*You've got this.* The thought flowed through his mind, and he could hear his father saying it in that voice that sounded halfway like Bear and halfway like Cactus. They'd gotten so much of their dad that it felt like there had been nothing left for Judge by the time he'd come along.

*Perpetually third*, he thought. The third son. Always third in the Christmas light show too.

*This is not going to be your third strike*, he told himself. *It's not.*

He got out of the truck and reached back in for the flowers. He gripped the glass, thinking it slick, and turned toward the house. June kept a pretty yard in the spring and summer. She loved putting bulbs in the ground in the fall and seeing what would poke its head through the dirt in March. She'd planted a few trees when she'd moved in, and Judge would like to see them in twenty years when they were fully mature.

Deep down, though, in twenty years' time, he wanted to be married to June for a good long while, the two of them living in the Ranch House at Shiloh Ridge. There were plenty of mature trees up there, and Judge could just see June in his life permanently.

*You're going to keep that to yourself,* he commanded himself silently. *No emotional outbursts tonight, John. None.*

He cursed his emotional side from time to time. Other times, he didn't mind that he felt things so keenly. Tonight, though, he needed to be one cool cowboy.

He stepped down the sidewalk at the same time another car turned into the driveway. He looked over his shoulder to see a little blue car pulling all the way into the garage. A moment later he heard a car door slam, and he expected to see June's daughter come out to greet him.

She didn't come, and Judge waited a few more seconds just to be sure he wouldn't be rude to her. Surely she'd seen him—no way she could've missed his giant pickup truck in the driveway.

Lucy Mae didn't come out front, and he assumed she'd gone into the house through the garage entrance. He continued toward the front door, and the moment his boot touched the top step, he knew something was wrong.

Yelling came from the house. Female yelling, and it sounded very much like Lucy Mae shouting something. Since only two people lived here, Judge could only assume she was yelling at her mother, and his heart did a full somersault in his chest. Maybe tonight wouldn't be a good night for a date.

He didn't hesitate as he reached for the doorbell. Lucy Mae had already seen him. The *ding-ding-doooong* sounded behind the door, and the yelling stopped. In its place, however, a round of barking started.

Judge smiled, because he loved June's dogs. He'd met them before, and they'd loved him. They'd loved him so much and obeyed him so well that it had actually annoyed June.

Footsteps sounded, and June yelled, "You be nice!" to her daughter. Or maybe the dogs. Either way, she opened the door a moment later, and her two rascals bolted straight at him.

"Hey guys," he said, laughing as they both tried to jump up on his legs. Holding the slippery vase and trying to pat two crazy, whining dogs didn't seem like a good idea, so he met June's eyes.

Boy, he could lose hours looking at her. "Hey, beautiful." He extended the flowers toward her. "Rescue these so I can get your beasts."

She smiled at him, but Judge saw how tired she was. His heart bled for her, but he wasn't going to offer her a shoulder to cry on. Not tonight. He was going to play the perfect gentleman, and see what her next step was. After all, when he'd tried to dictate the steps, she'd broken up with him.

She took the flowers with a "Thank you, Judge. They're beautiful," and he bent down to pat the toy poodle and the Bichon Frise. The little dogs kept jumping up, and he finally scooped them both into his arms, where they simultaneously tried to lick his face.

He laughed as he dodged their attempts and realized that June had disappeared from the doorway. The door still stood open, and Judge could only assume that meant he was supposed to enter the house.

So he did, hoping he wasn't walking into something he shouldn't.

# Chapter Twenty-Nine

Juniper Nichols gave her sixteen-year-old her best *you-better-watch-it* look as she re-entered the living area of the house. She carried the flowers, and she wished with everything inside her that her life were different.

*No, you don't*, she told herself, though she would love to be gazing down at these gorgeous flowers while still standing in the foyer of the house. Then she'd look up into Judge Glover's gorgeous face and smile all flirtatiously. She'd murmur something about how beautiful they were, and he'd tell her how stunningly beautiful she was just before he kissed her.

Wow, her fantasies about the tall, sexy cowboy picking her up for a dinner date had really gotten out of hand.

She banished the thoughts of kissing Judge to the far recesses of her mind and set the vase of flowers on the piano.

"Do you play?" Judge asked from behind her, and she

spun to face him. He'd taken off his cowboy hat and set it somewhere, and not a single hair on his head sat out of place. With his perfectly styled beard, his long legs in those blue jeans, the polished cowboy boots, and a dark brown leather jacket where a blue plain collar peeked through at the throat, he was cowboy perfection right there in her house.

"A little," June said, trying to keep her head on straight as her hormones buzzed. She'd been out with this man before. She'd kissed him before, for crying out loud. He'd kept calling her for her wireless services even after she'd broken things off with him. He'd been nothing but kind and polite when she'd gone up to his ranch for business.

Nervous was an understatement for how she felt in this moment, watching him gaze around her house. She'd never invited him in before, and she told herself she hadn't tonight either. She'd simply walked away and left the front door open. What had she expected him to do? Meet her in the truck?

"You've met Lucy Mae," she said, sweeping her arm around her unhappy daughter. "Lucy Mae, you remember Judge Glover."

"How could I forget?" the girl asked, plenty of acid in her tone.

June put in her mama eyes and set them on laser-mode. She was not going to ruin this for June. Not again.

Judge juggled the two ten-pound dogs in his arms and stepped toward Lucy Mae. "Nice to see you again," he drawled, that Texan accent dang near perfect. "I saw your momma's post about you graduating early. That's highly impressive."

Lucy Mae brightened considerably at that, and June could've scripted what her daughter said next. "Thank you, Judge. Will you please tell my mother while you're out tonight that I'm old enough to do the summer engineering program?" She moved her gaze back to June, and Lucy Mae had plenty of lasers in her expression too.

June supposed she had learned from the best, and she sighed as Judge's eyes cut back to hers. "You don't have to hold the dogs," she said, moving toward him. She took them from him, the silly babies. They'd want him to hold them and carry them around every time he came over if he did it once. "You guys aren't coming tonight. Stay."

She deposited them on the couch and turned toward Lucy Mae. She wouldn't leave without hugging her daughter, but Lucy Mae looked like she'd rather slice out her own tongue. Still, she let June embrace her though she didn't return it. Hugging a board wasn't all that fun, so June ended the touch quickly and said, "You know where everything is?"

"Yes, Mom," Lucy Mae said with a hefty roll of her eyes.

"In case I die," June said, putting a smile on her face. "You're going to live with Grandma, and all the papers are in the bottom drawer of the nightstand." She plucked her coat from the back of the dining room chair and started to put it on.

Judge stepped forward and helped her, and June quickly pulled her hair out from under the collar. She'd worked on her curls for an hour, and they'd barely last through an appetizer as it was.

"I love Lucy," June said, giving her daughter the line they'd been using since she was old enough to understand English.

Lucy Mae rolled her eyes again. "I love you too, Mom."

Satisfied, June grinned at her daughter and then turned toward Judge. She pulled in a breath, because oh, my, she'd forgotten how magnetic and dashing he was in the flesh. She could tell herself she wasn't attracted to him when she wasn't face-to-face with him. It was why she'd let his calls go until the very last day she could stand it. Why she only went to Shiloh Ridge when she only had a two-hour window to stay. Why she'd said yes when he'd asked her to dinner on Christmas Day.

She hadn't been able to say no. He'd been pulling on her for months now. Years, and June was tired of resisting the man. He called to every female cell in her body, and she reminded herself to stay cool.

Judge offered her his arm, and June slipped hers through it. "Good to see you, Lucy Mae. I like what you've done with your hair." He smiled at her with the wattage of the sun, and June couldn't help smiling again.

"Thanks, Judge." Lucy Mae cocked her left eyebrow at June, who chose not to say anything. The walk to the front door seemed to take an hour instead of ten steps, and the moment he'd closed the door behind them, June exhaled.

"We don't have to go to dinner." Judge didn't touch her again as he went past her to the top of the steps.

"Why wouldn't we go?" She moved to stand beside him,

her right hand twitching toward his left. He really was a North pole to her South.

"I don't know," he said quietly. "Seems like you and Lucy Mae might need to have a little talk."

"She's real mad at me over this summer engineering camp." June sighed. "I also didn't tell her about this date...." She let the words trail off, especially when Judge turned and looked at her. She really couldn't stay standing with the weight of his gaze on her face.

"Why not?" he asked.

"I don't know," June said, though she did know why. "Actually, I wanted to keep you all to myself." She tucked herself back into his arm and put her other hand on his forearm too.

Judge leaned down, creating an intimate space. "June, you best not say things like that if you don't mean them."

She swallowed, because he was absolutely right. She couldn't lead him on again, and guilt stuttered through her that she'd done so last time. It had been a few years now, but that didn't mean her gut felt good about what she'd done.

June cleared her throat and said, "I mean it, Judge."

He nodded, lifting his head to face the front yard again. He was so handsome, so strong, and so amazing. He went to church every week, and she'd heard him singing last time she'd gone up to the ranch. He'd very nearly lost his jeans that day, but tonight's pair seemed solidly in place.

She grinned out into the night, the possibilities stretching for miles in every direction.

"All right," he drawled, taking the first step down to get

to the sidewalk. "Maybe you should start by tellin' me about this summer engineering camp and your reservations about it."

June appreciated that he wasn't just going to sweep away her concerns. He wasn't going to focus the date on himself, though Judge never had. She hadn't been out with anyone but him in a solid eight or nine years, and her dating skills felt as rusty as her aging body.

"For starters, the one she wants to attend is in California," she said. "And she's not a legal adult until way next year."

"Mm." Judge opened her door for her, and June boosted herself up and into the truck using the runner. He moved into the doorway after her and leveled his gaze at her. "I think those are valid concerns, June. Doesn't her father live in California?"

How Judge had remembered that, she wasn't sure. The man had a memory like a vault, because she'd told him that years ago, on perhaps their third or fourth date. They'd only had a couple more after that before she'd ended things with him.

"Yes," she said. "And that's reason number three I don't want her to go." June had a handful more, but they were mostly trivial things that Lucy Mae and any other reasonable person could explain away.

"Reason number four is that you'll miss her," Judge said. He gave her a soft smile that made him even more beautiful, stepped back, and closed her door. She watched him round the front of the truck with calm, cool strides, and she mentally commanded herself to be the same way.

She'd called him "cowboy" last summer, and she'd told him to keep his pants on when he was literally losing his. Up at the ranch, June was in charge. He called her to come fix his WiFi network and upgrade his systems so he could run his Christmas light display for the annual contest Three Rivers sponsored.

To her knowledge, he'd never won, but he sure did try hard. June had seen every one of his light displays for the past four Christmases, and they got better and better each year. Judge possessed some serious tenacity, she'd give him that. He had to, because he was still interested in her, all these months later.

He got behind the wheel of the truck and buckled his seatbelt. June watched his every move, including how he reached to twist the key in the ignition and then reach to turn down the volume on the radio.

"You're right," she said. "I will miss her. It's just been me and her forever, it seems."

"How long?" Judge asked, glancing at her. "I should've asked first: Is The Tea Room okay?"

"The Tea Room?" June had never heard of it. "Sounds fussy."

"I think it is kind of fussy," Judge said with a smile. "But I wore my best boots and my dress hat." He reached up and touched the dark brown cowboy hat, drawing June's attention there.

For some reason, she licked her lips. "I suppose I can handle fussy food tonight."

"I've heard the soup is good," he said. "That's what they're saying on Two Cents anyway."

And June loved soup—another little tidbit she'd told him eons ago. June shifted uncomfortably in her seat. Would she be able to remember little facts about him? Her mind blanked, and June simply stared out the front windshield.

"Do you help Ranger with the app at all?" she finally asked. Her phone buzzed in her purse, and June wished she'd employed her selective features before leaving the house. That way, she'd only get calls or texts from Lucy Mae, not all of her employees or her neighbor who constantly lost her cat and wanted June's help to find it.

Judge cleared his throat. "No," he said simply, but it almost sounded like he'd barked the word.

"Is that a sore subject?" she asked, almost a teasing lilt to her voice. Before Judge could answer, her phone started buzzing in earnest. "Just a sec. Someone's calling me." She tugged her phone free of her purse to find Lucy Mae's name on the screen. "It's Lucy Mae."

"Answer it," he said.

She swiped the phone icon up to connect the call. "Hey, baby. What's going on?"

"Mom, I'm so sorry, but I think you better come back."

"Why?" June asked, signaling to Judge that he better slow down and turn around. He did, no questions asked.

"The cops just showed up," Lucy Mae said. "They want to talk to you."

"I'll be right there," June said. "I'll stay on the line, okay?" She pulled the phone away from her ear. "I'm so sorry, Judge, but apparently, there are some police officers at my house who need to speak with me."

"I see," he said, sliding her a grin while he flipped around. "Something you need to tell me, June?"

She gaped at him and then burst into giggles. He laughed too, and while June really wanted to go to dinner with him, and talk with him, and get to know him, she told herself there would be another opportunity.

She'd make sure there was another opportunity.

As they quieted, and Judge went back the way they'd already come, June said a silent prayer that the cops weren't there for her or Lucy Mae, but only to get information about someone's network or Internet usage.

*Please, please, please*, she thought, hoping the Lord wouldn't think her too dramatic. He pulled into the driveway and June found the three cops sitting on the steps with Lucy Mae, the four of them laughing about something.

She turned toward Judge. "I'm so sorry. Raincheck?"

"Name the date and time," he said with a perfect smile.

She leaned over the console, and he leaned toward her too. She kissed his cheek and said, "You're the best, cowboy. I'll call you," before sliding out of his truck and facing the cops as they stood.

June needed to be sure that Judge would call her should she stay silent for longer than he'd like, so she added a bit of sway to her hips as she approached the police officers. "This better be good," she said. "You just cost me a first date with a *very* handsome man."

# Chapter Thirty

Mister Glover couldn't believe he'd showered, shaved, and slathered himself in cologne. "She's going to say no," he muttered to himself. Yet he couldn't stop himself from leaving Bull House and getting behind the wheel of his truck.

He should be washing the blanket on the bed where he'd stayed last night, and where he'd be sleeping tonight too. He felt like a ping pong ball, bouncing around from one side of the ranch to the other.

But Preacher and Charlie had been married yesterday, and a man and his new wife required some level of privacy. Judge and Mister had moved down the road to Bull House just for a few nights, as the newlyweds would be leaving for their honeymoon on New Year's Day.

Tomorrow night, the Glovers were throwing a New Year's Eve party at the ranch, and Bear had invited everyone he knew. Since everyone in Three Rivers knew

Bear, it felt like the whole town was coming. Mister didn't want to go at all, but he'd promised to be there to help with the refreshments.

He told himself that was why he'd worked all day, showered, shaved, and slathered. So he could go to the grocery store…to pick up trays of cheese and vegetables.

When he got to the highway, he turned left, as usual. He pretended he was going straight to Wilde & Organic. He swore the truck slowed down all by itself, and he didn't even tell his hands to turn the wheel right.

He drove past Seven Sons Ranch on the left and kept on going. The east highway where Preacher had gone off the road several months ago loomed in front of him, but another right turn took him away from that scene.

And straight to the Bellamore Ranch. Brit Bellamore was Mister's father's age, and his eldest two sons worked the ranch with him. He also had two daughters, and they worked on the family land as well. The Bellamores were a lot like the Glovers in that regard, and Mister couldn't believe he hadn't ever seen the youngest daughter, Liberty, as more than a friend.

She sure seemed determined to keep him in his place, and Mister sighed as he approached the fence that marked the perimeter of the Bellamore land.

The ranch was actually named the Golden Hour, as Britt's land sat out on the plain and seemed to be bathed in sunlight twenty-four hours a day. Mister had always liked coming here, as his dad had brought the kids to help at other ranches whenever necessary. Sometimes when it wasn't necessary, as Stone Glover believed in being neighborly and helpful.

*It's never a bad idea to serve someone,* Mister heard in his dad's voice, the truck moving right onto the Bellamore's land. *You might need help one day, boys, and who's going to be there?*

Mister could see his dad's bright blue eyes glancing around the room as he waited for one of his children to answer.

"Family," Mister said, just like he had when he was six years old.

Dad had smiled then, and he'd nodded. *Family, yes. And those who love you, because you've showed them they're important to you too. How do we make sure people know we care about them? That they're important to us?*

Bear had raised his hand and said, *We serve them, Dad.*

Mister couldn't believe the seventeen-year-old Bear had even been in the meeting. When Mister had finally reached seventeen, the last place he wanted to be was in the living room with all of his siblings. Of course, Cactus was gone by then—off to college. Bear was working the ranch full-time. Dad would be gone in only three more years.

Mister's chest caved in, but he inhaled, trying to puff it out again. "You can't get inside your head like this," he said. "Get your game face on. You're about to ask out Libby. Really ask her."

He thought about all of the advice Preacher and Judge had given him. *Get over there and tell her how you feel,* Preacher had said.

*No more beating around the bush*, Judge had said. His brother had a date with June Nichols that night, and Mister could admit he'd taken some of his brother's courage and somehow infused it into himself.

He parked in front of Libby's tiny little house before the main homestead on the ranch. She lived there with her older sister, Mildred, and Mister knew both of them really well. He'd been inside Libby's house dozens and dozens of times. They'd climbed the trees on this land—and his ranch—and they'd gone to church youth groups together for years.

When they'd become adults, Mister had asked Libby to dance at the summer dances held in the downtown park. He'd asked her to help him get other girl's numbers, and he'd asked her to all of the big parties and get-togethers at Shiloh Ridge Ranch—the ones that other townspeople attended.

This was no different.

Except this was wildly different.

He looked up to the house, seeing Libby's touch everywhere. A flagpole extended from one of the columns, a flag in the white and blue shape of a snowman flapping in the breeze. The Texas Panhandle always seemed to have a wind blowing, and Mister had seriously considered leaving the ranch during the two days they'd had to shelter during the windstorm.

He'd never do it, and he knew it. His father had ingrained the importance of family into Mister, and he did like spending time with his brothers and their wives, Arizona and Duke, and all of his cousins.

He didn't mind the loud laughter and the annoying way Ida and Etta had to explain every item of food on the buffet before anyone could eat. He liked that there was always food at the homestead, and he loved being able to go to people he trusted for advice.

He and Judge had not gotten along for years, but Mister had accepted his apologies, and he'd made some of his own too. They'd started getting along better the past few months, and Mister had done what his father had always told him to do.

Forgive.

Things weren't perfect, but they were both trying. Judge had changed a lot in the past year or two, and Mister felt like he had too. He was trying to be more patient with himself and with others. He was trying to work hard. He was trying to take care of problems before someone asked him to. He was trying to be there for his family members as the number of people who had Glover for a last name continued to grow and grow.

He did want someone to call his own, and he'd love to have a tiny human with the last name Glover too.

The bright yellow door on the house swung in, and Libby came out. Mister dang near ducked down in his truck, as if she wouldn't know he was there if she didn't see him sitting behind the wheel.

His heart boomed like a big bass drum in his chest, especially when Libby moved to the top of the steps and leaned against the pillar there. She folded her arms, not a smile in sight.

Mister sighed, his nerves making his palms sweat.

He told himself he'd ridden championship bulls. He'd broken six bones. He had four huge belt buckles sitting in a box in Bull House, and he'd been a national bull riding champion for four straight years.

He could face Libby Bellamore.

*Don't let your head get too big*, he told himself as he unbuckled his seatbelt and got out of the truck. "Heya, Liberty," he said.

"Mister Glover," she said, and sometimes he really hated his first name. Every male in his family could be called Mister Glover—except Cactus, as he was technically a doctor—but Mister was better than Michael.

Mister tucked his hands in his pockets, having left the giant belt buckles at home. "I wanted to come apologize for yesterday."

Libby deflated, and Mister actually smiled. "Come do it then." She sat down on the top step, and Mister made his way over to her. He sat next to her, a sigh coming from his mouth. He didn't know what to say next.

"How many times have we sat here?" Libby asked, drawing in a big breath. She exhaled it out and didn't look at him. "How many times have I cried on your shoulder over some boyfriend who liked Mildred more than me?"

Mister chuckled, though he didn't really want to spend time in the past. With Libby, he wanted a future. At least he thought he did. "A lot of times," he said.

He swallowed, because there were some things he'd done that he wished he hadn't. He could ask her how many times she'd set him up with the women she knew in Three Rivers, the answer to that would be a lot too.

"I'm sorry I said you were being impossible," he said. "I was frustrated that what I wanted to say wasn't coming across." He cleared his throat, because he'd asked her to go to breakfast with him after they'd cleared the road onto the ranch, and she'd argued back that they wouldn't be able to do that for days. Maybe weeks.

He'd growled at her that she knew what he meant, and she'd glared right on back. Then stupid Wyatt Walker had shown up with doughnuts and juice and food, and Libby had said they had no need to "waste time" going to town when there was breakfast—and lunch— right there.

Mister had called her impossible and stomped away. They hadn't spoken, though that had all just happened yesterday morning.

"I don't like it when I can't text you," he said, looking down to his cowboy boots. He used to own twenty pairs of them, and he'd stand in front of the row of boots for ten minutes before choosing. Now, he wore the same ones all the time.

Dad had taught him not to be pretentious. Not think of himself as better than others. His father had seen the talent in him at a young age, and Mister had competed in junior rodeo for a decade before his dad died. That year, Mister had gone pro, and he was fairly certain he'd stayed on some of the bulls he'd ridden because his angel father had held him up with his wings.

"I'm sorry I said you were a brute," Libby said, inching a bit closer to him.

He reached over and took her hand, sighing with how

comfortable that made him. "Will you come to the New Year's Eve party tomorrow?"

"Mildred and I wouldn't miss it." She squeezed his hand, her happiness obvious in her tone.

Mister turned toward her, the beauty in her face making him suck in a breath. She wore her sandy blonde hair half-up and half-down, and Mister wanted to reach out and flip back a long piece hanging over her shoulder. He wanted to kiss her. He wanted to tell her—really *tell* her—what was going on inside his head.

*You have to tell her*, he thought. *Tell her what you're thinking. Tell her you want to come pick her up. Like it's a date.*

"Oh, I was thinking—" Mister started.

"What time does it start?" she interrupted, releasing his hand and putting several more inches between them.

Mister noticed all of it, and his words died in his throat. A lump formed there, and he swallowed against it. "Eight," he managed to say.

"I'll drive," she said. "Mildred doesn't like to drive at night."

"I could come get you," he said, clearing his throat again. "Maybe Scott and Alli could bring Mildred." He met her eyes, and Mister knew Libby Bellamore. He'd known her for thirty years. She was smart and articulate, and there was no way she didn't know what was happening here.

"We could go to dinner first," he said. "There won't be real food there. Just party food, you know, like popcorn and brownies and stuff." His throat felt so dry. "There's a new place in town, in one of those high-rise buildings? Bishop and Montana went with Aurora and Ollie, and they said it's real nice. They have vegetable tempura, and I thought since you like that so much, we could go."

He dropped his eyes to his hands, his chest vibrating strangely now. Mister wasn't even sure why. He'd been out with plenty of women over the years, and he was usually so smooth. "Say, like, six? I'll come get you, and we'll go. It'll be a date." The last word scraped his throat, and he cleared it a moment later.

Libby sat in silence, and Mister didn't dare look at her.

"What about Mildred?" she asked.

"She can get a ride with Scott and Alli," Mister said again. "I know they're coming, because I saw them on Bear's list." Surely her brother could give Mildred a ride. They lived two hundred yards down the lane.

Libby stood up. "Mister, I...I already told Mildred we'd go together if you invited us."

Mister stood too, his frustration blooming. "I'm not inviting the two of you," he said. "She can come or not. I don't care." He faced the ranch, wishing he could communicate better. "I'm inviting *you*," he said. "And not just to the party, Libby. To dinner. On a date." He cleared his throat. "I want to go on a date with you. The two of us."

He faced her, feeling strangely powerful now that some of the hard words had left his mouth. "You know how I've asked you to set me up with other women before?"

Libby wore fear in her eyes, which were as wide as the full moon. She didn't nod or shake her head or speak. Her chest rose and fell in spurts, and Mister hated that he'd caused her nerves to fire.

"I don't have you to set me up with you, Libs." He

reached for her hands, taking them in both of his. "I like you, Libby Bellamore. Will you go out with me, please? Not as friends."

"Not as friends?"

He shook his head, a smile filling his soul. He'd said all the things Preacher and Judge had told him to. This had to work.

"There you are," Mildred said, and Libby yanked her hands away from Mister. "Daddy's on the radio, carrying on about the goats gettin' out again." She wore a cross look on her face, and she switched her gaze to Mister. Her expression changed in that instant too. "Oh, hi, Mister. Sorry to interrupt."

"It's fine," Libby said, darting away from him. "He was just inviting us to the party up at Shiloh Ridge tomorrow night." She linked her arm through her sister's and faced him, those dark brown eyes wide and begging him to corroborate her story.

"Yeah," Mister said, his voice actually squeaking. "Starts at eight."

"Perfect," Mildred said with a smile. "That gives us time to try that new pizza place, Libs. Pie in the Sky? You've wanted to go."

"Yes," Libby said. "We should do that." She lifted her free hand in a wave, but it was such a jerky motion that it felt like a military salute. "Bye, Mister." She spun and hurried inside the house, leaving Mildred looking after her in confusion.

She swung back to Mister. "What has her scared as a jackrabbit?"

Mister shook his head. "I told her to try the new Japanese place," he said, the words just flowing from him. No matter what, he wasn't going to sell Libby out to her sister. "I think she's afraid of sushi." He grinned, though his heart felt like Libby had stabbed it with a fork, ripped it from his chest, and tossed it into a food dehydrator. When —or if—he got it back, it would be shriveled and dry, brittle, cracked, and broken.

Mildred giggled and shook her head. "She's not adventurous with her eating."

"Don't I know it," Mister said, thinking he did a pretty good job of joking. "Hey, I'll come pick y'all up tomorrow. She says you don't like to drive at night, and I think that's code for the fact that *she* doesn't like to drive at night."

"You are such a code breaker," Mildred said, laughing again. Mister joined in with her as he went down the steps. He got behind the wheel of his truck, staring at the house while he buckled and started the vehicle.

He couldn't believe Libby had said no.

She hadn't used that word, but the implication was as tall and as wide as a mountain. It screamed down at him from the wide sky overhead, and he hurried to get off the ranch. The moment his tires hit the asphalt on the highway, he jabbed at the button on his steering wheel and said, "Call Judge Glover."

"Calling Judge Glover," his truck said in a cool female voice. The line rang and rang, and Mister remembered his brother was on his own date with the woman of his dreams. He quickly stabbed at the screen to get the call to disconnect.

He pressed the button again. "Call Preacher Glover."

"Calling Preacher Glover."

This brother answered after the second ring with a, "Hey, Mister. How did it go?"

"How did it go?" Mister repeated, his anger and irritation shooting to the top of his head. "I'll tell you how it went, Preach. She said no."

"What? That can't be true."

"Well, I'm driving her and Mildred to the party tomorrow," he said. "We're not going to dinner."

"Did you ask her?" Preacher asked. "Did you tell her? *What* did you tell her?"

"I said everything you guys said to say." Mister sighed, feeling worthless and oh-so-foolish. "Dear Lord, I told her I liked her. I said I wanted to date her. I used the words 'not as friends.' I did everything—and more—that you guys said to do."

Preacher exhaled, and the line scuffled, which meant Charlie was listening too. "And she said no?"

"Her sister interrupted, and Libby ran away from me. She told Mildred I'd invited them both to the party—and that was after I'd said I wasn't inviting Mildred. Only Libby."

"Come back to the Ranch House," Preacher said. "We'll go over everything you said and she said. Surely she didn't say no."

Mister shook his head and gripped the steering wheel as he drove. He looked down at the speedometer and eased off the accelerator when he realized how fast he was going. "No," he said. "I have to pick up some food for the party tomorrow night. I can't go over it again. It was humiliating enough the first time."

"Mister," Charlie said. "Maybe you misunderstood."

"Nope," he bit out. "I have to go." He hung up while Preacher was in the middle of saying something. Guilt strung through him, but Mister could apologize later.

He couldn't believe she'd said no.

# Chapter Thirty-One

Ward rolled over as his alarm filled the bedroom with birdsong. He silenced it and listened to the furnace blow hot air through the vents. The house wasn't empty this morning, as Judge and Mister had come to stay for a few nights before Preacher and Charlie left on their honeymoon, but it wasn't the same without Dot here.

She hadn't called last night. He hadn't called her. There had been no texts, and he told himself that a woman like Dot needed some distance. For him, though, the silence and distance between them signaled a problem. He hated it. He wanted to solve the problem and get her back into his life.

Judge had returned early from his date, saying that June had been called on by the cops to help with a case. Mister had stormed in several minutes later, yelled that Libby Bellamore had rejected him, and disappeared into the basement with the words, "I don't want to talk about it."

Ward didn't blame him. Sometimes the Glovers—particularly Judge—could talk things to death.

He sighed as he got out of bed and went down the hall to the kitchen. He made coffee and started to preheat the oven. Mister had brought back a quiche that just needed to be reheated, and Ward had said he'd get it ready for breakfast that day.

They'd put in a full day's work on the ranch, just like always. The New Year's Eve party didn't start until eight. Ward couldn't believe Bear thought it was a good idea to host a party at Shiloh Ridge, but the light parade had been cancelled this year due to the wind damage, and Bear said it was tradition to get together as a family to welcome in the New Year.

They did usually go down to Three Rivers for the light parade, with sandwiches and snacks and glow sticks. This would be the same party, but in True Blue instead of on the side of the road with the parade for entertainment.

"Bear wants to do a talent show tonight," Judge said, entering the kitchen. He'd slept in a bedroom downstairs instead of Dot's, and Ward quickly told himself it was not Dot's bedroom. It was the bedroom where she'd slept for a few days. He'd stripped the bed and washed the sheets and blanket, pillowcases and shams. Everything.

"Oh, so that's going to be the entertainment," Ward said, reaching for a coffee mug. He did like having other people in the house, and he didn't like the idea of living in Bull House alone.

"Yep," Judge said. "Want to do a duet with me?" He got

down a mug too, then turned to the fridge to get out the cream.

"Sure," Ward said. "What do you think of me comin' to live in the Ranch House?"

Judge set his mug down, along with the jug of cream. "Why?"

"Where's Preacher gonna be when he gets back from Europe? The Ranch House?" Ward shook his head. "They've got two years before their place is done. He's the foreman. He can't live an hour away in Charlie's house."

Ward got out a couple of spoons, his mind whirring. He'd laid awake last night, thinking about Dot, and he supposed he'd worked out a few other things too. "I think he should live here. I moved over with you guys when he was hurt. There's room for me and my guitar there. They'll let me keep the office here. Or I can move it."

"Don't move it," Judge said. "At most, it'll be two or three months." He turned to get the coffee that had been made so far. The burner hissed as a couple of drops hit it while Judge poured himself what he could. He replaced the pot and faced Ward again. "Zona and Duke's house will be done by the end of March. She's due in April, and I know she's planning to be settled in that house long before the baby comes."

"So Preach and Charlie could then move into the Top Cottage," Ward said.

Judge nodded as he added about the same amount of cream to his mug as there was coffee. "But yeah, maybe you'd like to come to the Ranch House. Might be easier than me and Mister moving here."

"Let's talk to everyone today," Ward said. "I'm easy. I just need my clothes, and I do need to use the office." It would be easier if he didn't have to relocate it, but he'd make the situation work. He'd want to have a place of his own for himself and his new wife, and Preacher should have that even if he had gotten married six months earlier than planned.

"Sounds good," Judge said. "Have you seen Mister this morning?"

"Nope." Ward bent to put the quiche in the oven. "Don't ask him about Libby, okay? Preacher texted last night, and he said Mister told her everything and Libby rejected him."

Judge shook his head. "He could talk to me about it. I know exactly what that feels like."

Ward nodded. "You and me both, brother."

"Really?" Judge asked. "You and Dot seemed to be getting along real nice. *Super* cozy." Judge's eyes sparkled as if he knew Ward and Dot had been kissing quite a lot over the past week.

"Yes, well," Ward said, exhaling heavily. He leaned into the counter, searching his thoughts for the right way to explain things. "She left yesterday. I know she's busy—she runs this huge landscaping company, right? But she didn't call or text. I didn't either. It feels...it feels like a rejection. Like she's saying, 'hey, it was super fun while I *had* to be up there, but I'm not really interested in you.'"

His chest pinched with the reality of the words he'd just spoken. He turned away from Judge, suddenly understanding Mister on a whole new level. The pain in his soul went on and on, and Ward finally looked up when Judge's hand landed on his forearm.

"Are you okay?" Judge asked.

"No," Ward said. "I'm in love with her." He forced a chuckle that sounded as miserable as he felt. "I'm in love with her, and I'm not okay."

Judge studied his face. "I knew you didn't hear a thing I said."

"What did you say?"

"I asked if you were just going to let her put you on hold."

"What am I supposed to do? I can't make the woman talk to me."

"No," Judge said slowly. "But you can talk to her."

Ward let Judge's words sink into his brain. "You have some experience with this."

"I've been in love with Juniper Nichols for four years," Judge said sadly. "Sometimes she talks back to me, and sometimes she doesn't." He hung his head. "I'm pathetic, I know. I should've moved on a long time ago. But last night...." He let the sentence trail off, his smile real and bright as it filled his face.

"I know it's not real love yet," he said. "But she's just as beautiful as I remember, and I want to know everything about her just as strongly as I always have." He shrugged and reached for the coffee pot again, his eyes down. "I'm hoping the crush can turn into love, and I'm hoping she'll feel the same. I can't *stop* hoping and praying for that, so I've just tried to listen to the Lord and reach out to June when it felt right."

Ward appreciated Judge's emotions, and the way he could articulate them so well. "You're not pathetic," he said quietly.

"Thank you, Ward," Judge said. "I'm going to go get Mister, and I need some reinforcements. You in?"

Ward grinned at his cousin. "So in. I need help knowing what to do with Dot, and I'd love to know what Mister said to Libby that made it clear he liked her. Maybe then I can say the same things to Dot."

"You know what to say to her," Judge said, turning toward the doorway that led into the basement. "So you'll work really fast today, and you'll come back here and shower. You'll get yourself down to town and to her front door, and you'll lead with 'I love you, Dorothy. I love you, I love you, I love you.'" Judge burst out laughing, but Ward actually thought his suggestion had merit.

"You love her?" Mister asked, his voice coming from behind Ward. He and Judge turned to find the man fully dressed, wearing a coat, and closing the front door behind him. He faced the two of them and added, "The sunrise is gorgeous this morning."

"The sun rises over the back yard," Ward said.

"I went up to Ace's," Mister said. "He said I could sit on his back deck any time I wanted."

"How long have you been up?" Judge asked as he walked through the living room and toward Mister.

"Hours," Mister said, accepting the hug from Judge and then collapsing onto the loveseat. "I hate feeling like this. Why did she have to say no?" He closed his eyes, but the pain coming from him echoed Ward's.

"Ward feels the same way," Judge said, also taking a seat. "Bring me that coffee, would you, Ward?"

He moved over to the counter and collected the mug for Judge. "All right, Mister. You're going to tell Ward everything you said so he can repeat it to Dot and get her up to the party tonight."

"You haven't invited her to the party yet?" Mister asked.

"It's very last-minute," Ward said, a bit defensively. He didn't rush to sit down and hear Mister's sad tale but busied himself with making a cup of coffee. He took it to Mister and returned to the kitchen to make one for himself.

"Seems like you'd invite the woman you loved," Mister said.

"Dot's...different," Ward said.

"She's a woman," Mister said. "She's probably thinking you should call her first."

"We live in the twenty-first century," Ward said, rolling his eyes. "Women call men all the time." He sat down on the couch, his mind only on Dot. Could he just call her out of nowhere?

*It's not out of nowhere*, he thought. *She kissed you, and she said she'd call. You're dating. It's somewhere.*

Would she come back up to the ranch?

Ward could worry about anything, and he stewed while Mister started his story.

"Go," Preacher said later that day. He moved to stand right in front of Ward. "You are yelling at everything. Can you please go shower and go talk to Dot already? You're driving me insane." He wore a stern look, his eyes filled with fire as he glared at Ward.

Ward could only blink at him. "I'm yelling at everything?"

"For an hour," Preacher said. He reached up and ran his hand under his hat and then down his face. "Haven't you noticed that I've assigned all the cowboys somewhere else?"

"This stupid pigpen won't cooperate." Ward kicked the nearest board, realizing that he'd practically yelled. At a piece of wood.

"Please go," Preacher said. "You'll feel so much better, and we're done here anyway. I'm going to have Bishop come deal with it, as we're both obviously dunces with hammers."

Ward looked at the hammer in his hand, and Preacher quickly reached for it. "I'll take that." He plucked it out of Ward's hand and backed up. "Judge filled me in, and I really appreciate you, Ward. I know you like your space, and I got married too soon."

Preacher looked away, something storming on his face now. "Charlie and I are leaving tomorrow. You'll have your house back—at least for a week or so."

"I don't care about any of that," Ward said. "I want you and Charlie to have Bull House until you can move into the Top Cottage."

Preacher nodded, his gaze still far away, out on something on the ranch only he could see. Ward looked that direction too, wishing the Lord would write in the sky what he should say and do. "I'm nervous," he admitted. "I've been out with a lot of women in the past four or five years, and I haven't felt as strongly for any of them as I do for Dot. What if...?" He exhaled and stopped talking. He didn't need to finish anyway.

"I showed up on Charlie's front step and just told her," Preacher said. "It worked for me, and I thought it would work for Mister."

"Yeah, well." Ward blew out his breath, and it didn't hover in the air in front of him, so that was something.

"Want to say a prayer real quick?" Preacher asked. "I'll say it for you?"

"Thanks." Ward bowed his head and pressed his cowboy hat to his chest.

"Lord," Preacher said. "Ward is the best man I know. Well, besides Bear. And Ranger. And maybe Judge." He started to chuckle, and Ward smiled, all of the tension and frustration leaking out through the gesture. "The point is, Lord, Ward's good. He took care of me when others didn't know how. He sacrifices for this ranch, and he has for a lot of years. He's got a lot of points built up with Thee, and he'd like to cash in just a little. He loves Dot Crockett, and if there's any way for the two of them to be together, I know he'd appreciate it. Give him courage. Give him the right thing to say. Give him increased faith in Thee and Thy plan for him."

Preacher paused, and Ward thought that was a pretty dang perfect prayer. He waited, though, because Preacher had strong faith that had only increased over the past several months since his accident, and Ward wanted to hear what he had to say.

"Bless Mister. We know he's hurting, and we want to do what we can for him. Help us to support him in the best way for him, not us. Bless Etta, as she has some tough things she's dealing with."

Ward swallowed hard, thinking he better stop by the French fry shop on his way back to the ranch tonight. Etta loved the Cajun fries, and Ward had been so consumed with Dot and then the road off the ranch that his sister's troubles had fallen by the wayside.

"Bless Judge," Preacher said. "With his new relationship with June. Bless Sammy and her new baby." Preacher sighed. "We could go on and on, Lord, as even when things look so great from the outside, we know there is trouble and heartache behind closed doors. We love Thee, and strive to live Thy will, no matter what it is. Amen."

"Amen." Ward replaced his hat and studied the far sky again. Several long seconds passed, and then he said, "I guess I'll go shower and go invite Dot to the party tonight."

"Good luck."

"Thanks, brother." Ward grabbed onto Preacher and hugged him tight. "You're the best man I know." He smiled at him and turned to go.

An hour later, he pulled up to Dot's house, having been there several times for dates in the past. The windows sat in darkness, and he had the distinct feeling she wasn't home. He rang the doorbell anyway and listened to it sing through the house.

Even George didn't bark, and an increased intensity of frustration filled Ward. "What do I do now?" he asked, tilting his head back toward the sky.

The immediate thought came to go see Ida and the twins, so Ward shuffled back to his truck, put the box of sugar-free fruit snacks he'd found in his pantry back on the passenger seat, and drove around the corner to his sister's house.

Her and Brady's windows shone with cheery, yellow light, and Ward went toward the energy pulsing from the house at a quick clip. He knocked and then simply entered the house, the sound of one crying newborn meeting his ears.

"It's just me," he called.

"Ward, thank the Lord," Ida said, tears in her eyes. "Take Johnny, would you? Judy just made a huge mess." She handed Ward the screaming baby boy and started wiping at something viscous and off-white on her black blouse. "This is a new shirt too."

She bustled off, still sniffling, and Ward glanced around for Brady. He didn't seem to be home, so Ward focused on the tiny baby in his arms. "Hey, now," he said soothingly to Johnny. "You don't need to be makin' such a fuss."

He bounced the boy and stepped further into the house, looking for a blanket or a pacifier. A bomb looked like it had gone off in the living room, and Ward could only stare for a moment. There were two baby swings, two baby seats, a playpen where Judy flailed her arms and legs, her own wail starting to fill the air, and plenty of other baby paraphernalia.

He spotted a pacifier and reached for it, slipping it into Johnny's mouth. The baby tried to grab onto it immediately, but it took him a couple of tries to really get the suction going. Ward picked up a blue blanket and started to hum the tune he'd been working on for the past couple of weeks. Maybe months.

The boy quieted completely, his eyes drifting closed as Ward continued to bounce him. He wrapped the baby up tightly and tucked him into his arm like a football before turning to the little girl working her way toward a scream.

"Come on now, Judy." He bent to get the little girl out of the playpen and spotted the bottle sitting on the windowsill. He suddenly knew what Ida had been cleaning off her blouse, and he reached for the bottle too.

He took both babies to the rocking chair Ida obviously used, as her phone sat on the nearby table, along with a big glass of water, and her reading glasses. Ward settled into the chair, the song already coming out of his mouth again.

He grabbed the blanket from the side of the playpen and tucked Judy into his body too. "She always drives away when she should stay," he sang, his tenor voice barely hitting the lower notes. He slipped into a hum, wishing the song he'd written wasn't about Dot.

But it was. Everything in Ward's life had become about Dot. He fitted the bottle into Judy's mouth, and she started eating again. Ward toed himself and the twins back and forth, back and forth, the way he had with Etta and Ida when they were newborns and he was five years old.

Of course, Mother had swaddled them like dolls and set them in his arms, but Ward had wanted to hold them so badly. He had pictures of himself beaming at the camera with one twin in each arm, and he'd loved his sisters from the moment he'd met them.

Ida's heels clicked as she came back down the hall, and she paused, looking at him. He smiled at her and said, "Judy's eating, and I hope that's the right thing to be doing. Johnny seemed hungry too, so maybe I should've fed him."

Ida burst into tears and threw both hands into the air. "It's official." She marched toward the kitchen. "I have no idea what I'm doing. I've been trying to get those silly babies to stop crying for an hour. Brady got called into work, and now we're going to be late to the party, and honestly, I can't wear these heels."

She kicked them off, her voice becoming high enough to audition for the part of one of the Chipmunks. "I won't let Etta come over, because then she'll see what a mess everything is." Ida kept her back to Ward and leaned into the counter in front of the sink.

He wanted to get up and go soothe her, but the babies....

He'd been led to Dot's, and she wasn't home for a very specific reason. He'd really been led to Ida's, so he could help her with the babies.

"Come sit down," he said, and Ida turned toward him.

By some miracle—perhaps his father with his angel hand held Judy's bottle for her—Ward managed to get up without disturbing either baby. "Right here, Ida."

She did, tears covering her crumpled face. "Take Johnny," he said, slipping the baby from his arms to hers. "I'll get him a bottle, because I think he has to eat too."

"He does," Ida said. "I started to make it when the water boiled over on the stove." She sobbed as she looked down at her son. "I think it's still in the microwave. I'd just fixed the stove when Judy woke up. She's so shrill, so I fed her first. By then, Johnny was pretty mad he had to go second again, and then she threw up all over me, and by then I seriously thought—is this my life now? How did I get here?"

She sobbed again, and Ward wished he could take her desperation and despair from her. "It's all right, Ida. You cry as much as you want." He turned to get the bottle from the microwave. He took it to her so she could feed her son, and then he noticed that Judy's bottle was almost gone.

"You're done, Little Miss," he told her, slipping the nipple out of her mouth. "You give me a big burp now, okay?" He put the little girl over his shoulder, and she molded right to him, melting and stealing his heart all in one single second. He patted her back as he stutter-stepped back into the kitchen.

A pot sat on the dormant stove, pasta water spilled all around it on the burner. The oven clicked, indicating it was on, and Ward bent to open it. Meatballs and sauce boiled inside, and Ward quickly turned the oven off and left them.

With one hand, he lifted the pot and poured the water and noodles into the waiting colander in the sink. Judy burped, and he laughed quietly. "What a good girl. Yes, that was a good one."

He cradled the baby in his arms, and he could've sworn

she smiled. He bundled her up tight in the pink blanket and took her back to the playpen.

Ida had her eyes closed, and even still she looked exhausted. Johnny sucked away at his dinner, and Ward started cleaning up. He folded burp cloths and blankets, took tiny pajamas into Ida's laundry room, and straightened the pillows on the couch.

He tackled the kitchen next, pouring the slightly overdone pasta back into the pot and adding the meatballs and sauce to it. With that all stirred together and steaming hot, he put the lid back on and started doing dishes. He filled the dishwasher with bottles and nipples, all the plates and bowls in the sink, and started the machine. He washed the counters, throwing away plastic cups and empty water bottles, paper plates and takeout containers. He scrubbed the flat surface of the stovetop and rinsed out the washrag just as Ida said, "You don't have to clean my house."

"I sure don't," Ward said, laying the rag out so it would dry. "Dinner's ready. Are you ready for it?"

She folded Johnny over her shoulder and patted his back too. She glanced at the sleeping girl baby in the playpen. "How do you do this?"

"I've been here for thirty minutes," Ward said. "You do it twenty-four-seven. You just had a bad ten minutes."

"It's been so hard," Ida said quietly. "Don't you dare tell Etta I said that. She'll hate me forever."

"She will not," Ward said. "Even if I did tell her, which I won't." He smiled at his sister and dished up a bowl of spaghetti and meatballs. "Is Brady going to make it to the party?"

"He doesn't think so." Ida stood and laid Johnny beside his sister in the playpen. "Thank you, Ward. I needed help, and you showed up."

He nodded and put the bowl of food on the now-clean counter. "I'm staying for dinner, by the way." He got himself a bowl too, his phone chiming several times in a row, one practically on top of the other.

"Someone's trying to get in touch with you," Ida said, twirling her first bite of pasta around her fork.

"Someone's always trying to get in touch with me." Ward didn't take his phone out of his pocket. "Are you okay now?"

She nodded and finished chewing. After she swallowed, she said, "Please don't think badly of me. Brady's been gone a lot the past couple of days, and I really have no idea what I'm doing."

"I don't either."

"Sure," she said dryly as his phone chimed again. Then it started to ring. She looked down toward his back pocket, but he simply took another bite of pasta. He didn't want to talk to anyone right now.

"It's probably Bishop or Cactus with some *big* emergency," Ward said, really laying the sarcasm on the last two words. "Or Judge or Ranger, calling to ask me to stop at the grocery store and get something for them."

"It might be important."

"I'll check before I leave town."

The ringing stopped, and Ida smiled. "You've always been so good at being present."

"This is the best meal I've had in weeks," Ward said, smiling at her.

"Oh, please, I know Holly Ann presented her Christmas dinner for Preacher's wedding." Ida grinned and started giggling. Ward smiled back at her but wouldn't confirm that Holly Ann's cooking was better than Ida's.

They settled into silence and ate, and Ward sure did like the comfortable silence. He'd just finished his last meatball when another flurry of texts arrived.

"Ward, I really think you should get it." Ida's phone rang too, and she glanced at it. "It's Etta."

Ward sighed and pulled his phone out of his back pocket as Ida answered. "I've got Ranger calling." They lived together, so something major must be happening. He swiped on the call and stood up from the bar.

"What's up, Range?"

"Where are you?"

"He's sitting right here," Ida said, and Ward turned toward her.

"I'm at Ida's."

Ida opened her mouth and said the same words Ranger did over the phone. "Dot's looking for you."

Ward's heartbeat kicked into an extra gear. "Where is she?" he asked.

"Standing in front of me," Ranger said. "She said she texted and called you when she didn't find you at Bull House."

"I'll call her," Ward said, his hands starting to shake a little bit. "Thanks, Ranger."

"I'll tell her," he said.

Ward ended the call, almost simultaneously with Ida. "I came down to talk to Dot," he said. "She wasn't home, so I came to you."

"I needed you more for a few minutes." Ida stepped into him and hugged him tight. "Thank you, Ward. You saved me."

He held her tight. "I love you, Ida. I love those babies. I'll come any time." He stepped back and held onto his sister's shoulders. "Etta will too. You're probably hurting her feelings by not letting her come."

Ida's chin shook, and she nodded. "I told her I'd call her right back." She half-laughed and half-cried. "Now that the kitchen is clean, I'm going to tell her she can come."

Ward leaned down and pressed his lips to her forehead. "Okay, I've got to go talk to Dot." He couldn't believe she was up at the ranch. She hadn't called or texted until she was there, but he reminded himself that he hadn't either.

He hadn't wanted her to tell him not to come.

He dialed her as he stepped out onto the front porch.

"Ward," she said. "Did you get any of my messages?"

"I didn't look," he said, smiling into the night. "I guess you're up at the ranch?"

"Yeah, where are you?"

"At your house, sweetheart." He started to laugh, and Dot did too. Everything tight inside Ward released, and he said, "Tell me where to meet you, Dot, and I'll be there."

# Chapter Thirty-Two

D ot pulled into the grocery store, her chest expanding and collapsing at a rate that made her light-headed. She wanted to check her blood sugar, but she had twenty minutes ago when she'd left Shiloh Ridge Ranch.

She was trying so hard to be the woman Ward deserved. She took care of herself, so he wouldn't have to. She'd driven away from him, the same way she'd driven away from her business and life in Albuquerque, and she'd been miserable.

So she'd gotten in her car and driven back toward him, something Dot had never really done in her life before.

The double doors ahead of her slid open, and Ward exited. Dot sucked in a breath and stalled, the sight of him so glorious it was as if heaven itself had opened the clouds and let a little divine light shine down on him.

She grinned and broke into a run, laughing as he opened his arms to her.

"Oh, I missed you," he said, gripping her tightly and turning her around. She could only breathe in the scent of his clothes, his hair, his skin. He pulled away and kissed her right there in the parking lot. Dot normally hated public displays of affection, but right now, she didn't care. This was the man she loved, and she didn't care who saw them in this moment.

"I'm sorry," she whispered against his lips. "I should've called you last night, but I didn't."

"Why didn't you?" he asked.

"There you go again, asking the hard questions." She grinned up at him. She drew in a breath and blew it out. "My house felt so...dead. So lonely. I went to my parents', and I was there for a long time talking. When I got home, Tyson was there, and he met someone he wanted help talking to. So more talking." She rolled her eyes, but Ward just grinned at her.

"You don't like talking that much," he said.

"Not for hours," she said.

"So I should get straight to the point."

"It's advisable." She swallowed as she stepped back and took his hand. "I have some things to say too."

"But you want your own private New Year's Eve party." He turned with her, and they went into Wilde & Organic. It was almost a question, but Dot didn't think it really was.

"Yes," Dot said. "I want to go to your family party for a little bit. I want to get to know the people who live up there with you. I know they're important to you, and honestly, I could use some friends."

"You have friends at work," he said. "I've seen them."

"I suppose I do." Dot steered him over toward the fresh produce side. "After we go to your family party, I do want my own private party at Bull House. Just me, and you, and the stars." She twirled away from him, feeling lighter than she had in a long, long time.

Ward chuckled and hung back. Dot faced him again, and she wondered if it would be considered lame or stupid to tell him she loved him in a grocery store. She bit the words back, hoping the actions she'd exhibited in the past hour spoke enough for now.

"So we're getting dinner here?" he asked, reaching down for a bagged salad.

"They have these great ready-to-eat meals," she said. "Heat and eat."

"Are we eating at your place?"

"I can do heat and eat, Ward," she said, adding some sarcasm to her tone.

"I'll be there to supervise." He grinned at her. "Get what you want, sweetheart. Some of these look like they take an hour or so."

Dot moved down the refrigerated unit to find her favorite one. "I love this chicken Picatta with wild rice and mushrooms." She picked up two containers of it, because each one only had a single chicken breast in it. "Sound good?"

"Yep. I'm easy to please."

Dot almost teased him that that was so far from the

truth, but she held back those words too. She smiled at him, let him buy a salad to go with it, and they got out of the grocery store. Since they both had vehicles there, they had to drive separately to her house, and she realized she'd have to drive herself up to the ranch too.

"No," she said as she pulled into her driveway. "Just ask if you can stay with him." A smile bloomed through her whole body, and she ran into the house to get the oven preheating while Ward parked behind her.

She let him in the front door, and Dot's nerves suddenly took over. He stepped past her to the kitchen counter and set down the food. "I like your place," he said, turning back to her. "But you'll come live with me on the ranch when we get married, right?"

He took her into his arms, shocking her with his words and his actions. Before she could answer, he bent his head closer and kissed her. This was a different kind of kiss than what he'd done in the parking lot. Different than what she'd felt at Small Plates. Different than any kiss they'd shared at the ranch, even the one before she'd left.

"I love you, Dot," Ward whispered, leaning his forehead against hers, their breath mingling and his lips still so close. "I know it's fast, and I used to care. I hope it doesn't scare you, but I love you, and I think you should know."

He kissed her again, and Dot *knew*. She felt the love of this amazing cowboy drifting through her, and she desperately wanted him to know she loved him too.

"I'm sorry I come off as arrogant," he said, moving his lips to her neck. She clung to him. "I don't mean to be demanding." He pushed his hands through her hair. "I am going to fuss over you, Dorothy. I'm really good at it, and I can't help doing it for the people I love." He smiled at her. "Can you put up with me?"

"I can try," she said, her throat so dry.

He chuckled and tried to step away from her. Dot increased her grip on his shoulders, drawing his attention back to her. "I'm sorry I didn't call."

"It's not important."

"It is to me."

"All right, then," he said. "I accept your apology."

"I'm sorry I drove away."

"From the ranch?"

"From you," she said. "You specifically." She swallowed and told herself not to look away from him. "When I realized I was in love with you, I got behind the wheel of my car and drove as fast as I could to tell you. Then you weren't there, and then we were at the store...." She reached up and traced her fingertips down the side of his face.

"You're so good-looking, and you so know it." She smiled at him, glad when the storm that had come into his face when she'd told him that previously didn't arrive. "I like that you're confident. I like that you demand high quality. I'm trying, Ward. I take my blood sugar all the time to make sure you won't have to watch me go into a diabetic coma. I'm so sorry about that."

Remorse moved through Dot, and Ward shook his head. "It's not your fault. I'm an idiot for making it sound like it was." He looked down and back up. "Forgive me for that, please."

"Already forgiven," she said, feeling brave and bold and everything Ward always felt. "If you'll have me, I'll come live with you in Bull House after we get married. Heck, I'd like you to drive me to the party with your family and let me stay in that bedroom I slept in over Christmas. Maybe we could do a late breakfast tomorrow."

He nodded, already dipping his head to kiss her again. She stopped him, those delicious lips only a millimeter from hers. "I'll let you fuss over me, Ward Glover, because I love you, and I know it's how you show people you love them."

"I love you too, Dot." He kissed her then, and Dot lost herself to the taste and touch of Ward Glover.

---

"OH, MY GOODNESS." DOT STALLED IN THE DOORWAY with Ward. The music pumping from the barn had alerted her to the vibrant atmosphere of the New Year's Eve party, but she'd been completely unprepared for so much silver. So many sparkles. "I guess this year's color is pink."

Ward laughed and tugged her further into the room. It was a large space, and Dot had been in True Blue for Preacher and Charlie's wedding. So many people had gathered to Shiloh Ridge that it looked like standing room only, which worked because they weren't serving dinner.

Chairs lined the wall to Dot's right and left, surrounding the doorway, but most people either danced near the front of the hall or stood in groups talking near the back.

"There's Mother," Ward said. "Let's go talk to her." He wove through a few people, saying hello and smiling. Dot couldn't erase the smile from her face if she'd tried.

She'd met Ward's mother before, but Ward had simply introduced her as Dorothy Crockett and nothing else.

She was something else now. Someone else.

"Mother," Ward said, releasing Dot's hand to hug his mother. Ace and Holly Ann backed up to make room for Ward and Dot, and she smiled at them. Holly Ann was a taller woman too, and she returned Dot's grin.

"This is quite the party," Dot said, glancing around. Streamers hung from the ceiling stories above, and a legit disco ball had been installed at some point over the past couple of days.

"Bishop says if you're going to have a party, you might as well go all-out," Ace said, smiling. "He and Cactus and Judge have been working on this all day."

"It's great," Dot said. "I don't think I've ever been to a party with this many people before."

"I ran the Christmas Festival a couple of years ago," Holly Ann said. "I've had my share of people." She leaned into Ace, and he put his arm protectively around her waist.

"I thought you guys were kind of isolated up here," Dot said as Ward stepped away from his mother.

"Don't buy into that," Holly Ann said. "There's people up here constantly."

"Yeah," Ward said, facing them. "Like your dad and sister." He indicated the doorway behind her with his head.

Holly Ann's face lit up, and she and Ace hurried toward the three people who had arrived and stood in the doorway as if they'd never been to a party with this many people before either.

"Dot," Ward said, grinning. "This is Dawna, my mother. Mother, this is Dot, and I'm going to marry her one day soon."

"So lovely to have someone who's finally captured Ward's heart," Dawna said, extending both of her arms out to Dot. She hugged her, and Dot sank into the matronly embrace.

"Thank you, ma'am."

"He adores you," Dawna whispered in Dot's ear. "I've been praying so hard for him to find the right woman, and I'm thrilled he did."

Dot wasn't sure if she was really "the right woman" for Ward or not. Was there one right person for everyone? If so, why did people get married more than once? Why wasn't everyone with their exact right person?

"Do you want to dance?" Ward asked as Dot separated from his mother.

"I do," his mother said before Dot could even consider dancing with him. She beamed at her son and linked her arm through his. "I'll bring him back in one piece, dear." She laughed and Ward did too, giving Dot a look of joy over his shoulder as his mother led him toward the front of the hall.

Dot migrated toward the outside edge of the party, spotting Arizona, Montana, and Willa sitting in a cluster of chairs near the refreshment tables. Her first inclination was to turn around and find somewhere else to be.

She told herself that these women would be her family

soon, and she'd be living up here at this ranch with them. She best get to know them now.

"Hello," she said as she approached.

Arizona looked up, her eyes widened, and then she jumped to her feet. Jumped might have been an overexaggeration, but she got up fast. "Dot," she said. "Come sit with us."

"Yes," Montana said, sliding her chair back. "Sammy is going to be so mad she's not here yet."

Arizona dragged over another chair and put it between her and Willa. "Yep, she is."

"I'll text her," Willa said. "And Oakley."

"Why?" Dot asked as she sat down. "What's the big deal?"

Arizona exchanged a glance with Montana, who started tapping on her phone.

"She says they're ten minutes out and to please wait." Willa looked up. "We can wait, right?"

"I'm dying," Arizona moaned.

Dot looked around at the three of them. "I'm so confused." They each wore a look of keen interest in their eyes, and while she wanted to be one of them—she *would* be one of them once Ward asked her to marry him properly—she wasn't sure what they were talking about.

"Ward sent this on the family text," Montana said, passing over her phone. "Zona, put her on the wives string."

"Oh, I'm not a wife," Dot said.

"We put Charlie on when she wasn't even talking to Preacher," Willa said. "I'm adding her right now."

"Good," Zona said. "Because I can't seem to add people to the group chat."

Dot stared at Montana's phone, sure she'd read the message wrong.

"What's your number, Dot?" Willa asked, but Dot's brain wasn't functioning properly.

"It's that stupid SIM card you have," Montana said. "You know who you should talk to? June." She half-stood, which was impressive for someone with the size of her pregnant belly. "Judge said he was bringing her tonight."

"I'm not talking to June," Zona said. "Judge would fillet me alive."

"He would?" Willa asked. "Why's that?"

Dot finally looked up from Montana's phone and handed it back to her. "He sent that everyone?"

"Mm hm."

*I'm real sorry if I've been short with any of you. Or acted arrogant. Or demanded something. Dot put me in my place, and I'm going to do better.*

Questions had come in after that, along with reassurances that Ward hadn't done anything wrong.

"So," Montana said. "We've all been dying to hear how you put the mighty Ward Glover in his place." Her bright blue eyes held more sparkle than all the tinsel and streamers currently decorating the barn.

*Because I love her, and she expects me to be better than that.*

That had been his answer when someone had asked him why he needed to do better.

*I love her.*

"Oakley says she's just going to bring Wilder, so she'll

be here with Sammy. And yes, she wants us to wait if we can," Willa said. She put a friendly smile on her face. "Tell me about your family, Dot."

"Okay, well." She slid her hands down her thighs, glad she'd worn jeans tonight. "I have this really annoying older brother named Tyson. Once, when I was kissing this really amazing man in the parking lot, he flashed his police siren and lights...."

# Chapter Thirty-Three

Liberty Bellamore loved to dance. She'd been on a team growing up, and she'd danced in high school too. She'd only gone away to college for one year—two short semesters—but she'd been on a folk dance team there too. In fact, that had been the hardest thing to give up when she'd returned to Three Rivers and her family's ranch.

She laughed as she danced with Beau Peterson. He'd never asked her out, and he wouldn't either. He was far too old for her, and they both knew it. So many people had come to the party with a date, though, and the choices for single men to dance with were slim.

Her eyes automatically moved over to where Mister stood with his brother, Preacher. He sipped something out of a clear plastic cup, and Libby's throat was suddenly so dry.

Beau spun her, and she squealed, coming right back

into his strong chest and arms. The song ended, and they both separated to clap though there wasn't a live band.

"Thanks, Libby," he said, reaching up to touch the brim of his hat. "I'm gonna sit the next one out."

The song started to play, but it wasn't a quickstep or a upbeat tune. A ballad. A love song. Libby turned away from Beau, only to come face-to-face with Mister Glover.

"Oh." Her hand went to her mouth, and her eyes rounded in surprise.

"Will you dance with me?" he asked, his voice deep and rich and wonderful. Libby wanted to dance with him. Only him. Always him.

She absolutely could *not* let him know it.

*Not as friends.*

His words from yesterday evening played on repeat in her head, but she nodded anyway. He extended his hand toward her, and the moment she put hers in his, her skin sizzled. Could he feel that too?

*Of course he can't*, she told herself. She'd had feelings for Mister for at least three years. Maybe a little longer. They'd touched plenty of times over that course of time, and he'd never once noticed her.

Never once.

Hurt ran through her, and she could admit that she might be holding a grudge against the man who'd once been her best friend.

Libby had grown up now. She knew men and women didn't remain best friends for life, and it was a stupid idea to think she was somehow different.

Anxiety ran through her as Mister encircled her in his

arms. Everything he did seemed so easy, like breathing or blinking, and every step Libby took weighed at least a hundred pounds.

"Are you having a good time?" he asked.

"Yes."

"Did you get some of that caramel and cheddar popcorn mix? I know you like that."

"I think I ate the whole bowl by myself." She managed to laugh, but she wasn't kidding. She'd gone straight to the treat table when she'd arrived, because a twenty-minute drive with her sister in the back seat and Mister behind the wheel had been akin to torture.

She'd needed a salty and sweet escape, and Libby could hear her sister-in-law telling her that popcorn put on an extra twenty pounds. Libby knew she carried too much weight; she simply didn't care.

Lizbeth said it could be why she hadn't been able to find a husband yet. Libby knew that wasn't true. She hadn't found a husband yet, because she was waiting for Mister Glover to open his eyes and see her standing there.

"I'll send some to you," he said.

"Please don't," she said. "I already binge on this sea salt and lime popcorn, and it's added plenty to my hips."

"It has not," he said with a scoff. "You look great."

"You can't be serious." She couldn't believe she was talking about her weight with Mister. At the same time, she and Mister used to talk about everything. Literally, everything. When he'd left for the pro rodeo circuit, he'd called her every night for a year. After that, he'd texted or emailed after every rodeo. Sometimes he'd call too.

They really had shared everything—except a kiss. They'd never held hands, and he'd never shown up on her stoop to ask her to dinner...until yesterday.

*Not as friends.*

"I'm serious," Mister said now, bringing her closer to him. Her first instinct was to pull back. Shy away. She wasn't going to give into the urge to be with him, because she didn't want to lose him as a friend.

With her nerves bouncing in the back of her throat, she let him pull her closer. She let herself rest her cheek against his chest, where his heart boomed in her eardrum. He said something, but she couldn't tell what. It didn't matter. She was safely encircled in his arms, and she wanted to stay there for a good long while.

The music quieted, and Libby lifted her head. Mister had danced them right out of the main hall and around the corner at the back of the room.

"Libby," he said. "I have to talk to you." He released her, and she stumbled slightly, catching herself against the wall behind her.

Mister sighed and paced away from her. He took off his cowboy hat and ran his hands through his hair. He usually took off his hat inside, but most men had left theirs on for the party. A man did want to look his best on the dance floor, and Libby was a sucker for a man in a cowboy hat.

*Wrong,* she thought. *You're a sucker for Mister in a cowboy hat.*

"We already talked," she said.

"No," he said, turning to face her. "We didn't. I asked

you out, Libby. I stood on your porch and said I liked you and wanted you, and you scampered away from me."

"You did *not* say that."

"What did you think I meant by 'not as friends'?" His eyebrows dropped, and his expression darkened. She'd seen this frustrated, irritated, angry version of Mister a lot over the past six months.

"What did you think I meant when I said we should go to breakfast the other day? Or when I asked you to the wildflower festival? The tree lighting?"

Libby rolled her hands over and around one another. "I don't know." She knew, but she absolutely would not admit it out loud. She hadn't once, not even to herself.

"Libby." Mister approached slowly, which was probably a good thing. "I'm standing right here, and I'm telling you in plain English that I'm interested in you. I like you. I want to date you. I think about kissing you all the time. Holding your hand. Holding you close, like I just did." His chest heaved, and his eyes seemed a bit wild. "Tell me you don't think about the same things. Tell me that, and I'll leave you alone."

She'd been taught not to lie, but she couldn't get her voice to work.

He trailed the back of his fingers down the side of her face, and oh, Libby couldn't help herself then. She leaned into that delightful touch and closed her eyes.

That must've been some sort of signal for Mister, because the next thing she knew, he'd cradled her face with one hand and touched his lips to hers.

*No!* her mind screamed. Libby had started to sink into

the kiss, but she stiffened. She pushed both palms against Mister's chest and sent him stumbling back away from her.

"Stop it," she said, her voice coming out so much like her mother's. Scathing and tight. "Don't you dare kiss me, Mister Glover."

"Libby," he said, and he wore shock and hurt in his eyes.

Libby had had enough. She was tired of playing the weak woman. Tired of pretending like she didn't know what Mister was doing when he asked her on dates. She was really tired of saying no or making up excuses, but she wouldn't be played for a fool.

She marched toward him, and back he went again, almost like he expected her to hit him.

"Libs," he said, his voice holding plenty of warning.

She kept going, backing him against the opposite wall. She grabbed a fistful of his shirt and held it tight. "I know what you're doing, Mister."

"What am I doing?"

"You don't see me. You aren't standing in front of me. Don't make it sound like you're this poor, poor man, pining away for the woman who won't give him the time of day. That's what *I've* been doing, Mister, and everyone knows it."

"I have no idea what you're talking about."

Libby forced her fingers to uncurl. Tears pressed behind her eyes, but she would not cry in front of him. "We've always been honest with each other, right?"

"Until the last few months, I thought so, yes."

"I only need a yes or no answer," she said. "To one question."

"Fine." Mister reached up and pulled his shirt down, straightening it and putting everything precisely back in place. How did cowboys know how to hit all the hormones of a woman? It really wasn't fair.

"If I hadn't messed up and said what I did to Preacher last year, would you even be standing here in this hallway with me right now?"

Mister looked like she'd hit him with a two-by-four. That was the only answer she needed, and it wasn't the right one.

She'd suspected as much, which was why she'd put him off about going to the wildflower festival. Why she'd made up a reason she couldn't go to the tree lighting ceremony with him. Why she'd picked a fight with him instead of agreeing to go to breakfast. Why she'd insisted Mildred ride with them tonight.

He wouldn't have seen her if she hadn't indicated her feelings for him first.

"The only reason you 'see me,'" she said. "Is because Preacher told you I liked you. If I hadn't been so stupid as to ask about you when he'd come to the ranch last year, you would've *never* known. You would've had me set you up with some other pretty girl for tonight. You'd be back here with her, trying to sneak a kiss."

"That's not true," he said, but he didn't provide any evidence to the contrary.

Libby raised her chin and looked him straight in the eyes. God would have to forgive her for lying, just this once. "I don't think about kissing you. I don't want to hold your hand. I want you to leave me alone."

The words took everything from her, and Libby didn't have the strength to hold back her tears any longer. But if she cried, he'd know what a liar she was. "Excuse me."

She marched away from him, from her sister, from the party. She burst into the night, the air cold and crisp. It burned her throat and lungs as it entered them, and she gulped at it, needing more and more and more.

The door banged closed behind her, and she flinched away from the sound of it. "I'm sorry," she said to the sky above. "Please forgive me for lying." Then she ran toward the corner of the building just in case Mister followed her and demanded she tell him the truth.

---

"THANKS, JUDGE," SHE SAID FORTY MINUTES LATER. Mildred got out of the back seat of Judge's truck, but Libby needed one more minute with him. Mildred seemed to know something major had happened, and Libby would have to answer a bunch of questions once they were alone.

She didn't care about that. She could handle her sister, who was sometimes even more clueless than Libby herself.

"I won't say anything to Mister," Judge said.

"You live with him," Libby said. "I know you two haven't always gotten along, and I don't want to be the thing that comes between you again." She reached over and put her hand on his. "I'm sorry if I've put you in an awkward place."

"It's fine," he said. "I can handle Mister." He'd been standing outside, hugging the front corner of the barn as

Libby had come around the back one. Apparently, June had canceled on him last-minute, and he couldn't stand to go into the party alone.

She'd asked him for a ride home, and if he could please go inside and tell Mildred to get a ride with one of their brothers. They'd both come to the party with their wives and kids, and surely they'd have one more seat for her.

It was barely ten o'clock, and at this rate, Libby would be in bed when the New Year's bell rang. She didn't care. She didn't understand New Year's Eve anyway.

"If it's a problem, you tell him to come talk to me again." She looked at Judge. "Okay?"

"You don't have to tell me, but what happened? He likes you so much."

She shook her head. "No, he doesn't. He likes the idea of a woman liking him. He likes the idea of having a girl-friend who has this big crush on him." She shook her head, aware that her voice had turned hard again. "He doesn't like *me*, Judge. He never has."

"I think you're wrong. I've seen him over the past six months. He's miserable trying to get your attention."

"We'll agree to disagree." Libby unbuckled her seatbelt and looked at him again. "Thanks again for the ride. I apol-ogize in advance for any trouble it might cause you." With that, she opened the door and got out of the truck. Judge said nothing, but Libby had been prepared to slam the door if he had.

She went up the steps and into the house, where Mildred had started the electric kettle and then probably gone to change. They'd talked of watching *Little Women* when they got home, and Libby hurried through the living room and kitchen to the hallway too. Her bedroom sat just off the main part of the house, and she ducked inside without having to face her sister.

She'd changed out of her party dress and into her silk pajamas before her phone chimed. She knew exactly who it would be, and she rolled her neck and gave an exaggerated sigh.

Mister never knew when to stop. Never. It was why he'd broken his femur—the injury that had ended his rodeo career. It was why they'd argued in front of everyone the other morning. It was why he and Judge hadn't gotten along for years.

It was why the text she'd find on her phone would be from him.

Sighing, she picked up her device and read his message. She sucked in a breath at the same time Mildred opened the door. "You ready, Libs? I've already got the lime popcorn popping, and I found some of that Mexican hot chocolate mix in the cupboard." She beamed like this Old Maids party between the two of them was better than what was happening at Shiloh Ridge Ranch, in that beautiful, remodeled barn that housed all their family parties.

"Yeah," Libby said, silencing her phone and placing it face-down on her nightstand. "I'm ready." She left the phone in her bedroom as she entered the hall and pulled the door closed behind her.

She didn't have the brain cells to deal with Mister's text right now anyway.

## Chapter Thirty-Four

Ward moved the picture of Ida and Etta into the pile for the twins. It was rare to have a photo of one of them alone, and he had no idea how he was going to finish a book for each of them.

The next picture showed him and his dad, both of them beaming out at the camera. Ward smiled at the teenage version of himself, his arm slung around his father's shoulders. Dad had his arm around Ward's too, and he remembered taking this picture vividly.

He was only fourteen, but already so tall. As tall as Dad, which was why Mother had made them pose one morning as they'd come in from the early chores on the ranch.

Ward didn't remember being so thrilled about getting up at four a.m. to milk the few dairy cows they had, feed horses and pigs, move sprinklers in their pastures, or haul hay. He'd done it though, and then he'd gone to school all day long.

At this age, Ranger or Bear would've been driving them down to the high school, and his mother had liked that. She had plenty of work to do around the house, yard, and ranch too, and an hour round trip—twice a day—had freed up plenty of her time.

"I love you, Dad," Ward said to the picture. His father had been the steady foundation in Ward's life. For a while there, after he'd died, Ward felt like he'd been made captain of a boat he didn't know how to sail. The crew had deserted him, and he was left alone to make his way through stormy seas to safety.

Ranger had been that place of safety, and Ward had the thought that he should text his brother and tell him as much. Since Ward was trying to do the good things that popped into his head, he paused in his picture-sorting and sent the text.

He snapped a picture of the old picture and sent it to Ranger. *Look at me and Dad. This was the day Mother realized we were the same height.*

*This is amazing*, Ranger sent back. *I needed to hear that today, Ward. Thank you. And thanks for the picture. Dad looks good, doesn't he?*

In the picture, he did look good. His smile filled his whole face, and Mother had fancied herself an amateur photographer, which meant she'd made them face the sun before she'd snap the button. That way, they didn't have shadows from their cowboy hats falling across their faces.

Dad's hat always sat perfectly straight on his head. He used to joke that the top of his head was flat, and that was why his hat sat so nicely. But Dad never wore his hat inside the house, and he didn't have a flat head. Ward still hung his hat by the door whenever he walked into Bull House, and that was a habit his father had drilled into him.

*Show respect, Ward. Always kiss your momma hello. Help your siblings.*

"I'm trying, Dad," he said. "How do you think I'm doing?"

Mother had called him a couple of times since Ward had asked about his name, and he didn't really have any insecurities about it. From time to time, something pinched in his chest. Right now, he could breathe easily, and he closed his eyes, trying to hear his father's voice.

He'd died almost seven years ago now, and Ward had lost so much in that time. The scent of his father's shirts. The sound of his voice. The cadence of his step as he strode down the cement aisles in the stables. The hearty laugh his father would bellow out whenever Uncle Stone told a joke.

Ward did not want to pass away as early as they had. For one, they'd finished having their families, and Ward hadn't even started yet. Dad had only been fifty-three when he'd lost his battle with prostate cancer. Uncle Stone had only been forty-five.

For Ward, that was only five years from now. If he and Dot got married by summer and had a baby right away, if he passed at forty-five, his child would be four years old.

A strange, peaceful feeling came over him. His father was telling him he was doing okay. Doing great, actually.

"Thanks, Dad."

A new thought entered his mind, and Ward once again picked up his phone. He called the doctor's office and let the phone ring. It was too early for anyone to be in, but if he didn't call now, he'd forget. They'd call him back, and the appointment would get set.

"Hey, this is Ward Glover. I need to come in for my annual physical and do a check on everything. Can you call me back to set up an appointment?" He left his number and once again hung up.

He stood and left the pictures on the back half of the dining room table. He, Mister, and Judge hadn't had any problems using the table with everything where it was, so he'd left it.

Ward went through the living room to the sliding glass doors that led onto the back porch. His guitar stood next to the exit, and he picked it up on his way out.

He sat in the chair on the edge of the porch and settled the guitar across his lap. He plucked the strings, the sun just barely starting to rise over the eastern edge of Texas. He'd finished the music for the song he'd been working on for the past few months, and he'd completed the lyrics last night too.

Now, he just needed to perfect the song before he sang it for Dot.

He'd spoken to her every day since New Year's Day, when she'd come out of the bedroom where she'd slept the night after their private New Year's Eve party at Bull

House. They'd gone to breakfast—which was more like brunch—and she'd shown him around her office at From the Ground Up.

She'd been working steadily since then, as had Ward, but he made a point to text or call her every single day. The next time she came up to Shiloh Ridge with a load of gravel, he was going to ask her to marry him.

He just needed to get all the pieces in place, and for the first time in his life, he prayed that the gravel would take its sweet time arriving.

"She braids her silver hair before leaving the house," he sang, holding onto some notes and rushing right past others. "And she has no idea that she shines like the stars."

Ward had never loved anyone the way he loved Dot, and a smile touched his heart, soul, and face as he thought of her.

"She thinks no one sees her,

That she can disappear as easily as a light goes out.

She thinks her past defines her,

That she can't overcome the loss and pain and disappointment."

His voice increased with each word on the last part, and his fingers knew exactly when to hit the strings hard and when to back off to create a high and low in the music.

"She's wrong, because he sees her.

He wants to call her,

He wants to know her,

He dreams of the silver between his fingers,

And the touch of her smile against his,

And the sound of her truck as she drives down his street."

He played the bridge notes, the part of the song that connected one part to another, in this case the chorus back to the verse.

"She always drives away

When she should stay,

Because he wants for-ev-er with her."

He drew in a breath while his fingers slid, played a chord, and held it.

"He wants forever with her."

Ward let his fingers finish the song without his voice, because that was all he was going to sing during the proposal. He glanced up as Mister came out onto the porch, but since his cousin said nothing, Ward played all the way through the end of the tune before stopping.

"That's amazing," Mister said. "Are you gonna sell that one to Nashville?"

"No," Ward said.

"He's gonna ask Dot to marry him with it," Ranger said, and both Ward and Mister turned to the right where his voice had come from. He was cutting across the back lawn, his baby boy in his arms. "I heard you playing and came back here." He came up the back steps, and Ward stood to put the guitar down so he could take Wilder from his brother.

"Morning, brother." Ward hugged Ranger, who held him tight for an extra moment. There was something going on with him, but Ward usually let Ranger come to him and tell him things over prying and asking.

"Morning," Ranger said. "I'm surprised you're not out on the ranch already."

"It's Tuesday," Ward said, stepping back and taking his nine-month old nephew from Ranger. "Preacher takes the early crews on Tuesday." He sat back down and sighed as he gazed out into the golden sunlight. "Look, Wilder, there's a bird." He pointed to the black, nearly flat M in the sky, but the baby just babbled to himself.

"When are you going to propose?" Mister asked.

"I don't know," Ward said.

"Do you have a ring?" Ranger asked.

"I ordered it," Ward said. "It said three to five days, so probably by the weekend."

"You ordered an engagement ring?" Mister ased.

"You can buy anything online now," Ranger said. "I need some help with the language on the update." He handed Ward his phone and pulled over another patio chair. "I don't want it to be too harsh, but it has to be super clear that we're not a dating website or app."

Ward scanned the message on Ranger's phone. "Is it going to look like this?" He glanced up.

Ranger nodded. "That's the design, yes."

A row of horses ran along the top of the message, stark black silhouettes against the white pop-up window. "Two Cents is not a dating app. The app or anyone affiliated with its creation is not responsible for meetings, phone number exchanges, flirtatious comments, or anything that may arise from them. See our Fair Use Policy here, and our Privacy Policy here. If someone leaves a comment that goes against our Community Standards (found here), please report it using the Help button in the right menu."

Ward read over it again, aware that Ranger wanted his opinion. He tried to find the flaws, but he didn't know legal language. "What did Michelle say?"

"This is what she came up with. I want it to sound... normal. Not like a lawyer wrote it. Can you understand it?"

"Easy to understand, yes," Ward said. "Two Cents is not a dating app, and if people want to exchange numbers or leave comments to get a date, that's fine as long as everything being said follows the Community Standards."

"Right." Ranger took the phone back from Ward, who leaned down and snuggled Wilder.

"Did you have a bath this morning, bud?" he asked. "You smell good."

"He did have a bath last night," Ranger said, smiling at his son. "Oakley is already talking about having another baby." He sighed like this was the worst thing that could happen to him.

"Why do you not sound happy about that?" Mister asked.

"It...cost us a great deal to get Wilder," Ranger said. "I'm worried about what the price will be for a second child."

Ward simply watched Ranger, as the man let trouble roll across his expression before he snuffed it out. Ranger wasn't talking in monetary terms, but emotional ones. Spiritual ones. Mental ones. And for Oakley, physical ones, as she'd suffered through a miscarriage before being able to maintain her pregnancy with Wilder.

The three of them sat there and watched the sun rise, the baby as happy as can be on Ward's lap. His phone rang, and he pulled it out from his back pocket to find Dot's name on the screen.

He handed Ranger's son back to him, stood, and swiped on the call. "Hey, sweetheart."

"Guess what I have on my lot?" she said in a sing-song voice.

Ward's heart fell to his boots and then started thrashing its way back to the right spot in his chest. "My gravel." He turned and faced Ranger. He shook his head, though a smile stretched across his face.

"Your gravel, cowboy." She drew in a breath and sighed it out. "Unfortunately, I'm pretty booked out on scheduling deliveries."

"That's no problem," he said, relief filling him. He'd like to have the ring before he proposed. He'd also like to have hundreds and hundreds of her favorite flowers—which he'd have to order in from California—and a big red bow to tie on Brutus. He needed to make a plan with Ranger, Bear, Bishop, Mister, and Judge to keep Dot away from the dump truck for a little bit while he prettied it up and got his guitar.

"What does next Wednesday look like for you?"

"Next Wednesday is fine," he said. "Tell me what time."

"Well, if I schedule you second, that's my delivery right before lunch, and maybe we can spend a couple of hours together."

"I like the way that sounds," he said, grinning at his family members.

"I should be up there by eleven," she said.

"Eleven," he repeated. "Next Wednesday."

"Yep." She popped the P and giggled.

"What about dinner tonight?" he asked, turning away from Mister and Ranger now. "I haven't seen you in a few days, and I'd love to take you somewhere nice."

"How about somewhere with my parents?" Dot asked. "It's my dad's birthday tomorrow, but I have that webinar on native plants, so we're going to dinner tonight."

"I'm invited to that?"

"I'm inviting you right now," she said. "Fair warning, Tyson's gonna be there, and so is my sister. She's coming from Amarillo with her husband."

"Oh, boy," Ward said, chuckling. "Won't Tyson feel awkward without someone with him?"

"Hmm, I'll call him and tell him to invite Melanie."

"The woman he hasn't even been out with yet? To a family dinner for your dad's birthday?" Ward shook his head. "Bad move, Dot."

They laughed together, and Ward agreed to pick her up at six so they could get to the restaurant on time to meet her family. When he turned back to Ranger and Mister, he said, "The delivery is eight days away. Can I call an emergency planning meeting to make sure this proposal goes exactly right?"

Ranger lifted his phone. "I've got Bear, Bishop, Ace, Etta, Ida, Mister, Preacher, and Judge on this text."

"And me," Ward said. "And Cactus."

"So the only person you're not going to invite is Zona?" Mister asked. "She won't like that."

"Put it on the family string," Ward said. "I'll take all the help I can get." He was sure he was going to regret that, knowing the women now in this family, but Ward really did want to pull out all the stops for Dot when she came to the ranch for the delivery.

And twenty heads had to be better than one...right?

# Chapter Thirty-Five

Dot could barely get Brutus around the turn that led across the eastern part of what used to be the lawn at the Ranch House. The main road that went right by the homestead still hadn't been fixed, though progress had been made.

Someone had come to clear the debris and start making the road bed again. She knew it couldn't be done overnight, not if the people driving on the road wanted it to last and be right, and of course, the Glovers wanted everything to be right and last forever.

"Come on," she said, cranking the wheel so hard to the left that Brutus groaned and the steering wheel shivered beneath her fingers. "There you go," she said as she made it around the sharp turn. "Good boy, Brutus."

She hadn't brought George with her today, because she really just wanted to have Ward feed her something warm and delicious and then kiss her for an hour or two. She hadn't seen him since Sunday when he'd accompanied her home after the sermon and heated up lunch for the two of them.

He'd stayed that afternoon, and there had been plenty of kissing. Dot smiled just thinking about the tall, dark cowboy, and she rumbled to a stop in front of Bull House a few minutes later.

She called Ward as she slipped from the truck to the ground, and he answered with, "I'm so sorry, Dot, but we've got an issue out in the hay loft. Do you wanna come out here for a few minutes? Then I promise lunch will be ready, and you can drop that gravel on the road out to the Edge. I'll have my cowboys move it."

"Sure," Dot said, facing the house and catching a whiff of something browned and meaty. He'd put something in the oven or slow cooker, and her stomach growled at her to find it and eat it before she went out to the hay loft. "I'll see you in a minute."

She rounded the truck and started the walk to the loft. It sat to the southwest, on the other side of the cowboy cabins in the middle of all the outbuildings. It was probably a decent fifteen-minute walk, but Dot took her time, so it would likely take her twenty minutes to get there.

The breeze up in the hills played with her hair, and Dot adjusted her sunglasses on her nose. Shiloh Ridge Ranch was a gorgeous piece of property, with owners who knew how to take care of things. Every building was in good repair, and those that weren't got fixed quickly. She passed several cowboys and a couple of cowgirls working with horses and cleaning out the stables. They all acknowledged her happily, and Dot did like the familial atmosphere up here.

"Dot," someone called, and she turned toward the male voice. Cactus jogged toward her. "Can you come look at this with me?"

"I guess," she said, wondering what in the world the veterinarian would need her to look at.

He grinned at her and gestured for her to follow him. She did, going past a couple of hen houses to a well. It sat in the shade of one of their bigger barns, and Dot almost felt like she'd entered a fairy land. "Oh, this is beautiful back here."

"I want to fix it up," Cactus said. "As a surprise for Ward. He loves a good sit-down by the fire, with that guitar of his in his lap. We've talked about it, and we're thinking benches, decorative rock, maybe making this well a fountain...."

She approached the well, her eyes searching the land-scape and surrounding area. "You could put picnic tables here, and have a really nice lunch area." She reached the cobbled well. "Is this not functional?"

"Not anymore," Cactus said. "But we like to keep the charm of the ranch, obviously. You've seen True Blue. We were thinking with this, we could do the same thing. Keep the old, but make it new."

"It's amazing," Dot said, peering down into the well. It had been blocked off, which was smart, considering they wouldn't want a child or an animal falling down inside it. "How much room do you want to take up?"

"Bishop mentioned picnic tables," he said. "Like an

outdoor eating area. Let me call him." Cactus got busy doing that, and while he did, Dot paced off the area she could see in her mind's eye.

She made a few notes on her phone and said, "We could easily fit five or six picnic tables here." She indicated the large trees on the other side of the small clearing. "The trees are nice for morning shade, and the barn provides afternoon and evening shade."

"Hey," Bishop said, approaching from the east. "Heya, Dot." He moved right over to her and hugged her. "What do you think?"

She thought she was surprised by his embrace, but she covered over that and started talking again. "Rock is best for picnic areas," she said. "Then you don't kill the grass. We've got nice pea gravel that would work. Or you could do something more decorative, but you don't need to."

"Do you sell picnic tables?" Ranger asked, stepping out of the barn. Preacher and Mister came with him, and Dot started to suspect something was up. She looked around at the five men standing in the clearing with her.

"No," she said slowly. "Don't you guys build stuff like that yourselves?" She looked at Bishop and cocked her eyebrows. "Where's Ward?"

Ranger grinned at her. "He ran back to the house to check on lunch."

"He said we could steal you for a few minutes," Preacher said, grinning like a fool too.

Something was definitely going on, and Dot narrowed her eyes at the lot of them. "Okay, tell me what's going on."

"Nothing's going on," Bishop said, stepping in front of

Preacher as if Dot wouldn't be able to see his face then. "Montana and Micah Walker helped with the redesign of the barn, but neither of them are that great with outdoor spaces. We were talking about it in our Friday meeting, and Ward suggested you'd be the one to talk to about outdoor spaces."

"Funny." Dot folded her arms. "He didn't mention it to me."

"He probably just forgot," Ranger said. "He says you guys don't do a lot of...talking when you're together."

Dot sucked in a breath, her eyes flying open even wider. "He says what?"

"No," Cactus said, practically growling at the others. "It's a *surprise* for him, you guys. Of course he didn't tell Dot. He *doesn't know*."

"Be quiet, Ranger," Mister said. "He doesn't say anything, Dot." He stepped in front of Ranger now. "So should we make the well the center of attention? Or have it be an accessory?"

Dot wasn't sure what to do—step over to Ranger and demand to know more, or go with Mister and let him distract her from this otherwise embarrassing conversation?

"It's kind of off to the side," Preacher mused.

"I think it should be a fountain," Cactus said. "Just think of the tranquility of running water while we eat lunch outside." He sighed like no greater thing existed in the world.

"We can make it a water feature," she said. "Easily. You can put a firepit right next to it too, and make a small seating area around that. Then the main picnic area over here." She could see it all in her mind, and she suddenly wanted to work on this project very much. "It would be beautiful."

"Can you work us up a quote?" Ranger asked as he moved over to the well.

"What's the ground like here?" Dot bent down and pinched some dirt between her fingers. "It's pretty hard. We'd want to cut some of this out—get rid of the grass and weeds. Make it a real area. Put down that weed preventer. Rock it. You could even anchor the picnic tables to cement blocks if you want."

She looked at Bishop, who she assumed would make the picnic tables.

"Lots to think about," he said.

"Could you design us a couple of options?" Cactus asked. "The fire pit is essential for Ward. But you know, with a fountain and without. How many picnic tables? That kind of thing?"

"Sure," Dot said. "I can do that."

"Great," Cactus said. "Well, boys, we've taken enough of her time. We'll let you get back to Ward, Dot."

"Yeah, thanks," Bishop said, and he and Cactus walked away together, mostly in the direction of Bishop's house, which wasn't that far away. Ranger and Preacher left with their heads bent together about something, and Dot met Mister's eye.

"I can give you a ride back to Bull House if you want," he said.

"That would be great," she said, giving him a smile. "I'm

pretty hungry and feeling a little low."

"My truck is right over here." Mister led her around the barn to a big, black pickup Dot could barely get into. Mister patted his pockets for the key and rolled his eyes. "I think I left it on the shelf in the office. Give me two minutes." He jogged back into the barn and Dot looked out the windshield.

An electric charge rode in the air that hadn't been there before. "You're just excited about this new, shiny project," she told herself. But it felt like something more.

Mister was gone long enough that Dot started to wonder where he'd gone. She could've walked back to Bull House by now. He finally came back out of the barn, his phone pressed to his ear. He wore a sourness to the set of his mouth and a dark cloud hung over his eyebrows.

"...talk to you later," he said as he opened the driver's door. He ended the call and nearly threw his phone in the console. "Sorry, someone called."

Dot looked at the name on his screen, still hovering there. Libby Bellamore. Ward had said a few things about the troubles between Libby and Mister, so Dot smiled brightly at him. "It's fine. I'm fine."

Mister grunted and got the truck started. He stuck to the road that led through the middle of the barns, cabins, and stables, so she couldn't see Bull House until he made a right turn and headed in the same direction she'd gone to park Brutus in front of the house.

"Here we are," he said, parking behind her truck instead of passing it and pulling into the driveway, something she found odd.

"Thanks." She got out of the truck, nearly breaking her ankle in the process, and started across the lawn toward the house.

Behind her, the first notes of a song filled the air.

Dot paused and turned to find Ward standing on Brutus's hood, his guitar slung across his shoulder. Someone—probably Ward himself—had tied a huge red bow around the truck, as if gifting it to Dot for the first time.

The tension and energy in the air tripled. A smile burst onto her face. "Ward," she said. "What are you doing up there?"

He started to play the song she'd heard him working on over Christmas, and when his beautiful tenor voice filled the sky with sound, Dot fell in love with him all over again. And then again.

"She braids her silver hair before leaving the house," he sang, and Dot hadn't heard the lyrics with the tune yet. Tears pressed behind her eyes, a battle she knew she'd lose. Ward was singing about her.

Her.

A nobody. Certainly not anyone worthy of a song.

"And she has no idea that she shines like the stars." He smiled with those lyrics, and Dot's breath hitched in her chest. She pressed one hand against her lungs as if that would get them to work properly, but the emotion continued to swirl through her.

"She thinks no one sees her,

That she can disappear as easily as a light goes out.

She thinks her past defines her,

That she can't overcome the loss and pain and disappointment."

Dot began to cry, because Ward had identified the deepest parts of her in only a few words. How did he do that? How could he see what she hadn't shown anyone but him?

The music swelled up with his voice, and then he released it, letting the guitar go quietly into the next notes. He was such a talented musician, and so good with his voice too.

"She's wrong, because he sees her.

He wants to call her,

He wants to know her,

He dreams of the silver between his fingers,

And the touch of her smile against his,

And the sound of her truck as she drives down his street."

People started to come around the front and back of the truck—the truck she drove down his street—and every single member of his family carried a bird of paradise in their hand.

"She always drives away

When she should stay,

Because he wants for-ev-er with her."

Dot had always driven away when she should stay, but this time...this time, she hadn't. This time, she was going to get her happily-ever-after with the sexy cowboy.

"She *used to* drive away," he sang next.

"When she knew she should stay." He held that last note a little longer, and Dot realized he was compensating for the human part of this show—his brothers and sisters and cousins and in-laws who were still gathering between her and Brutus and Ward.

She couldn't believe they had birds of paradise. She loved that flower with her whole heart, and she'd told Ward that months ago.

"Now she drives down his street,

She stays when she wants to flee,

Because he wants forever with her." He picked out the last few notes of the guitar, his eyes dropping to his fingers for a moment. He looked up again, hope in those brilliant blue eyes. In the semi-silence, with the chord hanging in the air, he repeated, "He wants for-ev-er with her."

Dot wasn't sure if she should wipe her face, rush his family, or sob uncontrollably into her hands.

"Dot," Ward said in a loud voice as he set his guitar against Brutus's windshield. He bent down and took something from Ace, who held it up for him. "I love you completely. I want forever with you. Will you marry me?"

He held up a little black box and opened it. Though she couldn't see the diamond, that certainly wasn't the deciding factor.

Her throat felt like she'd swallowed something the size of Brutus, and she cleared it away and shook her silver blonde hair over her shoulders. With his entire family standing there, all of them smiling at her, Dot knew what she was stepping into.

This huge Glover family. All those women who seemed so different from her. Dogs, and cats, and chaos. Cowboys and cowgirls.

They were perfection, and they didn't even know it.

"Yes," she said in the loudest voice she could. "Yes, I'll marry you."

Ward whooped and tossed his cowboy hat into the air. Ranger and Ace reached up to help him down, and he jumped from Brutus's hood and ran toward her. "I love you," he said as the first wave of cheering started.

"I love you too," she whispered, letting him slide the engagement ring onto her finger. She looked from the sparkly diamond to the perfect man who'd given it to her. He grinned, wiped her tears, and matched his smile to hers as he kissed her.

His family went nuts then, and Dot couldn't hold the kiss as she started to laugh. "Where did you get those flowers?" she asked as Ace and Bishop arrived on the scene and handed them to her.

"I had them delivered from California," Ward said, refusing to let her get too far from him though his family was like a tide that couldn't be stopped. At the end of it all, she held a couple dozen flowers that reminded her of paradise, wore a new weight on her left ring finger, and had the best memory to reflect on for the rest of her life.

"All right, all right," Ward said. "You guys are savages. Back up." He shooed them away from her and took the big bunch of flowers. "Let's go put these in a vase and eat lunch."

"Congratulations," a few people called, more and more joining in as they started to walk away to go back to work.

Inside Bull House, Dot leaned her back against the

door while Ward took the flowers to the kitchen counter and a ready-made vase.

He returned to her and cradled her face in his hands. "Did you like the song?"

"It was beautiful," she whispered, tears gathering in her eyes again. "And you know it."

He smiled down at her. "So are you." He kissed her again, and this time, it was a proper engagement kiss, with plenty of love and passion, no interruptions, and exactly what Dot wanted every kiss to be for the rest of her life.

---

Read on for a sneak peek at **THE BLESSINGS OF BABIES,** Book 8 in this series, which will keep you updated with all the babies and happenings with the women at Shiloh Ridge Ranch.

If you just want to go to the next Glover cowboy romance, **get THE NETWORKING OF THE NATIVITY**, and you can get a sneak peek at the first two chapters of that too!

I hope you enjoyed this snowed-in romance between Dot and Ward! I love that they made the best of a tough situation and grew closer because of it.

**Reviews are welcome and appreciated.** They can be as long or as short as you'd like. Even a star rating is amazing and appreciated. Thanks in advance.

## Sneak Peek! The Blessing of Babies,
### Chapter One:

❧

Etta Glover pulled up to her sister's house, a police cruiser parked in the far half of the driveway. Ida's husband, Brady, worked for the Three Rivers PD, so Etta wasn't surprised to see the cop car.

Her heart did beat out a staccato rhythm, a fact she actually hated. She shouldn't be nervous to visit her twin. She and Ida had been through everything together, right from the moment of their birth.

"You will not clean her house," Etta told herself as she lifted her water bottle from the cup holder. She took a sip and replaced the bottle. "You won't comment on her clothes. Or the twins' clothes. Or anything. You're here to show her unconditional love and support. That's all. You're here to listen to her talk about whatever *she* wants to talk about. Not yourself. Not your job. Nothing about you."

Etta was trying really hard to show Ida that she wasn't

jealous, as Ida had tried to keep Etta away immediately following the birth of Johnny and Judy. She knew the deepest desires of Etta's heart, and she hadn't wanted Etta to see how very hard it was to have two babies.

Etta already knew becoming a mother would be phenomenally hard. She wanted it anyway, and she didn't care if her sister had a week's worth of dishes in the sink, baby puke on her clothes, hadn't showered in days, or that the twins didn't wear matching outfits.

Ida had hated the matching outfits growing up, but Etta secretly loved them.

She got out of the car and made the trek up the front sidewalk, noting that the lawn was already starting to green, though it was only mid-January. Ida's flowerbeds waited, the earth rich and deep, and they'd planted bulbs last fall so Ida wouldn't have to do so much this spring.

She and Etta had put up a month's worth of freezer meals, but Ida had confessed that she'd only used a few. *They just aren't what I want to make*, she'd said. Etta didn't understand that, but she didn't need to understand it. She wasn't the one with a husband that worked long and odd hours, or the one trying to take care of two babies simultaneously.

Etta had learned so much in the past nine months, and one of the biggest lessons was that she didn't need to understand everything. She hadn't been able to walk down the aisle and marry Noah Johnson—a man she loved—and she still didn't fully understand that.

She only knew that she couldn't do it; that it wasn't the right thing for her, despite loving him so much. He'd loved her too, and she sent up another prayer that the Lord would bless him with happiness and anything he needed to find it.

Etta couldn't remember the last time she'd knocked or rang the doorbell at Ida's, and she didn't today either. "It's me, Ida," she called as she entered the house. The last time she'd come, both babies had been asleep in their swings, and Ida had been frantically scrubbing the couch to get something out of it.

She'd cried on Etta's shoulder for a good, long while, and Etta's whole heart had swelled with love and compassion for her sister.

Today, Ida came out of the kitchen, both twins strapped to the front of her body. She wore hope in her expression and all of her dark hair piled up on top of her head in the messiest, most elegant bun Etta had ever seen.

She grinned at her sister. "Look at you and those babies."

"This sling has literally saved my life," Ida said, returning the smile. "I can get so much more done, and they like being close to me."

"I bet they do." Etta set her purse on the floor near the side table just inside the door and went further into the house. "I'll take them if you want."

"We've just been waiting for Auntie Etta to show up, haven't we?" Ida rushed toward her and hugged Etta. The scent of lemons and soap came with her, and Etta scanned the kitchen behind her. It didn't look terrible, but it wasn't professionally cleaned either.

It was exactly how a kitchen should look that had a busy family living out of it.

Ida stepped away and started to untie the sling around her waist. "If you'll just grab Johnny," she said, and Etta reached to do just that.

"He's so big," Etta said, taking the three-week-old into her arms. "I almost brought Stetson, but Sammy says they're going to take him to cut his hair today when they pick up Lincoln from school."

"His first haircut," Ida said, smiling fondly. "I don't think these two will do that for a while. Poor Judy is still bald as a billiard ball." She laughed lightly as she removed the sleeping baby girl from the sling. "Go sit down, Etta. I know you want them both."

Etta did what she said, because she did want both babies on her lap. She sighed as she sat down, though she'd been driving for thirty minutes in a seated position. She shifted Johnny to her right side, and Ida settled Judy on her left.

She grinned down at the babies, both of whom remained asleep. "You must've worn them out this morning already." She beamed over to Ida, who'd sank into the recliner, her legs tucked underneath her.

"I took them to get their pictures done," she said. "Whitney Wilde has this whole studio over on the east side of town, in the cutest little farmhouse. You would love it, Etta."

"Yeah? Does she just shoot there?"

"She does all of her wedding photography there. Her newborns can be outside or inside, and we did some in both areas. She's got these antique milk cans with wheat coming out of them, and tons of cowboy props."

"Sounds amazing," Etta said. "Did you do cowboy pictures?"

"No, I talked to Whitney several times, and we wanted something a little more classic." Ida continued to talk about the photos, and how they'd taken a duo shot with Brady's police hat.

"I can't wait to see them," Etta said as Johnny grunted and groaned, pulling his tiny little legs up into his body. She tucked him closer and wobbled her elbow to bounce him back to sleep. He yawned, and that was the cutest little action Etta had ever seen.

Her heart melted, and a longing sigh came out of her mouth.

"Tell me what's new with you," Ida said, and Etta looked up.

"When do you take the babies in again?" she asked instead. "I can come help you."

Ida blinked at her, her smile faltering. Etta wished she could pull the offer back inside her mouth, but she'd also learned not to try to cover up a blunder with more words. So she remained silent too.

"You don't have to—I want to know about you too," Ida said. "I literally can't talk about the babies all day, every day." She reached up and released her hair from the pretty bun. "It's all anyone wants to know about. *How's Judy eating now? Is Johnny still hogging all of your milk?*" She shook her head and looked up at the ceiling.

Etta knew that tell, and that look meant Ida was trying to get her tears to go back inside her eyes.

"I don't want to talk about the babies. You're my best friend and my sister. Tell me something that has nothing to do with a pregnancy, a baby, a sister-in-law, a brother, a cousin, or anything at the ranch."

Etta's mind raced. "That's my whole life, Ida."

"No, it's not," she said firmly. "We've always had more to our lives than family and that ranch."

"I live there now," Etta said. "I don't think I'm as separated as I used to be." She shrugged and snuggled Judy closer too. "I don't hate it. I get to bring Stetson down to my suite some nights, and it's nice to not be alone in the room."

Ida gave her a soft smile. "Remember when you told me you couldn't wait to graduate so you could finally have a bedroom of your own?"

Etta's smile popped onto her face. "You're kind of a slob, Ida."

"And you're so proper and prim," she shot back.

"I'm trying to loosen up," she said, the one thing she hadn't told anyone yet coming to her mind.

Marshall Redmond.

"In fact, I'm getting so loose that I'm going to meet a man for a date that I met on Cowboy Connection."

Ida opened her mouth to respond, then only sucked in breath. "What?" exploded out of her mouth as she exhaled. Her eyes rounded and held only shock. "You're using Cowboy Connection?" Ida actually leaned forward. "Didn't you say you wouldn't be—and I quote—caught dead with that app on your phone? That it was too kitchy with that alliterative name?"

Ida's expression harbored delight now, and Etta held her head high and rolled her eyes as if this conversation was ridiculous. "I'm aware of what I said."

"Where's your phone?" Ida got ot her feet, searching the couch near Etta, and then the end table.

"Don't you dare look at my phone," Etta said as Ida made a dash for Etta's purse by the door. "Ida." She tried to get up, but two tiny humans severely restricted her.

A cry of triumph filled the air, and Etta heaved a great sigh of frustration. It was too late; Ida had the phone, and only an act of God would stop her from looking at it now.

"Listen," Etta said. "It's a dating app, okay? You're supposed to flirt on it. You say things you wouldn't normally."

"I can't wait to see what you said," Ida said, plenty of glee in her tone.

"Ida," Etta pleaded, and that got her twin to slow down and stop. Their eyes met, and Etta could see the moment Ida came back to reality. She lowered the phone to her lap. "Tell me about him."

Relief filled Etta. Ida had always respected Etta's privacy, and she knew her better than anyone else on the planet. "You have to promise not to let your eyes get all big like they just did."

"I won't," Ida promised.

"And I don't want you to interrupt me a thousand

times." Etta glanced down at her niece and nephew. "No questions until the end. And if you ever find yourself starting a sentence with 'you should' or 'you should have,' stop. Instantly."

Ida made a crisscrossing motion over her heart and nodded soberly. "You got it."

Etta took a moment to decide if she needed any more rules for Ida. Satisfied, she said, "I started talking to him on Christmas. He's got a nice profile picture, with a big, black cowboy hat. So I tapped on the heart. He responded within five seconds, and we've been talking here and there."

"Can I call a lie when I hear it?" Ida asked.

"Is that a question?" Etta fired back.

"I'm just saying that you just lied," Ida said, settling back into the recliner and folding her arms. Etta noted that she still had the phone secured in her hand.

"Fine," Etta said. "We chat quite a lot these days."

"Every day," Ida said.

"Yes, every day. Happy now?"

"Multiple times?"

"You're asking questions."

"They're valid questions."

"Yes, multiple times. He's up early because he's got a small farm on the highway going toward Amarillo. I'm up early because I can't sleep. So we talk in the morning. I usually send him a little picture of what I've made for lunch."

Embarrassment flooded Etta, though she did love to

cook, and she loved to make her dishes prettier than they tasted.

Ida's eyes sparkled like blue diamonds. "So exciting."

"He responds to that, and usually asks me a couple of questions about what I like to eat, what's the worst thing I've ever cooked, my favorite candy, that kind of thing."

"So he's not just some creep. He's trying to get to know you."

"Seems that way," Etta said. "So it's been a few weeks, and he asked me if I'd like to go to dinner this weekend, and I said yes." She lifted her chin again, feeling the need to defend herself. "We're going casual. Pizza and salad at The Pepperoni Garden."

Ida squealed, and Etta realized she should've made that a rule. No squealing. "I haven't even been out with him yet," she said. "He could show up and be twenty years younger than he said he was. He could have six kids I don't know about."

"You love kids."

"I don't want six from the moment I say I-do," Etta argued.

"Would you date a single dad?" Ida asked, in classic Ida style.

Etta had the thought to tell her that she'd said no questions, but she didn't really mind it. "I'd date a single dad, yes," she said. Noah had children. She didn't mind a man who came with kids. She wanted a man who wanted *her* kids.

"I really just want someone with a good heart. Someone

who loves Texas, loves God, and can put up with literally twenty-five people at family dinners."

"Someone who can make you a mom," Ida added quietly.

Etta took a breath. "Who knows if that will even happen?" she asked, vocalizing the thought that had been plaguing her for months. "I mean, look at Oakley and Ranger. They want kids so badly. More than me, even. And they have such a hard time getting pregnant."

Judy squirmed, her face scrunching up as she started to cry. Etta's focus shifted, and Ida got up and took Johnny. That way, Etta could focus on the fussy little girl.

"She needs to be fed," Ida said. "Then she'll sleep for a little bit, and we can talk about your outfit and what you're going to do with your hair on Friday."

Relief hit Etta again, because she did need help with her clothes and hair. "I don't want to come across as too stuffy."

"I won't let you," Ida promised as she moved into the kitchen.

Etta got up and followed her, and together, they made a bottle each for the baby in their arms. "Don't think I don't know that you gave me the pukey baby," Etta said, hipping her sister as she took Judy back into the living room.

"I don't have a clean shirt in the whole house," Ida said, following her. "I can't afford for her to throw up on this one."

Etta giggled and gave the bottle to Judy. "Here you go, baby. You're such a good girl, aren't you? You aren't going to puke on the bestest aunt in the world, are you? No. No, you're not."

"Oh, she is," Ida assured her. "Count on it."

Etta smiled at the little girl, because she was perfection, with Ida's nose and a tiny little chin the shape of all the Glovers she'd have to grow into. "Ida?" she asked, looking up.

Ida looked up from her son. "Hmm?"

"I don't want a word about me using the app or going out with Marshall at the luncheon."

"Cross my heart and hope to die," Ida said, repeating something they'd said as little girls. Etta grinned at her, and they both went back to taking care of the baby in their arms.

Etta had held onto her relationship with Noah Johnson too, and she couldn't help thinking that maybe she *should* tell all the ranch ladies about Marshall. She'd have gone out with him by the time they met next week.

Willa was hosting the luncheon this month out at the Edge Cabin, and it would be easy for Etta to tell them all on the group text they shared only with each other. Her brothers and male cousins wouldn't need to know.

*They wouldn't care anyway*, Etta thought. She'd considered telling Cactus, who was the best of anyone at keeping secrets. He also had great advice, and Etta had grown closer to him since she'd left Noah standing at the altar by himself, her entire family staring him in the face.

In the end, Etta decided she'd keep Marshall a secret for just a little longer. She wanted to meet him first, and she didn't need the pressure of eight people asking her how the date had gone before it had even ended.

That decided, Etta went back to her duties of bestest aunt, a title she took seriously and would be working to maintain for years to come.

**THE BLESSINGS OF BABIES,** Book 8 in this series, is coming soon and will keep you updated with all the babies and happenings with the women at Shiloh Ridge Ranch.

Sneak Peek! The Networking of the
Nativity, Chapter One:

*✿*

Judge Glover put the last bite of his scrambled eggs in his mouth just as the door that led into the garage opened. Out of the two men he lived with—his cousin Ward and his brother Mister—he'd prefer it to be Ward.

He'd been getting along just fine with Mister since they'd made up several months ago. The younger man annoyed Judge from time to time—or all the time lately—but he kept his mouth shut.

He didn't tease his brother the way he would've in the past. He didn't play tricks on him—or anyone—anymore. It had taken him an extra-long time to mature, but he'd done it.

Mister walked in, a sour look on his face. Instant annoyance sprouted inside Judge. Still, he said, "Morning," and got up to wash the ketchup off his plate. Mister had said plenty of things over the years about how Judge ruined perfectly good eggs by putting ketchup on them.

He washed the red stuff down the drain and bent to put his plate in the dishwasher. He noted that Mister had not done that with his dishes that morning, and another dose of annoyance washed through him.

"Is June coming to Ward's wedding with you?" Mister asked, the chair scraping as he pulled it out from under the table. He sat in it with a big sigh. "I don't want to be the only one at the wedding without a date."

"I honestly don't know," Judge said, his mood only worsening with this topic of conversation. His relationship with June over the months could barely be categorized as such. She'd been called back to her house by her daughter and the police on their date after Christmas.

She hadn't been able to come to the impromptu New Year's Eve party they'd held at Shiloh Ridge Ranch, due to some previous plans she'd made with friends.

Judge hadn't given up there, but he probably should have. Days bled by, turning into weeks, and months, and while he sometimes talked to June on the phone, and they texted fairly regularly, he'd only seen her a few times.

He wasn't even sure he'd call running into her at the diner a date.

He'd asked her out a few times. She'd said yes. They'd made plans.

Something always came up—and not just on her end, so Judge didn't believe she was putting him off.

Lucy Mae had a band concert she hadn't put on the calendar. Judge had six calves born in the same day, so there was no way he could leave the ranch. June's car got hit in the parking lot, and she needed to take it to the body shop. Bear had called a family meeting after church, and Judge couldn't miss it. June had a massive system failure at her office in Oklahoma City, and she'd had to leave immediately to go fix it.

The list went on and on for what had gotten in the way of him taking her to dinner, going to her house after church, or the two of them simply getting together.

He was starting to think the Lord simply didn't want him to be with June. He'd backed off on texting and calling, and she hadn't made much effort to reach out to him either.

"Have you asked her to attend with you?" Mister pressed.

Judge cast him a glare, but the other man was staring at his phone. Probably looking through the long list of women's numbers he owned, trying to find someone he could ask to Ward's wedding. "Not exactly."

"Why not?" Mister looked up.

Judge turned back to the sink with a sigh. "Because, Mister, if I don't ask, then she can't tell me yes and then cancel later."

"At least she tells you yes," Mister grumbled as Judge picked up a butter knife. He contemplated stabbing it through his own eye, but just held it under the hot water and let the mayo melt off of it. He put it in the dishwasher as Mister continued, "Libby still refuses to tell me anything else about why she doesn't believe I like her. I've asked her out a couple of times, and she just says no."

"Maybe it's time to move on," Judge said, and he was telling himself as well as Mister.

"I don't want to move on."

"We don't always get what we want."

"Thanks, Dad," Mister said sarcastically.

"At least I don't," Judge said as if Mister hadn't even spoken. His chest vibrated in a strange way, and something told him not to say another word. "You seem to though."

The chair scraped again as Mister stood. "What does that mean?" He came closer to Judge, who twisted away from him to put a rinsed plate in the dishwasher. Probably Mister's, but who was keeping track?

Judge was, that was who.

"It doesn't mean anything."

"Yes, it does," Mister said. "If you have something to say, just say it."

Judge paused, cocked his head to the side, and flew backward in time to another argument they'd had. He'd lost his temper; Mister had too. Cruel things were said. Judge wasn't going to do that again.

"I'm sorry," he said slowly. "I shouldn't have said that." He met Mister's eye, noting the darkness and unhappiness there. His heart ached for his brother, because Judge knew what bitter feelings came with unhappiness. He and Preacher had talked about how to help Mister, but they'd come to no conclusions or solutions yet.

"It means something," Mister pressed, and he was never one to let anything go. That was why he couldn't just let Libby walk out of his life, despite her rejections. He'd gotten one kiss, a while ago, after he'd successfully sold an article she'd helped him edit to *Modern Rodeo*.

Since then, Mister hadn't been able to let go of Libby, no matter what anyone said. No matter that she'd broken their dinner date and then refused to go out with him. She'd said she just wanted to be friends, and that rejection had almost killed Mister.

Judge had been rejected too, and it was never pleasant. "I just...I don't want to hurt your feelings. It doesn't really matter what I think."

Mister nodded, his expression softening. "Will you tell me anyway?"

Judge paused, only the sound of the hot water running between them. "What if it upsets you?"

"I'm already upset," Mister said. "What's one more thing?"

He did seem to walk around in a perpetual bad mood lately. Maybe since New Year's, when everything with Libby blew up.

"I think you missed out on learning some things when you were younger," Judge said, trying to be delicate. He kept his voice low and his eyes trained on the mugs in the sink. Dark liquid spilled from them when he turned them over, and he rinsed them out. "Because you didn't have to go live in the cowboy cabin for a year, and you never had to work the ranch like a regular cowboy."

"I work the ranch just fine," Mister said, his default always defensive.

"I didn't say you didn't work hard," Judge said.

The door opened again, and Judge prayed it would be

Ward. Preacher walked in, and that was ten times better than Ward. He was the perfect buffer between Judge and Mister, and he paused instantly. "What's goin' on?" he asked, looking between the two of them.

"Nothing," Judge said, reaching to turn off the water.

"Judge was just telling me how lazy I am."

"That is *not* true," Judge said. "At all."

"What did you say?" Preacher asked, his eyes still zipping from brother to brother.

"I said he missed out on learning some lessons because he went straight into the rodeo. The rest of us had to go live in the cowboy cabins, draw the cowboy's daily wage, and learn how other people live and work." He glared at Mister. "That's what you don't get. Not everything goes your way all the time. I learned that while sharing a cabin with three other men and barely having enough money to pay for groceries." He drew a deep breath. "Or waiting for the shower, only to find out there was no hot water left for me."

"It was a tough time," Preacher said, committing to entering the house. "What do you guys have to eat here? We haven't been to the store in a while, and Charlie's promised to bring you back whatever you want." He smiled at Judge and hugged him quickly.

Judge hugged him back and watched as he stepped over to Mister too. Mister stood unyieldingly in his arms, his frown still pinned on Judge.

"There's bagels and cream cheese," Judge said, moving back to the table to get his coffee mug. He started rinsing that too.

"What other kinds of lessons?" Mister asked.

Judge sighed and looked up to the ceiling, wishing he could see all the way to heaven. He needed some help from On High right now, that was for sure.

"Patience, for one," Judge said. "And for two, you have no idea how regular people live. What they have to deal with."

"I'm a regular person," Mister said.

"No," Judge said with a laugh. "You're not. We're not. None of us up here are. You learn that in the cabins."

Mister looked at Preacher, who set two halves of his bagel into the toaster. "What does he mean?"

"The fact that you don't know is how I know you don't get why Libby won't go out with you."

"Is this about Libby?" Preacher asked.

"It's always about Libby," Judge said, and a bit of sarcasm crept into his voice. He cleared his throat to tame it. He wasn't going to poke fun at Mister for his crush on Liberty Bellamore. He wasn't, because that was cruel, and not what brothers should do to one another.

"Mister," Preacher said, turning toward him. "He's right, bro. We're not normal."

"In what way?"

"In the billion-dollar way," Preacher said. "In the way that if we want a new house, we just build it. We don't have to get a loan. We don't have to worry about making mortgage payments. We don't worry about anything, really. At least not when it comes to how things will get paid for. Things like medical expenses or new cars or...whatever."

"That's not how normal people live," Judge said gently.

"They have more bills than money. They have to decide if they should pay their electric bill or the prom dress their daughter wants. Sometimes it's medical care or groceries. I learned that in the cowboy cabins. I met men who were desperately trying to provide for themselves or a family."

"You think I got off easy." Mister folded his arms and glared.

"You did," Preacher and Judge said together. They exchanged a glance, and Preacher's jaw tightened. Judge had seen that look before, and he knew Preacher was done talking. Judge should be too.

"You learn to lean on yourself," Judge said quietly. "Or the Lord, even though Dad is just a few steps away. That's what he wanted us to learn." Judge had learned it too.

"You think I'm spoiled," Mister said.

"You have a lot of money, and a lot of shiny belt buckles, and a lot of titles," Judge said.

Mister folded his arms and glared. "Do you think I never had to lean on anyone while traveling the rodeo circuit by myself?" He threw his arms up. "Because that was no picnic, Judge. I was alone all the time. There's *so* much pressure out there."

"I think it's different," Judge said. "Out here, when it's just you, and you have nothing? You have no idea what that's like. You've been privileged your whole life, even while on the rodeo circuit." He pointed toward the door, toward the whole ranch. "Those men we employ? That's all they have. They don't have big bank accounts waiting for them at home or glitzy belt buckles. You walk around here like you own the world, and that's fine. You're a great guy, and you help others. I'm just saying...."

"What?" Mister demanded, dropping his arms and clenching his fists. "What are you saying?"

"I'm saying you're hard to relate to," Judge said, committed now. He swallowed and glanced at Preacher, who seemed to need to stare unblinkingly at his bagel while he spread cream cheese on it.

"It's no wonder Libby thinks you don't get it. You don't. You've been spoiled rotten your whole life. You work, but you don't have to, and you know it. For some of us, we had to live and breathe and work like a cowboy for a year, and all we got was the twenty grand."

"You knew you'd have a big bank account afterward," Mister said with a scoff. "Don't give me that."

"Okay," Judge said, holding up both hands. "I'm not going to argue with you about it anymore. I think you missed out on learning some really valuable life lessons. Stuff Dad and Uncle Bull *wanted* us to experience and learn. You never did, and in my opinion, it shows." He started for the front door, but he kept his steps slow and even. He wasn't mad. Mister could think what he wanted. Judge was just tired of listening to him moan and complain about how everything didn't go his way.

*Welcome to the freaking club.*

Judge had learned while living in a two-bedroom cabin with three other men that compromises could and should be made. He didn't have to get his way all the time. He could put his needs aside in favor of someone else's.

He'd learned to truly share—and not just his toys like

when he'd been a kid. But share parts of himself with other people. Share his resources so they could all have a good life. Share the workload so one of them wasn't left doing all the dirty dishes.

No, he didn't have the bejeweled belt buckles or the titles Mister did. But he had more wisdom and knowledge that actually helped him in the life he was trying to live now. He didn't complain that life got in the way of him and June being together. Life did that sometimes. It happened, and it didn't always go the way he wanted it to.

He knew his life was charmed too. He wasn't delirious or blind to that fact. But he had put himself in someone else's boots and walked and worked for a full year. Mister never had.

His life had been, and still was, all about *him*. What he wanted. What he didn't have. Why Libby wouldn't go out with him.

"I'm gonna go get started with the horses in six," he said. "Is that where you want me, boss?"

"I'm not your boss," Preacher said.

"But you are," Judge said. "I know you and Ward are the boss, and that's another thing I learned in the cowboy cabins. The work is hard, and it never ends, and the boss tells you what to do, and you do it."

Judge actually didn't mind that. He knew who he was, and it wasn't to be Preacher or Ward. He'd never survive as a leader the way they did. He didn't like all the pressure on him when tough decisions needed to be made.

He could work like a dog, and he often had around the ranch. He had around other ranches when their owners needed help. Judge liked to work. He just didn't want to be in charge.

"I follow orders too," Mister said.

"I'm not saying you don't," Judge said. "I'm saying I don't think you have any idea what it means to bend your will to someone else's. After all, you're *still* asking Libby out, and she's still telling you no."

"You are?" Preacher asked. "Didn't she tell you no like six months ago?"

"The horses in six?" Judge asked.

"Yep," Preacher said, and Judge reached for the doorknob. He yanked the door open and stepped outside—and right into someone standing there, their hand reaching for the doorbell.

Their fingers hit his shoulder, and he grunted at the same time the woman there yelped. He reached out and grabbed onto her so he wouldn't knock her down, and that was when Judge looked into the gorgeous, brown eyes of Juniper Nichols.

In the flesh.

His heart leapt to the back of his throat. "June," he gasped out, his hands moving down her arms and settling on her waist. He looked over his shoulder, quickly dropping his hands from her body so he could close the door.

He faced her, noting the nerves—and tears?—in her eyes now. "What are you doing here? Is everything okay?"

## Sneak Peek! The Networking of the Nativity, Chapter Two:

⚜

Juniper Nichols told herself to *be cool. Play everything so cool.* In reality, she was hot under the collar, with burning tears behind her eyes.

"You look upset, June," Judge said. "What can I help you with?"

"I was just down the lane at Ace's," she said, stepping with him as he pressed her toward the edge of the porch. This one only had three steps leading to it, and it was clearly decades older than the house she'd just visited. "They needed some help with their WiFI. I got them a new cord, and they're good as new."

"Great," he said with a smile. "I'm headed over to the stables. Do you have a minute to walk with me?"

"No," she said, and Judge continued down the steps before he turned back to her. "I just heard that Ward is getting married this weekend. Holly Ann was on the phone with someone."

"Yes," Judge said, looking toward the homestead. That house dwarfed this one, though where Judge lived was twice as big as what June had.

"Why didn't you ask me to go with you?" June went down the steps too, and when she reached Judge, she laced her arm through his. "Can I go with you?" Her voice broke on the last word, drawing the cowboy's attention.

"Can you come with me to the wedding?" he asked. "Of course you can come with me." He leaned down and touched his lips to her forehead. "I didn't ask you, because I was afraid you'd say yes, and then cancel on me."

Instant defenses flew into place. "I didn't cancel any of the times because I didn't want to go out with you."

"I know that."

"You canceled on me too."

"I know that."

June let the morning silence settle over them. "Life has been really funny the past six months."

"Yes, it has." Judge tucked her arm closer to his body. "Plus, I don't believe you didn't know about Ward's wedding. You're on that text with all the women." He looked at her, his eyebrows cocked.

June's emotions stormed through her like an army of soldiers. "Actually, I asked Willa to remove me," she whispered. "It was too hard, knowing all the amazing stuff they were doing together and not being able to do any of it. I didn't...I don't...I don't belong with them."

"You could," he said.

"Judge Glover," June said, a smile dancing across her face. "You best not be sayin' things you don't mean."

He started to laugh, and June joined him. "It's been an interesting ride with you, Juniper."

She liked it when he used her full name, and she'd hated her full name since grade school. Somehow, when Judge said it, it became a term of endearment.

He drew in a deep breath. "I also didn't ask, because I know Lucy Mae graduates on Friday. I believe you told me she was leaving for California the next day—and that's the day Ward is getting married."

Those pesky tears entered her eyes again. She knew if she spoke, Judge would hear them. He'd look at her and see them again. "Yes," she said anyway, and he did exactly what she feared he would.

She let him look, and she let him see, and he did exactly what she hoped he would. He gathered her close to his chest, enveloping her in his strong arms, and whispered, "It's okay, June-Bug. It's all going to be okay."

She pressed her eyes closed, because her only daughter leaving Three Rivers wasn't okay. Such a thing wasn't even in the same realm as okay. "I don't know how to be alone," she said.

"Maybe you won't have to be," he said.

"I don't know how to have enough faith that she'll be okay in California."

"Maybe I can help," he said.

June pulled away slightly and looked up at him. "Why won't you go out with anyone else?"

"Have you?" he asked.

She shook her head. "I sort of have a policy about that."

"Yeah, but you'll break that policy for the right guy," Judge said, dead serious. "Right?"

"I guess."

"Have you been asked out in the past six months?"

"Yes," she said.

"By someone other than me?"

"Yes."

Judge frowned, and he obviously didn't like that. "Did you say yes?"

"No." A relationship with him felt impossible. It was exactly as she'd told Ida a couple of months ago. Maybe God simply didn't want June to have someone as amazing as Judge in her life.

"I don't want to ask you to come to the wedding," he said. "If you're available and you want to come, that's fine. No one's going to turn you away." He stepped gently away from her, and they both looked up to the door when it opened again.

Preacher came outside, and he paused, surprise evident on his face. "Hey, uh, when you're done here, can I talk to you for a sec?"

"Sure," Judge said, looking from his brother to June. "I think we're done. Miss Nichols surely has a full schedule today to be at the ranch so early." He reached up and tipped his hat to her, his smile gorgeous and perfectly symmetrical, with all those shiny, white teeth.

She watched him go up the few steps and say, "What's up? I overstepped with Mister, didn't I?" before the two of them went inside and the door closed behind them. She knew Judge and Mister didn't always get along, and she wanted to know what boundary he'd overstepped.

She wanted him at her side this summer while Lucy Mae was gone. She'd wanted more of a relationship with him the past few months, but she'd let the tides of life push her this way and then that one.

She wanted to see his Christmas display, and help him upgrade his network to make it run flawlessly.

She wanted to tell him that Adam was coming to pick up Lucy Mae, and she was scared out of her mind to see her ex-husband for the first time in thirteen years. She'd spoken to him when she'd had to, but she hadn't been in the same physical space as him since he'd left her and Lucy Mae all those years ago.

While still standing on the front sidewalk in front of Bull House, she sent a text to Judge. *Can you go to dinner tonight? I'll be done by five-thirty, and I have something I want to tell you.*

*Sure,* he said almost instantly, and she could hear it in his cowboy twang. The man said "Sure," as easily as he breathed, and with a date with him on the horizon, June finally felt like *she* could breathe again.

---

"DID YOU GET YOUR CAP AND GOWN?" JUNE ASKED WHEN her daughter walked in from her after school job. She pulled the pan of lasagna from the oven. "Dinner's almost ready."

"I'm going out with Timmy tonight, remember?" Lucy

Mae dropped her backpack by the door and kicked off her shoes. "Yes, I got my cap and gown. You would not believe how many cars came through the line today." She smiled and reached for one of the caramels June had gotten out for herself.

"I forgot about Timmy." June frowned and looked at the pan of lasagna. She wouldn't have made it if she'd remembered. After all, she had a dinner date tonight too.

*Maybe Judge could just come here,* she thought, and she reached for her phone as Lucy Mae filled a glass with water.

"And some of them went through the line twice, saying we had to give them a free wash, because the first one didn't get the mud off."

"What are you and Timmy doing?"

"I argued with this one guy until Gerome came out and said to just give it to him." She shook her head and took a big drink. "But honestly, the entire town got the mud rained on them. It's all over everything, from the garbage cans to the fence posts. I should work on tips." She grinned, and June smiled back at her.

Lucy Mae had always been a talker, and she could go on and on—and on—about almost anything. When she'd been obsessed with Broadway, June had listened to the plot of every play Lucy Mae could get her hands on. And not a short synopsis either.

"Timmy's taking me to the senior hot dog roast," she said. "Tomorrow is the all-nighter."

"I don't want you out all night."

"I know, Mom. We already talked about it." Lucy Mae

rolled her eyes and put her glass in the sink. "Sorry about the lasagna. We'll eat it, I'm sure."

"I'm thinking of having Judge come help." She looked from the Italian dish to her daughter.

Lucy Mae's eyebrows soared toward the ceiling "Judge Glover? I thought you'd decided to let life play its course, and he wasn't included."

"Maybe he still is," June said. "I saw him today."

"Where?"

"The ranch. I had a job up there."

Lucy Mae cocked one hip and put her hand on it. "Did you, Mom? Or did you go seek him out?"

"What if I did?" she asked. "People can alter their course in life, you know." She put the oven mitts back in the drawer next to the stove. "I'm letting you go to California, and that's a complete life course deviation." She gave her daughter a glare, not wanting to admit how much she still liked and thought about Judge Glover.

"I will text you every hour," Lucy Mae said.

June scoffed, caught her daughter's grin, and drew her into a hug. "I love you so much, Lucy Mae."

"I love you too, Mom."

"I can't believe you're graduating and moving out. Moving on. You're going to have such an amazing life." She stepped back, used to letting her daughter see her tears. She didn't let them slip down her face, but they definitely brimmed in her eyes.

"So are you," Lucy Mae said. "You'll finally be free to do what you want."

"You have never been a burden to me," June said firmly. "Never."

"I know." Lucy Mae hugged her again, and June felt something extra in the touch. Her daughter held her tighter, and June did the same in return.

They stepped apart, and Lucy Mae wiped her eyes. "I'm going to go shower. If Timmy gets here before I'm done, please be nice to him."

"I'm always nice to him," June said.

"Mom, last time you told him you could find out where he'd been on the Internet. 'Two clicks, Timmy, and that history is mine.' That's what you said." Lucy Mae rolled her eyes again, but June only smiled.

She knew better than most the dangers out there on the Internet, and she knew about the enticing things that teenage boys could get into.

Her daughter went down the hall to her bathroom, and June muttered, "That *was* me being nice, baby." She knew the ins and outs of routers, networks, security systems, and backend servers. She could sit outside Timmy's house and, within five minutes, be spying on what he was doing on his computer.

She wouldn't, of course. But she could.

She picked up her phone and called Judge, hoping he wasn't up to his elbows in manure or something. Now that summer had arrived, Judge would be pulling his Christmas supplies out of the basement, and the more likely scenario would have him wrapped up in old strings of Christmas lights.

"Heya, June," he said, and it sounded like he was

running. "Can I call you back in maybe ten minutes?"

"Sure," she said quickly, and he said, "Great, thanks," and the call ended.

June smiled to herself, because it sure felt like Judge would provide a life for her that would never have a dull moment. She looked around her house, feeling very much like a boring, old maid.

She needed some excitement in her life—and not the kind where her entire Oklahoma City office was offline.

But the cowboy kind.

The *sexy* cowboy kind, and she grabbed her phone and went down the hall to her bedroom and bathroom. If Judge was coming over, she needed to freshen up a little bit. She caught sight of herself in the mirror and gasped.

The manly polo with *Nichols Networking* stitched over the breast came right off. "I need new company shirts," she muttered to herself. Something with a V-neck or some-thing that didn't make her look so boxy.

She stepped out of her work boots and pants and slipped into some black slacks made of something silky.

"Mom?" Lucy Mae called.

"I'm changing," she said, turning her back toward the door, as her daughter would come in whether she was changing or not. She searched her limited closet space for something appropriate for a date in her own home.

She glanced at her daughter as she entered the closet. She must've been able to read June's mind, because Lucy Mae said, "You want something to bring out your eyes." She stepped over to the rack and started flipping. "And since it's the beginning of summer, and you're a little pale from winter, you want—"

"I am not pale from winter," June said. "The sun's been shining in Texas for months."

"Something blue or purple, I think," Lucy Mae continued, not bothered at all by June's protest. She plucked a purple blouse from the options and held it up. "This one's really cute."

The blouse had little white confetti blotches all over it, and June reached out to touch the material. It was light and airy, and June would feel confident in it. "Okay," she said, taking the blouse off the hanger. She pulled it over her head and then took the ponytail holder out of her hair.

"Up or down?"

"Down, Mom. Always down when you're trying to impress a man."

June's lungs seized. "I've always had it up when I've seen him before."

Lucy Mae smiled and reached over to fluff June's hair. "Then he'll be doubly impressed tonight."

"Yeah, the way I heated up that frozen lasagna is going to win him over for good."

Lucy Mae giggled and kept arranging June's hair. "Looks good now. Come and let me do your makeup."

"I don't want a lot of makeup."

"I'll choose three things," Lucy Mae said. "I won't do a single thing more." She opened the top drawer in June's vanity and started digging through her makeup bag. "Mascara, foundation, and lip gloss." She held them up, and the makeup looked so innocent. "Doable?"

"Doable," June said, and she followed Lucy Mae back into the kitchen. She sat at the dining room table, and she closed her eyes and let her daughter start to paint her face.

The doorbell rang, and Lucy Mae left quickly to go answer it. As she greeted her boyfriend, June's phone rang. Judge's name sat on the screen, and she hurried to answer the call.

"Hey," she said. "You really called back."

"I was chasing a turkey, believe it or not," he said with a laugh. "Stupid thing got into some cord, and we needed to get it off his feet."

"Sounds exciting," she said. "I didn't know you had turkeys."

"We have a little bit of everything up here," he said with a sigh. "Let me guess—something came up?"

"Yes," June said, grinning to herself and then looking at Lucy Mae and Timmy as they came into the kitchen. "I forgot my daughter had a date tonight, and I made dinner for her so we could go out and I wouldn't feel guilty. I'm wondering if you'd like to come to my place to eat instead of going out."

"Absolutely," Judge said. "I'm headed home now, so I just need to shower and make the drive. Say, an hour?"

"Can't wait," June said, hoping she'd used a flirtatious voice.

"Wow, Mom," Lucy Mae said as Judge said good-bye, and June hung up.

"What?" she asked. "You can't leave until you finish my makeup."

"Can't wait," Lucy Mae said in a falsely high voice, a

poor imitation of June. She giggled and waved with the mascara wand. "Eyes closed. I'm going to make your face match that flirty tone, and you're going to show this cowboy he shouldn't let a day go by without talking to you."

"From your lips to God's ears," June sad, immediately following that up with a silent prayer that the Lord would indeed help her with her at-home dinner date with Judge Glover in only an hour.

---

## THE NETWORKING OF THE NATIVITY -
### *coming soon!*

**The Mechanics of Mistletoe (Book 1):** Bear Glover can be a grizzly or a teddy, and he's always thought he'd be just fine working his generational family ranch and going back to the ancient homestead alone. But his crush on Samantha Benton won't go away. She's a genius with a wrench on Bear's tractors...and his heart. Can he tame his wild side and get the girl, or will he be left broken-hearted this Christmas season?

**The Horsepower of the Holiday (Book 2):** Ranger Glover has worked at Shiloh Ridge Ranch his entire life. The cowboys do everything from horseback there, but when he goes to town to trade in some trucks, somehow Oakley Hatch persuades him to take some ATVs back to the ranch. (Bear is NOT happy.)

She's a former race car driver who's got Ranger all revved up... Can he remember who he is and get Oakley to slow down enough to fall in love, or will there simply be too much horsepower in the holiday this year for a real relationship?

**The Construction of Cheer (Book 3):** Bishop Glover is the youngest brother, and he usually keeps his head down and gets the job done. When Montana Martin shows up at Shiloh Ridge Ranch looking for work, he finds himself inventing construction projects that need doing just to keep her coming around. (Again, Bear is NOT happy.) She wants to build her own construction firm, but she ends up carving a place for herself inside Bishop's heart. Can he convince her *he's* all she needs this Christmas season, or will her cheer rest solely on the success of her business?

**The Secret of Santa (Book 4):** He's a fun-loving cowboy with a heart of gold. She's the woman who keeps putting him on hold. Can Ace and Holly Ann make a relationship work this Christmas?

**The Harmony of Holly (Book 5):** He's as prickly as his name, but the new woman in town has caught his eye. Can Cactus shelve his temper and shed his cowboy hermit skin fast enough to make a relationship with Willa work?

**The Chemistry of Christmas (Book 6):** He's the black sheep of the family, and she's a chemist who understands formulas, not emotions. Can Preacher and Charlie take their quirks and turn them into a strong relationship this Christmas?

**The Delivery of Decor (Book 7):** When he falls, he falls hard and deep. She literally drives away from every relationship she's ever had. Can Ward somehow get Dot to stay this Christmas?

**The Blessing of Babies (Book 8):** Don't miss out on a single moment of the Glover family saga in this bridge story linking Ward and Judge's love stories!

The Glovers love God, country, dogs, horses, and family. Not necessarily in that order. ;)

Many of them are married now, with babies on the way, and there are lessons to be learned, forgiveness to be had and given, and new names coming to the family tree in southern Three Rivers!

**The Networking of the Nativity (Book 9):** He's had a crush on her for years. She doesn't want to date until her daughter is out of the house. Will June take a change on Judge when the success of his Christmas light display depends on her networking abilities?

**The Wrangling of the Wreath (Book 10):** He's been so busy trying to find Miss Right. She's been right in front of him the whole time. This Christmas, can Mister and Libby take their relationship out of the best friend zone?

**The Hope of Her Heart (Book 11):** She's the only Glover without a significant other. He's been searching for someone who can love him *and* his daughter. Can Etta and August make a meaningful connection this Christmas?

**Rhett's Make-Believe Marriage (Book 1):** She needs a husband to be credible as a matchmaker. He wants to help a neighbor. Will their fake marriage take them out of the friend zone?

**Tripp's Trivial Tie (Book 2):** She needs a husband to keep her son. He's wanted to take their relationship to the next level, but she's always pushing him away. Will their trivial tie take them all the way to happily-ever-after?

**Liam's Invented I-Do (Book 3):** She's desperate to save her ranch. He wants to help her any way he can. Will their invented I-Do open doors that have previously been closed and lead to a happily-ever-after for both of them?

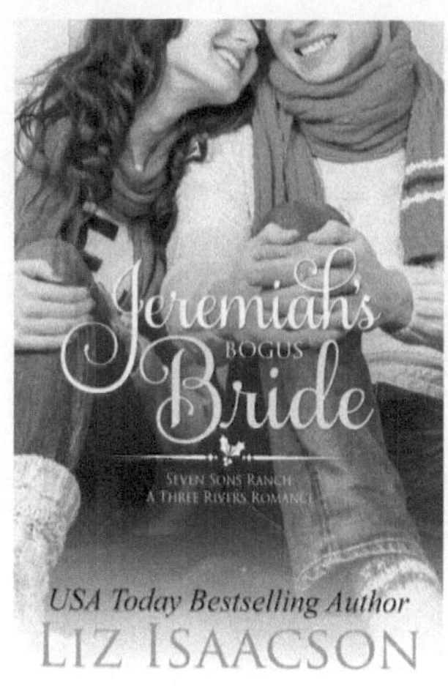

**Jeremiah's Bogus Bride (Book 4):** He wants to prove to his brothers that he's not broken. She just wants him. Will a fake marriage heal him or push her further away?

**Wyatt's Pretend Pledge (Book 5):** To get her inheritance, she needs a husband. He's wanted to fly with her for ages. Can their pretend pledge turn into something real?

**Skyler's Wanna-Be Wife (Book 6):** She needs a new last name to stay in school. He's willing to help a fellow student. Can this wanna-be wife show the playboy that some things should be taken seriously?

**Micah's Mock Matrimony (Book 7):** They were just actors auditioning for a play. The marriage was just for the audition – until a clerical error results in a legal marriage. Can these two ex-lovers negotiate this new ground between them and achieve new roles in each other's lives?

**Her Cowboy Billionaire Birthday Wish (Book 1):** All the maid at Whiskey Mountain Lodge wants for her birthday is a handsome cowboy billionaire. And Colton can make that wish come true—if only he hadn't escaped to Coral Canyon after being left at the altar...

**Her Cowboy Billionaire Butler (Book 2):** She broke up with him to date another man...who broke her heart. He's a former CEO with nothing to do who can't get her out of his head. Can Wes and Bree find a way toward happily-ever-after at Whiskey Mountain Lodge?

**Her Cowboy Billionaire Best Friend's Brother (Book 3):** She's best friends with the single dad cowboy's brother and has watched two friends find love with the sexy new cowboys in town. When Gray Hammond comes to Whiskey Mountain Lodge with his son, will Elise finally get her own happily-ever-after with one of the Hammond brothers?

**Her Cowboy Billionaire Beast (Book 4):** A cowboy billionaire beast, his new manager, and the Christmas traditions that soften his heart and bring them together.

**Her Cowboy Billionaire Bad Boy (Book 5):** A cowboy billionaire cop who's a stickler for rules, the woman he pulls over when he's not even on duty, and the personal mandates he has to break to keep her in his life...

**Her Cowboy Billionaire Best Friend (Book 1):** Graham Whittaker returns to Coral Canyon a few days after Christmas—after the death of his father. He takes over the energy company his dad built from the ground up and buys a high-end lodge to live in—only a mile from the home of his once-best friend, Laney McAllister. They were best friends once, but Laney's always entertained feelings for him, and spending so much time with him while they make Christmas memories puts her heart in danger of getting broken again...

**Her Cowboy Billionaire Boss (Book 2):** Since the death of his wife a few years ago, Eli Whittaker has been running from one job to another, unable to find somewhere for him and his son to settle. Meg Palmer is Stockton's nanny, and she comes with her boss, Eli, to the lodge, her long-time crush on the man no different in Wyoming than it was on the beach. When she confesses her feelings for him and gets nothing in return, she's crushed, embarrassed, and unsure if she can stay in Coral Canyon for Christmas. Then Eli starts to show some feelings for her too...

**Her Cowboy Billionaire Boyfriend (Book 3):** Andrew Whittaker is the public face for the Whittaker Brothers' family energy company, and with his older brother's robot about to be announced, he needs a press secretary to help him get everything ready and tour the state to make the announcements. When he's hit by a protest sign being carried by the company's biggest opponent, Rebecca Collings, he learns with a few clicks that she has the background they need. He offers her the job of press secretary when she thought she was going to be arrested, and not only because the spark between them in so hot Andrew can't see straight.

**Can Becca and Andrew work together and keep their relationship a secret? Or will hearts break in this classic romance retelling reminiscent of *Two Weeks Notice*?**

**Her Cowboy Billionaire Bodyguard (Book 4):** Beau Whittaker has watched his brothers find love one by one, but every attempt he's made has ended in disaster. Lily Everett has been in the spotlight since childhood and has half a dozen platinum records with her two sisters. She's taking a break from the brutal music industry and hiding out in Wyoming while her ex-husband continues to cause trouble for her. When she hears of Beau Whittaker and what he offers his clients, she wants to meet him. Beau is instantly attracted to Lily, but he tried a relationship with his last client that left a scar that still hasn't healed...

**Can Lily use the spirit of Christmas to discover what matters most? Will Beau open his heart to the possibility of love with someone so different from him?**

**Her Cowboy Billionaire Bull Rider (Book 5):** Todd Christopherson has just retired from the professional rodeo circuit and returned to his hometown of Coral Canyon. Problem is, he's got no family there anymore, no land, and no job. Not that he needs a job--he's got plenty of money from his illustrious career riding bulls.

Then Todd gets thrown during a routine horseback ride up the canyon, and his only support as he recovers physically is the beautiful Violet Everett. She's no nurse, but she does the best she can for the handsome cowboy. **Will she lose her heart to the billionaire bull rider? Can Todd trust that God led him to Coral Canyon...and Vi?**

**Her Cowboy Billionaire Bachelor (Book 6):** Rose Everett isn't sure what to do with her life now that her country music career is on hold. After all, with both of her sisters in Coral Canyon, and one about to have a baby, they're not making albums anymore.

Liam Murphy has been working for Doctors Without Borders, but he's back in the US now, and looking to start a new clinic in Coral Canyon, where he spent his summers.

When Rose wins a date with Liam in a bachelor auction, their relationship blooms and grows quickly. **Can Liam and Rose find a solution to their problems that doesn't involve one of them leaving Coral Canyon with a broken heart?**

**Her Cowboy Billionaire Blind Date (Book 7):** Her sons want her to be happy, but she's too old to be set up on a blind date...isn't she?

Amanda Whittaker has been looking for a second chance at love since the death of her husband several years ago. Finley Barber is a cowboy in every sense of the word. Born and raised on a racehorse farm in Kentucky, he's since moved to Dog Valley and started his own breeding stable for champion horses. He hasn't dated in years, and everything about Amanda makes him nervous.

**Will Amanda take the leap of faith required to be with Finn? Or will he become just another boyfriend who doesn't make the cut?**

**Her Cowboy Billionaire Best Man (Book 8):** When Celia Abbott-Armstrong runs into a gorgeous cowboy at her best friend's wedding, she decides she's ready to start dating again.

But the cowboy is Zach Zuckerman, and the Zuckermans and Abbotts have been at war for generations.

Can Zach and Celia find a way to reconcile their family's differences so they can have a future together?

**Second Chance Ranch: A Three Rivers Ranch Romance (Book 1):** After his deployment, injured and discharged Major Squire Ackerman returns to Three Rivers Ranch, wanting to forgive Kelly for ignoring him a decade ago. He'd like to provide the stable life she needs, but with old wounds opening and a ranch on the brink of financial collapse, it will take patience and faith to make their second chance possible.

**Third Time's the Charm: A Three Rivers Ranch Romance (Book 2):** First Lieutenant Peter Marshall has a truckload of debt and no way to provide for a family, but Chelsea helps him see past all the obstacles, all the scars. With so many unknowns, can Pete and Chelsea develop the love, acceptance, and faith needed to find their happily ever after?

**Fourth and Long: A Three Rivers Ranch Romance (Book 3):** Commander Brett Murphy goes to Three Rivers Ranch to find some rest and relaxation with his Army buddies. Having his ex-wife show up with a seven-year-old she claims is his son is anything but the R&R he craves. Kate needs to make amends, and Brett needs to find forgiveness, but are they too late to find their happily ever after?

**Fifth Generation Cowboy: A Three Rivers Ranch Romance (Book 4):** Tom Lovell has watched his friends find their true happiness on Three Rivers Ranch, but everywhere he looks, he only sees friends. Rose Reyes has been bringing her daughter out to the ranch for equine therapy for months, but it doesn't seem to be working. Her challenges with Mari are just as frustrating as ever. Could Tom be exactly what Rose needs? Can he remove his friendship blinders and find love with someone who's been right in front of him all this time?

**Sixth Street Love Affair: A Three Rivers Ranch Romance (Book 5):** After losing his wife a few years back, Garth Ahlstrom thinks he's ready for a second chance at love. But Juliette Thompson has a secret that could destroy their budding relationship. Can they find the strength, patience, and faith to make things work?

**The Seventh Sergeant: A Three Rivers Ranch Romance (Book 6):** Life has finally started to settle down for Sergeant Reese Sanders after his devastating injury overseas. Discharged from the Army and now with a good job at Courage Reins, he's finally found happiness—until a horrific fall puts him right back where he was years ago: Injured and depressed. Carly Watters, Reese's new veteran care coordinator, dislikes small towns almost as much as she loathes cowboys. But she finds herself faced with both when she gets assigned to Reese's case. Do they have the humility and faith to make their relationship more than professional?

**Eight Second Ride: A Three Rivers Ranch Romance (Book 7):** Ethan Greene loves his work at Three Rivers Ranch, but he can't seem to find the right woman to settle down with. When sassy yet vulnerable Brynn Bowman shows up at the ranch to recruit him back to the rodeo circuit, he takes a different approach with the barrel racing champion. His patience and newfound faith pay off when a friendship--and more--starts with Brynn. But she wants out of the rodeo circuit right when Ethan wants to rejoin. Can they find the path God wants them to take and still stay together?

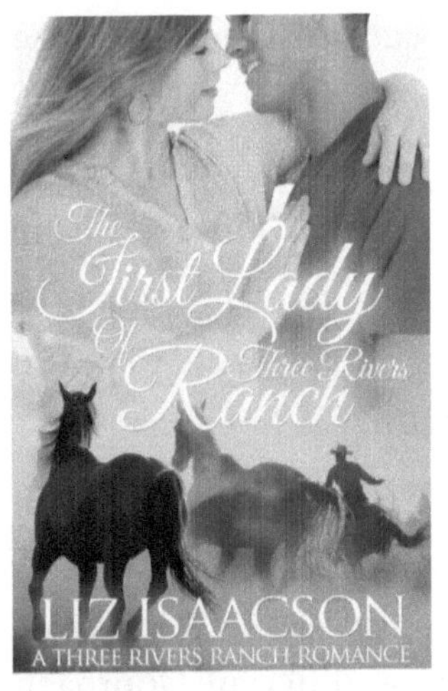

**The First Lady of Three Rivers Ranch: A Three Rivers Ranch Romance (Book 8):** Heidi Duffin has been dreaming about opening her own bakery since she was thirteen years old. She scrimped and saved for years to afford baking and pastry school in San Francisco. And now she only has one year left before she's a certified pastry chef. Frank Ackerman's father has recently retired, and he's taken over the largest cattle ranch in the Texas Panhandle. A horseman through and through, he's also nearing thirty-one and looking for someone to bring love and joy to a homestead that's been dominated by men for a decade. But when he convinces Heidi to come clean the cowboy cabins, she changes all that. But the siren's call of a bakery is still loud in Heidi's ears, even if she's also seeing a future with Frank. Can she rely on her faith in ways she's never had to before or will their relationship end when summer does?

**Christmas in Three Rivers: A Three Rivers Ranch Romance (Book 9):** Isn't Christmas the best time to fall in love? The cowboys of Three Rivers Ranch think so. Join four of them as they journey toward their path to happily ever after in four, all-new novellas in the Amazon #1 Bestselling Three Rivers Ranch Romance series.

THE NINTH INNING: The Christmas season has never felt like such a burden to boutique owner Andrea Larsen. But with Mama gone and the holidays upon her, Andy finds herself wishing she hadn't been so quick to judge her former boyfriend, cowboy Lawrence Collins. Well, Lawrence hasn't forgotten about Andy either, and he devises a plan to get her out to the ranch so they can reconnect. Do they have the faith and humility to patch things up and start a new relationship?

TEN DAYS IN TOWN: Sandy Keller is tired of the dating scene in Three Rivers. Though she owns the pancake house, she's looking for a fresh start, which means an escape from the town where she grew up. When her older brother's best friend, Tad Jorgensen, comes to town for the holidays, it is a balm to his weary soul. A helicopter tour guide who experienced a near-death experience, he's looking to start over too--but in Three Rivers. Can Sandy and Tad navigate their troubles to find the path God wants them to take--and discover true love--in only ten days?

ELEVEN YEAR REUNION: Pastry chef extraordinaire, Grace Lewis has moved to Three Rivers to help Heidi Ackerman open a bakery in Three Rivers. Grace relishes the idea of starting over in a town where no one knows about her failed cupcakery. She doesn't expect to run into her old high school boyfriend, Jonathan Carver. A carpenter working at Three Rivers Ranch, Jon's in town against his will. But with Grace now on the scene, Jon's thinking life in Three Rivers is suddenly looking up. But with her focus on baking and his disdain for small towns, can they make their eleven year reunion stick?

THE TWELFTH TOWN: Newscaster Taryn Tucker has had enough of life on-screen. She's bounced from town to town before arriving in Three Rivers, completely alone and completely anonymous--just the way she now likes it. She takes a job cleaning at Three Rivers Ranch, hoping for a chance to figure out who she is and where God wants her. When she meets happy-go-lucky cowhand Kenny Stockton, she doesn't expect sparks to fly. Kenny's always been "the best friend" for his female friends, but the pull between him and Taryn can't be denied. Will they have the courage and faith necessary to make their opposite worlds mesh?

**Lucky Number Thirteen: A Three Rivers Ranch Romance (Book 10):** Tanner Wolf, a rodeo champion ten times over, is excited to be riding in Three Rivers for the first time since he left his philandering ways and found religion. Seeing his old friends Ethan and Brynn is thera-puetic--until a terrible accident lands him in the hospital. With his rodeo career over, Tanner thinks maybe he'll stay in town--and it's not just because his nurse, Summer Hamblin, is the prettiest woman he's ever met. But Summer's the queen of first dates, and as she looks for a way to make a relationship with the transient rodeo star work Summer's not sure she has the fortitude to go on a second date. Can they find love among the tragedy?

**The Curse of February Fourteenth: A Three Rivers Ranch Romance (Book 11):** Cal Hodgkins, cowboy veterinarian at Bowman's Breeds, isn't planning to meet anyone at the masked dance in small-town Three Rivers. He just wants to get his bachelor friends off his back and sit on the sidelines to drink his punch. But when he sees a woman dressed in gorgeous butterfly wings and cowgirl boots with blue stitching, he's smitten. Too bad she runs away from the dance before he can get her name, leaving only her boot behind...

**Fifteen Minutes of Fame: A Three Rivers Ranch Romance (Book 12):** Navy Richards is thirty-five years of tired—tired of dating the same men, working a demanding job, and getting her heart broken over and over again. Her aunt has always spoken highly of the matchmaker in Three Rivers, Texas, so she takes a six-month sabbatical from her high-stress job as a pediatric nurse, hops on a bus, and meets with the matchmaker. Then she meets Gavin Redd. He's handsome, he's hardworking, and he's a cowboy. But is he an Aquarius too? Navy's not making a move until she knows for sure...

**Sixteen Steps to Fall in Love: A Three Rivers Ranch Romance (Book 13):** A chance encounter at a dog park sheds new light on the tall, talented Boone that Nicole can't ignore. As they get to know each other better and start to dig into each other's past, Nicole is the one who wants to run. This time from her growing admiration and attachment to Boone. From her aging parents. From herself.

But Boone feels the attraction between them too, and he decides he's tired of running and ready to make Three Rivers his permanent home. **Can Boone and Nicole use their faith to overcome their differences and find a happily-ever-after together?**

**The Sleigh on Seventeenth Street: A Three Rivers Ranch Romance (Book 14):** A cowboy with skills as an electrician tries a relationship with a down-on-her luck plumber. Can Dylan and Camila make water and electricity play nicely together this Christmas season? Or will they get shocked as they try to make their relationship work?

**Last Chance Cowboy (Book 2):** A billionaire cowboy without a home meets a woman who secretly makes food videos to pay her debts...Can Carson and Adele do more than fight in the kitchens at Last Chance Ranch?

**Last Chance Wedding (Book 3):** A female carpenter needs a husband just for a few days... Can Jeri and Sawyer navigate the minefield of a pretend marriage before their feelings become real?

**Last Chance Reunion (Book 4):** An Army cowboy, the woman he dated years ago, and their last chance at Last Chance Ranch... Can Dave and Sissy put aside hurt feelings and make their second chance romance work?

**Last Chance Lake (Book 5):** A former dairy farmer and the marketing director on the ranch have to work together to make the cow cuddling program a success. But can Karla let Cache into her life? Or will she keep all her secrets from him – and keep *him* a secret too?

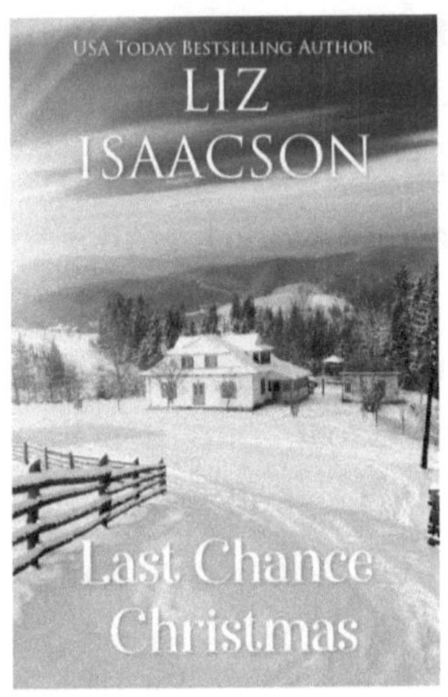

**Last Chance Christmas (Book 6):** She's tired of having her heart broken by cowboys. He waited too long to ask her out. Can Lance fix things quickly, or will Amber leave Last Chance Ranch before he can tell her how he feels?

**Her Billionaire Cowboy (Book 1):** Tucker Jenkins has had enough of tall buildings, traffic, and has traded in his technology firm in New York City for Steeple Ridge Horse Farm in rural Vermont. Missy Marino has worked at the farm since she was a teen, and she's always dreamed of owning it. But her ex-husband left her with a truckload of debt, making her fantasies of owning the farm unfulfilled. Tucker didn't come to the country to find a new wife, but he supposes a woman could help him start over in Steeple Ridge. Will Tucker and Missy be able to navigate the shaky ground between them to find a new beginning?

**Her Restless Cowboy: A Butters Brothers Novel, Steeple Ridge Romance (Book 2):** Ben Buttars is the youngest of the four Buttars brothers who come to Steeple Ridge Farm, and he finally feels like he's landed somewhere he can make a life for himself. Reagan Cantwell is a decade older than Ben and the recreational direction for the town of Island Park. Though Ben is young, he knows what he wants—and that's Rae. Can she figure out how to put what matters most in her life—family and faith—above her job before she loses Ben?

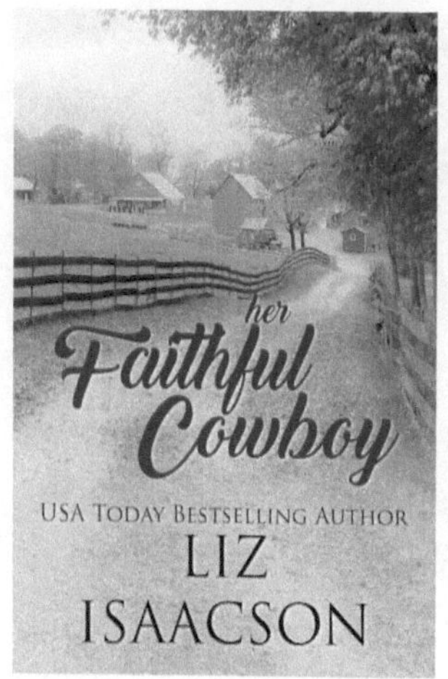 **Her Faithful Cowboy: A Butters Brothers Novel, Steeple Ridge Romance (Book 3):** Sam Buttars has spent the last decade making sure he and his brothers stay together. They've been at Steeple Ridge for a while now, but with the youngest married and happy, the siren's call to return to his parents' farm in Wyoming is loud in Sam's ears. He'd just go if it weren't for beautiful Bonnie Sherman, who roped his heart the first time he saw her. Do Sam and Bonnie have the faith to find comfort in each other instead of in the people who've already passed?

**Her Mistletoe Cowboy: A Butters Brothers Novel, Steeple Ridge Romance (Book 4):** Logan Buttars has always been good-natured and happy-go-lucky. After watching two of his brothers settle down, he recognizes a void in his life he didn't know about. Veterinarian Layla Guyman has appreciated Logan's friendship and easy way with animals when he comes into the clinic to get the service dogs. But with his future at Steeple Ridge in the balance, she's not sure a relationship with him is worth the risk. Can she rely on her faith and employ patience to tame Logan's wild heart?

**Her Patient Cowboy: A Butters Brothers Novel, Steeple Ridge Romance (Book 5):** Darren Buttars is cool, collected, and quiet—and utterly devastated when his girlfriend of nine months, Farrah Irvine, breaks up with him because he wanted her to ride her horse in a parade. But Farrah doesn't ride anymore, a fact she made very clear to Darren. She returned to her childhood home with so much baggage, she doesn't know where to start with the unpacking. Darren's the only Buttars brother who isn't married, and he wants to make Island Park his permanent home—with Farrah. Can they find their way through the heartache to achieve a happily-ever-after together?

**Craving the Cowboy (Book 1):** Dwayne Carver is set to inherit his family's ranch in the heart of Texas Hill Country, and in order to keep up with his ranch duties and fulfill his dreams of owning a horse farm, he hires top trainer Felicity Lightburne. They get along great, and she can envision herself on this new farm—at least until her mother falls ill and she has to return to help her. Can Dwayne and Felicity work through their differences to find their happily-ever-after?

**Charming the Cowboy (Book 2):** Third grade teacher Heather Carver has had her eye on Levi Rhodes for a couple of years now, but he seems to be blind to her attempts to charm him. When she breaks her arm while on his horse ranch, Heather infiltrates Levi's life in ways he's never thought of, and his strict anti-female stance slips. Will Heather heal his emotional scars and he care for her physical ones so they can have a real relationship?

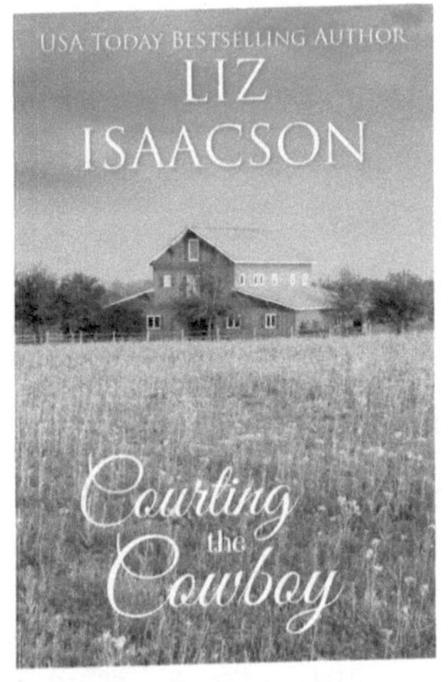

**Courting the Cowboy (Book 3):** Frustrated with the cowboy-only dating scene in Grape Seed Falls, May Sotheby joins TexasFaithful.com, hoping to find her soul mate without having to relocate--or deal with cowboy hats and boots. She has no idea that Kurt Pemberton, foreman at Grape Seed Ranch, is the man she starts communicating with... Will May be able to follow her heart and get Kurt to forgive her so they can be together?

**Claiming the Cowboy, Royal Brothers Book 1 (Grape Seed Falls Romance Book 4):** Unwilling to be tied down, farrier Robin Cook has managed to pack her entire life into a two-hundred-and-eighty square-foot house, and that includes her Yorkie. Cowboy and co-foreman, Shane Royal has had his heart set on Robin for three years, even though she flat-out turned him down the last time he asked her to dinner. But she's back at Grape Seed Ranch for five weeks as she works her horse-shoeing magic, and he's still interested, despite a bitter life lesson that left a bad taste for marriage in his mouth.

Robin's interested in him too. But can she find room for Shane in her tiny house--and can he take a chance on her with his tired heart?

**Catching the Cowboy, Royal Brothers Book 2 (Grape Seed Falls Romance Book 5):** Dylan Royal is good at two things: whistling and caring for cattle. When his cows are being attacked by an unknown wild animal, he calls Texas Parks & Wildlife for help. He wasn't expecting a beautiful mammologist to show up, all flirty and fun and everything Dylan didn't know he wanted in his life.

Hazel Brewster has gone on more first dates than anyone in Grape Seed Falls, and she thinks maybe Dylan deserves a second... Can they find their way through wild animals, huge life changes, and their emotional pasts to find their forever future?

**Cheering the Cowboy, Royal Brothers Book 3 (Grape Seed Falls Romance Book 6):** Austin Royal loves his life on his new ranch with his brothers. But he doesn't love that Shayleigh Hatch came with the property, nor that he has to take the blame for the fact that he now owns her childhood ranch. They rarely have a conversation that doesn't leave him furious and frustrated--and yet he's still attracted to Shay in a strange, new way.

Shay inexplicably likes him too, which utterly confuses and angers her. As they work to make this Christmas the best the Triple Towers Ranch has ever seen, can they also navigate through their rocky relationship to smoother waters?

**Choosing the Cowboy (Book 7):** With financial trouble and personal issues around every corner, can Maggie Duffin and Chase Carver rely on their faith to find their happily-ever-after?

A spinoff from the #1 best-selling Three Rivers Ranch Romance novels, also by USA Today bestselling author Liz Isaacson.

**The Redesigned Ranch (Book 1):** Jace Lovell only has one thing left after his fiancé abandons him at the altar: his job at Horseshoe Home Ranch. Belle Edmunds is back in Gold Valley and she's desperate to build a portfolio that she can use to start her own firm in Montana. Jace isn't anywhere near forgiving his fiancé, and he's not sure he's ready for a new relationship with someone as fiery and beautiful as Belle. Can she employ her patience while he figures out how to forgive so they can find their own brand of happily-ever-after?

**The Snowstorm in Gold Valley (Book 2):** Professional snowboarder Sterling Maughan has sequestered himself in his family's cabin in the exclusive mountain community above Gold Valley, Montana after a devastating fall that ended his career. Norah Watson cleans Sterling's cabin and the more time they spend together, the more Sterling is interested in all things Norah. As his body heals, so does his faith. Will Norah be able to trust Sterling so they can have a chance at true love?

**The Cabin on Bear Mountain (Book 3):** Landon Edmunds has been a cowboy his whole life. An accident five years ago ended his successful rodeo career, and now he's looking to start a horse ranch-- and he's looking outside of Montana. Which would be great if God hadn't brought Megan Palmer back to Gold Valley right when Landon is looking to leave. Megan and Landon work together well, and as sparks fly, she's sure God brought her back to Gold Valley so she could find her happily ever after. Through serious discussion and prayer, can Landon and Megan find their future together?

Be sure to check out the spinoff series, the Brush Creek Brides romances after you read FALLING FOR HIS BEST FRIEND. Start with A WEDDING FOR THE WIDOWER.

**The Cowboy at the Creek (Book 4):** Twelve years ago, Owen Carr left Gold Valley—and his long-time girlfriend—in favor of a country music career in Nashville. Married and divorced, Natalie teaches ballet at the dance studio in Gold Valley, but she never auditioned for the professional company the way she dreamed of doing. With Owen back, she realizes all the opportunities she missed out on when he left all those years ago—including a future with him. Can they mend broken bridges in order to have a second chance at love?

**The Wedding in the Winter (Book 5):** Caleb Chamberlain has spent the last five years recovering from a horrible breakup, his alcoholism that stemmed from it, and the car accident that left him hospitalized. He's finally on the right track in his life—until Holly Gray, his twin brother's ex-fiance mistakes him for Nathan.

Holly's back in Gold Valley to get the required veterinarian hours to apply for her graduate program. When the herd at Horseshoe Home comes down with pneumonia, Caleb and Holly are forced to work together in close quarters. Holly's over Nathan, but she hasn't forgiven him—or the woman she believes broke up their relationship. Can Caleb and Holly navigate such a rough past to find their happily-ever-after?

**The Long Way Home (Book 6):** Ty Barker has been dancing through the last thirty years of his life--and he's suddenly realized he's alone. River Lee Whitely is back in Gold Valley with her two little girls after a divorce that's left deep scars. She has a job at Silver Creek that requires her to be able to ride a horse, and she nearly tramples Ty at her first lesson. That's just fine by him, because River Lee is the girl Ty has never gotten over. Ty realizes River Lee needs time to settle into her new job, her new home, her new life as a single parent, but going slow has never been his style. But for River Lee, can Ty take the necessary steps to keep her in his life?

**Christmas at the Ranch (Book 7):** Archer Bailey has already lost one job to Emersyn Enders, so he deliberately doesn't tell her about the cowhand job up at Horseshoe Home Ranch. Emery's temporary job is ending, but her obligations to her physically disabled sister aren't. As Archer and Emery work together, its clear that the sparks flying between them aren't all from their friendly competition over a job. Will Emery and Archer be able to navigate the ranch, their close quarters, and their individual circumstances to find love this holiday season?

**The Love of a Cowboy (Book 8):** Cowboy Elliott Hawthorne has just lost his best friend and cabin mate to the worst thing imaginable—marriage. When his brother calls about an accident with their father, Elliott rushes down to Gold Valley from the ranch only to be met with the most beautiful woman he's ever seen. His father's new physical therapist, London Marsh, likes the handsome face and gentle spirit she sees in Elliott too. Can Elliott and London navigate difficult family situations to find a happily-ever-after?

**Brush Creek Cowboy: Brush Creek Cowboys Romance (Book 1):** Former rodeo champion and cowboy Walker Thompson trains horses at Brush Creek Horse Ranch, where he lives a simple life in his cabin with his ten-year-old son. A widower of six years, he's worked with Tess Wagner, a widow who came to Brush Creek to escape the turmoil of her life to give her seven-year-old son a slower pace of life. But Tess's breast cancer is back...

Walker will have to decide if he'd rather spend even a short time with Tess than not have her in his life at all. Tess wants to feel God's love and power, but can she discover and accept God's will in order to find her happy ending?

**The Cowboy's Challenge: Brush Creek Brides Romance (Book 2):** Cowboy and professional roper Justin Jackman has found solitude at Brush Creek Horse Ranch, preferring his time with the animals he trains over dating. With two failed engagements in his past, he's not really interested in getting his heart stomped on again. But when flirty and fun Renee Martin picks him up at a church ice cream bar--on a bet, no less--he finds himself more than just a little interested. His Gen-X attitudes are attractive to her; her Millennial behaviors drive him nuts. Can Justin look past their differences and take a chance on another engagement?

**A Cowboy Proposal: Brush Creek Brides Romance (Book 3):** Ted Caldwell has been a retired bronc rider for years, and he thought he was perfectly happy training horses to buck at Brush Creek Ranch. He was wrong. When he meets April Nox, who comes to the ranch to hide her pregnancy from all her friends back in Jackson Hole, Ted realizes he has a huge family-shaped hole in his life. April is embarrassed, heartbroken, and trying to find her extinguished faith. She's never ridden a horse and wants nothing to do with a cowboy ever again. Can Ted and April create a family of happiness and love from a tragedy?

**A New Family for the Cowboy: Brush Creek Brides Romance (Book 4):** Blake Gibbons oversees all the agriculture at Brush Creek Horse Ranch, sometimes moonlighting as a general contractor. When he meets Erin Shields, new in town, at her aunt's bakery, he's instantly smitten. Erin moved to Brush Creek after a divorce that left her penniless, homeless, and a single mother of three children under age eight. She's nowhere near ready to start dating again, but the longer Blake hangs around the bakery, the more she starts to like him. Can Blake and Erin find a way to blend their lifestyles and become a family?

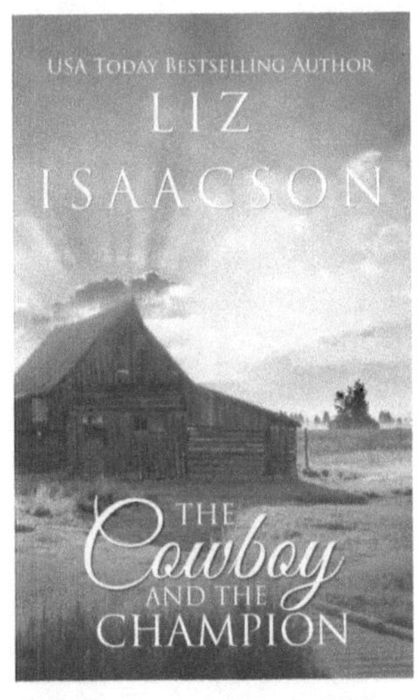

**The Cowboy and the Champion: Brush Creek Brides Romance (Book 5):** Emmett Graves has always had a positive outlook on life. He adores training horses to become barrel racing champions during the day and cuddling with his cat at night. Fresh off her professional rodeo retirement, Molly Brady comes to Brush Creek Horse Ranch as Emmett's protege. He's not thrilled, and she's allergic to cats. Oh, and she'd like to stay cowboy-free, thank you very much. But Emmett's about as cowboy as they come.... Can Emmett and Molly work together without falling in love?

**Schooled by the Cowboy: Brush Creek Brides Romance (Book 6):** Grant Ford spends his days training cattle—when he's not camped out at the elementary school hoping to catch a glimpse of his ex-girlfriend. When principal Shannon Sharpe confronts him and asks him to stay away from the school, the spark between them is instant and hot. Shannon's expecting a transfer very soon, but she also needs a summer outdoor coordinator—and Grant fits the bill. Just because he's handsome and everything Shannon's ever wanted in a cowboy husband means nothing. Will Grant and Shannon be able to survive the summer or will the Utah heat be too much for them to handle?

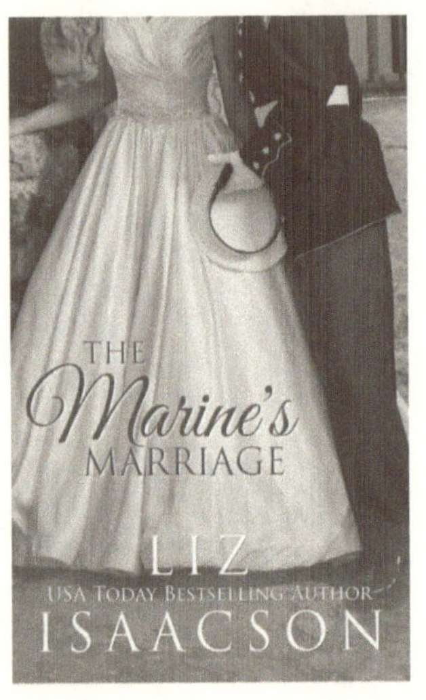

**The Marine's Marriage: A Fuller Family Novel - Brush Creek Brides Romance (Book 1):** Tate Benson can't believe he's come to Nowhere, Utah, to fix up a house that hasn't been inhabited in years. But he has. Because he's retired from the Marines and looking to start a life as a police officer in small-town Brush Creek. Wren Fuller has her hands full most days running her family's company. When Tate calls and demands a maid for that morning, she decides to have the calls forwarded to her cell and go help him out. She didn't know he was moving in next door, and she's completely unprepared for his handsomeness, his kind heart, and his wounded soul.Can Tate and Wren weather a relationship when they're also next-door neighbors?

**The Firefighter's Fiancé: A Fuller Family Novel - Brush Creek Brides Romance (Book 2):** Cora Wesley comes to Brush Creek, hoping to get some in-the-wild firefighting training as she prepares to put in her application to be a hotshot. When she meets Brennan Fuller, the spark between them is hot and instant. As they get to know  each other, her deadline is constantly looming over them, and Brennan starts to wonder if he can break ranks in the family business. He's okay mowing lawns and hanging out with his brothers, but he dreams of being able to go to college and become a landscape architect, but he's just not sure it can be done. Will Cora and Brennan be able to endure their trials to find true love?

**The Trooper's Treasure: A Fuller Family Novel - Brush Creek Brides Romance (Book 3):** Dawn Fuller has made some mistakes in her life, and she's not proud of the way McDermott Boyd found her off the road one day last year. She's spent a hard year wrestling with her choices and trying to fix them, glad for McDermott's acceptance and friendship. He lost his wife years ago, done his best with his daughter, and now he's ready to move on. Can McDermott help Dawn find a way past her former mistakes and down a path that leads to love, family, and happiness?

**The Detective's Date: A Fuller Family Novel - Brush Creek Brides Romance (Book 4):** Dahlia Reid is one of the best detectives Brush Creek and the surrounding towns has ever had. She's given up on the idea of marriage—and pleasing her mother—and has dedicated herself fully to her job. Which is great, since one of the most perplexing

cases of her career has come to town. Kyler Fuller thinks he's finally ready to move past the woman who ghosted him years ago. He's cut his hair, and he's ready to start dating. Too bad every woman he's been out with is about as interesting as a lamppost—until Dahlia. He finds her beautiful, her quick wit a breath of fresh air, and her intelligence sexy. Can Kyler and Dahlia use their faith to find a way through the obstacles threatening to keep them apart?

**The Paramedic's Partner: A Fuller Family Novel - Brush Creek Brides Romance (Book 5):** Jazzy Fuller has always been overshadowed by her prettier, more popular twin, Fabiana. Fabi meets paramedic Max Robinson at the park and sets a date with him only to come down with the flu. So she convinces Jazzy to cut her hair and take her place on the date. And the spark between Jazzy and Max is hot and instant...if only he knew she wasn't her sister, Fabi.

Max drives the ambulance for the town of Brush Creek with is partner Ed Moon, and neither of them have been all that lucky in love. Until Max suggests to who he thinks is Fabi that they should double with Ed and Jazzy. They do, and Fabi is smitten with the steady, strong Ed Moon. As each twin falls further and further in love with their respective paramedic, it becomes obvious they'll need to come clean about the switcheroo sooner rather than later...or risk losing their hearts.

**The Chief's Catch: A Fuller Family Novel - Brush Creek Brides Romance (Book 6):** Berlin Fuller has struck out with the dating scene in Brush Creek more times than she cares to admit. When she makes a deal with her friends that they can choose the next man she goes out with, she didn't dream they'd pick surly Cole Fairbanks, the new Chief of Police.

His friends call him the Beast and challenge him to complete ten dates that summer or give up his bonus check. When Berlin approaches him, stuttering about the deal with her friends and claiming they don't actually have to go out, he's intrigued. As the summer passes, Cole finds himself burning both ends of the candle to keep up with his job and his new relationship. When he unleashes the Beast one time too many, Berlin will have to decide if she can tame him or if she should walk away.

# About Liz

Liz Isaacson writes inspirational romance, usually set in Texas, or Montana, or anywhere else horses and cowboys exist. She lives in Utah, where she writes full-time, walks her two dogs daily, and eats a lot of peanut butter M&Ms while writing. Find her on her website at lizisaacson.com.